Dedicated to my wonderful parents

Philomena and Patrick

Thank you for all your wonderful and loving

support

CW01496456

CHAPTER ONE

Claire was usually in work by 8.15am each morning, which placed her in a prime position to tune into the daily office banter. One bright Monday morning the conversation was all about the contents of an email which Daniel, financial controller of Leictreach, had circulated around the finance department. He was taking on additional duties at head office and a new manager was taking over several of his responsibilities in the finance department. Reference was made to a revised senior staff organisational plan. The arrival of a new manager was news to the staff. They had sensed that change was in the air, but they had not been expecting to lose their most senior manager for most of the working week.

'I hope the new manager is better looking than Daniel', said Anna.

'It wouldn't be hard to look good, standing beside Daniel', guffawed Emmet, 'he has nearly as many wrinkles as myself and not half as good looking neither.'

'Oh, I don't know,' Joan mused, 'he is always on his bike and that keeps a body lean and keen. If he was few years younger I wouldn't kick him out of bed for eating a packet of crisps. He has plenty of money and could give me a bonus for brilliant performance in the bedroom.'
Anna sniggered. 'Please, you flatter yourself my dear…and it's not worth the effort. I bet Daniel is like a robot in bed. He is such an accountant he'd want everything to balance. You'd need to be an acrobat to keep him happy.'

'You lot can't go two minutes without lowering the tone. There is no respect or privacy in this office', groused Emmet.

'There is no privacy here because it is an open plan office and people are neither deaf nor blind', said Amy.

'Never mind all that nonsense' urged a businesslike Deirdre as she entered the room. 'I've just come from downstairs and Daniel is showing the new manager around. They will both be here in a few minutes'.

The ladies moved as one to settle themselves down at their desks, switching computers on, tidying desks and touching up the all-important lipstick.

Emmet, team player that he was, adjusted his glasses, straightened his back and reached for an A4 writing pad to carry about in his hand.

Questions about the new manager came thick and fast, with everybody talking over each other.

'What's her name?'

'Ashley Scanlon.'

'What's she like?'

'She's tall and blonde'.

'Every female manager appointed in this company these days is tall, thin and blonde. A fat brunette looking for promotion doesn't stand a chance.'

'Does anybody know anything about her? Where has she come from?'

'Give us a chance, we didn't know her name until a second ago'.

'Dublin is a small place. We'll find out about her. Somebody will know somebody who knows her.'

'I saw the job 'spec a while back and it was quite demanding; accountant with five years post qualified experience, ability to meet reporting deadlines, IT and system knowledge, supervisory experience, excellent communication skills, ability to manage change in the workplace', recalled Deirdre.

'Change? Crap. Any idea of what they want to change?'

'Why should they want to change anything? We all work hard and do our jobs well. We'll have to bring her up to speed, if anything.'

'One thing's for sure, she's bound to be making heaps more money than we're getting.'

'Daniel hasn't got many communication skills to speak of. Oh, hang on, he does leave his door open occasionally'.

'That's to see us when we creep in late.'

'Will you all button it and do some work. They'll be coming through that door in a minute,' warned an exasperated Deirdre.

It was enough to settle them down and turn their attention to the day's work. The chit chat ceased, and a totally different atmosphere spread through the room. Claire hurriedly raked a comb through her red gold hair to project a more professional image, but her curly locks were not easily tamed. Emmet went back into his own office across the hall and the girls concentrated on data input, their fingers flying over the keyboards, intending to appear as efficient as possible. The office staff wanted Daniel and the new manager to see nothing but workhorses when they strode through the door.

Daniel was a workaholic who was the first to arrive and the last to leave the department every day. He had spent all his working life in Leictreach and was regarded as the ultimate company man. He was an expert at identifying duds in the six-month probationary period undertaken by all new employees and he had no compunction about letting anybody go if they did not meet his high standards. He did not suffer fools gladly. Money and figures left a trail. His job was to watch the money and safeguard the cash flow and for that he needed competent, vigilant and responsible people in his team. He was well aware that good people, able to deliver on set targets within a tight time frame, made any manager look good.

Claire was not the only person to notice that Daniel had an uncanny knack of getting people to willingly consent to take on more work than was part of the original deal. He would appear at her desk just as she was finishing up an assignment, compliment her on a job well done, mention some other task which needed urgent attention and suggest that she, with her talents, was the ideal person to undertake it. Claire normally capitulated in record time, even if the task was unappealing to her, because she wanted to glow briefly in Daniel's presence. Once Daniel had her agreement he was gone, into the next office, onto the next item on his agenda, ensuring that he had every duty and responsibility covered. He moved quickly and silently and would materialise when you were least expecting it, like when you were on the phone to a family member for the first time that day. His words were few, but he led by example and he did command the respect and loyalty of his troops. People considered him a gentleman in the cut and thrust world of corporate politics.

The finance staff did not have to wait long before Daniel and Ashley entered the room together. They approached the desks one at a time, with Daniel making the introductions, smiling as he outlined each person's job to Ashley. The social niceties were all observed, and everyone spoke briefly but pleasantly to one another. Claire looked up from her computer when they stopped at her desk and shook hands with Ashley, noticing that her finger nails were immaculately manicured and that her handshake was purposely firm. She was dressed in a designer navy slim line dress with matching jacket. She appeared to be about five feet nine inches tall and she accentuated her height by wearing high heeled shoes. Ashley had a pale complexion, which gave prominence to her slate grey eyes. She probably came out well in photographs, but Claire thought that her skeletal frame and short, blonde bob accentuated the length of her nose and jaw line too much. She was the picture of a sharp faced business woman dressed to impress and succeed.

'This is Claire Howard', Daniel said. 'Claire has responsibility for the month end accounting for the central departments. She has in depth knowledge of the general ledger, which comes in useful for her business analysis work. She is also involved in payroll reporting, merger activity, problem reconciliations and basically any ad hoc project work I ask her to turn her attention to.'

'I look forward to working with you', said Ashley.

'Likewise' replied Claire, suspecting both of them were mouthing polite lies.

Once Daniel and Ashley left the room, Joan got up to close the door, freeing them to speak their minds.

'What do you think?'

'Too soon to say.'

'I'd say she is around thirty-three or thirty-four'.

'She looks older but then again, being skeleton thin adds years on you'.

'I thought she looked extremely confident and self assured.'

'She wouldn't have gotten the job if she wasn't confident.'

Claire stayed silent as she buried herself in paperwork. Something had bothered her about Ashley, but what was it? The realisation dawned upon her; when Ben was a baby he often sucked a soother in his mouth, but Claire always knew when he was happy because a smile first manifested itself as a bright gleam in his eyes. Ashley smiled with her closed lips curved slightly upwards, but her eyes remained cold and distant, as impenetrable and grey as a sleet laden sky. Claire felt an uneasy feeling stir deep within her.

'Don't be daft', she scolded herself, shaking her head 'haven't you got enough to do without inventing problems?'

Life in the finance department went on as usual as Ashley spent a lot of time in meetings with Daniel and the other senior managers, getting a handle on how the wider organisation operated and the reports she was expected to produce. She was also busy getting to grips with the management information systems in place and familiarising herself with the details of each person's job description. The staff for their part thought the transition was going smoothly but this proved to be the calm before the storm.

On a wet Tuesday morning, Ashley entered the general office and strode straight up to Tracey, the office junior.

She pressed the knuckles of her hands down on the surface of the desk, leant her upper body forward and thrust her head close to the younger girl's face.

'You're the person responsible for distributing the mail to all finance personnel, are you not?' she snapped.

'Yyyessss', Tracey stammered in surprise. Distribution of the daily mail did not normally rouse people's ire in the office.

'Then can you explain to me why the payroll office did not receive the letter instructing them to put Alex Brennan, the new Director of Human Resources onto the payroll and which also contained his personal bank details?'

'The email was sent to the wrong person by mistake?' suggested Tracey in innocent confusion.

The director did not want his personal bank details circulated via email', said Ashley, close to spitting. 'Confidentiality is of key importance to finance and human resource personnel. I put the envelope containing his details on your desk. All you had to do was hand it into the payroll office but no, that was too much trouble for you. You'd move fast enough if it was your own wage on the line.'

'But you never told me about the important letter', said a bemused Tracey.

'You weren't at your desk when I left the marked envelope here; you were most likely off on a lengthy coffee break. As a result of your carelessness and laziness, I have just had an uncomfortable conversation with a top director explaining why no money has gone into his bank account this month. We are trying to build up the finance department's reputation for efficiency throughout the organisation and your performance is dragging us down. You had better find that letter now', said Ashley, her flint eyes narrowed to slits in her closed, steely face.

'I didn't see it', squeaked Tracey. 'I never set eyes on it, I swear. I didn't mean to let the department down.'

Tracey started to fumble about with the sheets and paper folders lying on top of her desk, lifting them up high to flick through them, checking the contents of her 'In' and 'Out' trays. When this failed to reveal the missing envelope, she pulled open her desk drawers and began to frantically search through them. In her distressed state it was unlikely she was going to recognise the envelope, even if it materialised in bold print under her eyes.

'For God's sake, if you can't even keep your desk tidy how can you possibly do the job we pay you for? Clean up this mess while I fix the problem your inefficiency created', said Ashley in disgust. She marched out of the door with long, mannish strides, leaving a stunned silence in the room. Everyone looked at each other in disbelief, before they all began talking at once.

'She's a bitch'.

'She was exactly like my old maths teacher Ms. Riley in secondary school. What age does she think Tracey is? Twelve?'

'She can't talk to people like that'.

'Well, she did, and Tracey's been doing that job for a year, no problem to her. And we don't have a clean desk policy here.'

'But I didn't see any envelope', said Tracey, lip trembling. 'I know my desk looks untidy, but I know where everything is'. Two big tears dropped down her face before she buried it in a heap of paper tissues.

'I thought I knew where everything was but, I've been so wreaked, maybe I missed it', she whispered, more to herself than anybody else in the room.

'I'll help you look for it', Claire volunteered. She was the only one in the office who knew that Tracey was pregnant and grappling with morning sickness, but she was sworn to secrecy about it. Tracey was employed by an agency which supplied relief staff to Leictreach. She had worked in Leictreach for nearly a year and had reason to believe that Daniel intended making her a direct, permanent employee in the near future. She was afraid that the contract would never materialise if her pregnancy became public knowledge. The last thing Tracey needed was Ashley coming down on her like a tonne of bricks.

Claire began to go methodically through all the folders on the desk one by one, noting that Tracey was lifting the same bunch of papers up and down and around repeatedly, too upset to focus on them properly. When Claire reached for a red coloured paper folder, Tracey checked her, lightly placing her own hand on top of it.

'There's no point in going through that, I only put old junk mail in there, stuff that nobody wants'.

'Ashley doesn't know that', replied Claire. She had looked everywhere else in Tracey's desk, so the elusive envelope had to be in this last folder.

Sure enough, there it was, a white envelope, face down, marked with the word 'Payroll,' buried among all the flyers and notices contained in the battered folder.

'But I didn't put it in there, that's only for junk mail', cried Tracey.

'The folder was probably open on your desk when Ashley came along and dropped the envelope on top of it. You came back to your desk, closed over the folder and put it away, knowing nothing about it,' guessed Claire astutely.

'It was more Ashley's fault than yours Tracey; she should have mentioned it to you at the time. Go and tell her what happened, she was way out of order', urged Amy.

Tracey slumped further down in her chair, obviously distressed.

'I'm not going near her, she might give out to me again. No, I can't talk to her', she said tearfully. 'I don't feel well, I have a really bad headache... I don't feel well at all'.

'I have a packet of aspirin in my desk Tracey and you're to take one, it will help you feel better', said Anna firmly. 'Come to the canteen with me and I'll get you sorted out'.

'Give me that envelope and I'll take it along to Ashley now and explain to her exactly what happened', said Deirdre. 'I'm too long in the tooth for that madam to put the frighteners on me'.

The room was quiet for the rest of the day. Most people were genuinely shocked at Ashley's rough treatment of Tracey (who after all was an inoffensive, helpful young girl) but a couple were silently scornful of the manner in which she had crumbled under pressure.

The girls urged Tracey to report her conversation with Ashley to Daniel, but Tracey was horrified at this suggestion.

'No, he's too busy and important to take any notice of me. I'm only a temp. I'm going to say nothing and keep my head down and try to become invisible and then Ashley might leave me alone. Today was a bad day but tomorrow might be better.'

'Tracey must show more backbone and stop being such a mouse, or else Ashley will squish her for fun', commented Deirdre, after Tracey left for the day fifteen minutes earlier than usual.

'It's not her fault, it is Ashley who has caused this unpleasantness', said Claire, rushing in to defend Tracey. 'Besides, I don't think Tracey is feeling well, she looks dreadful. She has worked very hard to be made permanent and it is not surprising if she does not want to jeopardise it. We are all here because we need the money.'

The consensus of the group was that if Tracey was not willing to say anything to Daniel about Ashley's harsh treatment of her then the other members of staff felt they had better keep their mouths shut as well. They would wait and see what happened next.

'Besides', said Joan,' it might sound selfish, but it's up to everyone to fight their own corner. You have to be careful not to get yourself a bad name. If they don't like you, they can make your life here uncomfortable, no problem to them. There's no point in everybody being miserable.'

Tracey called in sick for the rest of the week and another person from the agency was drafted in to provide temporary cover for her absence. Claire was acutely aware that she was the only person in the office who knew about Tracey's pregnancy, but she had promised not to tell anybody. She was worried that the stress associated with the altercation with Ashley might have pushed up Tracey's blood pressure and that could be harmful for the baby.

Ashley Scanlon was just in the door and already she was sucking the fun and the camaraderie out of the office. It was even obvious to the cleaner that the good humour which had long existed among the co- workers was dissipating into thin air. It was rapidly progressing to the next step, which was the build up of tensions, complaints and bad tempers. Claire had never experienced anything like it before. She thanked her lucky stars that she was not reporting directly to Ashley, unlike the unfortunate Tracey. The younger girl had the right idea in staying as far away from Ashley as possible and, until Claire figured out the best way in dealing with the new boss on the block, she intended to do likewise.

CHAPTER TWO

Any dreams anybody might harbour about wearing a cloak of invisibility in Ashley's presence were torn to shreds from the outset. Ashley prowled around the office like a panther each day, eyeing Tracey as her prey, turning the girl into a nervous wreck. Nothing Tracey produced was enough to satisfy the new manager.

'I've just read the car leasing report you've been working on and it's so inaccurate and incomplete we can't use it. You'll have to stay late and do it again', snapped Ashley.

'But I can't!' stuttered Tracey, her face flushed red. 'I have a doctor's appointment at five, I have to leave early. I was in at eight this morning to make up the time'.

'Not that anybody would notice from the work you've produced today. You are more out than in these days Tracey', shot back Ashley. 'I can't depend on you. What good are you to me?'

'I have to leave early today as well Ashley', interjected Anna coolly. 'I worked late yesterday. I have to go to a parent teacher meeting'.

'I heard you have a house husband', said Ashley. 'Can't he go instead of you?'

Claire sucked in her breath, knowing Anna would be enraged by Ashley's careless question. Anna's husband had been employed as a car mechanic in a construction firm for twenty- eight years and they had been gutted when he was made redundant. He had not managed to secure a full-time job since then, railing against ageism in the workplace, and the family keenly felt their reduced economic circumstances.

'It is better that I go to see the teachers about my seventeen-year-old daughter, I have more of an understanding of her. It's her Leaving Certificate year and it's important that I be there for her', said Anna firmly.

'You can take every hour of every Wednesday off to infinity if you don't care about your job', said Ashley angrily. Just as she was about to exit the room, she spun around on her three-inch heels and looked thoughtfully across at Tracey.

'You're not permanent here, are you Tracey?' said Ashley, her sudden soft tone making the question more dangerous.

If Tracey was sitting any lower in her chair she would have been crawling underneath the desk. Her dark eyes resembled those of a rabbit caught in the headlights of a speeding car as she mutely shook her head.

'Are you permanent yet yourself Ashley?' challenged Anna bravely. 'Because I am and I'm leaving on the dot of four o'clock.'

'Since you wouldn't get much done anyway, I guess you can go', replied Ashley coolly, determined not to let Anna have the last word. Her managerial authority must be maintained.

The dislike between Anna and Ashley was palpable, it lingered in the air. War had been declared and the lines of battle were being drawn. People had to decide for themselves which side they intended to back in the conflict. Most put their heads down, uncomfortable, not wanting to get involved. It was not their business, not their battle and certainly not their war.

The atmosphere was terrible, and Claire was glad to get out of the office at lunch time to meet Andrew Kennedy, a close friend from her college days. The two friends had a long-standing arrangement to have lunch together every third week of the month to catch up with what was happening in their lives. She wanted to discuss her impressions of Ashley with him. He was a rock of good sense upon which she could always reply. Claire had learnt that when Andrew gave advice it tended to be solid and reliable or else he simply declined to comment, saying he did not know enough about the circumstances to offer an opinion. Just because he gave good advice did not mean that Claire always took it, it was usually a fifty – fifty situation. Andrew had observed that Claire listened to the part of his advice which suited her the best and ignored the rest, leading her onto a course of action which he never would have advocated. But he was a man and she was a woman and that fact alone ensured that they were going to respond to situations differently.

When Andrew left college, the economy was faltering but he was startled to discover that he was offered every job he interviewed for. The recruitment agency told him it was because of his exceptionally strong personality, a comment which Claire loved to tease him about. Secretly she could not understand why the recruiter had described him in those terms since she considered him to be a quiet person, a listener rather than a talker. Andrew once pointed out to her that for every person who talked, there should be somebody to listen. She talked, he listened, they got along fine together and in regard to their relationship, Claire adopted the old motif of 'if it ain't broke, don't fix it'.

Andrew was one of those rare people whom everybody liked, and he never seemed to have any trouble getting on with people at work.   He won respect by being technically competent and his affable demeanour disarmed the political players he encountered in the work environment.   Andrew did not aspire to be a fat cat in the world of finance, his secret lack of ambition was fuelled by his belief that banking and accounting were boring professions. He played the game at work and kept his opinion of the rat race to himself, primarily because his job paid the bills and was a means to an end. With turbulence in the world markets an ever-present danger to the operations of the banking system, it was best policy for a junior bank manager to hold fast and keep his own counsel whilst being a cog in the wheel.

At their last meeting Andrew had confided to Claire that he was six years out of college and looking for something more fulfilling than working a twelve-hour day compiling figures for a dried-up bank. No spreadsheet, no matter how good looking, could compete with having a beautiful woman in his life.

'But what about Susie? She's pretty isn't she?' a confused Claire understandably drew attention to his girlfriend.

'Very pretty', agreed Andrew. 'Why else would I be going out with her for the last two years?'

Why indeed?

Claire pushed open the pub door and scanned the room for Andrew, spotting him at a table reading the newspaper, putting small chunks of his dinner into his mouth and chewing it well, with no danger of any gravy spots landing on his pressed white shirt.   Andrew had three work suits which he rotated throughout the year, a black one, a blue one and a grey one which he wore as a uniform to blend in with the crowd. Claire much preferred to see his five foot, ten-inch-tall body dressed in the blue jeans and sport tops which he favoured out of the office.

Andrew acknowledged Claire with a movement of his hand before he was distracted by the girl behind him knocking over a chair as she tried to squeeze into a tight space at a small table where three of her girl friends were already sitting. Andrew immediately stood the chair upright and picked the girl's bag up off the ground to hand it over to her. She thanked him briefly for his help before turning aside to launch into an animated conversation with her friends. Claire caught a segment of the girls' conversation as she passed by their table.

'The good men are all taken.'

'They're so full of themselves, they don't make any effort. The last one told me I could text him if I was interested. In your dreams, pal'.

'I often text men first, it's an accepted norm. I'm fed up with it though. My mother told me to move out of Dublin to the country, I'd have a better chance of meeting a farmer or a policeman.'

'A nurse and a policeman, how old fashioned but cute is that?', teased her friend.

'I'd be able to buy a lovely house in the countryside with a policeman. I'm actually considering the move. My mother's no fool, she has a great life. Everything is cheaper in the country and the salaries are the same for nurses and policemen. My rent has gone up here again too. It is barely leaving me enough money to get my highlights done.'

Claire noticed that none of these girls had given Andrew a second glance. Each and every one of them could have been given a telescope and they still wouldn't be able to spot a good man free of a wedding ring on his finger.

They look but they do not see.

Andrew wore thick rimmed glasses which gave him a studious air, but Claire knew that when he laughed, his hazel eyes lit up his whole face. He had sandy hair and a fair complexion with freckles across the bridge of his nose. His features were boyish and symmetrical, pleasing to the eye but unremarkable. He stood up when Claire reached him, and she surprised him by planting a kiss on his cheek.

'I saw you help that girl out. Always the gentleman, Mr. Kennedy', she teased.

'I know, I know, they'll write it on my tombstone when they bury me with my dog, "Here lies Gentleman Andrew, he was a nice man", agreed Andrew ruefully.

'It will be a beautiful ceremony, I'll come with my twenty grandchildren and do a reading', promised Claire.

'Empty promises, you have one child, statistically you will be doing well to have four grandchildren. Eat up, I've got you your favourite beef sandwich and a bowl of soup, so you don't have to queue'.

'Thanks Andrew, I'm starving. Look at this place, it's mobbed. People obviously have money again'. The pub was hopping with people and the aroma of delicious food whetted their appetite.

'The economy is growing but wages are static or barely increasing for a lot of people and taxes are high. The banks are being careful about lending out money. I think a lot of people are weary of staying in to safe guard their money and they are going out and about again to have some fun.'

'I heard your bank was subcontracting its IT department to India. Your job is safe for now, isn't it Andrew?' queried Claire.

'I'm hoping it is secure, but it is impossible to be sure. A lot of the old timers are eying up redundancy deals but I'm not there long enough to get a decent package. It's a pity because I'd consider taking a lump sum to go trekking through the Himalayas'.

'How adventurous of you, most people still put real money into a house. Are they paying out bonuses again? That might fund a fabulous holiday', said Claire.

'They actually are paying out bonuses, but it is all very hush, hush, we are sworn to secrecy. How is it going for you at work these days?'

'I'm glad you asked because I want to talk to you about it. It looks like the bitch from hell has been appointed as a senior manager in Finance and her main objective is to wreak havoc in the place.'

'Are you sure she is not just shaking things up to make her mark?' queried Andrew.

Claire shook her head emphatically and filled him in on Ashley's rough treatment of Tracey.

'She treats staff as if they are handkerchiefs to blow her nose in before hurling them into the bin. I'm telling you Andrew, she is awful; I've never come across anybody like her before. I don't know what is the best way of dealing with her.'

'It is best to be professional and polite while keeping your distance. Keep a detailed diary of everything she says to you. You need to protect yourself by documenting everything that happens at work. I know it is not easy because it takes time to do, but it is worth the effort.'

'Have you ever had to keep that type of diary Andrew?'

'No, thankfully I have never needed to, but I know people who could not sleep at night if their work dairy was not fully filled in. It can be an effective bargaining tool when the shit hits the fan'.

'My mother believes it is better to work for a man than a woman any day of the week', divulged Claire.

'I've had two female managers and they've both been easy to work for. I could not help but admire the way they juggled heavy work commitments with kids and family responsibilities. You know better than anybody how difficult it is to pull that off Claire,' said Andrew.

'I can't imagine Ashley with children of her own. Maybe that's part of the problem, she's married to the job and trying too hard to climb the corporate ladder. She could be miserable in her private life and as jealous as hell, dragging it into the office to make us miserable too. I can't see her in a meaningful relationship or having anything outside of work which matters to her.'

Andrew shrugged his shoulders, making no comment.

'Does it sound like Ashley is some kind of aberration, a psycho?' mused Claire.

'Unfortunately, no. There is a new breed of "Leopard" manager coming along who is completely ruthless and unrelenting. They are the ones getting promoted because the people working under them are frightened into giving a hundred and twenty percent to keep them off their backs while the decent, more accommodating managers are only getting eighty percent effort out of their people. It is not just the woman, the men getting ahead are ball breakers too.'

'Their motto is to grab, gobble and go and then laugh about it. I for one wish Ashley would just go now, before she does any more damage,' said Claire.

'They will only leave if they get bigger and better remuneration packages elsewhere. Often, they know deep down they've got lucky. We're not talking Einstein sized brains here. They network madly, have thick necks, attack at strategic moments and can bluff or lie without blushing. They value themselves but not the people reporting into them. If their business strategy fails, then they change the discussion which surrounds it. Their philosophy is changing the culture in organisations for the worst and inevitably the workers feel they are easily replaced numbers.'

'It is a bit depressing isn't it? We should be able to respect the people we work for, they are meant to be better at their jobs than us. We all have to work and earn money to get by,' commented Claire. She paused for a second before asking the question which had been going around in her mind for some time:

'Do you suppose there's a different dynamic between a man reporting to a woman, compared to a woman reporting to another woman?'

Andrew threw back his head and laughed his hazel eyes merry behind the thick glasses.

'You mean, do I think women are different from men? Yes, I do. It seems to me that when it comes to the workplace, women who become managers display a preference for dealing with men. I don't know why, because outside work it is impossible to separate them from the sisterhood'.

'They don't mention women freezing out other women when they talk about the glass ceiling blocking off career advancement for women,' said Claire.

'Hell no, can you imagine any well-known personality sparking off such a debate? A man would be pecked to death by the birds on Twitter.'

'Ashley's like an eagle pecking at us little sparrows'.

Andrew's lips twitched.

'You are not that much of a pushover Claire. Look, behave in a confident manner around this Ashley person and you will have a much better chance of her leaving you alone. If she does manage to rattle you, act as if you have a massive secret like winning the lotto which you are hugging to yourself. If it helps to bolster your confidence, get your hair done and invest in chic outfits to wear at work. Strive to keep smiling and to remain calm. It is important not to show fear or nervousness when you are around her', he advised.

'But I think I am afraid of her Andrew. In the short time she has been in Finance she has shown a frightening lack of respect for people. I need my job, but I am not sure I can work for a person like her for any length of time,' Claire spoke in troubled tones.

'Listen to me Claire; you are working for Leictreach, not for her. She is only allowed to do what the organisation lets her get away with. If she behaves as badly as you say, then she might not be there long, the company might let her go during her probationary period.'

'And turkeys will vote for Christmas, you've just told me that ball breakers are the ones being promoted in organisations today. So back to Plan A, act confident around her, be calm, smile……… oh God, I'm not able to do it, I already keep my head down and my eyes glued to the computer screen whenever she comes into the room', Claire moaned.

'Of course, you can do it and remember, everybody has a boss and Ashley can do zilch without his agreement. Daniel is the big boss of your department and you get on well enough with him, don't you?' encouraged Andrew.

It was true, over the last two and a half years Claire had built up a huge respect for Daniel and she believed that he liked her and appreciated the work she did.

'There you go, problem solved. Daniel is the master puppeteer pulling the strings of the puppets and muppets in your finance department and Ashley will learn that truth sooner or later. In the meantime, you just have to put on an act and behave as if nothing fazes you. Smile and say nothing of any consequence, blend in and everyone will say you're a dream. If the going gets tough, just think that at five o'clock you can walk out of the office and go home to a small boy who is always thrilled to see you.'

Claire gave her friend's arm an appreciative squeeze.

'Thanks Andrew, you are the best, no, you are the best of the best.'

Andrew gave her a sudden shy smile. 'You're not so bad yourself. C'mon, we'd better get out of here before neither of us has a job to go back to.'

As Claire and Andrew stood up to put their coats on, the four young women at the next table were all motion too. The girl Andrew had previously helped turned around to acknowledge them and this time Andrew seemed to be much more to her liking. Claire found herself wondering if she had been busy ear wigging on them and had decided to give Andrew another look.

'Thank you for your help earlier', said the girl, beaming at Andrew.

'No problem', he replied.

'It's a nice place isn't it? I usually come here for lunch on Fridays.'

There was no doubt about it, the girl must have eaves dropped on their entire conversation and now she was definitely angling for an opening with Andrew. It was funny really, how quickly people's perceptions could change. Since Andrew was already in a relationship with Susie, this girl's romantic prospects would be better served by taking herself to the sidelines of the local GAA football club and supporting the team. Either that or follow the mother's advice and move to the countryside!

Andrew nodded agreeably and followed Claire to the door, where they hugged and quickly said their goodbyes. The lunch had lasted longer than normal and they both had to get back to work. Claire worked flat out in the afternoon and was nearly half an hour later than normal leaving the office. Ashley's door was open as she passed by and Claire had the misfortune of hearing her penetrating voice on the phone, dictating to the agency which supplied them with relief staff.

'I caught her as she was leaving disgracefully early and told her not to bother coming back here again. I don't care if she's been here a year, she's useless and totally unreliable. She's on your payroll, not ours, and that makes her your problem. Send me in somebody new first thing in the morning but this time make sure she's good'.

There was a brief pause, followed by the unlovely comment:

'Am I making myself clear? Don't make your problem, my problem. Otherwise we will switch to another agency for sourcing staff. That will put an end to your juicy placement fees.'

Claire felt sick to her stomach as she made her way towards the train station. Poor Tracey, Ashley had made mince meat of her. Ashley was a bully who had ruthlessly issued the order to terminate a vulnerable girl's employment and it made Claire fearful of the damage she was capable of doing to the rest of them. As she stood waiting on the platform for her train, she pulled her mobile phone out of her coat pocket and sent a text to Tracey.

Are you OK? I'm worried about U Claire.

Tracey's response came through seconds later.

.

I lost my baby, my baby's gone.

The noise of the approaching train exploded in Claire's ears and her stomach lurched and heaved as she pressed the phone so hard in her hand it was a wonder it did not smash into smithereens. Claire was a mother of a small child herself and she immediately felt empathy with Tracey for her huge loss. She recognised feelings of pity and sadness within her for Tracey, but she also detected stirrings of fierce anger. Had Ashley's unkind taunts and actions placed such stress on Tracey that she had suffered a miscarriage as a result? Or had the baby in her womb been biologically unfit to survive? Nobody would ever know but it was irrefutable that Ashley's horrible harshness had contributed to Tracey's anxiety levels going through the roof during her brief pregnancy. Ashley might as well do the world a favour and sew a large, capital "B" symbol on her designer suits, to mark her out as the bitch she was and make her easier to deal with. Instead, there was a real danger that Ashley was going to trample over the competition and end up the victor collecting the spoils at the top of the hierarchical heap.

CHAPTER THREE

'Zing…. Claire felt a deep sense of satisfaction as she emailed her latest report to Daniel. She had nailed that report; she sometimes amazed herself with her flashes of brilliance. She had mentioned this once to her father Tom, a practical man who had counselled her against being too brilliant; she got on fine with Daniel for now but one day she might need the support of other people with influence in the company and drawing attention to facts and figures which might threaten their bonuses was not the way to be going about it.

"People move around, and Daniel won't always be your boss. Don't be stepping on the wrong toes if you want a future in that company. People don't appreciate an analyst coming along and pointing out all they have done wrong', Tom cautioned. 'I know, I worked forty years in the same organisation and there were always people lying in the long grass, ready to get you if they thought you were responsible for making their lives more difficult. They turn the problem back on you and suddenly, you are the person who has to solve the problem they created because you were the one who pointed it out. People in high positions are thick skinned and brush over their mistakes. If they don't like you, they get rid of you, it doesn't matter how well you do your job.'

'Give over Tom,' instructed her mother Eileen. 'You can't put an old head on young shoulders. Let Claire find her own way. The world has changed, there are more opportunities for young people nowadays. Claire gets along well with people and she's a clever girl who is not afraid of hard work. She'll do just fine, given time and space'.

For the most part, before Ashley's arrival on the scene, Claire had succeeded in shutting out her father's words of warning; firstly, she fully respected Daniel and secondly, because she believed in the power of facts and figures to tell a straightforward story. It frustrated her to see senior mangers authorising actions based on their personal preferences and bias as opposed to an objective evaluation of the benefits versus the costs of a proposal, interpreting the data dubiously to rubber stamp a decision which had already been made. But she was aware too that large organisations employed HR specialists who were expert in managing exit strategies for members of staff who no longer pleased the reigning regime. Claire did want to please, and she worked extremely hard to make sure she met every deadline while producing figures she could stand over.

It was difficult to showcase her talents and ability in Leictreach, since its hierarchal structure ensured that recommendations had to be made by a person of more importance and authority than a junior financial analyst if they were to merit serious consideration. Every report she produced either fed into another report or had somebody else's name on it. When Claire was not being inspired to write reports which clearly showed that there were too many people in the mighty multinational being paid far too much to do their jobs, she was busy posting mundane entries in the system for the month end accounts. Those at the top had zilch interest in the plight of the employees who were paid too little for their work and were not mentioned in any report.

Claire's work ranged from complex projects to routine weekly tasks. Her own salary was paltry to begin with, but she had been given a big percentage pay hike at her performance appraisal a couple of weeks ago, at a time when most people in the company deemed themselves lucky to be getting minuscule rises. She had studied for years to gain employment in a job she relished, and her hard work was beginning to pay off. She hugged the memory of the great compliment Daniel had bestowed on her during her review:

'What I like about you Claire is that you rise to a challenge.'

Daniel had requested her to keep quiet about her salary increase and she had heeded his words, not wanting to stoke up resentment among her colleagues. She was also aware that when the financial controller instructed a minion in his department to keep a fact confidential, it was more than the person's job was worth to let it slip. It was onwards and upwards from here on in. Or at least it had been up, until Ashley had started work as a manager within the department. Perhaps she should have listened to her father more. It was Ashley's appointment that was causing these dormant worries about being unappreciated and under valued to emerge into her consciousness. Claire was quietly ambitious, and recognition of her work effort was important to her.

Claire looked around the empty room. She had been the first to arrive and the last to leave the general office again. Where had the day gone? She had intended to go out at lunch time to get her hair done but had ended up eating a sandwich at her desk. Her day had been spent answering unexpected queries from a programme manager; it had thrown her schedule out of kilter. She had better hurry up and leave, she had to collect Ben. They had left home at a time when the rain was driving down hard, most other households on their street were still slumbering and the cold blackness of the winter night had not yet lifted.

'It's still the middle of the night Mommy', protested Ben. 'I don't want to go. Let's stay. Take the day off.'

There was no school today, but she had to go to work, one day the child would understand. An image of Ben's earnest little face staring out of her parents' front bay window, watching and waiting for her return, came into her mind's eye. She knew Ben was much more likely to be engaged in an interesting activity with a doting grandparent rather than fretting for her, because he was a child with two homes and was happy in either one. The guilt of a working mother never fully went away, and it was a feeling which intensified in her own situation, where she had to be both father and mother to her child.

Ben was her white-haired boy of Irish folklore; he was her delight and could do no wrong; he was the sun in her sky; he formed the ground beneath her feet; he was responsible for the laughter and song in her voice. He had been born weeks after she had finished her business degree course in Trinity College Dublin and it was hard to believe he was already turning six. Ben's father had jumped on the fastest plane to America as soon as he had dotted the last 'i' and crossed the last 't' on his final exam paper, never setting eyes on his son. Thanks to the unstinting support of her parents, Claire had been able to study at night for her accountancy exams and then hold down a demanding job with long hours at Leictreach. Tom and Eileen unselfishly cared for Ben while Claire was at work and this gave her the peace of mind she needed to concentrate fully on her job.

Claire had not moved from her computer for hours and as she pushed herself away from her desk, she slipped her thumb into the waist band of her trouser suit. Judging by the fit of her trousers she had definitely put on weight. She had become suspicious when her elderly but active father had started advising her to take a brisk twenty-minute walk around the block at lunch time, saying it would sharpen her brain and result in her working more effectively throughout the afternoon.

'People make time for what is important to them', pronounced Tom.

If only she could invent time out of thin air. She made her way along the corridor to see Daniel approaching from the opposite direction, his shock of grey hair, rimless glasses and tall, lean body making him easily identifiable.

'I reviewed your report Claire. Good work, it was exactly what I was looking for', he acknowledged. 'Thanks Daniel,' replied Claire pleasantly, knowing he was heading back to his office for a few more hours of number crunching before heading home. He looked tired, as if the constant strain of juggling all the accountancy balls in the air was starting to get at him, knowing full well that he could not afford to drop any of them.

'Maybe he did need Ashley's help after all, it might prevent him from having a heart attack', reasoned Claire, in an attempt to reconcile herself to the changes taking place in the office.

Claire glanced at an ornate mirror hanging at the bottom of the stairway, a move which prompted her to dip into her bag in search of lip gloss and mascara. She rarely used any other make-up; her skin was lucent and did not need foundation. At least she was still pretty, even if she had put on weight. When she was a child, people were struck by her red corkscrew hair streaked with gold and her dark blue eyes set in a heart shaped face and frequently commented that she resembled a porcelain doll. Claire was concerned that lines were starting to show on her forehead, but lipstick certainly highlighted her beautiful bow shaped lips.

Claire jogged slowly to the nearby train station, the rain seeping steadily into the fabric of her winter coat. She was lucky and did not have to wait long for the train to arrive. As soon as Claire opened the door of her parents' four bed, semi detached house in the Dublin suburb of Raheny, her mother appeared in the hallway. Eileen was an older version of Claire, except that her hair was straight and ash white. She could have been a model for a skin care commercial for mature ladies.

'You're late Claire', said Eileen in greeting. 'I've told you before, go to work on time, do your work on time and leave on time. You know we love having Ben, but you are his mother and he needs to see you. Come into the fire child, you look worn out.'

'I know Mam, I'm sorry but I had to finish off my report. They expect me to work all hours if that is what it takes to get the job done, unpaid overtime is part of the deal', said Claire, placing her sodden coat over the warm radiator. 'Where's my boy?' she beamed as she entered the sitting room. Ben was nestled on his grandfather's lap in the big armchair in the corner of the room, watching one of 'his' programmes on the television. An open fire crackled in the fireplace, radiating heat which warmed Claire's cold body and boosted her mood.

'Mommy!' Ben's happy voice rang out. He launched himself off his Granddad's knee to run over and hug Claire around the waist, swaying his whole body backwards on his heels to look up at her face.

'Look what we done…look what we done', Ben chanted, pointing proudly to an impressive aeroplane taking pride of place on the small coffee table. Tom kept a number of unopened boxes of building blocks stashed away in cupboards, ready to be taken out and assembled whenever Ben got bored indoors. Claire considered some of the models were so complicated that only people with a mechanical engineering degree should attempt assembly. After forty years working as an electrician, with carpentry as a hobby, model building presented no difficulty to the skilled hands of her father.

'It's brilliant, darling, well done', she said. 'You and Granddad make a great team'.

'Of course we do', Ben said. "Of course" was one of his favourite phrases, which he determined to use as often as possible. 'Mom, Jack hit Dermot at school today'.

'And what did Dermot do when Jack hit him?' asked Claire.

'He kicked him', replied Ben.

'Good on him. If Jack hits you Ben, punch him on the nose', chimed in Granddad Tom.

Her father was still a big man, although at seventy years of age his burly frame had shrunk from the towering heights of his heyday. His once brown hair had turned grey, but it was still abundant for a man of his years. It was obvious he had been a handsome man in his prime with his deep brown eyes, prominent nose and cleft chin. Eileen joked that if she could not have Sean Connery, she would have to make do with Thomas Howard.

'Yes Granddad, I'll punch him on the nose', Ben promised, taking up a karate stance.

Claire laughed along with her father, but Eileen frowned.

'You must not do that Ben, we don't hurt anybody. You tell the teacher and let her sort it out,' said Eileen.

'You do what your Granny says Ben, but if that doesn't work out, punch him hard as you can on the nose', said Tom, swinging his own arm. 'We don't want him coming back at you.'

'Leave the child alone, the teachers are trained to deal with these things. Are you staying here tonight?' questioned Eileen as she handed Claire a cup of tea and a plate of sandwiches.

'Thanks Mam, but we're probably better going home and sticking to the routine.'

'Whatever you think is best, but you know there's always a bed for you here and it's dark and cold outside.'

After a brief chat with her parents she gathered up Ben and drove the short distance to their two up, two down house in Donnycarney. The heating was set to come on in the house at six o'clock and she had left the light on in the sitting room. She did not like returning to a cold, dark, empty house. She gave Ben a light supper and then it was time for pyjamas, teeth brushing and story telling. An hour and a half after arriving home, Ben was climbing into bed, yawning loudly. He reached up to lock his arms around his mother's neck, the unmatched elasticity and smoothness of his cheek pressed against hers.

'Do you know what?' whispered Ben, eyes huge in the semi-darkness.' I love you even beyond Heaven, to where the aliens are in space ships'.

'I love you beyond words and I'm very proud of you. Goodnight my angel, sleep tight,' said Claire, tucking the duvet around him.

'Don't let the bed bugs bite', the young voice lilted after her as she went down the stairs.

She was blessed to have her beautiful, healthy child safe beside her and her parents nearby to help her take care of him. None of it had been planned, but perhaps babies are destined to be born. Claire's pregnancy in her final year of college had come as a big disappointment to her parents; they had not expected their only daughter to have a baby with the father nowhere in sight. Luke Elliott had done a runner to America by the time Claire identified him as the father of her unborn baby. Tom threatened to wring Luke's neck if the "spineless pup" ever walked through his door again. In the absence of the child's father and with no money of her own, Claire had no option but to lean on her parents for support in rearing Ben. Life had gone on and it was obvious to anybody with eyes in their heads that Eileen and Tom adored Ben, they would not be without their grandson for the world. As for herself, Claire resolved to get serious about her life and her career. Her parents would not be around forever to take care of them. She had saddled Ben with the handicap of an invisible father. She owed it to him to provide him with the opportunities in life he deserved.

Claire hid the heartache, never mentioned Luke Elliott to anybody, the hurt caused by his abandonment of her and Ben ran too deep. Her failure to read his real character had shaken her to the core. She had always considered the name Luke had a solid, reliable ring to it. That was a laugh! When she told him about the baby he could not inform her quickly enough that he was going to America, a country where he had a right of residency. With his first class degree in physics, the world was his oyster and he was starting with America, the land of opportunity. He wanted money - bucket loads of it - and he couldn't wait to get started. A tiny baby didn't figure in his plans, nor of course did Claire.

In fairness to Luke, he had never told Claire that he loved her, but Claire had been besotted with him, intoxicated by the feel and smell of him. Luke had made no effort to contact her over the passage of six years. His silence in an age of global communications, where instant messaging was available to everyone, was painful. The world was being set on fire with the explosion in social media. Claire was aware that Luke had a social media profile and used it to keep in contact with many other people, but he had never used it to reach out to her. The truth of the matter was as clear as day; Luke did not want to acknowledge Claire or his son. Claire lived with that brutal truth every day and the hole that had been opened in her heart could not be filled in. It had eaten away at her, like a worm lodged inside an apple. Claire resolved that Luke Elliott would not cost her one more sleepless night. What a disappointment handsome Luke Elliot had turned out to be. If only her body had followed her brain, she would not have cried a stream of bitter tears into her pillow. Her mother had been right when she had warned her against the charming, feckless Luke Elliott, pointing out the merits of having a solid, dependable boyfriend like Andrew Kennedy instead. Andrew had only ever been a friend to her, but his girlfriend Susie was certainly trying her hardest to become the next Mrs. Kennedy, including tactics such as ingratiating herself with the elder Mrs. Kennedy at every opportunity.

Claire stirred restlessly in her bed, trying to blank out the images of the charismatic man who haunted her dreams. Her mobile phone bleeped, and she awoke groggily, wondering who on earth was texting her in the dead of the night. Was it from Tracey? But her mind was still full of memories about Luke. Her heart jumped. Was Luke finally reaching out to her from across the Atlantic, beseeching her to forgive him and begging her to let him see Ben? Not a chance, more fool she! The message came from Andrew.

Susie annoyed with me. I can't do right for doing wrong.

She blinked at the screen, trying to put order on all the jumbled thoughts milling around in her sleepy head.

> **U do a lot right. Susie mad about U.**
> **Relax, have a beer. U will sort it out tomorrow, C xx**

It was unusual for Andrew to mention Susie in this context to her. She hoped the text seemed caring, but the truth was that tonight Claire did not give a toss about the ups and downs of Andrew's relationship with Susie. She always had the feeling that Susie was friendly to her, not because she liked her, but rather because she was close friends with Andrew. Possibly a case of 'keep your friends close and your enemies closer'.

Claire continued to twist and turn, conjuring up an image of Luke lying down upon the ground and her reaching across to trace the laughter lines on his face with a blade of grass. She almost cried with frustration when her hand clutched at empty space. After all these years it was ridiculous that her dreams about Luke Elliott retained the power to disturb her sleep, like a spirit hovering over her. It was making her a prisoner of the past. She needed to be mindful of the present, not the past. Where had all the fun and energy gone?

In the morning, she felt tired and disgusted with herself. She must retrieve the merriment which had once defined her days. She must work harder at being happy. Enough was enough, she decided, it was time to progress, both at work and in her private life. Claire vowed not to mention Luke Elliott again to anybody, not even to her best friend Andrew and certainly not to her parents. The only exception to this vow of silence was Ben, for he had a right to question his parentage in the coming years. Luke Elliott was a Continent apart and had chosen not to be a player in Ben and Claire's world. Luke was one complication too many and it was more than time for her to move on mentally and emotionally from him. Claire realised it was time to sleep peacefully and wake up refreshed and undisturbed to the realities of life as a single mother to an adorable little boy, working in an office in Dublin

CHAPTER FOUR

As a matter of routine, the whole finance team trouped into the conference room once a month to be given a briefing on the key issues happening within the department and the wider company. Claire looked around the table, her eyes resting on Isabella, the petite dark haired Spanish girl brought in to replace Tracey. She had received a text message from Tracey's new husband Colin, thanking her for her concern but going on to convey the message that Tracey did not want to talk to anybody from Leictreach and she needed time to herself to get over her miscarriage. Claire tried to push thoughts of Tracey to the back of her mind and instead focused her attention on the present, noticing that Sandra had changed her hair colour from brown to black, Anna was platinum blonde again, Deirdre was showing off a smart new tartan jacket and red headed Joan should not wear that high necked ruffled blouse, it made her look like a stuffed hen. By contrast Amy, who was the other junior accountant in the department, looked sensational as she crossed her long supermodel legs, wearing a severe black high waisted tailored jacket, teamed with the shortest possible skirt a girl could get away with wearing in the office. A few people had sniffles and colds, not a good sign as it meant it was spreading through the office. Daniel would hate that, if people had to be sick, he preferred it to be on their holiday time. Claire had better snap to attention as the Big Boss had begun to speak.

Daniel began the normal quarterly power point presentation of charts and facts showing how all the divisions in Leictreach were getting on. He saved his bombshell to the end of the meeting, just as his restive staff were beginning to glance longingly at the door. It was a sure-fire way of getting their attention riveted on him again.

'As you may have heard, our finance director John Grayson is undergoing treatment for cancer and I have been asked to take over some of his duties for the foreseeable future. My input is also needed in the development of the new IT system to ensure that it will be able to meet the company's financial needs and objectives. These extra responsibilities necessitate me being based in the Ballsbridge office for four days out of five each week.'

A shocked silence greeted this news and the staff around the table all looked aghast at each other. What were they going to do without Daniel in the office; he had been there forever and was the font of all knowledge and the solver of all problems? Who were they going to go to in his stead? The unwelcome answer to the question was not long in coming their way.

'In my absence Ashley Scanlon will be in charge of Accounts Payable, Treasury, Payroll and Balance Sheet activity. Peter Jones will be responsible for the Debtors section and will liaise with the divisional managers over Income and Expenditure activity. All staff in Finance will report directly to either Ashley or Peter for their work in any of these areas. People will still report directly to me on matters concerning strategic planning and budgeting, as well as inter-company merger and de-merger activity', explained Daniel.

'So, it is still your department Daniel', drawled Deirdre laconically. 'We're not getting rid of you completely?'

Uneasy laughs floated through the room. Daniel smiled warmly back at her, aware that her easy familiarity had diffused some of the tension.

'It is still my department Deirdre and I'll be here one day a week to check in on everything and see that it is business as usual. You can appreciate that Ashley and Peter have difficult jobs to do and I know that I can count on you all giving them your full support.'

Claire looked around the table again to try to read people's faces as they digested the news. The department was already splitting in two on the issue. The people in Accounts Receivable were not too upset as they already reported directly to Peter Jones and he was regarded as an amenable manager. Ashley was a different kettle of fish and all those unfortunates in her line of command were already debating with themselves on their best line of defence. Was it better to suck up to her and get her to like you or should they keep their distance from her and hope for the best? Anna was looking at Ashley in open repulsion and the rest of the gang could at best be described as glum and unenthusiastic at the prospect of having her as their new boss.

Claire was trying to keep the distaste she felt at the prospect of Ashley being her direct line manager off her face. By contrast, Madam Scanlon was sitting there on her chair with the look of a Cheshire cat who had guzzled the cream on her face. She could not believe her luck on being presented with an excellent chance of empire building so soon after joining the company. Claire feared that Ashley was like a destructive child who had got her hands on the best toys in the shop, to be played with any which way she chose.

Daniel was in flying form and he had more in store for his captive audience.

'As you all know, Emmet is retiring on Friday after thirty years with the company. Nobody is sorrier than I am to see him go. He leaves big shoes to fill,' said Daniel.

'My shoes are too well worn to be used anymore Daniel', quipped Emmet.

'That's why you're retiring mate', joked Barry from Debtors.

'I'd still work you under the table lad, although I'd probably not drink you under it', Emmet came back at him good humouredly.

'We don't doubt your capacity for hard work Emmet, no man has earned his retirement more, I've seen to that', said Daniel smiling. 'We'll all be there on Friday to raise a glass to you. You know how well regarded you are in the company. There isn't a person in this room who won't miss you.'

This was indeed fulsome praise from Daniel and everybody in the room knew it.

'Getaway outta that. I know memories are short in this country, unless we're talking about the great players in the GAA. But I'll leave a picture of myself with my teeth in for you all to remember me by, for when Daniel comes looking for you all to do the loaves and the fishes,' said Emmet gleefully.

Everybody laughed when they heard the habitual lament which broke from Emmet's lips whenever management asked him to perform the impossible in a given time period. They were all genuinely sad to see him go. Emmet was one of a kind and his retirement marked the end of an era in the department. When he left, Deirdre would be the only person over fifty in the department, although Daniel and Anna were coming up to that age.

'There is a new supervisor starting in Accounts Payable next Monday. Her name is Karen Woods and I expect you all to welcome her in her new position. She will be sharing an office with Ashley while she learns the ropes. Ashley has ultimate responsibility for Accounts Payable and, given that space has become tight and is at a premium, it makes sense for them to share until we can organise new offices in the building,' continued Daniel.

A dozen people in the room immediately made up their minds to be as nice as pie to the luckless Karen Woods. They imagined the poor girl starting work on a Monday and walking unsuspectingly into the lioness' den. It was enough to make a person weep, as the new girl would, in all probability, be doing all next week.

Claire was expecting Daniel to adjourn the meeting, enabling them to get back to work. It was not like Daniel to keep them away from their desks for longer than was strictly necessary. But no, Daniel had another card up his sleeve.

'The general office room on floor two has become too crowded to be an efficient workspace for everybody in it. It has therefore been decided to move Claire and Anna into the room adjacent to Ashley's office', he said.

Claire's mood completely nose dived when she heard this unexpected news. She immediately realised that the room Daniel was referring to was tiny for two people. She did not want to move out of the general office. She was quite happy being part of the group, joining in and out of the banter as work pressures allowed. All in all, it had turned out to be a rotten meeting.

'Hasn't that room always been used for storage Daniel?' Claire asked.

'The porters are clearing the boxes out as we speak Claire. Facilities are going to put up shelving in the room and the IT people will fix up your computers. It will be made as comfortable as possible for the two of you.'

'When are we to move in Daniel?' Claire had a sinking feeling she knew the answer. With Daniel, it was always 'as soon as possible'.

'I expect you and Anna to be based in your new office by the end of the week. That's about it. Thank you for your time,' Daniel dismissed the troops.

The finance team slowly pushed their chairs back and were subdued as they walked away. Daniel's news had shaken everybody. The vast majority had worked in Finance for at least two years or more. Although people groaned about the quantity of work they had to get through and griped that just because Daniel was a workaholic it did not mean that they had to all become one too, there was not a person in the finance department who did not trust or respect him. They did not like to think of Daniel being out of the building for four days out of five, especially when it entailed them being left to the less than tender mercies of Ashley.

It signalled a big change for Claire. Daniel had been her direct line manager since she had started work in Leictreach and from now on she would have to report into Ashley for a sizeable portion of her work. It was unusual for somebody in a non-managerial role in a large finance office to report directly to the financial controller, but it was down to the type of work Claire was involved in. At least she would still have some contact with him, but she had to accept the fact that Ashley was to be her new line manager on a day to day basis.

'He could have told us', complained Claire to Anna, resenting the manner in which Daniel had presented the office move as a fait accompli to them during the meeting.

'Ah, it will be fine once we get used to it', Anna replied brightly. 'Give us some peace and quiet from the grousing that goes on around here. C'mon, let's go and have a look at our new home from home. It's only a pity it is next door to the Queen Bee'

The nearest staircase was at the side of the building, as opposed to the main stairway which was used by the majority of people in Finance and this added to Claire's sense of separation from her peers. Unbelievable as it sounded, being in close proximity to Ashley was not the worst thing about their new office; that distinction belonged to the ten square metre size of the room. The room was a good space for one person but for two people with rows of folders and files and a printer to accommodate it was going to be a tight squeeze. They were going to have to draw in their breath and be careful not to brush off each other when entering and exiting the room. When the door was closed the room was definitely claustrophobic. Claire was sure that the dimensions were restrictive enough to breach office floor space and freedom of movement regulations. Options were limited as lodging a formal complaint about being cooped up like chickens could have unpleasant consequences. It was well known that it never paid anybody in Finance to make waves with Daniel and question his dictates.

Claire trailed her finger along a shelf coated with a think layer of dust, noticing that the paintwork was stained with dirt from the boxes which had been stacked upon them. It must have been years since this room was used for anything but storage.

'It's very dark in here Anna. Do you think they could give the walls a fresh coat of paint before we move in?' said Claire.

'There's no harm in asking, they can only say no and might say yes. It makes sense to do the painting before the shelving. It will make a big difference in here and a few plants and pictures will do the rest. It could be a right cosy den for us', said Anna optimistically. She was much more positive about the proposed move than Claire.

Anna bleeped for Dave the facilities manager and he obliged them by coming up to see them in their new office.

'A paint job can be done handy enough. A tin or two won't break the budget. Is it alright to put the shelves up from top to bottom on those two walls? We can get started on the job today and we should be ready to move the desks in by Wednesday', said Dave.

'Any chance of a partition between the desks?' requested Claire, causing Anna to spin around in surprise.

"Best to get settled in before you decide on anything like that, it might block the light. There is one little thing I should mention to you both".

The phrase **'one little thing'** usually spelt trouble.

'Go on, let's hear it', said Claire, her antennae quivering in the dust bowl.

'It's the overhead lights in the ceiling', responded Dave, sheepishly pointing upwards.

'What's wrong with them? Surely the lights aren't going to fall down on top of us, are they?' enquired Anna.

'That should only happen if the roof fell down too. No, no, that's not the problem. The lights are embedded in the ceiling and they are special lights which only come into the country from Germany,' replied Dave.

The two women looked at him uncomprehendingly.

'Can you not fit them with a regular light bulb, which you can buy from any corner shop?' asked Claire.

'No, that's what I'm trying to tell you. You can't buy the lights which fit into that ceiling in this country. They have to be imported from Germany. That's why this room hasn't been used as an office for so long. It's the lights you see, they are the difficulty.'

'Dave', Claire felt surreal disbelief that she even had to ask the question,

'Are you telling us that we are being put in a room with no lights, in the middle of February, and that we're expected to work on computers all day long in those conditions?'

'Yep, I guess you've just about summed up the situation. That's about the height of it. Don't you worry now, I've put the order in already and the lights should be delivered within the next three months. In the meantime, I'll bring you both up a desk lamp which you can use as you need it.'

'Three months! I don't believe this. This is a multinational company with huge resources, and we can't even get a proper light in our office'. Claire was disgusted at the turn of events. 'Is Daniel aware of the problem with this room?'

'He was up with me the other day, giving it the once over. He thought you could make do with it, because of the large window and the lamps. And neither of you wear glasses, so that's a plus', said Dave.

'We will need binoculars for eye strain if the ceiling lights take three months to come on! It can't possibly take that long. What's the real amount of time we can expect to wait until they're fixed Dave?'

'Honest to God, they took three months to arrive the last time they were ordered, not many must use them. They're worth it though; they last years once they're put in. In the meantime, I'll get you those desk lamps, as many as you want. There's no problem getting our hands on them'.

'Thanks Dave, we appreciate your help', said Claire. The affable Dave was their only hope of a quick delivery and it would be pointless to take out her frustration on him. Everybody had to carry out their jobs within company constraints.

'Ah we'll get it sorted, maybe sooner than we think', reassured Dave, before taking his leave.

'Why did you ask for a partition between the desks Claire?' asked Anna, feelings wounded.

'It's a small space Anna, I just thought we might be able to concentrate more on our work with a partition between us. It is normal practice for people working in close proximity to have a divider between them.'

Anna looked unconvinced, as if they were both young kids in the playground and Claire had told her they were no longer best friends.

'Oh dear', Claire inwardly signed, 'not a good beginning'.

Claire looked through the windows and spotted a skinny young man dressed in nothing but boxer shorts, ironing his clothes in front of the upstairs window of the house directly facing them.

'Look Anna', she gestured over to the man, guessing the sight of him could lift Anna's mood. Anna immediately brightened up and waved energetically over to the guy, who responded to his new audience by tossing his shirt up high and swinging his hips.

Ashley must have had her ear pressed against the dividing wall between the two offices because no sooner had they shared a laugh then she appeared silhouetted against the doorway, reminiscent of Cruella de Ville come to inspect the 101 Dalmatians.

'So, I find my staff here, loitering about instead of working at their desks', she drawled.

'We are not loitering Ashley. We came to view our new office in order to determine what needs to be done to it before we can move in', said Claire, immediately defensive.

Ashley gave the room a quick scan and smirked.

'It was my idea to put the two of you together in here. There was far too much talk going on in the general office and the atmosphere was polluted. I expect a more helpful attitude to emerge there over time', she said.

'Are you implying Claire and I are pollutants to be removed Ashley? ', said Anna, spots of red appearing on her face.

Ashley considered Anna coolly for a long moment, before smiling faintly.

'You're being very sensitive Anna, I was merely expressing the view that the general office will be quieter with fewer people in it, making it easier for people to concentrate on their work.'

Her bony finger drew a circle through the layer of dust on the desk, putting two dots inside for eyes and a semi circle curved upwards for the mouth.

'So, what's it to be?' Will you be happy here?' mused Ashley.

She drew another circle face, this time with the mouth turned downwards.

'Or will you be all sad?' she tutted.

'Better not give up the day job Ashley. Those pictures wouldn't win a child's art competition', sniped Anna.

'As usual, Anna, you miss the point', sneered Ashley. 'How you feel in this office will be essentially your own choice'.

'Wow Ashley, I hope for your sake that you're a better accountant than pretend psychologist', Anna hit back.

The half-smile vanished off Ashley's horsey face.

'The room does need to be cleaned up but then it will be fine. The most important thing is to get the computers functioning as normal. Log a call with IT support and get it sorted. Do you intend doing any work today or are going to dawdle around the place until you move in?'

Claire looked around the dank room, not yet an office and smaller than a prison cell for two. The disorder in the room offended Claire. She was an accountant by training, and she appreciated order, neatness, balance and logic, none of which was apparent to her in the current setup. Claire deliberately wiped her hand on the desk, obliterating the mad happy/unhappy circle faces which Ashley had drawn in the dust with such relish.

'We're leaving now Ashley, but the room does need a lot of work done to it before it will be fit for purpose', replied Claire with dignity.

'You heard Daniel, you are expected to be in it by the end of the week. Deadlines are deadlines in this department, with no exceptions', emphasised Ashley.

'I hate her already and she is just in the door', muttered Anna as they made their way back to the general office. The two women looked at each other and chanted in unison:

"And she's only going to get worse."

CHAPTER FIVE

Claire's initial sense of foreboding at the imminent move returned when they stepped back into the light filled general office. She was comfortable in this room, settled in her corner. It reminded her of gracious living in bygone days, when a well to do family were served afternoon tea on a silver platter by an attending maid, before the building was enlarged and remodelled into offices. The centre piece of the room was a magnificent mahogany fireplace, which had its grate boarded up and Anna's desk placed in front of it. The office furniture could not hide the fine Victorian features of the room, with its spacious dimensions, tall windows flanked by wooden shutters, and intricate coving decorating the high ceiling.

Claire could not admit it to Anna, who obviously thought differently, but she would have been much happier to remain in the large general office with the others, rather than for the two of them to move out and share such a small room together. She found it a daunting prospect, given the number of hours the two of them would have to spend closeted together in each other's company. There was a big age difference between the two women and they would not have sought out each other's company under normal circumstances. There were also privacy issues around interacting with one person in a tiny restricted space for forty hours a week; it meant more intimacy and time together than most people in relationships shared with each other by choice. Anna and herself normally got on well together but it was possible they would grate on each other's nerves when they were forced to spend so much time alone in each other's company. In a large, general office a person could choose to flit into and out of the conversation. Claire feared that in sharing an office for two it might be deemed impolite or unfriendly of her to ignore the other person, even when she had to work flat out to meet a deadline. Even though all these fears milled around in Claire's head, she did not realise the real threats which separation from her co-workers posed to her wellbeing; isolation and lack of support.

Emmet was standing chatting to the others as Anna and Claire entered the general office. He stretched out his long gangly arms with the dexterity of an octopus and gave them both a warm hug.

'Me auld flowers, why are youse looking down hearted? You've been promoted into your own office. It's a great day for youse both.'

'You haven't seen the office Emmet, or you wouldn't be saying that', replied Claire darkly.

'You're not seeing the bigger picture. The main thing is that Daniel has put you in an office for two. It's a step up. I've always been part of the crowd myself. Mark my words, the next thing is you'll have an office of your own with your name on the door. You've a bright future in this company my girl.'

'I'm going to miss you Emmet. The place just won't be the same without you', Claire returned the hug.

'Just make sure you don't miss my farewell party. Book your Ma to look after your little fellow on Friday,' instructed Emmet.

'I'll be there Emmet, I wouldn't miss your send off for anything', promised Claire.

''We'll all be there for you Emmet', affirmed Amy.

''I heard there's going to be a free bar in your honour Emmet. The place will be mobbed by people who've done nothing but give out yards about you for years'', teased Joan.

Everybody in the finance department was sad to see Emmet retire. They had known with the inevitability of night following day that the date of his departure would come, and some people had even joked with him that it could not come fast enough for all concerned. Emmet was one of the last of the old-timers in the place. Everyone knew him and had a high regard for him. Emmet was a true-blue Dub, born and bred in the city, as were his parents and grandparents before him. He was imbued with a Dubliner's wit and always lightened the mood within the office with his kind words and benign presence.

By any reckoning Dublin fifty years ago was a hard place to live in, with a pittance for pay if a person was lucky enough to find employment. Emmet once told Claire that he had made a pet of a rat when he was a boy, because a dog was too expensive to feed. A boy would not dare to touch a morsel of food kept in a cupboard without first getting permission from the mother of the house, for fear of being skinned alive. He was a Celiac whose condition was only diagnosed as an adult. He had suffered severe malnutrition as a child and was only saved by being sent to live for a couple of years with a kind aunt who had married a farmer in county Wicklow, where the food was plentiful. He maintained that a poor person had a better chance of getting by living in the countryside rather than the city because at least in the countryside you could grow your own food in a corner of a field and burn a fire made of sticks and turf in the fireplace to ward off the bitter cold of a winter's night.

Emmet had defied the odds and ended up with a cosy job as an accounts clerk in a big corporation. Those were the days when working as a clerk in an office was the equivalent of being an accountant in an organisation today. A person could guess by looking at the premature aging of the lines in Emmet's face and the hunched shoulders pushing down hard on his tall frame that he had endured tough times. Emmet was proud of his good respectable job, which paid a salary sufficient to buy a modest house and rear a family, and Claire could not recall him ever being in a bad humour.

Most of Emmet's conversation was about politics, centring on his die-hard loyalty to the Fianna Fail political party, GAA football and hurling and his "piéce de resistance", all the impossible things management were asking him to do in the time available for him to do it. He liked to find out what was happening in the lives of the people around him in the workplace, but he did not gossip about what he was told. He adored his wife and five children and worshipped his grandchildren. He made a special effort to be warm and friendly to prickly women at work, genuinely seeming to like them and to want the best for them. Anna was of the opinion that some men inexplicably liked bitches and Emmet was one of those men. Claire thought Anna was wrong about Emmet preferring nasty over nice because his wife was absolutely lovely, warm and artistic. It was more the case that Emmet was able to charm women with bitchy tendencies and dampen down their fire to a non-threatening flame, making the environment more comfortable for everybody. If anybody could have played Ashley and teased out her better nature, it was Emmet.

At the end of the day, Claire knew that the younger newcomers like herself had only seen glimpses of the real Emmet, despite his gregariousness in the office. She recognised that he preferred the company of men to women but had got used to dealing with women on close terms in the workplace. Claire would certainly miss him when he left, she had always found him interesting to talk to and liked the way he reached out occasionally to give her a friendly, paternal hug. There was nothing sexual or untoward about it. She was certainly not alone in the organisation in feeling that Emmet's retirement signified the passing away of the old guard.

There was a big turnout for Emmet's going away party and it was all great fun. The company had hired out a room off the main lounge in the Shelburne hotel in the city centre and they had also splashed out on food and drink. This was not normal practice and showed the regard in which Emmet was held throughout the organisation. Even Daniel attended the function, which was an unusual occurrence in itself. People from each of the five different geographical locations in Dublin and from every division of the company turned out in droves to bid him a fond farewell. The main man himself arrived with his wife and a couple of his children in tow, and they were regaled with stories of their loved one's exploits and foibles, collected in the company through the years.

'He had some great sayings all the same, I'll always remember him saying 'if the cat has kittens they'll put it into the computer', Claire smiled over at Emmet, who was bent over from the waist down, laughing and holding onto the shoulder of a man she did not recognise but guessed was based in one of the other divisions.

Laughing voices immediately chimed in with other phrases associated with Emmet: -

'He's a nice enough fella but has he got fire in his belly?'

'You're a right molly'

'There's women for you'

'Speed without accuracy is no speed at all'

'There's a man driving a truckload of hubris'

'They're leading me up the yellow brick road'

'You can't pluck feathers off a frog.'

'Don't turn puce on me, cough it up' (when asking for money).

Emmet with all his sayings would be long remembered with fondness by the people who had enjoyed the privilege of working with him. Claire thought it would be wonderful if Emmet was being replaced with somebody equally as warm and upbeat, but it was unlikely. The human resources department seemed to be specialising in recruiting go getters in their late twenties and early thirties, cool customers who were all out for themselves and their own remuneration packages. They needed to read the word empathy off a cue card; it was a learned response for many of them. They could pretend to project empathy for their colleagues, but they did not instinctively feel it.

Claire spied Ashley standing close to Daniel, smiling up at him in an attractive manner as if butter would not melt in her mouth. Daniel was about to be based in head office for the majority of the working week and his people in Finance were feeling more than a little bereft about it. He was always courteous when approached, no matter how much pressure he was under and members of the department felt they knew him and could depend on him if they had difficulties in work. The thirty-three people in Finance realised it was essential for the good of the reporting structures in the company that he should go, and spear head the development of the new ICT system, but they would miss him. As they were prone to giving out about all the work he expected them to do, most felt too sheepish to express their dismay at the thought of him leaving them for eighty percent of the working week. As Claire scrutinised Ashley's charm offensive on Daniel, Amy came up to stand beside her. The two girls were at a similar level in the department and often had lunch together. They got on well and shared a mutual liking and respect for each other.

'Don't say anything for the moment Claire, it's Emmet's night but, I'm leaving too,' revealed Amy.

Claire looked at Amy in dismay, totally thrown off balance by her news.

'You're not, Amy! When are you leaving? Why are you going?'

'Two weeks from now, I've handed in my notice, but I asked Daniel not to mention it till after Emmet's retirement party. I probably would have stayed longer but I was at a meeting with Ashley recently and she tried to make it look like it was my fault that something wasn't done. I'm not hanging around working for her. Lots of my friends are in Australia and I'm joining them there on a holiday visa. I can't wait to go, it will be a blast.'

'Amy, you can't go. I'm going to miss you and Emmet so much, you are the best people here', said Claire, genuinely upset to hear of Amy's planned departure.

'Thanks Claire, you've been great to work with too. I've passed my exams and I want to travel and see the world. We can keep in touch on Facebook. You'll never be without friends Claire, you're too nice,' said Amy. 'Come on, let's dance and have fun, we could all be dead tomorrow.'

Claire watched Amy dancing beside dumpy Dympna from Debtors for a moment, struck once more by her light gracefulness, a sunflower beside a tulip. Amy had sized Ashley up and decided to have no more dealings with her. The girl was brimming with confidence and refused to let anybody diminish her stature. Amy was choosing to leave in search of a bigger and better life, seizing opportunities as they presented themselves. Claire had the responsibility of rearing a child and did not have the freedom to toss in a letter of resignation and jump on a plane out of the country to go exploring with Amy.

Claire spotted Ashley standing on the opposite edge of the dance floor, taking in all the action, her coral lipstick a slash of colour in her thin, hardened face. She reminded Claire of the Queen of Hearts in 'Alice in Wonderland' who loved shouting 'off with their heads' to anybody who displeased her, although in Ashley's case the message was more likely to be 'off out the door'. Emmet and Amy were pure gold and they were both leaving, making the company a poorer place to be without the glow of their rich presence. Claire could only hope that, at the end of the day, it would not be only the dross or pliable 'yes, sir/mam, whatever the circumstances' protectionist brigade who remained.

CHAPTER SIX

Ben's party for his sixth birthday was being held at Tom and Eileen's house to take advantage of their long back garden, which could comfortably hold the all important bouncy castle. It had the added bonus of being located close to the national school and therefore his school friends all lived in the neighbourhood. Birthday balloons were blown up and tied with ribbons, ready to be hung on the garden gate to signal the party location. Eileen lit a candle in the local Church every day for a week praying that it would not rain on the Saturday, as she feared for her prized china if twenty children ran riot within the confines of the house. If God owed anybody a favour it was Eileen Howard and she was intent on cashing it in.

Claire and Ben were staying the night at her parents' house. Claire was glad when the time came to send her excited son off to bed, with Granddad Tom volunteering to read him a story. Mother and daughter stood back and proudly surveyed the fruits of their labour with pleased smiles on their faces. The floor and surfaces of the kitchen were spotless. Food and drink had been prepared for both adults and children, from rice crispy buns, popcorn, crisps, bowls of sweets, to food such as chips, cocktail sausages, chicken nuggets, fish fingers and pizza packed in the fridge freezer ready to be popped into the oven. Eileen had also made an apple tart, lemon cake, Victoria sponge and a berry pavlova and there was jelly and ice cream tucked away in the fridge, ready to be spooned out. There were jugs of juice for the children and bottles of mineral water and wine for the adults standing on top of the worktops. Party bags were packed for the visiting children to take away with them. In the centre of the table stood a magnificent chocolate cake, crafted in the shape of a spaceship. There was no way all the food could be eaten at the party, but Eileen intended to bring the bountiful leftovers to the parish community hall on Sunday for people to enjoy after Mass. This eased her conscience, given she was a woman who did not approve of waste.

The phone rang, and Eileen wiped her hands on the front of her pink stripped apron.

'I'll get it Claire. Be a good girl and make us a pot of tea. We deserve it after all our hard work'.

She went out into the hall to answer the phone and Claire did as she was told, carrying a tray full of tea and biscuits into the sitting room. Tom had made it back to his favourite armchair in time to watch the nine o'clock news.

'Thanks love', he said, taking his cup of tea.

'What are the headlines?' Claire asked.

'All bad news as usual, politicians out of their depth, children with no homes to go to and murder and mayhem happening throughout the country. I don't know what the world is coming to', said Tom, shaking his head.

Eileen came bustling into the room, wound up tight as a spring after her conversation with Claire's older brother Martin.

'Turn that telly down, it's too loud. Martin says he's not coming to Ben's party. He hasn't got the time! Did you ever hear such rubbish? It's a Saturday, what else has he got to do on a Saturday? It only takes three hours to drive from Sligo to here, that's nothing for a young man like Martin. He could make the effort to come to his only nephew's birthday party and see us all.'

'Martin never said he was going to come to the party Mam. It's okay, there is going to be plenty there,' said Claire, trying to placate her mother.

'Well, he didn't say he wasn't going to come', snapped Eileen. 'Of course we were expecting him. I've only two children and I want him to be there. The last time we saw him was Christmas. Your father and I could be dead and buried since then. Remember when he jumped on a plane and it only took him half an hour to get here from Sligo? And now he says he has no time to join us for Ben's party!' Eileen's chest swelled in indignation.

'It was a ridiculous extravagance flying from Sligo to Dublin', said Tom. 'Martin is better off keeping his hands in his pockets and saving his money. Ben won't know the difference, he'll be playing with the other children and ignoring the adults.'

'I know the difference. I'm his mother and I say Martin should be taking an interest in his nephew, especially since the poor little mite has no father. Ben is a boy, and growing boys need men in the family to show them the right way to behave,' said Eileen firmly.

'Ben sees Dad nearly every day of the week and he is a man. He could not want for a better role mode than Dad', Claire interjected, not liking the way the conversation was going.

'Your father is getting older and he won't be around forever', said Eileen. 'We might be too old or too sick to guide Ben properly when he's a teenager and needs a firm hand. The world is changing fast. We know nothing about social media or bullying on phones. Martin needs to get close to Ben while he is still a child, to be ready to step into your father's shoes when the time comes.'

'I look after Ben. Plenty of women have brought up boys on their own and made a fine job of it. Men have always gone away either to work or to fight. I'll do what needs to be done, at any given time, to see that Ben is fine,' said Claire defensively.

'Certainly, a woman can bring up a boy on her own, I'm not disputing it. But I think it is better if the mother has a good man in the family close by, somebody the boy can talk to and copy as he grows. You are a wonderful mother Claire but, if you don't mind me saying so, sometimes I think you are too strict with Ben. You can pick at him to behave perfectly, as if you are trying to make a girl of him, rather than let him act like a boy. You have a little boy, not a little girl. Let him jump and make noise and take things apart. And he doesn't have to have more manners than anybody else in the room, including the adults. With the best will in the world, you can't show him how a man thinks and behaves', said Eileen.

Claire's temper was rising and luckily Tom intervened before matters got out of hand and things were said that could not be retracted. He got out of his armchair and walked over to Eileen and put both his hands on top of her shoulders, giving her his full attention.

'I'm still very much here you know', he smiled. 'Don't you be worrying about Martin or Ben, or Claire for that matter. I've just been watching the news and I can tell you that, in comparison, we're the lucky ones. Have a little faith woman. Our family is having a party tomorrow and from the looks of the kitchen, we'll be welcoming an army of guests. You are disappointed Martin is not coming but I am sure he has his reasons and we will see him soon. We have to enjoy the good times while they are here and not be worrying about the future. We've got our health, haven't we?'

Eileen held her husband's eyes and then relaxed her body against his tall frame, letting go of her anxiety, glad to feel his arms encircling her. It was unusual for Claire to witness such a tangible display of her parents' affection for each other.

'You're right, my dear. But I believe Martin is troubled. Whatever is causing it, it is the same thing as what is keeping him away from us. I won't rest easy until I see him with my own eyes.   If he won't come to us, then I'll go to him. We are a family and we look out for each other. It's what we do. That's part of my faith. In the meantime, we'll enjoy Ben's party. The child deserves it, for all his hard work at school and for doing all we ask of him.'

Observing her parents, Claire acknowledged that their love for each other had endured through all the ups and downs of their lives together over forty years, as they remained steadfast and true to each other and the vows they had taken on their wedding day. It was only recently that Claire was beginning to see Eileen and Tom as a couple in their own right, as opposed to thinking of them as being her parents. They were devoted and kind to each other, respectful and considerate. Where was she going to find a man of similar calibre to her father? Did they even make men like him anymore? But then again Claire could not possibly want a younger version of her father for herself because that would be just plain weird and (cringe) possibly involve her turning into a mini version of her mother.

 What Claire wanted was a man who was one of a kind, a staunch ally who she could joyfully commit to with body and soul, one who could make her laugh in the face of the unexpected complexities that life threw up around them. She refused to settle for less, even if it meant she might be forever looking over the menu instead of consuming the meal.

At 6am the next morning, Ben came hurling into her bedroom full of birthday bounce, proclaiming 'Get up Mommy, it's morning time'. To prevent Ben from waking her parents, Claire had no option but to shake off her drowsiness and begin the day. Thank the inventors for the wonderful babysitting prowess of television and screens. Around noon, when the sun emerged as a real presence in the sky, a deeply satisfied Eileen gave thanks to the Lord who had heard her for dry weather and congratulated herself on been born into the right religion all those years ago. Small things going right always brightened up Eileen's day.

From the minute the party swung into action, it was relaxed and fun. Claire's main duty was to keep an eye on the food in the oven and dole it out on paper plates when it was fully cooked. Tom took up the post of sentry in front of the bouncy castle, encouraging the children to jump and climb safely and sternly rebuking attempts to perform wild gymnastics or contortions upon it. Children liked her father, thought Claire, observing them laughing and chatting away to him. The boys were definitely more boisterous than the girls, but Tom was well able to keep them all good humouredly under control.

Andrew and his girlfriend Susie arrived together, with Andrew exchanging a wrapped present for a plateful of food. 'Your mother is a foodie Goddess', said Andrew. 'I'll go outside and help your father. It looks like every kid within a radius of two miles has squeezed themselves onto that bouncy castle.'

Susie stayed beside Claire in the kitchen, but she seemed distracted and unhappy, surreptitiously watching Andrew through the open kitchen door. She reached for a glass of white wine and gulped it down thirstily before filling it up again and swirling it around. Predictably Susie ignored the food, for she did not eat by the clock nor upon its availability; rather food was ingested when darts of hunger pangs assaulted her stomach. Her straightened black hair fell in a thick curtain onto her slender shoulders, but it looked too heavy for her petite frame. Susie enjoyed the process of layering on makeup, experimenting with different looks and colours and showcasing her brown eyes with lashings of mascara. Her nails were always a work of art to be noticed and admired.

Today her golden nails matched her patterned sequined top, which she wore over blue jeans and high heeled brown fringed boots. She was usually perky and upbeat, full of "hi's" and hugs, but for once she was subdued. It brought to mind the late-night message Andrew had sent to Claire, which implied that there was trouble in paradise. Claire hesitated about voicing any inquiry or concern, since she considered Susie to be more of an acquaintance than a friend. It might be better for her to leave well alone and concentrate on overseeing the children attending the party. She wanted to enjoy Ben's special day but, in spite of herself, she could not totally ignore Susie's obvious agitation.

'How are you Susie? I haven't seen you for a while. I hope everything is well?' asked Claire.

'No, it bloody well is not. Isn't it obvious that I'm upset?' snapped Susie. Claire's eyes widened in startled surprise at her hostile tone and Susie immediately apologised.

'I'm sorry, that was rude of me. But you and Andrew are such good friends, I expected him to have filled you in on what we're rowing about.'

'Andrew hasn't said a word to me about you', replied Claire. A flicker of annoyance flashed across the other girl's face. 'Other than that, you're great', Claire tagged on hurriedly. 'There's no pressure, you don't have to say anything to me either. I hope it all works out between you and Andrew, whatever it is'.

'Andrew is leaving me!' burst out Susie. 'Can you believe it? He is moving back home to live with his mother. He says it is just until he saves up for a deposit on a house and he will never get the money together while he is paying such high rent. I think he's using it as an excuse to break up with me.'

'I'm sure that's not the case Susie. Just because he wants to move back home for a while to save on rent and other bills does not mean he is leaving you. Lots of people move back into the family home for a period of time, so they can save up for a place of their own. It's the next big milestone. Have you ever discussed buying a house or apartment together?' queried Claire. Susie's eyes flashed dangerously, which meant that question was obviously a mistake. Claire wished she had kept her thoughts to herself until she had a better sense of what she was dealing with here.

'It was the first thing I suggested when he floated the idea. I was actually excited about it for all of two minutes, before he burst my bubble. I know Andrew earns more money than me, but we could afford to buy a nicer place if the mortgage was assessed on our joint incomes. But Andrew wants to buy a place of his own, without me. We've been living together for over a year but apparently that counts for nothing. I count for nothing!', ground out Susie angrily.

'That is simply not true, Andrew thinks more of you than any other girlfriend he has ever had', placated Claire.

'How many has he had?' screeched Susie. 'A jolly hockey team?'

Claire had to stop her lips from twitching at such an incongruous suggestion. This was Andrew they were talking about; did Susie not know him at all?

'Susie, from what I've seen there are two types of men; type A is a serial cheater on the woman in his life, type B cares about his family and his job and that's about it, nothing else comes close. Andrew belongs very definitely to the second category and you can fully trust him', said Claire emphatically. 'I can't help feeling there must be some misunderstanding.

Did Andrew definitely tell you he does not want to live with you anymore?'

'He's probably afraid I'll clobber him with a shoe if he breaks the news that bluntly to me', sniffed Susie. 'No, apparently I'm welcome to live with him once he's purchased his new pad, whenever and wherever that turns out to be. In the meantime, he'll be living with Mommy dearest while I can bugger off and sort myself out. I don't want to leave our rented apartment. I've decorated it exactly how I like it and it is perfect.'

'Except that it belongs to somebody else, who can ask you to leave with a month's notice', pointed out Claire.

'Nearly perfect then. I can live with it', sniffed Susie.

'As a short-term solution, can you and Andrew both move into his mother's house?' asked Claire.

'Are you kidding me? Have you met his mother? She has an opinion on everything. We'd kill each other within a week. Besides, his mother does not want me to move into her house with Andrew because we are not married. How old fashioned is that? I think the old bat simply does not like me and is using that as a pathetic excuse; she does not think I'm good enough for her precious son. He should side with me, not his mother. bristled Susie.

Andrew's mother was a strong character. His father had died from leukaemia when he was seven years old, making it essential for Mrs. Kennedy to get a job to make ends meet. As the manager of the local newsagent shop in Raheny village, she became known to hordes of people in the community. She was bored since her retirement, with not enough to occupy her alert mind. Mrs. Kennedy treated Andrew like a king whenever he called around to see her. It had not always been thus; she had allotted him plenty of jobs to do around the house to keep him busy when he was growing up.

'I seem to recall Andrew mentioning that his mother was going into hospital soon to have a hip replacement?' queried Claire.

'That's right, her operation is in two weeks time. That's another reason Andrew gives for moving back home, he says his mother will need help and support after the operation. But we don't live in Outer Mongolia, he can visit her in the evenings, can't he?' said Susie.

'He often works very late. I know all this is annoying for you Susie but a man who cares for his mother is meant to be great husband material. Try to see the positives in the situation, they do exist. Like, consider how much rent money you will save once Andrew buys a place of his own,' pointed out Claire.

'Yeah well, I don't see it happening. The mortgage will be huge, and Andrew won't have the money to go out and do fun stuff for years. Where am I going to live and rent in the meantime? He is not considering my feelings at all and he should, because he's my boyfriend. And he actually said he had no idea I could be this moody. Me, moody! After I've put up with him working day and night for that bloody bank. He must be gay if he prefers to live with his mother instead of me. Do you know if Andrew is secretly gay, Claire?'

'No, I don't think Andrew is gay, He likes women, not men', replied a flabbergasted Claire. She had never questioned Andrew's sexual orientation before but surely Susie should have a more informed view of it than her. 'What makes you wonder if he's gay?'

'Well, once when we were out at a disco and a guy pinched his bum at the bar. Andrew was mad about it and he wanted to punch the dude but, I dunno, it set me thinking. I mean, I know he's not built like a body builder but, do you think he looks gay?' mused Susie.

The probability of Andrew and Susie's relationship being doomed had suddenly shot into the stratosphere. Claire gave Andrew an appraising look though the open door and liked what she saw. Andrew jogged four times a week and this kept his five-foot ten-inch frame trimmed and toned. He was wearing faded Levi jeans, Nike trainers and a multicoloured Timberland jersey. He was slim, fair skinned and pleasant looking, although he could do without the thick rimmed glasses sitting on top of his fine boned nose.

'I don't know what constitutes a gay look, but Andrew looks very well. Don't pay any heed to the drunken antics of a complete stranger', advised Claire.

'There's something else, he wants to do acting classes on Friday nights. What am I meant to do by myself at the end of a long week? I suggested us both taking salsa lessons as an alternative but no, he's not interested. He's meant to be my boyfriend but there's no compromise', said Susie, knocking back another glass of wine, before continuing with her unexpected confidences.

'We usually have sex on a Friday night but that's not going to be happening either. I'll be either asleep, pissed off or out clubbing myself when he crawls into bed after tearing himself away from his acting buddies. He's going off me, I know. Or else I was wrong about him and he's nothing but a selfish loser. I want a real man, not a Mammy's boy', said Susie, her tough words at odds with the tremble in her voice. She had made some valid points but nonetheless Claire felt compelled to defend Andrew vigorously.

'Andrew is a kind, thoughtful person but that does not make him a mother's boy. Obviously he wants to care for his mother while she is recovering from her operation. He is an independent thinker who quietly goes his own way. Acting will allow him to express his emotions more. Here is what I do know about Andrew: he would never betray you by having an affair with another woman when he is seeing you, it simply isn't in his DNA to behave dishonourably'.

'Yeah, sure, Andrew's a great guy. Everything's peachy. I'm raining on your parade. I'd better go. You've put up a great party for Ben. He is a lucky boy, I don't remember having a party like this when I was a kid. Thanks for listening Claire but, please say nothing to Andrew. Tell him I'll see him later. Maybe….. If he is really lucky.'

Susie daintily dabbed a napkin against her coral coated lips, before disappearing out through the door on a waft of citrus scented perfume. Not a happy bunny, perhaps gone for the last time. Claire walked towards Andrew, opting for the strategy of least said, soonest mended. She did not want any words of hers to cause further strife between him and Susie.

'Susie has left, she has a few things to do but will catch up with you later. I hear you have been very busy Andrew, making plans to take up acting lessons', she said lightly. 'I had no idea I might be talking to the next Bradley Cooper'.

'Even better if it's the next Leonardo DiCaprio', grinned Andrew.

'All the men want to be Leonardo. What makes you want to try your hand at acting Andrew?' asked Claire lightly, choosing the safe topic, compared to the thorny issue of house relocation which was plaguing Susie.

'I think it will be fun and it is something different. It's nothing to do with work, although learning acting techniques might boost my presentation skills. I'm hoping to get a role where my character treats girls mean and keeps them keen', joked Andrew.

'I can't wait to see that performance. Susie also mentioned you were moving back home to save money for a deposit on a house. It's more likely that, after living long term with your mother, you'll be able to portray Norman Bates in a play to perfection', bantered Claire.

Andrew's smile disappeared, and he hit his hand against his head.

'Susie is giving me hell over my intention to move back home for a couple of months. It makes sense, Mam will need help and company around the house while she recovers from her operation and I will be able to save some money. Susie has the option of moving in with her sister but she's being ridiculous about it; it's almost like she is jealous of my relationship with my own mother. There is no talking to her about it.'

Claire felt relieved when Ben choose that moment to appear in their midst, catching hold of both of their hands.

'Come on Mommy and Andrew, it's time for my birthday cake. I have to blow the candles out and make a wish, but I can't tell you what it is. We want to eat the cake too, Granny's made me a marvellous cake', he said, pulling them towards the kitchen door.

Claire and Andrew rounded up all the children and went inside to take pictures of Ben blowing out the six candles on top of the cake in one breath, cheered on by his pals. It was unlikely that Ben was old enough to store the day into his long-term memory, but Claire wanted to remember the happy occasion. Andrew stayed around all afternoon, being friendly to everybody and providing backup to Tom's kids' patrol agenda in the garden. Before they knew it, the parents were lining up at the front door to collect their children, all of whom were protectively gripping on tight to a goody bag.

'I like your Granddad, he's cool', said a little boy to Ben.

'I have the best Granddad', replied Ben proudly. 'You know, not everybody has a Granddad and my Granddad is the tops'.

'Your Daddy is nice too, I never met him before', chimed in another boy. Ben looked confused, but his friend had already darted away to catch up with his own father at the gate and the moment of clarification was lost.

Claire realised that some of the children and their parents had gained the impression that Andrew was Ben's daddy because of the family's easy familiarity with him and his stewardship in the garden. It was a situation which she had not expected to develop at the beginning of the day. Claire held her tongue and smilingly waved the rest of the visitors away. Let them think that Andrew was her partner and Ben's father if that was what they wanted to believe. She was under no obligation to explain her private business to the world, although the day was approaching when she might have to discuss it with her son.

CHAPTER SEVEN

Claire and Anna moved into their new office on the same day Karen Woods started work in Leictreach. They paused at the threshold of the room for a moment before entering, with Claire immediately sending a silent 'thank you' floating the way of David Maguire, the maintenance manager who had kept his word and seen that the dank walls of the long-neglected office space were given a fresh coat of cream paint.

'It's better than I thought it would be, Dave has done a good job in getting it ready for us', Claire breathed a sign of relief as she dropped a large cardboard box filled with documents onto the desk.

'Wow, that box is heavy, and we probably have twenty more of them to go. I'd better ring Dave to see if he has a trolley we can use to move all our folders in here'.

'That's a good idea Claire. You watch out that you don't lift up Ben now he's six and getting bigger by the day. I'm sure that's how I did my back in years ago, lifting up the kids when they got as heavy as baby elephants', advised Anna. Claire reflected wryly that, since there was only going to be the two of them in the office, she would be on the receiving end of plenty of motherly advice from the older woman, whether she wanted it or not.

'I'll bear it in mind Anna. Some nights when he is very tired, he wants me to help him up the stairs, but he is too heavy to carry,' acknowledged Claire.

'I'm telling you Claire, you'll put your back out that way and it will never be the same again. We've never seen what your Ben looks like, you'll have to bring in a picture of him and put it on your desk. Does he look like you or his father?' asked Anna, unable to keep the note of naked curiosity out of her voice. 'I always put up pictures of my kids no matter where I am, it makes me feel more settled'.

Claire certainly was not going to get into a discussion about Ben's father with Anna just because they had been thrust together in a hole of a room. She used her tried and tested technique of diversion to turn the conversation around to a safe topic.
'Talking about being more settled, how is Frank getting on these days?', asked Claire. Unlike her, Anna was never happier than when she was discussing her family.

'Better than I expected. He's done work in the garden and cut the bushes right back cos' over the years they grew too big and took up too much space and blocked off the light. He might even put up decking for the summer if it isn't too expensive. He's got the time to do work around the house since he lost his job, but we have to watch the money. He'd do a carpentry course, but they don't seem to be available, worst luck. He's painting the whole house an' he's doing a lovely job. We had every wall in the house painted magnolia because it's a clean colour, but it got boring, every room the same. Last week Frank painted one whole wall in the sitting room bright red and it's only gorgeous', said Anna.

Anna had the ability to outdo the radio for chat. She looked around the room in satisfaction, blissfully unaware of Claire's uneasiness.

'I'm glad Dave stuck to his word and got this room painted for us, it makes it much brighter.
And it's great that they put up all the shelves along the walls, though we'll need every one of them for the filing. A few plants and pictures and it will be right homely. Some blinds for the windows wouldn't go astray either or we'll be half blinded by the sun, when it decides to come out. It's just our bad luck to be beside dragon lady next door', she nodded to the partition wall which separated the two offices. 'God help the poor creature they've put in with her, she'll be a basket case in no time'.

Claire flicked her finger at the switch on the wall but to her disgust no overhead lights came on. She was finding it hard to get her head around the fact that they needed to use desk lamps when the natural light in the room dimmed. The paint job and new shelving did not change the fact that the room was the size of a postage stamp for two people to share and that their desks were facing and touching each other with no dividing partition between them. The full sized, perfectly proportioned window was the only saving grace of the room.

Claire and Anna spent the entire morning moving their stuff into the room and settled down to work as best they could in the afternoon. Andrew emailed Claire a joke which made her laugh, causing Anna to swing her head up on her side of the desk.

'Why are you laughing?' asked Anna, her body practically quivering with anticipation.
'It's a joke, I'll forward it onto you.'

The nature of capitalism…..two workers leaving after a 12-hour shift

stop to admire the boss's spanking new yellow Mercedes car. Boss, 'If you continue to work long hours, improve your productivity 130% and do all I ask of you, then I'll have an even better one next year.'

'Ha, ha, very good. Is that Andrew bloke a good friend of yours?'

'Yes, I've known him since college', said Claire, not raising her head. What business was it of Anna's why she laughed or who her friends were? 'I'm sorry Anna but I have to concentrate on this spreadsheet or I won't get it finished today. Perhaps we can talk later?'

'Suits me, I've plenty to do, they keep me busy too', sniffed Anna.

The ensuing silence was strained. Anna had worked in a large office for years and had become used to making a short, casual comment about every ten minutes to break up the monotony of the day. There had always been somebody glad of a distraction and ready to reply back to her. Claire was different, she preferred to concentrate fully on a task and engage in casual conversation only when there was a natural break in her work, which could take a couple of hours. She did not appreciate her train of thought being needlessly interrupted with boring trivia.

Claire came across an inconsistency with the figures in a spreadsheet she was analysing and thought it was a possibility that Ashley could have the information she needed to explain the discrepancy. She got up to leave the room.

'Where are you going?', asked Anna.

Claire had never felt this claustrophobic before, not even when she got stuck in a hotel lift and had to be physically hauled out. She did not want to have to account to Anna for her every movement.

'I have to ask Ashley about a problem with the figures', Claire answered, trying to ignore the exasperation she felt.

'You're wasting your time, even if she knows the answer she won't help you', said Anna with a shake of her head.

'She's our manager Anna, it is in her own interest for us to get our work done as quickly and as efficiently as possible', said Claire. She refused to believe that Ashley would hinder the work itself, bad as she was.

'You still don't understand, do you? Ashley has no scruples. She wants you to look bad and will do nothing to help you. But if you don't believe me, you'll have to learn how she operates the hard way for yourself.'

Anna pursed her lips, gave Claire a long pitying look and turned her attention back to the computer.

Claire knocked on Ashley's door before opening it. The room was at least three times the size of Anna and Claire's office, making it comfortable for two people. Karen Woods and Ashley sat at their desks with their backs against the wall, facing each other across a narrow space. Claire did a double take at the similarities between the two; both were wearing grey trouser suits and white tops, with their jackets hanging from the back of their chairs. They were both rhythmically pealing oranges for their morning ten-minute break. They could be twins. Neither woman smiled when Claire entered the room.

'This is Karen Woods, she is going to be working with me.' Ashley made the introduction without bothering to give Claire's name to Karen.

Claire registered the phrase *'working with me'* as opposed to *'working with us'* or *'working for me'* as being of interest but she was not sure what it signified. She guessed that Karen was close to her in age, but she appeared aloof. Karen was not as tall as Ashley, but she was nearly as thin. She wore her mousey coloured hair in an elfin style and her nondescript hazel eyes were framed by light rimmed glasses which sat on top of a pointed nose. Ashley clearly intended the recruit to be her protégé and in return Karen's body language was shouting that she was more than happy to model herself on her new mentor.

'I'm Claire Howard and I am part of the finance team. I hope you will be happy here', Claire addressed Karen pleasantly.

'Thank you. I expect it to be a worthwhile experience. Leictreach ranks highly in surveys evaluating employee satisfaction levels,' replied Karen, speaking with a northern Irish accent.

'A lot of people have worked here for years, I always take that as a sign of a good company to work for,' commented Claire.

'It's a pity more of the deadwood won't up sticks and leave but unfortunately they are the very ones we're stuck with. The one thing the over fifties brigade are busy with is building up their pension rights. They lose out big time on their pensions if they leave and well do they know it,' jeered Ashley. 'Where else can they go, when companies are able to get a bright graduate with cutting edge knowledge to do the job for a fraction of their salary?'

'Older people who have worked long term for a company are very committed to it. Among other things, they know its customers, its systems, its key values, other staff members and who best to contact when things go wrong', retorted Claire.

'All those things can be learned in a few months. They are no big deal. What do you want Claire? Or did you come in here to give Karen the once over, so you can gossip about her to the others at lunch time?' enquired Ashley.

'Can you take a look at these figures please Ashley?' said Claire in a much stiffer tone of voice. 'The numbers in column two do not make sense when you compare them with the data in column five.'

Ashley gave the sheet of paper the briefest of scans, not attempting to explain or solve the riddle. She did not access the repository of information which flowed from the departments into her office for the monthly report preparation and review.

'I see what you mean. Show it to Karen, see what she thinks', said Ashley.

What was the point of showing it to Karen? The girl had just started working in the company that morning and knew nothing about the company and how it operated. Detailed data from one of the Divisions had to be meaningless to her. Nonetheless Claire did as she was instructed and handed the sheet over to Karen to read. The latter took a cursory glance at the paper before handing it back to Claire.

'It does not look familiar to me' said Karen, as cool as a breeze.

There was a surprise! It might look familiar to Daniel or to another senior manager in the organisation, but Karen would have to have a genius IQ for it to make sense to her. But Claire noticed that Karen did not say 'Sorry, I haven't a clue about it' which was the reality of the situation. No, she used the phrase '*it does not look familiar to me*'.

The phrase '*phraseology and codology*' flashed through Claire's mind as she gazed at Karen.

'Okay then, sorry for disturbing you during your morning break', said Claire.

'Next time ring before disturbing us Claire, we are not in the business of time wasting', instructed Ashley.

Oh, she was charming! Worse still, Anna had been right about Ashley. Their so-called manager had not the slightest interest in helping them provide explanations or solutions to problems. Claire had to take the next step of contacting the divisional manager to try to get to the bottom of the anomaly in the figures.

As Claire left the room, she tucked away in her mind's eye the image of the two clones smirking at each other, their fingers tearing into the juicy flesh of the dripping, half pealed oranges, which both of them had placed centre stage on their desks.

'Well?' said Anna, as soon as Claire entered the room. The younger girl replied with a sideways shake of her head.

'Told you so', nodded Anna vigorously. 'She's never going to help you or me with our work Claire. Ashley is no use. She will suck all of our knowledge up but pass none of her own information down. She's like a vampire. We'll only hear about what's done wrong, not right. What's the new girl like?'

'Awful' was the word which sprang to mind but Claire preferred Anna to come to her own conclusion.

'You'll see for yourself soon enough Anna, but one thing I will say is that she isn't a patch on Emmet. It's such a shame we've lost him at this time', said Claire.

When anybody put an unintelligible sheet of paper under Emmet's nose, the old Dubliner would snort and proclaim that he'd have to be God Almighty to know the impossible. Emmet had to be approached sensibly or he would suggest a consultation with his good friend, the man in the moon. He would not have calmly uttered the words *'it does not look familiar to me'*. In Claire's opinion, Karen Woods was a totally unsatisfactory replacement for the wonderfully forthright, good humoured Emmet. It was outrageous that Ashley spoke about older people in the workplace with such contempt.

Claire's pang of loneliness for the much-missed Emmet was interrupted by the shrill tones of the telephone ringing on her desk. She reached out to pick up the receiver, recognising Daniel's number immediately.

'Yes, I'll come up to see you now', she said into the mouthpiece. It was a while since Daniel had called her into his office for a one to one conversation and Claire wondered what was up.

Anna arched her eyebrow in enquiry as Claire went to the door.

'Daniel wants to have a word with me', said Claire, resigned but not reconciled to Anna's constant curiosity.

The infringement on her personal space was driving Claire crazy, as she was a private person who was more introvert than extrovert. The words *'mind your own business'*, were on the of her tongue but she did not want to fling them out. Anna was sensitive, and Claire did not want to upset her. It was not Anna's fault that they were stuck in each other's company for hours on end in a glorified storage facility; no, that had happened courtesy of Ashley's meddling. It was essential that Anna and Claire develop a harmonious relationship together or else the work atmosphere could become truly unbearable.

Despite the prickles of irritation tingling down Claire's spine, she did like Anna and knew her to be a good person. It was a pity that the concept of privacy had flown out of the window. What was it with older people watching her every move and giving her unsolicited advice? First her mother at home and now Anna at work. She did not need the hassle, she really didn't! She did not go around telling other people what to do, questioning them all the time. Claire would appreciate them getting off her back and leave her to live her own life, without having to put up with a running commentary in the background. But she did not say the words aloud, for fear of causing upset and sullen silence in their claustrophobic office cell.

CHAPTER EIGHT

Claire felt inexplicably nervous as she walked along the corridor towards Daniel's office. What did Daniel want to see her about? He was keeping a low profile in the finance department since he made the announcement of the changes in the managerial positions. Daniel's office door was open when she approached, and he nodded at her to come into the room. Claire could see cream cracker crumbs scattered on the edge of his desk which he had obviously been nibbling on and she recalled Deirdre mentioning to her that Daniel was a diabetic.

Daniel got straight to the purpose of the meeting in typical fashion.

'We have taken over a small company called ZFixitz based in Northern Ireland and I'm putting Joan in charge of all its accounting operations. But first we have to incorporate their accounts into the main general ledger. I want you to show Joan how we code and set up the new accounts for the company in a merger situation, transferring over all the balances.'

'Certainly Daniel, that's no problem' replied Claire serenely.

'Good. How are you getting on in your new office?', enquired Daniel.

Claire hesitated, aware that this might be the only chance she had to voice her disquiet but fearing Daniel might interpret her concerns as being mean spirited and nit picking. The seconds ticked away, and she chose to let the opportunity to speak freely slip away.

'Fine, there are a few settling in problems like the overhead lights not working properly in the ceiling, but Dave has promised us he will get it sorted.'

'Glad to hear it. It is quieter in that office, you should find it easier to concentrate on your work compared to the noise level in the general office. Best of luck with it.'

Daniel gave her a fixed smile before turning back towards his computer, his mind already going onto the next task. Claire was not surprised; the sky would have to fall in or the building collapse before people in Finance could turn their attention away from their computer screens for more than a few minutes. Even in those circumstances they would probably run away clutching the computers to their chests, as if they were rescuing the family pet from a fire.

Claire enjoyed merger and de-merger accounting work and was extremely competent at it. These types of projects broke up the monotony of carrying out her routine work. In multinational companies' mergers and de-mergers happen on a worldwide basis, which like everything else had positive and negative repercussions. Claire had seen first hand how a merger might be good for a company on an international level but could have negative consequences for subsidiary companies at a national level. This unfortunate side effect of a global merger can be a striking feature when a smaller sized company takes over a bigger company in a country. Most of the top managerial positions in the merged company go to the managers which are employed in the company executing the takeover on a worldwide basis. The senior managers of the company taken over find that their positions in the organisational hierarchy have been downgraded and are faced with the decision of whether to stay or to go. They often put considerable effort into leaving with a golden handshake.

Claire was fascinated by the psychology behind the merger and de-merger process. A corporate brain drain, and corporate memory loss can develop when the managers with the most intricate knowledge of operations in the company being assimilated decide to leave en-masse with handsome payoffs. Alternatively, there are the senior managers who decide to remain on in the new organisation for a couple of years until they can collect on their early retirement packages. Claire had seen a head of departmental, in the year of his retirement, release provisions which had been built up over many years because the performance of the division in the three years preceding his retirement fed into his bonus and pension entitlements. The executive had no concern about massively boosting his department's profits in the year of his retirement, even though there was inevitably going to be an adverse effect on performance in the management reports of the following year. He had taken care of his pension requirements for the future financial stability of his family and the company was big enough to take care of the department.

Some of these managers are happy to sow the seeds of discontent and resentment felt by the staff of the company being taken over because the plum jobs in the new combined enterprise have been given to the personnel in the takeover company. Leictreach, as a huge multinational company, was constantly going through a merger or de-merger process. In the two years Claire had spent working with some exposure to the merger/de-merger processes she had been struck by the value lost as well as gained in the companies taken over by a dominant player in the marketplace.

Claire and Joan immediately got working on the project together, with Claire taking complete command of it. It was a very tight squeeze because Joan spent most of the week holed up in the new office with Claire, who took her through the entire process step by step. Claire was glad to have a third presence in the room as it meant she could unapologetically focus her attention away from Anna, who in fairness appeared to enjoy having the extra company and chat. Joan was good fun to be around and they worked productively together, focused on their common task. Claire set up the new accounts on the system and transferred the data into them once she was satisfied that the figures were correct. She made sure that the accounts all had the proper back up documentation attached, and she wrote up all the explanatory notes as she went along. She designed multiple excel spreadsheets and saved them in a shared drive on the system to help Joan going forward. The nominal journals were entered in the system, printed off and signed by Claire. In short Claire did all the work and trained Joan into the role by the time-honoured method of 'sitting next to Nellie'. They finished the project on the Friday just before lunch time.

'Perfect timing Claire. Let's go out for a celebratory lunch', suggested Joan, stretching her arms out and holding her hands together to flex her fingers.

'Do you want to join us Anna?', invited Claire.

'No thanks, I'm saving my money. I can't afford to pay for lunches out in restaurants when I have four kids and a husband to feed at home', said Anna.

'If you come out to lunch with us Anna, you might find yourself a rich lover and not have to worry about dinner, let alone lunch', joked Joan.

'I couldn't be bothered with one. I'm happily married, thank you very much, and my Frank is man enough for me', said Anna dismissively.

'There's no harm looking at the menu, even if you don't want to eat. Suit yourself. See you later,' Joan shrugged.

When Claire and Joan were walking to the local pub for sandwiches and soup, they passed a new Pop Up shop, which had opened its doors early on in the week. Pop Up shops had a novelty appeal and enabled vendors to rent the outlet in a prime retail district for a short period of time, in order to display their wares and get publicity for their businesses. After a couple of weeks everything would be taken away and a different business would take its place, displaying and selling its products in the shop. For the customer it lent extra variety to the thrill of window shopping. When Claire had passed its doors last week it was filled with hand crafted jewellery and animals shaped out of glass, wood, bronze and wrought iron. A stunning coral necklace had transfixed her to the spot, but she reluctantly forced herself to walk away, in the knowledge that she had not got the money to spare on such a beautiful luxury item. She dreamed of being able to walk into a store and buy whatever item she coveted without troubling about the cost.

This week the shop window was completely changed, filled with rows of mannequin heads showcasing a variety of wigs in all lengths and colours. It was impossible for two women to walk by without taking a glance and what they saw was enough to entice them inside the shop. Joan immediately reached out for a wavy blonde wig to plop on top of her short dyed red hair. She opened her bag to fish out a purple lipstick stick which she lavishly applied to her anchor shaped lips. She wasn't finished yet and she jammed a glittering costume jewellery ring the size of a Fabergé egg onto her index finger.

'Look at me Sugar. I'm Atomic Kitten all ready to be stroked and diamonds are my best friend', she pouted playfully in a sing song voice.

Claire emitted a gurgle of laughter.

'That wig suits you Joan, you look really good in it'.

'I know. I think it's time I went blonde again, it's true they have more fun. I've tried red but it's no good. You don't have to wait as long to get served in a bar when you have blonde hair. You try one on Claire, it's surprising how much a wig can change your whole appearance', urged Joan.

Claire did not need to be told twice, it would be a shame to pass up on the chance to experiment. She made straight for the long blonde wig on a mannequin's head on the middle shelf close to the door. She had long harboured a secret fantasy that she would look drop dead gorgeous, if only she had long, golden tresses instead of curly, red locks. Claire gasped at the high price tags attached to the wigs but was even more taken aback to discover that she looked distinctly less attractive to the eye than she had before she put the wig on.

How could this be? Blonde women were meant to be the most attractive females the world over, adorning magazine covers and irresistible to men. Millions of women spent fortunes of money dyeing their mousey brown hair blonde. Little girls play with Barbie dolls and listen to the fairy tale stories, where the most beautiful princesses were blonde like Cinderella.

'Nope, it doesn't do it for you Claire. Try on the long, straight, black one instead', suggested Joan. 'We'll get you a fabulous new look too'.

Claire did not want to take the chance of looking good in the Morticia Addams styled wig. Perhaps reality was to be preferred to fantasy. She knew that most people considered her to be pretty with her curly reddish/gold hair, dark blue eyes and full lips. It was true that she would never make it onto the cover of Vogue since she liked eating chocolate too much and had not got the requisite height. She could accept that Barbie-like long blonde tresses had not transformed her into a supermodel, but she had not expected to look drab.

'Why am I a bad blonde?' she asked.

'It's because, like, your eyebrows are too dark for the blonde hair colour, you'll have to dye them to get a match and your skin tone is all wrong, it's too pale and the wig drains it. You need to layer on the right make up to get the look you want', explained the bored shop assistant.

Claire pointed to the mannequin head at her right-hand shoulder which was crowned with a pageboy styled blonde wig.

'That mannequin has black eyebrows and a very white face, but the blonde wig still looks great on it', Claire observed.

'That's because it's a mannequin, not a person', said the salesperson witheringly. 'Maybe your friend can do you a favour and teach you about makeup.'

Honestly, with such rude customer service, the retailer should stick to selling her products over the internet and not bother renting a place for a couple of weeks to directly interface with the buying public.

'It's been a good week so I'm going to buy this', Joan approached the sales assistant carrying a blonde ponytail extension. 'I'll dye my hair the exact same shade and it will turn long the instant I attach it. I can't wait to glam up. Ken better not let me out of his sight Saturday night.'

Joan caused a sensation when she arrived into work on Monday, with her hair dyed blonde and wearing the ponytail extension. For good measure she wore a top which showed off her ample cleavage as much as was permitted in a professional environment. The guys in the Debtors section threw off political correctness enough to give her a couple of 'wows' and winks as she slowly strolled by, swinging her ponytail and hips, but did not dare risk wolf whistling in the office.

'You're wasted in Finance looking like that Joan, you should be on the telly'.

'Yeah, behind the bar in a soap opera, any of them will do.'

'I'll take that as a compliment, I wouldn't mind the money those actors are earning', parried Joan as she made her way to her own office, thrilled with herself and the reaction she had received. She called into Claire and Anna's office much later on in the day, trying to sound low key but glowing with satisfaction.

'Just letting you know Claire that I decided to use pink coloured journal pages to record the transactions for ZFixitz making it easy for me to identify them easily from the main white coloured company journals. I printed out all the journals we did again and wrote them up nice and neatly and I brought them into Daniel to sign as well. He was very pleased, said we had done great work', said Joan.

'That's good to hear, Daniel only gives praise when he thinks it is due', Claire looked up from her computer and smiled at Joan.

'I know, but he said it was one less thing he had to worry about'. Joan relaxed at Claire's easy response and let her delight show as she danced out of the room.

Immediately after Joan had closed the door behind her, Anna turned towards Claire.

'You have to go straight into Daniel's office and clearly tell him that it was you who did all that work Claire and not Joan. Go today, before he disappears on us for the rest of the week' instructed Anna firmly.

'He knows I did the work Anna, he asked me to show Joan how to do it', replied Claire mildly.

Anna looked at her incredulously, gasping at her naivety.

'Look Claire, I'm telling you, Daniel won't realise that work is yours. He'll think Joan did it all. People have short memories and seeing is believing. Joan's waltzed into him all pleased and proud, hugging bunches of paperwork, with notes written out in her own handwriting and her signature on the end of every journal, asking him to double sign everything. Your writing or signature is nowhere in sight on any of those pages. There is no stamp of you on the job, nothing to remind him that you were involved in it. Daniel will give Joan all the credit for doing that job, not you. Get yourself up to that office now and tell him it was your hard work and knowledge that got the job done and that Joan was just looking on over your shoulder'.

'There is no need to do that Anna', replied Claire, surprised at Anna's insistence.

'There is a need, a real need!' Anna nearly shouted. 'Don't be stupid Claire'.

'There's no need for you to insult me', protested Claire, face reddening.

'I'm sorry, but this is important. You're too quiet about the good work you do Claire. It's not only Joan, other people are taking advantage and passing projects off as their own, when they depended on you to put them on the right track and keep them on the straight and narrow. They'd have been all over the place without your help. You have to put yourself about more and speak up at meetings. The ones who talk big at meetings using fancy words and buzz phrases are the very ones doing the least and taking responsibility for nothing. They are the ones getting the big pay rises and bonuses, not the quiet ones sitting in a corner actually doing the work.'

Anne paused a split second for breath before continuing to share.

'I'll tell you something else while I'm about it. You're too generous with your knowledge and information, you share it with anybody who asks. But I don't notice other people rushing to give you information, to share it with you. Knowledge is power, and people keep it to themselves unless they are forced to give it up. I've seen you having to beg for information from others, information that you need to do your job as an accountant. You should not have to apologise for asking for information, people ought to respect your right to ask.'

'We are all working in Finance for the same organisation Anna. We are all working for common goals, to accomplish the same company objectives', reasoned Claire.

'Bollocks! Will you get that foolish idea out of your head? People are out for themselves, not the company. They always put their own interests ahead of the company's interest and the people at the top are here to line their own pockets. It's like you thinking Ashley will help you solve a problem because she is your manager and that is what a good manager should do. Problem is, she is a lousy manager, she makes our jobs ten times harder than it need be. She doesn't want to help you, she wants to make your position as uncomfortable as she can. It's simple, she wants us out, because she doesn't like us, and she wants to put her own people in. Joan is intent on being part of the IN crowd. Mark my words, the time will come when you ask Joan for help and she won't give it to you. She will say NO. I don't care how nice you think she is, when it comes to work, it is dog eat dog and Joan's a Rottweiler. Joan wants to keep in with Daniel, especially now with Ashley here, and she will sell you down the river without a qualm, if it helps her to do it.

'It all sounds very dramatic Anna and it is hard to believe you are right about Joan', said Claire. 'She has always been good humoured.'

'Claire, I'm older than you. To me, a job is just a job. I don't care what they have me doing as long as I get my pay cheque at the end of the month. If they paid me the same money and asked me to clean the toilets, then that is what I'd do. I'm here because I need the money, for no other reason. But most of the others here aren't like that. They are ambitious, they want to get on, they want to have careers. They'll walk all over you if you let them. Joan has stampeded through you today, doing what she's done, and you don't even realise it. Go on! Get up to Daniel's office and tell him all about the work you did on that Northern merger. Walk him through every last detail and show him how Joan was only looking on. You have to fight your corner because nobody else will do it for you'.

'Honestly Anna, Daniel must realise I took control of the merger/ demerger project, not Joan. She didn't have the basic tools or knowledge to do the job by herself and Daniel has to know that already, since he asked me to help her. I appreciate your concern but there is no need for me to say anything to him. Don't worry about it anymore,' responded Claire.

Anna shook her head with tightened lips and swivelled around to her computer. She had tried her best to make Claire understand the wider dynamics operating within the department. She could not make Claire listen to her, if the younger girl had set her mind against it. Claire truly did not comprehend how coldly calculated and devious some people could be in their pursuit of career objectives.

As events unfolded and time went by Claire acknowledged to herself that she had made a grave error in judgement by not heeding Anna's wise words of advice to claim her work as her own. It turned out that Daniel did credit Joan (not Claire) with completing the merger/demerger accounting for the Northern Ireland subsidiary and he was impressed with the technical proficiency and accuracy displayed. Claire's stewardship of the project was erased from his memory. From this time forth, Daniel began to allocate more of the interesting analysis project work to Joan and much less to Claire. For her part, Joan worked extremely hard to impress when she was presented with any opportunity to shine before Daniel and she made a concerted effort to be charming and pleasant to him. Henceforth, whatever time and attention he had to spare for project supervision and meetings was directed at Joan, not Claire.

The rot had set in.

CHAPTER NINE

The phone rang on her work desk late on a Tuesday afternoon. Claire picked the receiver up and smiled when she heard Andrew's voice at the other end of the phone.

'I haven't heard from you for a while. Any news?', said Claire.

'You could say that. I've living back home with Mam. Susie and I have split up', answered Andrew.

'Wow, break it to me gently, why don't you? Susie and you breaking up is huge news. How are you feeling?' asked Claire.

'Okay I guess. It has been on the cards for months. Susie wanted to get engaged and all that jazz, but I just could not bring myself to do it. Once the split happened, I felt relieved, although she did use me as a punching bag before I could get away. I've decided to take my mind off it by going speed dating this Thursday.'

Claire gave a snort of laughter.

'Courage in the face of adversity, way to go Romeo. Where are you going to get the energy and space to date hordes of women through speed dating, since you're living with your Mama?'

'I'm not going to tell her a thing about it of course. I'm doing it for acting experience, not for a real date, though I'm not ruling it out either. I want you to come along to it with me. The best bit is that it is themed as a masquerade, so nobody will recognise us', said Andrew.

'No way, it's not going to happen', said Claire.

'I insist. You took every excuse to dress up when we were in college. Don't be boring. Are you going to stay in and watch television every night until Ben turns thirty? It's time for you to get back into the saddle before you forget how to ride. C'mon Claire, it will be a laugh. Don't think about it, just do it. Your mother will baby sit Ben, she's been encouraging you to get out and about more.'

Andrew's dart about her becoming boring found its mark.

'I will go with you on Thursday. It had better be fun though or you owe me big time', she capitulated impulsively.

'Atta girl', whooped Andrew. 'I knew you had it in you.'

Claire put the phone down and looked ruefully at Anna, who never made the claim of being deaf.

'You're right to go, you're only young once. Though meeting a stranger in a pub worked well enough for my generation', said Anna.

'My generation is hooked on internet dating but that does not appeal to me. I met Ben's father in college and I have not bothered much with dating since we broke up', confided Claire. So much for wanting to keep her private life, well private.

'Do you see much of him now', asked Anna, very interested.

'No, he lives in America', said Claire.

'That's far enough away for it not to be a problem when you meet somebody new', said Anna.

At least the practical Anna was optimistic about Claire having a relationship with a man some time in the future, which was the very thing her own mother was beginning to doubt. Claire was not expecting any romance to come out of her speed dating evening but, with Andrew for company, the night was guaranteed not to turn into a disaster.

Claire got to the hotel with five minutes to spare on Thursday evening.

'Am here, where RU? she texted Andrew.

'Dawn Suite', replied Andrew. **'UR already winner, I pick U'**.

Andrew was sweet and, more importantly, he had her back. She drew in a deep breath, feeling as brave as a lioness about to go hunting.

There were two long tables in the suite, one marked out for the ladies and the other for the men. A woman handed Claire a gold mask which covered the top part of her face and gave her the option of wearing a voluminous purple cloak over her outfit. She was also given a numbered score card and told to pick out a name tag from a list of titles, which might help bolster conversation during the match making evening.

Claire was not going to risk picking out the name of a Disney princess because who knew what type of nutter that might attract? She was not going to risk cute, tacky or risqué tonight, no, she was going to play it safe. As she cast her eye down the list of character descriptions she noticed a section halfway down devoted to the arts, like 'Writer, Muse, Poet, Artist, Singer' and then came across the label 'Blythe Spirit', which conjured up a sense of classy joie de vive.

She pinned 'Blythe Spirit' onto her cape and was ready for action.

The men were similarly dressed, but with blue masks and grey capes and their name tags included sportsmen, cars, actors, superheroes and animal descriptions. Claire spotted that the name tag of one man passing by stated **'No.1 Golfer'** and made a mental note to strike him off her list; she did not trust golfing fanatics because they were forever going off on trips abroad with the boys. Every wife at home believed that at least some of the group were playing more than golf away from home but not one of them believed it was their own husband. The golfer was a no-win prospect because, even if the guy was not a philanderer, he would be spending all his spare time on the golf course instead of dedicating it to his new girlfriend.

The score card was simple to fill out: -

YES: (she was interested in meeting the guy again on their own for a date).

NO: (she had no interest in meeting him again, not now or ever).

FRIENDSHIP ONLY- Y/N : (if she was interested in meeting up with the guy again with a view to platonic friendship).

Claire was surprised at the third category and was not interested in it at all, she didn't have enough time or energy to keep up with the friends she already had, let alone make new ones from an evening such as this. Friendship usually was not the problem for people; it was a desire for lust, love and companionship which had drawn the punters into the hotel tonight, like bees circling the honey pot.

When the bell rang to signal for the women to take their seats, a frisson of excitement and anticipation ran through the packed room. Let the games begin! The room was darker than Claire had expected and, given the disguises, she had not got a hope of recognising Andrew until it was his turn to sit at her table.

To Claire's relief most of the men appeared to be normal. The disguises made it more difficult to assess the men's ages, but she judged most of them to be under the thirty-five mark, complying to the advertised age profile of the event. Most of the questions did not surprise her, although the casual curiosity of some of personal questions in a four-minute time interval slot did cause her to blink and draw back. People were braver when they wore masks.

'What age are you?' asked **'Star Striker'**, with a guerrilla like hunch to his shoulders. *In times gone by that question would never have been addressed to a lady. It should not be allowed today.*

'I'm too old for you. I love watching television. I can't stand football. You wouldn't like me'.

'What kind of work do you do?' asked **'Action Hero'**. *Is this a job interview? How boring are you? You are dishonouring your badge.*

'I work in an office but would like to own my own pottery business one day.'

Claire considered that sounded much more arty and interesting than Finance. She had taken evening pottery lessons in her college days as a pastime and had produced cups, plates, bowls, wine goblets and vases, which she was rightly proud of. She was talented at pottery and when she had more money and time she intended to invest in a kiln of her own and develop her old hobby further.

'Why have you not got a boyfriend?' asked **'Heavy Weight Champion of the World'**. *Ah, he sounds puzzled, that's kind of nice. He's big though, one squeeze and I'm dead.*

'I have no idea, I'm lovely. Why have you not got a girlfriend?'

'In my country, the sun is hot, and we love to sing and dance in the streets and fall in love', said **'Music Mogul'** lyrically. 'I know by your eyes that I could fall in love with you. I think I am already in love.'

'I'm flattered but I'm not musical and I'm from Dublin, where the weather leaves us in a perpetual state of confusion.' *Yeah, in love with yourself mate.*

'What's your favourite colour?' asked **'Heavy Metal Rocker'** desperately, after swallowing nervously and staying silent for two whole minutes with his head down. *Claire sympathised with his discomfort and decided to work with his comment.*

'Red, I like the colour red. It goes with so many things and it's a warm colour. Like many people I always associate it with Christmas. From the time I was a little kid, I always loved Christmas'. *Everybody is able to talk about Christmas. Surely we can get one minute of conversation on the topic*

'I don't like Christmas, my dog died at Christmas. But red goes with coca cola and, and ...... red bull', Rocker burst out inspired. *Saved by the bell He's a lost cause, time to move on to* **Master Chef**.

'I'd cook up a storm in my kitchen for you, anything you wanted, starters, main course, deserts....I'll cook you a banquet. What's your favourite food?'

'There's so much to choose from, it's difficult to say. Red meat cooked tenderly can be better than chocolate.' *It's true, food does lend itself to flirting.'*

'Are you interested in politics? enquired '**Radio Head'**. *I'm a politics junkie.*

'It depends on the issues and the politicians. I have become more aware of how the decisions made by politicians affect our lives. I wish they had to pass an IQ test before they were able to stand for election.' *Most of them are incapable of passing the civil service exams.*

'I disagree', replied Radio Head. 'If the people want to be represented by a thick fool then that is their prerogative.' *Interesting point.*

'Have you got children? asked '**King of the Jungle'.** *I don't choose to talk about my child. You are too old to be here tonight and probably have four kids tucked away in the attic.*

'Kids and romance don't go well together, as I'm sure you know.'

'Yeah, you're right there, alright. Do you smoke?'

His teeth are as yellow as parchment paper, he must smoke sixty ciggies a day.

'No.'

'Would you go out with a smoker?'

'No.' *I am not going out with you.*

Claire's father Tom had never smoked cigarettes, but it was his routine on a Friday night to relax in his armchair beside the fire and reach out for the tin of tobacco and worn wooden pipe which he kept on a side shelf. The distinctive smell of pipe tobacco hanging in the air always reminded Claire of her father and she savoured the scent. She knew that smoking was a health hazard and society frowned upon it but for Claire the smell of tobacco evoked images and memories of men pulling on pipes and being at peace with their world. That was not to say that a man had to smoke for Claire to find him attractive, but she certainly did not hold smoking against a man. She did not smoke herself, mainly because she feared that if she did, she would be puffing on forty cigarettes a day before she knew it.

'Do you like travelling? I've travelled the world a lot',' **World Explorer** wanted to know.
'No but I've travelled through Ireland a lot, it's such a beautiful country.' *I haven't had the money to do much travelling.*

Claire was glad of the halfway interval. It was very warm in the room and she was sweltering under the cloak. Claire gulped down her drink. The questions were getting exhausting and she resolved to turn the focus away from herself and onto the man after the break. Where the hell was Andrew? There was still no sign of him. He was a dead man if he had done a runner on her.

The girls seemed nice enough and the consensus was that it was nearly obligatory for a single girl living in the city to try speed dating and internet dating at least once. People were enjoying the added mystique that the cloaks, masks and name tags bestowed on them. Before they knew it, the bell rang and round two of the marathon evening began.

'Bird Watcher' man approached and, given the night that was in it, Claire assumed he meant it ironically. She soon discovered he had a consuming passion for birds of the feathered variety.

'Sometimes I get a call that a rare bird has been spotted in a radius within two hundred miles and I get up and leave my desk to go see it. If it's a rare bird it's worth the effort, you might never get the chance to see the little beauty again. I plan all my holidays around bird watching. There are billions of birds on the planet and sadly I'm only going to see a minuscule fraction of them. Have you ever seen the manner by which a bird ingests food or water through its beak? It's amazing'.

'I can imagine. Maybe you will find your perfect woman in a bird watching club. It's good for couples to share interests together, especially when it is more of a passion than a hobby.' *I'd be better off taking my chances with a golfer, fewer birds to compete against.*

'How do you spend your free time?' asked **'Martial Arts Expert'**. *What free time? I have a child and a full-time job. Time for myself is the ultimate treat.*

'I like walking, swimming, reading, watching films, music'. *You go girl, you energetic, mad thing.*

'Golfer No. 2' sat down opposite Claire. For devilment she asked him about his views on men only golf clubs.

'The furore about men only clubs is political correctness gone mad. Men have a right to play a round of golf together without having to listen to women going on incessantly about their weight. There's nothing wrong with their bloody weight unless they're obese and women golfers don't have that problem. We're not interfering with the ladies, let them do their own thing and leave us alone.'

No trouble, I'll give you all the space you will ever need. Oh goody, is that a real live Mr. Darcy approaching?

'Are you Mr. Darcy from Pride and Prejudice or Mr. Darcy from Bridget Jones?' *Either one of them ticks my box. Pity both Mr. Darcy are dead.*

'Since I am addressing 'Blythe Spirit', I will lay claim to the first title. Your humble servant Madam', he said in a best of British accent. When he flashed a smile displaying large, protruding teeth, Claire was knocked backwards. *Mr. Darcy is not meant to have prominent teeth.*

'Mr. Darcy only stumbles towards humility at the end of the book, not the beginning', parried Claire.

'True, but some women can't resist skipping chunks of the book to get to the ending quickly'.
Perceptive

'And may I ask you Mr. Darcy is your ideal woman like Elizabeth Bennett?' she asked.

'You mean beautiful, intelligent, strong and diverting?' he replied. 'Yes, I'd chase after her'.

Claire got a tingling feeling in her spine, there was suddenly something familiar about this Mr Darcy.

'Andrew?' she said tentatively.

The bell to switch places rang out loud and clear and she was not sure he heard her.

'I've got your number Blythe Spirit, it's been a pleasure.' He flashed his enormous dentures and **Champion Rider** approached in his stead.

'There's nothing like the feel of riding out with the horses and the hounds on a fresh Spring day. The sport has been around for centuries. The hunts are well organised, and they contribute to the community. Those people ringing up radio stations to object are ignorant, they don't know one end of a horse from another. If they want to better society let them vent their spleen on drug pushers.' You probably *have thighs like tree trunks, country boy.*

'My marriage has broken up.', confided '**Motor Racing Legend'.** 'We split the house fifty- fifty, she got the inside and I got the outside. I'm back in the family home with the parents. The wife makes it difficult for the kids to visit me but they're great, they keep me going. The wife's a lethal weapon, she wants to leave me with nothing.' *You are in a bad state, you poor man.*

Claire brightened up when she saw **Bugs Bunny** approaching her table. The guy was tall, with buck teeth and glasses and mousey brown hair. What was it with gigantic teeth tonight? Ireland must either have the worst dentists in the world or they are too expensive for ordinary people to afford to go and get their unsightly teeth fixed. Claire was glad to see him because nobody expected a sad story from Bugs Bunny. She wanted her novelty night out to end on a happy note.

Bugs had a stream of jokes. 'What did the bunnies say when the farmer caught them kissing in the garden? Lettuce alone. What are four hundred rabbits hopping backwards? A receding hare line. What did the bunny give his girlfriend when he asked her to marry him? A thirteen-carrot ring.' *He wasn't going to challenge the kings of comedy, but he was harmless*

The bell rang signalling the end of the four-minute introductory chats. It had certainly been one of the more interesting evenings Claire had experienced in the last couple of years. She had quite liked Master Chef and there had been something intelligent about Bird Watcher man but the only name she ticked on the list was Mr. Darcy's.

'Will you not tick more names, my dear? I can see from the cards handed in already that you are popular tonight. There is sure to be a match if you select four or five names and after all, that is what the evening is all about', encouraged the lady collecting the cards.

Her words fell on deaf ears because, when it came down to it, Claire did not feel ready to go on a date with a stranger. She had dipped her toe in the water tonight and she did not care to start swimming yet. The organiser confided in her that Mr. Darcy had been a popular choice, which was a surprise given his frightful teeth. Claire was not to be disappointed if he did not give her a call.

Once the masquerade costumes were removed it was impossible to distinguish the participants of the speed dating event from the casual clientele of the hotel. Claire made a bee line to the bar in search of Andrew and found him there, thirstily downing a pint of lager and ready to push a glass of red glass in her direction.

'Where have you hidden them?', Claire asked straightaway.

Andrew put his hand in his inside pocket and drew out the set of enormous false buck teeth.

'Good, aren't they?' he grinned.

'The organiser said you were the hit of the evening, which stretches all credibility with those monstrosities in your mouth. Did you put them in just for me?'

'Yes. I wanted to see if I could fool you', laughed Andrew.

'You fraud, Mr. Darcy with buck teeth! I'll never be able to think of him in the same way'.

'But did you pick him?'

'Of course, I couldn't say no to Mr. Darcy. Did you pick me?'

'There were so many to choose from, hmm, I'm not sure. I could have gotten you mixed up with Black Widow or Foxy Transformer. The Ice Queen was tempting too,' teased Andrew.

'Andrew,' said Claire warningly, giving him a dig in the ribs.

'Mind the glass with your elbow! Of course, I choose you, I've got some sense'.

'Thanks Andrew. You know I love you', she hugged him.

'Not as much as I love you', Andrew's softly spoken words floated over Claire's head.

Her attention was caught by two girls who were still wearing masks at a nearby table, one of whom was giving her the thumbs up sign. They appeared to be congratulating her on a successful hook up. Except for Claire, the evening was no more than a rare night out on the town with her good friend Andrew Kennedy, to be talked and laughed about afterwards. But a tiny spark was lit deep within her and she suddenly realised that she no longer believed that romantic love was dead and gone. Hope did indeed spring eternal.

CHAPTER TEN

Daniel called Claire into his office and cut to the chase as soon as she walked through the door, as was his typical mode of operation.

'A discrepancy has emerged between the costs incurred in the development of the new IT system as reported into the top management steering committee compared to the costs coming through the general ledger. I want you to take a look at it and see what figures we can rely on.'

'How big is the discrepancy?'

'Over half a million and growing by the day'.

'I'm onto it', replied Claire promptly.

'Thanks Claire. This is a priority, clear the decks and work on nothing else for the week', directed Daniel.

Claire felt the adrenaline pumping through her body as she walked back into her office with a smile on her face. She knew she was good at this type of work. She immediately got on the phone and set up a meeting in the afternoon with the accounts assistant for the ICT project. It meant her going out to the Ballsbridge office which was where the ICT development and implementation project was based. She met with a pleasant girl called Ruth who was in charge of keeping track of the costs of the project, under the management of the Executive Director of the project, a Mr. Frederick Knowles.

Knowles was an outside consultant from the United Kingdom who had been brought in to oversee the ICT project. He reported into the steering committee of the Irish division of Leictreach.

'Every day brings its own surprises and pleasures', said Knowles, putting his manicured hand out to greet Claire. She was nearly blinded by the flash of his brilliantly white, cosmetically enhanced teeth, set against tanned skin. Since English and Irish people were usually milky white after winter, she suspected the tan came from sun beds and his black as coal hair came out of a bottle. She rarely trusted men who dyed their hair.

'I hear you are here because we've regrettably become a negative variance.

Let me assure you my team are all intent on becoming positive variances against budget.'

Claire smiled politely at Knowles little accounting joke, noting that he held onto her hand too tightly for comfort. Her instinctive reaction to Frederick Knowles was that he was capable of knifing his granny in the back if it could be turned to his advantage. Knowles knew why Claire was there and who had sent her. If he obstructed Claire in her investigations, he would in effect, be challenging Daniel's authority, and he always made it his priority to stay on the right side of the big players in the game. Knowles was adept at playing his cards close to his chest and Claire did not expect him to volunteer any information. No sooner had he said hello than he was waving goodbye to her. Whatever Claire found out, she would have to do it on her own.

Claire tracked through the methodologies employed in recording the costs of the IT consultants and then she reviewed the spreadsheets which collected the data. She collected and checked through a big sample of the invoices and expense vouchers from the consultants brought in from abroad to work on the project, whistling soundlessly when she saw what they were charging for their services. Leictreach was being billed by the day for each of the consultants and the time they spent travelling from their country of origin to Ireland was also being charged. Throw in the costs of their flights and accommodation and the bills were quickly mounting up to significant amounts. Knowles himself had been working at the company for nine months, at a rate of €1,700 a day.

Claire assumed that the consultants must have brains the size of Britain to justify such massive salaries, but she soon discovered that this was not the case. She witnessed one of the consultants, who was paid an hourly rate of €150, take half an hour before he was even able to get into one of the sandpit sites to begin any kind of work. She sat quietly for three days at a desk in the corner of a room surrounded by these highly paid consultants and came to the conclusion that if somebody was lucky enough to be hired as a consultant they could add on a couple of zeros to the wages they would command if they were a salaried employee. Most of the consultants she observed were not Einstein's, they simply had garnered IT knowledge in a specific area before it got to the masses.

As for 'Know it All Knowles', Claire heard him talk more about rugby to the men working in the section rather than the intricacies of the information management system. Given that he was the Executive Director of the ICT project, most of the people working in the department paid him remarkably little heed. She did hear Frederick Knowles lecture a young guy who was wet behind the ears and who hung on his every word about the *'need for autonomy but with that comes responsibility'* but she doubted if he practiced what he preached. She did not see Knowles engage with any of the team of consultants in any problem solving capacity. Instead Fingers Freddy spewed business strategy jargon and sound bites as he waltzed around the office, waiting for the next meeting, concentrating on style rather than substance.

On her third and final day in the ICT department she went for coffee with a group of the consultants working under Knowles. Were her instincts about him right or wrong? Claire did not automatically respect a person because he held a post or role in the organisation, he had to earn her respect by the manner in which he carried out his job. Knowles' technology underlings were not long in telling her that he brought nothing to the table, and they had found it better to ignore him. He was full of bluff. With Knowles, it was always going to be somebody else's fault if things did not pan out as planned.

Claire was left with the impression that Knowles would not take responsibility for feeding a cat, let alone the responsibility for delivering a project which cost millions of euro on time and on budget. In Leictreach, Knowles was fortunate to be supported by a team of hardworking, technically proficient specialists. Knowles had got on in the world and was handsomely paid because he used the business terminology beloved of academics and top managers, who soaked up his "rugger bugger" conversation and did not want to see past his smooth smile and brass neck. The chancer moved around a lot, not staying too long on a project and moving from country to country. If the project succeeded, he took all the credit and if it failed, he blamed it on the incompetence of the ring of people reporting into him.

Claire put her report together, identifying the key cost differences in a detailed reconciliation. Basic errors of omission contributed to the differences, such as Knowles not including the VAT element in his costings or the travel time of the many consultants working on the project. It clearly showed that the true costs of the ICT project were more accurately reflected in the invoices coming through in the general ledger rather than in Knowles' figures. She knew that Knowles would not welcome her report since its findings confirmed that he had been consistently understating the cost of the ICT project to the top management steering committee.

She mitigated against the errors she had identified from occurring again by designing a new template for accurately collecting the costs of the ICT expenditure. She emailed the much improved template to Ruth and was pleased with her reply:-

Thanks a million Claire, your template will definitely make my job easier and it has been a while since I can say that about anything. Don't forget to call in and see us the next time you are in the building and we will have a coffee together.

Regards,
Ruth

Claire sent the report to Daniel, feeling a sense of satisfaction for a job well done. She knew she had identified the causes behind the problem and put forward its solution. She was sanguine when Daniel summoned her to his office.

'Claire, I showed your report to Frederick Knowles and he did not understand it', said Daniel without preamble.

Claire's first reaction was to bite on her lip to prevent a laugh breaking out from her. Of course, Frederick Knowles was going to prevaricate, the man was responsible for delivering the project on time and within budget and instead her report had shown that costs were going sky high. He had a thick neck saying he did not understand her crystal clear report because it risked revealing the depth of his ignorance.

'What did he not understand about it?' she asked.

Daniel did not provide an answer to her question.

'Perhaps you need to go on a writing course', he suggested instead.

Claire sucked in her breath in disbelief. She had expected to hear words of praise coming out of Daniel's mouth, not disparagement. She had produced an accurate, informative report and Knowles was trying to deflect attention away from its legitimate findings. Daniel, the financial controller she admired and trusted, was helping Knowles to do this by making it *'shoot the messenger time'* instead of focussing in on the message. For the first time ever with Daniel, Claire had to control the sensations of anger and indignation swelling up within her at this unfair criticism. She focused on defending her report, unwilling to let the insult to her professional ability pass by without protest.

'Daniel, I wrote that report on the assumption that since Frederick Knowles is in charge of an ICT project worth millions, he has the ability to understand basic financial data. The report has a table of contents, executive summary, each section is headed and referenced, and it ends with a clear conclusion. He should be able to understand the report, it is very clear' she defended herself.

'Look Claire, all I know is that I had to draw up a one page summary of the report for Frederick Knowles, which took up time I needed to use for something else', snapped Daniel, face tight, not appreciating his authority being questioned.

Claire had included a one page summary, which had all the main points on it, if anybody had bothered to read it. She'd put money on it that there was very little difference between her summary and Daniel's one. Why was she being chewed out because Fingers Freddy admitted he was too stupid to comprehend a report with some financial detail in it? Having come to the conclusion that Knowles was a waste of space, the next step for Claire was to try and reason out why top management was supporting and retaining him in his lucrative position.

Ultimately of course the real culprit was the CEO of the company, for it was he who had appointed Knowles to the important position of Executive Director in the first place and had been listening to his drivel for ages. Maybe the top brass were loathe to fire Knowles because it would mean publicly admitting their own mistake in appointing him to the job and they guarded against anything which reflected badly on their own judgement. Contract stipulations might also make it difficult and expensive to sack Knowles and hire a replacement for him. Daniel was the stalwart company man and dissent from the senior management team was not part of his mentality.

Claire strove to look at the situation logically from another angle.

'Is the report and its findings of any use?', she asked, wanting to determine if her good work counted for nothing.

'The financial findings presented in the report are valid and I presented them to the steering committee on Wednesday', acknowledged Daniel. It was good that he had make use of her findings, not that anybody would have guessed it by the displeasure stiffening his spine.

'That's something then', said Claire, relieved.

There was nothing more Claire could say about this matter without risking an explosion. There was however a topic she wanted to discuss with Daniel, in the interests of career development. It probably was not the best time to bring the issue up but, as he was away from the office so much, it might be ages before she got the opportunity of a one to one conversation with him again.

'Daniel, you mentioned during my last performance review that you were considering incorporating treasury and cash flow operations into my remit. I do want to gain experience in those areas. Can I be involved with the treasury function going forward please?'

'Ashley is in charge of overseeing Balance Sheet activity and therefore manages the treasury function. I will mention your request to her but any change there needs her consent', replied Daniel.

Claire left the office glumly. Daniel had only grudgingly acknowledged the usefulness of her report for presentation to the senior management team. It was completely unfair, she had actually done everything right and yet, instead of praising her, Daniel had dragged her in to haul her over the coals for somebody else's limitations.

She had seen this tactic before, with the people on the higher rungs of the hierarchy placing the blame for the failure to get the job done right onto the drone worker beneath them. It was unfair because the manager controlled the system and his/her subordinate had no control. Lack of control leads to increased stress levels in an individual. It was often the case that the lowly administrator could not process the data because the system was originally designed for a different purpose and was adapted too poorly for the current task in hand. When the work inevitably did not get done, the lowly data processor was blamed for either not understanding how to use the system properly or being too lazy to be productive. Valuable time was wasted while senior management refused to recognise the reality of the situation, which was that the system itself had been ill devised and had broken down. Claire had never, ever thought that Daniel might fall into this category of bad managers and she had to get her head around the fact that his judgement about people and the way they operated could be unsound. Anna was more pragmatic about the situation.

'What do you expect Claire? He's a bloody accountant, not a psychologist. A lot of the time Daniel only sees his spreadsheets, his nose is buried in them. Also, managers stick together. If one of them gets the sack the others don't like it, they think they'll be next on the hit list. Don't expect too much of Daniel or you'll be disappointed. He's a busy man, and only a man at that', remarked Anna.

As usual her words of advice gave no comfort to the agitated Claire. Another bum deal was that she needed Ashley's consent to be involved in the Treasury function and she might need to hire the services of a hypnotist to wangle that out of her.

Claire had no option but to bury herself as usual in her day job and try to push Daniel's startling support for Knowles, coupled with his lack of support for her, out of her mind. What about the concepts of loyalty and backup for his own team member? It appeared that in future she had to write reports for the most senior people in a multinational company in terms a ten year old child could read and understand. Was that what they wanted? Claire felt confused and her confidence in her own judgment was shaken. Perhaps after all she should go on the writing course for more direction on the appropriate level of complexity and language to use in preparing a report for senior managers. Could it be that she had overestimated the general intelligence levels of the people at the top? Was a Knowles type executive the exception to the rule or was he representative of the rule?

Claire had always assumed the brightest and the best rose to the top echelons of major corporations. The possibility that people of average intelligence and ability were running some of the big corporations was a concept that she was having huge difficulty in accepting. No wonder there was always a danger of the stock market tanking when people who lied about their capabilities and shook the right hands got ahead of people with real brainpower and honesty. No wonder the mantra 'greed is good' had gotten stuck in mainstream consciousness. What drove these people of average intellect but huge egos above all else was their intense desire to make money while the going was good. Claire had never before felt such disillusionment with the powers that be who ruled the world as she knew it and it left her feeling restless and downcast.

Meantime things were going from bad to worse for Claire at work, despite the high reliability of her output and through no fault of her own. Ashley's next email to her proved she was not letting her imagination go wild.

Claire

It has been decided that you are now responsible for doing the weekly stock reconciliation report, effective immediately.

**Rgds
Ashley**

Claire groaned when she read this email, which involved her having to do a detailed, repetitive, time consuming reconciliation each week which people only noticed if stock levels went under or over by extremes. It was not a hard task to do, simply a time consuming one. She would learn nothing new doing this work, the Treasury gig would have been much more engaging. Taxation was another interesting area she would like to learn more about. For an accountant, nothing was more boring than stock. She gnawed her lip before deciding to take the plunge and typed the following,

Hi Ashley,

I am requesting involvement in Treasury as opposed to monitoring the inventory levels, which is more of a purchasing function. Treasury activity is a much better fit for my accounting background and financial analytical skillset, therefore the potential for me to add value to the company is greater in this function.

Regards,

Claire

She hit the send bottom on the email as nothing ventured, nothing gained. This was no time to be hiding her light under a bushel. Involvement in Treasury meant daily contact with Ashley but at least she would be learning something new and interesting. The response to her request came back quicker than she could blink.

Claire

**Karen has been appointed to take over the Treasury function and monitor the daily cash flow under my direction.
I urge you to apply the same level of due diligence to the monitoring of the inventory levels.**

Rgds
Ashley

Ashley's email seemed innocent enough on the face of it, but it was actually full of gleeful spite; both women were well aware that the treasury role in a finance department was more prestigious than the stock monitoring one. If the company had too little money overnight in its current accounts, it encountered difficulty in meeting its payment obligations and if it had too much it was losing out on earning interest in its deposit accounts. It also transferred a percentage of its money out of euros at the weekends because if the currency collapsed the senior management reckoned the catastrophe would occur on a Saturday or Sunday rather than during the standard Monday to Friday business week. If the stock figure was wrong in the balance sheet for one month nobody really cared that much, unless it had a material effect on the cash flow figure. In short, the Treasury job was interesting, the stock one was not, and Claire had lost out on a job she wanted to the new kid on the block, aka Ms. Karen Woods.

Claire's fingers hovered over the keyboard as she considered sending Ashley another email to express her eagerness to gain new experiences in financial management activity within the company. Or would she sound desperate and begging? She pulled her hands away and bunched them under her chin. There was no point in holding her hands out again, for them to be smacked back down. The jobs had been allocated and the deal was done. Without a doubt she had been given a repetitive, tedious task but she must get through it as quickly as possible so that she could move onto her more interesting work. Claire was a realist and she knew that nearly every job had some boring elements to it. If a person was feeling under the weather, it could actually be quite handy to have some brain dead work to get through.

One of the things Claire was concerned about was that she was becoming very busy on time consuming tasks which nobody high up in the organisation gave any thought to. For instance, the purchasing manager might give the summary stock reconciliation report a quick review to check that his own departmental operations were on target, but Claire doubted if Daniel had given the report a glance since the year dot; such detail was beneath his attention.

Senior management were turning their attention to devising the next three year strategic plan for the company. Input into the strategic plan was great experience for any accountant in a company the size of Leictreach. Claire would have jumped at the chance to be repositioned to work on a section of it, but pigs would fly before that was going to happen this time around. She was being pushed into the wrong square of Leictreach's activity grid, the one that kept her frantically busy with tasks below the radar of senior management. If she was not seen to add value to the organisation, she became easily replaceable and disposable. Claire did not need to work in Human Resources to realise that a combination of 'very busy' with 'unimportant stuff to tick an audit box' did not augur well for her career development prospects in Leictreach.

CHAPTER ELEVEN

Claire must have been born optimistic because even though she realised things were bad she was still totally unprepared for the bomb shell Joan dropped on her.

'Claire, did you hear the news? Daniel has asked Karen to take control of the de-merger of the TvQuinno division from the company', said Joan, rushing into the room. She was practically quivering with excitement from head to toe as she broke the news to Claire, keenly watching her reaction.

'That can't be right, Claire does all that kind of work here. Where did you hear that news from Joan?', Anna asked sharply. The ambitious Joan was not one of her favourite people and Anna had distrusted her since she had swiped the credit for Claire's work.

'She's in our office now, asking Orla about the invoices. There's no mistake, she announced it clear as day and for all to hear that Daniel had asked her to take charge of the de-merger. I thought Claire should know about it, that's all, you know, as a friend, because the whole of the general office is talking about it', replied Joan, with her nose in the air, not appreciating Anna's sharp tone. She swung around to face Claire again.

'Unless you knew about it already from Daniel?' Joan probed.

Claire shook her head and tried to keep the bewilderment she was feeling out of her voice.

'No, I didn't know about it. If Daniel has given Karen the job, then that's it. Nobody argues with Daniel, he's the boss', said Claire, a tremor in her voice. Joan oozed satisfaction as she sashayed out of their office, mission accomplished, leaving Anna gritting her teeth and Claire reeling from her shock.

'Ashley is promoting Karen every which way she turns. They are sharing that office together and they are as thick as thieves. Orla was looking at the sundry creditor list yesterday and spotted that the two of them are off together on a two day training course next week and it is costing the company €2,000. Have you ever been sent off on a course like that in the time you've been here Claire?' asked Anna.

'No', Claire shook her head slowly. 'But then I've never asked to go on one'. She wished Anna would stop rubbing salt into the open wound, it was giving her a pain in her head.

The wound left its mark. Claire had handled all the merger and de-merger financial accounting groundwork in the company for over two years. She was brilliant at it, speedy and accurate. There was no need to take it away from her and give it to somebody else.

'Karen is just in the door and they are spending money on her to go training. That's not like them, they penny pinch when it comes to formal training and spending days away from the office. They want us at our desks, not gallivanting on a course with a fancy lunch thrown in', stated Anna.

She eyed up Claire, ferociously protective.

'Now you listen here to me, for just this once. When that Karen comes in here looking for your help and advice on how to do that de-merger job and, mark my words she will, you are to keep your mouth shut. You are to tell her absolutely nothing. I will **kill** you if you give her one word of advice. To hell with *'team work'* and *'we're all in this together'* and *'it's for the good of the department'*, mocked Anna. 'They don't care about you or the department, they care about themselves.'

Claire looked dumbly across at Anna and nodded her head. She could not disguise the hurt of her displacement.

'At last you are showing some sense. It's dog eat dog, around here, my girl, and the blood has started to spill under the doors. People are holding their noses and ignoring the bad smell.'

Things were bad indeed if Daniel was taking this work away from her. How would Karen go about tackling the de-merger of TvQuinno? You had to take a very methodological, thorough approach and it was not as easy a task to execute as Claire made it look. Karen could easily tie herself up into knots with it if she did not approach it from the right angle. Yes, Claire expected Ms. Perfect to get quite stressed out doing it and she would get a bitter sense of satisfaction from witnessing it from the sidelines.

Karen knocked on their door later on in the day and approached Claire's desk, holding a printout of the control account of TvQuinno in her hand. She had never entered their office before, not even to greet them with a breezy hello as she passed by their door to get to her own each morning. Anna's eyebrows shot up and she winked at Claire out of Karen's sight line.

'I hear you have been involved with de-merger projects before Claire. I'd like us to discuss methodologies in order to determine the best approach to take for the successful accomplishment of our goals and targets. Two heads are better than one when it comes to creating synergies, don't you agree?' commented Karen with a smooth smile.

'I do indeed Karen. It's unfortunate that I have pressing deadlines to meet, and I have no spare time available for meetings this week. Isn't that the nature of our business, there's never enough time. What approach are you currently adopting?' Claire asked, politely professional.

'A top down approach, to get an overview of the business information. But surely with an element of organising and planning we can factor in a meeting together,' replied Karen, trying in vain to push the control account summary into Claire's hands.

'I'm afraid not, next week looks to be choc a bloc as well. The best planning won't create time that is simply not there. But it's great that you have decided on a definite strategy. It fits in well with senior management's preference for taking the panoramic view. Good luck with it, although I'm sure a person of your ability won't need it', Claire did her best impression of a porcelain doll as she blanked Karen politely. The other girl's lips noticeably tightened.

'Thank you Claire. I will surely remember all the help you've offered me today', said Karen, not too subtly threatening to be a lioness lying in the long grass waiting to devour her in the future, if Claire did not come up with the goods in the present. She left the room in disgust.

'Good girl, you're learning', muttered Anna out of the side of her mouth, amused.

'Thanks. At least I'm getting praise from somewhere. Karen looked like she was sucking on a lemon when she left', said Claire. 'I actually found it quite hard to refuse to help her, the words sounded odd to me, even as I spoke them.'

'She'll get over it. Let's see how well she does when she has nobody holding her hand. I bet you had to figure the methodology out for yourself the first time you did it', snorted Anna.

Anna was right on the money there, nobody had sat down with Claire to explain the best process to take. Karen definitely would not get far with her top down approach as the figures had to be built upon layer by layer from the bottom up in order to be reliable. It had to be done that way because the top down approach missed out on too much vital information, often hidden in the detail.

Claire got a much bigger sense of satisfaction when Daniel entered her office the following week. Anna was on her lunch break, but Claire was still working away on her computer. He spoke very nicely to Claire and it was music to her ears.

'I do not know if you are aware of it, but Karen is handling the accounting work for the de-merger of the TvQuinno division. She could use your expertise in the area. Are you willing to help her out with the project? I'd really appreciate it since the de-merger is a big undertaking', said Daniel, his manner all friendly.

'Of course I will help Karen, since *you* ask me to. I like and enjoy de-merger accounting and I am pleased to be involved in it again', said Claire, her face breaking into a sunny smile.

'That's great Claire', said Daniel, 'Karen will continue to do the payroll aspects of the job, but you can pull together everything else. Karen knows I am asking you to get involved in the project, so she is expecting your call. Make it your highest work priority until it's complete. As usual we're working to a tight deadline'.

With those words, he was off. Claire hugged herself in delight. This was simply wonderful. It was obvious that Karen had not got a clue about how to go about the de-merger process and was making a mess of it. Daniel had realised that he needed Claire's input and (wait for it) what was that delicious word he had used? Her *expertise*, in order to get the work delivered right and on time. Claire was suddenly like a greyhound in the trap with the scent of a rabbit in her nostrils. 'Let's go,' she said to herself as she drummed her fingers happily on the desk. She knew she was going to do a terrific job and she could not wait to get started.

Karen was quick to hand over control of the de-merger accounting project to Claire and then she completely backed away. Claire did not hear a peep out of her. The first thing Claire did was to contact Stephen Murray, the commercial manager for the TvQuinno division. He was going to be its new Finance Director, once it was a company in its own right. Vanessa Kimble, his most senior administrator, was also a valuable contact. Claire needed to liaise with them to make sure she had all the relevant data and they were all singing from the same song sheet. She was not surprised that Stephen wanted to be kept fully informed of developments, as he did not want any unpleasant surprises in store when it came to signing off on a set of accounts with Daniel. TvQuinno Ltd was going to be the first company Stephen Murray was put in control of; it was his baby and he wanted to make sure that its assets were greater than its liabilities in its new venture as a separate legal entity. He was not going to agree to take over any expenditure unless he was fully convinced it was incurred by TvQuinno and for that he wanted extensive invoice back up documentation for verification purposes, shelves of it. So much for Karen's top down approach! Value was built up, not down.

Nothing escaped Claire's attention. She analysed everything. Claire had an uncanny ability to scan through mountains of invoices in record time and identify anything that was out of the ordinary or which had not been originally dealt with correctly. Alarm bells rang in her ears, urging her to take a closer look and get the matter sorted out. Her unerring detection of errors resulted in specific costs and revenues been taken out and others being added in, which ultimately changed the end valuation of the de-merged division.

Claire had always found it easy to communicate with the divisional heads as they were invariably friendly and courteous in their dealings with her and thankfully Stephen Murray was no exception. She did not have to trouble the overburdened Orla in Accounts Payable for help with accessing and photocopying the invoices because she was able to rope in the services of an agency temp. A wall of folders comprising documentation relating to TvQuinno was handed over to Stephen Murray for examination and record-keeping purposes. Claire set up and filled in a summary spreadsheet of all the transactions. She worked quickly and efficiently with the singleness of purpose which defined the way she did everything, putting the whole package together, without input from Karen or Daniel. She arranged a meeting with Stephen and his assistant Vanessa to agree final figures. Once Stephen stated he was ready to sign off on the set of accounts, Claire emailed the completed files to both Daniel and Karen, delighted with her fait accompli. She really wanted Daniel to realise that she was responsible for preparing the financial package for the TvQuinno demerger, as opposed to Karen. She made sure to put a tracker on the email as she wanted to be notified when it was opened.

Days went by without Daniel reading her email. Karen opened it up the instant she received it, almost as if she was sitting by her PC watching and waiting for its delivery, but this was not the case with Daniel. Every day Claire checked to see if Daniel had opened the email, willing him to see it and congratulate her on a job well done. It did not happen. What did happen at the end of the week was that Claire was alerted by an email notification message that Daniel had deleted her TvQuinno file attachment without ever having opened it.

It was essential for Daniel to be aware of the information contained in her email in order for the demerger of TvQuinno to progress. If he did not derive it from Claire's email attachment, then it meant that Karen had affixed her minor piece of work on the salaries to Claire's major analysis of the division and forwarded it all over to Daniel. He had chosen to bypass Claire's email and go directly to open Karen's one. It was not an illogical thing for him to do as he was only interested in the final version. It did mean though that he was unaware of the extent of Claire's output on the project relative to Karen's paltry input.

This suspicion was confirmed when Claire passed by the open door of the office Karen shared with Ashley and heard Daniel's voice inside. She could not resist lingering outside in the corridor to eavesdrop on their conversation.

'I wanted you to know that I have met with Stephen Murray and we were both happy to go with your final figures. We were able to fully sign off on the value of the de-merged division as it transferred into the new company. It was a seamless process. Thank you for your excellent input and hard work. It greatly contributed to the success of the de-merger of TvQuinno division,' said Daniel warmly.

'It was no trouble Daniel. The whole project was a valuable learning exercise for me, in addition to being interesting and informative. I am delighted that it was completed successfully and on time', replied Karen with cloying sweetness.

Claire felt sick to the pit of her stomach. What about her trojan contribution to the project? There was no mention of her at all. Of course, it had been no trouble for Karen, it was Claire who had done all the work! Should she butt in on the cosy tête-à-tête and say something? But Daniel had to know the truth for he was the very one who had come into Claire's office to ask her to share her *expertise* with Karen, who was making a dog's dinner of the whole affaire when she was put working on it on her own.

A realisation hit Claire; Daniel must intend coming into her office next to thank her for all her outstanding work on the high profile project and for so generously sharing her knowledge with Karen. She scurried back inside her office, expecting Daniel to appear at her door any minute now to proffer his congratulations and appreciation of an important job well done.

The minutes ticked by, the hours dragged on. Claire waited and waited but Daniel never did approach her to congratulate her on her successful work on the TvQuinno de-merger. Daniel never once mentioned it to her in passing on the corridor. He did not acknowledge her involvement in the project with one word of praise and there was certainly nothing like the thanks he had lavishly heaped on the undeserving Karen's head. Claire digested the sickening truth; a pattern had emerged whereby Daniel was wrongly accrediting Claire's work to other people in Finance, partly because her colleagues were quick to accept the credit for work they did not do themselves. This was resulting in her output being unacknowledged and undervalued. Her future chances of any career development in the organisation were being sabotaged by more than one person. Any motivation to excel and accomplish had to come from within herself, for the organisation was rewarding her strong performances with precisely nought.

CHAPTER TWELVE

It had been four months since Claire's brother Martin had come home to visit his parents. Eileen was becoming distraught about the non-appearance of her only son. Elizabeth Sheridan, a neighbour's daughter from up the road, had come home twice from England to see her parents in the time which had elapsed since Tom and Eileen had last set eyes on Martin. Their son lived in Sligo, a three hour drive away from Dublin and he was not making the trip home to see them. It was not like him. Eileen knew in her bones that something was wrong with her boy and she wanted to see him, she could wait no longer. Tom said that he was not going traipsing half way round the country to see Martin. He was a fit young man with plenty of energy who knew full well where they lived, and it was up to him to make the effort to visit his parents. But there was no stopping Eileen once her mind was made up and, if need be, she would travel up to Sligo on the train, alone, to see her beloved son and find out what was wrong with him.

Claire stepped into their argument and offered to drive Eileen to Sligo. She was annoyed with Martin for his selfishness in not making the effort to visit their parents for months on end and she did not like to see Eileen fret needlessly. Part of her wanted to see Martin anyway, for he was her big brother and even as children they had got on well together. Neither of them had resented the unspoken assumption in the household that he was their mother's white haired boy and she was the apple of their father's eye. With only two children in the happy household, there was always one parent available for each of them and they knew their parents loved them both.

There was no point in meeting up with Martin in Sligo if the visit was ruined by a row about not seeing him for months. It was far better to travel with the intention of enjoying a lovely family get together. Claire could certainly do with a nice break herself, to recharge her batteries far away from the trials and tribulations of the workplace. She suggested that they take Ben with them and enjoy a full weekend break in a four star hotel in Sligo. People had been discussing different hotels and the special deals they were offering to entice people through the doors during the off peak season. This hotel ticked all the boxes; the food in the hotel was reported to be excellent, it had a leisure spa and swimming pool to relax in and it was located close to the beautiful Rosses Point beach. By staying there for a couple of nights, at reasonable room rates, they could enjoy a bit of luxury for once and might even treat themselves to a beauty treatment. It had the added advantage of not putting Martin to the bother of preparing bedrooms in his house for their stay.

At first Eileen demurred, uneasy at leaving Tom alone in the house for more than one night; he might forget to take his pills and have a heart attack if she was away from him for too long. If Tom was not too proud, he could come with them for the break but, there was no budging him. He was quite content to stay at home by himself for a couple of nights with the television and his newspapers for company. He could watch one of those blood and guts films his wife disliked so much and which out of consideration for her he rarely viewed. Eileen liked the idea of staying in the four star hotel, but only for the one night without her darling husband. It came to pass that Claire booked a family room in the hotel for the Saturday night only and the three of them set off eagerly in her car, on a mission to meet up with Martin and have a relaxing time. Ben was thrilled at the prospect of staying in a big, fancy hotel and he placed his swimming shorts in the suitcase himself, keen to splash about in the pool.

Although work was never far from Claire's mind, she made a decision not to talk about it to her mother over the weekend. This excursion was not about her and her troubles, no, it concerned her mother's attempt to quell a deep anxiety about Martin's wellbeing. Eileen knew of some men and women in the wider neighbourhood who tragically had committed suicide during recent years, and she had become sensitive about the sad topic, especially since it was mentioned regularly on the radio. When the Church had ruled the land, suicide had been seen as a shameful act which resulted in the person's body being refused burial on consecrated land. It was not talked about and consequently there did not seem to be as much of it around. Nowadays, thankfully and rightfully, the families of people who had taken their own lives had the deepest sympathy of their communities and their bodies were laid to rest in peace and love alongside deceased family members. Since an act of suicide had drained the last breath out of the body of a neighbour's good, sensitive son, Eileen Howard feared its shadowy presence like the devilish Grim Reaper himself.

Once she had expressed it as her deepest worry to Tom and Claire, only for them to scoff at her fear. Martin had never been a person to worry about, as far as they were aware, he was a stable guy. He had always made friends easily at school and at college. He was academically bright and had sailed through his architectural degree course with high honours and an enviable social life. He had been in gainful employment since college and he had always done really well for himself, no matter what he turned his hand to. Unlike Claire, who had put the cart before the horse with her pregnancy and single parent status, he had never done anything to worry or distress her parents in the thirty years he had lived on the planet. He was the model son, somebody his parents were justifiably proud of.

Ben sat in the backseat of the car and was soon preoccupied with watching a movie on his mother's mobile phone, using his ear plugs. Reassured that Ben had no interest in listening to the adult conversation, Claire gently probed her mother's sense of foreboding about Martin as they travelled to Sligo.

'I know you haven't seen Martin for four months Mam, but he is always busy, and time simply flies by. Martin has never given you a reason to worry, he is very sensible', said Claire.

'It's a feeling I have in my waters and I can't shake it off. It doesn't matter what age a son or daughter becomes, a mother worries about her child, from the cradle to the grave', said Eileen earnestly.

'I do sometimes worry about Ben and I know I always want the best for him. I could not bear it if anything bad ever happened to him', acknowledged Claire. 'It is a bit depressing to think that the worry will never stop. The doctor was teasing me about it the last time I brought Ben in to see her.'

'You never mentioned it. What did she say?' asked Eileen, who was always interested in the opinions of doctors. If she had her way, she would trot down every week to the doctor's surgery for a chat, if not about herself, then about the heart tablets Tom was on.

'Dr. Helen told me that she's '*seen it all*' in her years of practice and it is true what they say about Irish Mammies and their sons; the refrain is always 'My Son, My Son', and never 'My Daughter, My Daughter'.

Eileen threw back her head and laughed merrily.

'Maybe it's true what the doctor says'.

'Do you think so Mam? I thought I worried about Ben because he is my only child and I'm learning about him all the time. I wonder if I do the right thing or make the right choices for him. It did not occur to me that I might worry more about him because he is a boy, not a girl', said Claire.

'A mother worries about any sick child, be it a son or daughter. All our children are very precious to us. The son grows up and a wife replaces the mother, it is the nature of things. The daughter tends to stay closer to the parents. Every mother hopes that her son will get a good wife to stand by him, somebody who will support him when the going gets tough and not be too demanding or give him a hard time when it is not necessary. The most important decision a person will ever make is who they decide to marry or indeed, not marry. The right marriage is a marvellous thing. I see the deep loneliness in widowers' eyes, they are lost without their wives. A widow copes far better with her loss than a man, with some even going from strength to strength, but it does not happen that way for men. Your father would be lost without me,' said Eileen, nodded her head confidently towards Claire.

'We'd all be lost without you Mam', teased Claire.

'Well, I don't intend to kick the bucket any time soon. I want to see both my children married and settled before I go and meet my maker. I know a lot of couples aren't bothering getting married nowadays but they are losing out on a solid foundation to a relationship which others treasure. Tell people they can't get married and then they suddenly see the value in it. I believe marriage is the strongest bond a couple can have, helping the relationship to endure over the best and worst of times. Actually, one of the reasons I want to take this trip is to meet Martin's girlfriend, in case he ends up marrying her', said Eileen.

'You have marriage on the brain Mam, and I wish you hadn't. But I agree with you that it is about time we met Caroline since Martin has been seeing her for about a year. Do you know anything about her?' asked Claire. 'He has told me nothing.'

'Martin says she has a responsible job and that her career is important to her. She works in public relations for a big company, whatever that means. Or did he say human resources? It's something like that anyway. You should get on well with her', said Eileen.

Claire was not too sure about that, she did not consider herself to be a driven career girl. She wanted the fruits of her career to provide the funding for a comfortable lifestyle for Ben and herself and also to feel a pride and satisfaction in her work. She was not consumed with a burning ambition to blaze a trail, to rise to heights where few women had gone before. She was beginning to view ambitious, competitive, career women with deep suspicion. Rationally Claire knew that there were countless numbers of decent women working their way up the managerial ranks in organisations through nothing but hard work, polite manners and the ability to get the job done. Katie, a friend of hers from college days, was proof positive of it. It was difficult to meet a more genuine person than Katie and she had succeeded in securing a senior management position in banking in the city of London through her brilliance with figures and IT systems. Even though Claire had the misfortune to run across a nasty character like Ashley for a manager, it did not mean that all career minded women had to be avoided like the plague. It was possible that her brother's girlfriend could turn out to be a brilliant career person, the perfect match for him and a potential close friend of her own. They might be meeting Wonder Woman!

'I think perhaps this Caroline is preventing him from coming home to visit your father and me', confided Eileen. Claire nearly turned her eyes away from the road, she was so surprised.

'Why do you think that Mam?' asked Claire, aware that she should not dismiss Eileen's speculations out of hand. Her mother was nobody's fool.

'I was reading in the problem pages of the newspaper how older women like me are worried sick that they aren't seeing their sons and grandchildren because the sons were silly enough to marry mean minded women who keep them away from their own families. They can only see their sons and grandchildren when the wives are away. These poor women never see their grandchildren if the marriage breaks up, they have no legal rights. It has become a serious problem', said Eileen.

Claire tried to make light of her mother's concern.

'I thought all the jokes were about mothers-in-law, not daughters-in-law Mam.'

It was the wrong response.

'It's not a joke Claire. It is a very sad situation, where the parents can't see their own sons, let alone their little grandchildren. It is as I say; a daughter is a daughter for life, they stay closer to home. A son can go away and marry a possessive woman who won't share him with family or friends and that's the end of it, the parents hardly ever see him again. I don't want that to happen to my Martin'.

'I'm sorry Mam, I didn't mean to upset you. Look, all I'm saying is, don't go worrying about things that may never happen. Caroline may be a lovely person, the second daughter you never had. Or it is possible that Martin and herself have already broken up, they could have had a row last week and the relationship is over even as we speak. Let's wait and see and talk to him before trying to guess what's wrong.'

'I'm glad you admit there is something wrong Claire. A mother's instinct is a very strong thing', Eileen said solemnly.

Claire decided to change the subject, a tactic she often employed with her nearest and dearest.

'How is Dad getting on Mam? Any time I ask him he says *'Grand, it's another fine day, thank God',* said Claire, doing a spot of mimicking Tom's voice and was rewarded by her mother giving a snort of laughter.

'That's your father to a tee alright. He is doing grand, as long as he takes his pills for his heart and does his exercise. He insists on going out in the rain for his daily walk, no matter what I say. I worry about him catching bronchitis or pneumonia, they're easy enough for older people to pick up in our climate. But Tom laughs and says he has stomped in the rain all his life and a bit of water is not going to do him any more harm, no more than it ever did'.

'Dad is sensible enough to wear protective clothing and to change out of wet gear, he knows the drill. He spent most of his life working outdoors, fixing up electrical cables in all types of weather. You're always worrying about something Mam, you'll have me thinking that you're not happy unless you're worrying' teased Claire.

'You must take after me Claire for there is always something on your mind', sniffed Eileen. 'Your father thinks he is a young man and I have to remind him that he's not, especially since he is considering taking up hill walking in Wicklow. I'm not going to spend my Sundays clamouring over rocks on the hill sides, no thank you.'

'I heard those groups walk for ten miles before they take a break. You need to be young like me for that kind of exercise Mam,' teased Claire lightly.

'You're not that young, the years go by quicker than you think', replied Eileen tartly. 'There are plenty of young women married at your age or at least in sight of the altar.'

Eileen twisted around in her seat in the front of the car to check on Ben, oblivious to Claire's inwards groan. She smiled when she saw that the child had fallen asleep, with his head pressed back against the seat and his mouth fallen open. When Ben was asleep, he reminded her strongly of when he was still a toddler.

'You're getting a bit long in the tooth, you'll be thirty before you know it, then forty will fly in. You've no idea how quickly the years go by, it's one of the biggest mysteries in life. The majority of good men are taken by thirty and you had better get a move on or the ones worth having will be gone. Once you're stuck in middle age, you can forget it unless you'd accept somebody divorced or damaged. But you will never be better looking than you are now. These are your best years for attracting a man and all you're doing is wasting them twiddling on a computer, instead of touching up your lipstick and going out to enjoy yourself with single people your own age. I'll babysit Ben, no problem. I want you to be happy Claire. Shut the computer down at 5pm and leave it, walk away. Put more effort into finding a good man who will put his arms around you. Martin will be nabbed soon, you watch and see. He must have been very busy with his job for it not to have happened already.'

Eileen put her hand out to pat Claire reassuringly on the knee, warming up to her theme.

'You are not a free agent Claire, you have your child to consider. Ben won't accept a man in the house telling him what to do when he's a teenager, those are difficult years for a boy. But if the man is kind and decent, Ben is young enough to accept him in your lives now.'

'Thanks for the advice Mam. I'll just go up to the next thirty year old guy I spot without a ring and ask him to take me off your hands, will I?' said Claire sarcastically, stung by her mother's words. She had plenty of time to fall in love with a man, she was not even thirty years old yet, she was young! Did her mother not realise that women considered themselves to be fabulous at forty nowadays? She had years of opportunity ahead of her yet.

'Don't get cheeky with me for stating the truth, if your own mother can't tell you what's what, then who is going to do it? They can sprout all kinds of rubbish and call it research but nature is nature. People are looking out for their life partners from their twenties. The best fruit is plucked from the tree first. It's survival of the fittest and last place wins no trophies. What about Andrew? He's a good boy and he is always hanging around you.'

'Andrew is just a friend Mam' said Claire.

'You are a foolish girl Claire. Andrew is shaping up to be a fine man and many women would have him, if he happened to look their way. I'm not surprised that Andrew broke up with his girlfriend, for he's been mad about you for years. Ben likes him too, he's known Andrew for all of his short life. But if you aren't interested in Andrew, if he really is only a friend to you, then tell him straight and put him right. Don't spend too much time with him or other men will think he is your boyfriend and won't come near you. You are missing your chances and they won't be out there for you forever', said Eileen urgently.

'Don't hold back Mam', urged Claire sarcastically. 'Anything more to say, while you're on fire?'

'Yes, I do have something more to say because I have been silent for too long', said Eileen. 'Go in and do your job from nine to five as best you can and when you leave in the evening, forget about it. Don't give it a thought. Only work for the hours you are paid to put in. Why should you work for nothing? You'll get no thanks for it, they appreciate you more if they have to pay for your services. Let them hire an extra person if it is needed to get the job done, they have plenty of resources and money to pay for another like you. Find a good man with a secure job and then you will not have to work, you'll have the option of staying at home and minding your child yourself'.

Claire was nearly speechless; had her mother not heard about the women's liberation movement and that women were a driving force in the workforce of the twenty first century? What with Anna dishing out advice to her every time she turned around in the office and her mother taking it upon herself to critique her commitment to her job and non-existent love life at home, Claire was heartily sick of older women telling her about how she should live her life.

'Why did you have me educated if your main ambition for me is to stay at home and raise children?' queried Claire.

'Education is never wasted, it has a value of its own. It is society's great leveller. You can talk to both the poorest and the richest person on earth, if you have an education. I wanted you to have education to have options, not to slave away the best years of your life for a meagre wage. Perhaps you picked the wrong profession, maybe an occupation in the medical field is higher regarded and appreciated than working with accounts. Or maybe the problem is that Ireland has produced thousands and thousands of graduates for years and the employers don't want to pay the young people for their education. Frankly, I think a person with your qualifications should be paid much more for the hours you put in.'

Thank goodness they were pulling up at the hotel, although that did not deter Eileen from having the final say on the subject.

'I never worked after marrying your father and having Martin and I've had a happy, content life, thank God. I see women driving up to the school in big cars and they have a lovely life, with their husbands buying everything for them, having cleaners because they are too busy going off to the gym and don't want to ruin their nails. What they consider to be a busy day is easier than your day off Claire. It would make you laugh, if it was funny. Tina Anderson up the road never went to college and hardly worked a day in her life and she passed me the other day, driving a Mercedes no less. Her own mother told me she was a flighty thing with hardly a brain in her head. She was smart enough to make sure she kept her hair groomed and her make- up touched up and watched her figure like a hawk until she got her man, a butcher with three shops, and here she is whizzing by me with a Mercedes under her backside. You are a nice looking girl Claire, much better looking than Tina Anderson, for sure. Why kill yourself at work, if you didn't need to? Stop worrying about your work, you are only a number there. Anyway, there are easier jobs available to you if you choose to look for them. Be careful not to sit down at the wrong dinner table, girl of mine, for you won't get fed there.'

'Thanks for the kind advice Mam. Ben wake up, love, we're here. I think we all need refreshments, especially your Granny. Let's all go in. I'm going to get Gran a steaming cup of tea, with extra lumps of sugar in it to sweeten her up', remarked Claire. She definitely needed a bottle of wine to get into the holiday spirit after that charming chit chat with her mother. Ben shook off his drowsiness with a yell of excitement and the threesome happily trouped up the steps of the hotel, eager to experience the comforts which awaited them inside, ready to park the concerns of the world outside.

CHAPTER THIRTEEN

The Howards enjoyed a lovely relaxed afternoon using the facilities of the hotel. Eileen was delighted to discover that Claire had booked her a facial and a manicure in the hotel's beauty salon as a surprise. After settling into the room and tucking into a tasty lunch, Ben and Claire went down to the swimming pool in the leisure centre for an hour while Eileen strolled off for her beauty treatments. Claire was vigilant with Ben, who was ducking and diving like a duck. Eileen had a more soothing time and nearly fell asleep in the relaxation room after her treatments were complete, the whole experience was remarkably comfortable and peaceful. She had chosen a bright red colour for her manicure and she kept holding her hands up before her face to admire the painted nails. It was impossible to guess how many times she had put those hands into a basin of water to peel the potatoes for dinner. She was beaming with delight when she met up with Claire in the lounge.

'You and Dad could go on one of those short Mediterranean cruises Mam, you deserve to sample some of the luxuries of life after all your hard work down through the years', suggested Claire.

'I'd love to go, for the dancing and the glamour and to see the sights. I'm not sure if your father will agree to go on a cruise trip, there's been a few horror stories about how boats have hit the rocks and capsized. I might sell it to Tom on the basis that it's a history tour, he's always looking at those documentaries on the television', said Eileen twinkling up. 'Seriously, your father and I are talking about going to Rome for a holiday as we both want to visit the Vatican and hope to see the Pope on his balcony. We want to travel from Rome to Sorrento and the Amalfi coastline, taking in Pompeii along the way, that incredible city which was preserved by ash more than a thousand years ago. It will be an amazing trip, full of real history worth seeing. We'd like to go in early September and celebrate our wedding anniversary there in style. It will be exactly forty years since we were in Rome together, it has a special place in our hearts. Prices will be reasonable then because there will be less tourists about and the weather will be cooler, which will make it easier for us to get around. But is it possible for us to go there for about ten days at that time of year? You have to work and who will look after Ben in our absence?'

'It will be a wonderful trip for you and Dad to take together. You must go while you both have the good health to fully enjoy the experience', urged Claire. 'I will skip the usual two week summer holiday in July and book off the last week in August and the first week in September instead. It will fit in nicely with Ben's return to school after the summer break and I'd like to be around to settle him into his new school year. Go ahead and book your holiday of the decade.'

'Nothing is decided yet, your father and I are still discussing it. But if you're sure you can manage without us, we probably will go ahead with the trip. I think it will turn out to be one of our best holidays ever', enthused Eileen, eyes dancing. She was a woman still madly in love with her man, forty years on. How romantic and touching was that?

Later that evening Martin arrived in the hotel for dinner, accompanied by his girlfriend, who turned out to be the exquisite Ms. Caroline Freeney. Ben got off his chair to race towards his uncle, who caught him up in a bear hug.

'Uncle Martin, I haven't seen you for such a long time. I've got much bigger an' stronger an' good at football since you've seen me. And Teacher says I'm a clever boy an' gives me gold stars and stickers', gasped out Ben excitedly. He caught sight of the girl standing alongside Martin. 'Wow, look at her, she's really pretty.'

A child will always tell the truth and indeed Caroline's loveliness dazzled as much as a top model. Her blond tresses reached half way down her back, glistening in a golden veil under the light. She did not need cosmetics or adornment to be lovely. Delicate, arched shaped eyebrows framed her sparkling sea green eyes, which were set huge in a finely boned face. Her lips were as luscious as a blossoming rose, her nose was completely straight, her cheekbones highly sculpted and her lightly tanned skin glowed with health and vitality. She wore a knee length, layered, turquoise dress and her high silver sandal heels gave extra height to her perfectly toned five foot, nine inch frame.

Although Caroline was naturally beautiful, she still had to work hard at maintaining such a classic blonde image. Her body image was important to her; she took care to exercise intensively, manicure her nails and invest significant time and money on buying stylish clothes which she coordinated perfectly. The end result was that Caroline was a visual delight, a stunner who could turn the heads of any number of professional photographers, all desiring to immortalise her natural perfection through their camera lens. Not surprisingly she had been stopped in the street by model scouts many times since she was a child, especially whenever she visited London, all entreating her to embark on a professional modelling career. For a myriad of reasons, she had never pursued any of the offers which had come her way. Caroline was indifferent to the fact that every head in the restaurant was spinning in her direction as she followed Martin with the gracefulness of a dancer to the table where his mother and sister were sitting. For their part, Eileen and Claire's senses sprang to a high level of acute observation, for both instantly formed the opinion that they were looking at the woman who could chose to become the future Mrs. Martin Howard. What red blooded man alive would walk willingly away from a woman of perfect beauty?

'What on earth was she doing with Martin?' was Claire's uncharitable sisterly thought as she stood up to meet and greet Caroline. After the introductions were made, the social chatter began and gradually Eileen and herself got a sense of what the flesh and blood Caroline was like. She was an only child of a national school teacher and a lecturer in engineering in Sligo Institute of Technology. Caroline was pleasant during the meal, listened attentively to what was being discussed around the table and made a real effort to communicate with Ben and not ignore the child. The little boy responded positively to her friendliness and pointed out his brand new light- up- as- you-go trainers to her. Clearly taken with Caroline, Ben decided to share his new joke with her.

'Why did the crocodile go to the court room?' he asked.

'I don't know, why did the crocodile go to the court room?'

'He had to make a snap decision. Is that funny?'

Caroline looked doubtful but caught Martin's eye and nodded back at the child.

'Yes, that's funny. I've a joke, what did the man do when he saw a fly in his soup?

'What did he do?'

'He gave it a shake and said, 'spit it out'.

Ben looked confused and pushed his bowl of soup away.

'I don't think that's funny, I don't like flies'.

Claire looked at Caroline and explained:

'Ben is only six years old and he is going through a phase of trying to understand what people think is funny, or not. He loves to see people laughing. He is at a stage where he is enjoying slap stick humour'.

Caroline did something unexpected then which did not fit in with her ultra glamorous image. She put an empty glass to her mouth and sucked in her breath.

'Is this funny?' she mouthed in a deep voice into the glass.

Ben roared with laughter and promptly stuck a glass to his own mouth and started singing the chorus of 'We're going to the Zoo, Zoo, what about you, you' through it, which caused the grown-ups at the table to join in the merriment. She is good with children, Claire noted with surprise, trying to keep a quizzical look off her face as Caroline opened up to them.

'I like kids, I grew up surrounded by them. I had no choice in the matter, my parents took in foster kids. My mother is a national school teacher and every hungry child in the neighbourhood beats a path to our kitchen door. Mum is feeding milk and sandwiches to children whose parents she used to teach and feed'.

Claire knew her mother well enough to know that Eileen wanted to reach out across the table to give the girl a hug. Fostering was a noble and unselfish calling in life. It was remarkable to open up one's house to provide a safe haven for vulnerable children who had suffered either neglect or cruelty in the family situation they were born into. It was also tough and challenging, which was why few people opted to do it. Caroline obviously came from generous, loving people if they took in troubled children and cared for them in their home. There seemed to be everything to like about Caroline and nothing to dislike. It was unfortunate that Caroline's physical perfection set Claire on edge and reminded her that since Ben's birth she was unlikely to have a totally flat stomach ever again.

As much as she was interested in Caroline, Eileen was even more thrilled to see her son. She kept reaching out to lightly stroke Martin's hand during the meal, to which he responded with a smile and a slight pressing back of his own hand on top of hers. Eileen was reassured by the sight of her son in good health and spirits, with a wonderful girl by his side; surely no mother could ask for more. Claire was not as convinced, even though Martin did look well. He was not as tanned as normal, which indicated that he had skipped his ski trip this year. He was missing the spark of vitality which normally set him apart from the other men in the room. A duck made everything look smooth and effortless on the surface of the water but was actually paddling furiously underneath. Was her brother doing something similar?

The conversation was about general topics such as the best tourist spots to visit, how friends and relatives were getting on, Tom's health, Ben's activities and the merits of living in the West of Ireland compared to Dublin. There was no mention of work and this helped to ensure that a good time was had by all. After the meal, Eileen excused herself to make a phone call to Tom while Martin decided to use the short break to kick a football outside with Ben, who was growing increasingly restless. This left Caroline and Claire alone to have a glass of wine and a girlie chat together. There was a silence which Claire did not rush to fill. Caroline fidgeted with the stem of her wine goblet, before steadying her hands and lifting her head up.

'I am glad we have a chance to talk by ourselves Claire. I did not want to say anything to upset your mother, but I am worried about Martin. He is becoming distant and serious and he is working all hours at the office. He only comes back to the house to sleep. We used to go sailing at the weekend, but he does not want to make time for it anymore. The only sporting activity he is continuing with is running. We used to have great fun together, but it has all changed. I'm at my wits end,' said Caroline, her beautiful eyes troubled.

'If it is as you say, then something is indeed troubling Martin. Unfortunately, I have no idea what it is, I had not seen him for ages before tonight. He is usually an even tempered, rock solid guy', replied Claire.

'Exactly, that was one of the characteristics which really attracted me to him', said Caroline.
'I'm frustrated because he won't talk to me. I know he does not want to transfer his troubles onto my shoulders, but he won't let me help him. He wants to cope with shit on his own. I am supposed to be his partner and he is shutting me out. I want us to communicate better, but then he goes all quiet. I'm mad as hell about it. I'd walk away, but I'm in too deep.'

'I will try talking to him and getting to the root of the problem tomorrow', promised Claire.
'Will you Claire? I'd be so grateful. I want everything to go back to the way it used to be. It's driving me crazy. I even wondered if Martin was spending so much time in the office to shag his secretary. Then I calmed down and

remembered that she was a size fourteen and had a face like a hamster. I was being ridiculous, there was no way Martin could be interested in her, not after sleeping with me', confided Caroline.

Charming. Claire bit down hard on her lip as the mirror reflecting Caroline's aura of serene perfection shattered into a cascade of shards. She herself had been nudging towards a comfortable size fourteen before dear Ashley had caused her appetite to disappear. Caroline was oblivious to the fact that there were millions of women in the world who fitted into a size fourteen or greater dress size and who enjoyed healthy sex lives with their appreciative partners. Not every man chose to ride a bicycle, even if it was a model capable of winning the Tour de France. But Caroline's essential point was hard to dismiss; what man in his right mind and senses would desert Helen of Troy for a Jane Doe?

'The likely explanation is that Martin is swamped with work and needs some time and space to sort it out. The only other explanation is that he is unwell, but he looks perfectly healthy to me', advised Claire. 'I'll try and talk properly to him before I leave. We both have Martin's well being at heart. Take my phone number so that you have it if you ever want to contact me about him.'

While Caroline added Claire's phone number to her contacts in her mobile phone, Claire mulled over the realisation that her brother's girlfriend was a very human girl and not the real life manifestation of the fairytale Perfect Princess she had first appeared to be.

Martin, Ben and Eileen came back to the table to say their goodbyes and wrap up the evening.
Eileen gave both her son and Caroline a peck on the cheek, looking somewhat tearful. She impulsively pulled the younger girl into a warm embrace because it was not everyday a mother met a prospective daughter-in-law.

'Don't be a stranger Caroline. Martin will have to bring you to Dublin to meet Tom. I've told him what a lovely girl you are, and he can't wait to see you', said Eileen.

'You'll like Dad. Martin's cut out of him. It will give you a good idea of what Martin will be like in forty years time', teased Claire.

'Do you think your father will like me?' questioned Caroline.

'Of course he will dear, what's not to like?' scoffed Eileen. 'I'm sure we will like your parents too, whenever we are lucky enough to meet them.'

Caroline's face became guarded.

'Dad is sociable and easy to get on with, but my mother can be more distant with people she does not know', cautioned Caroline. 'She has great warmth and energy, but she tends to reserve it for my father and the foster kids and for her community projects'.

Caroline did not include herself as being one of the recipients of her mother's warmth, noted Claire astutely. It implied that her mother made little time for Caroline in her busy life. Had beautiful Caroline a fractured relationship with her own mother, leaving her with Mama issues? Some instinct told Claire that there was more water churning around in that well and her brother Martin had no idea of the insecurities lurking behind Caroline's perfect facade.

'I'm sure we will all get on famously together. Your mother is a wonderful woman dear, taking in foster children the way she does. It is an extraordinary act of kindness and it will be a privilege meeting such an admirable woman', said Eileen, blissfully unaware of any undercurrents. 'Drive carefully Martin, it has begun to rain and there are always drunk drivers on the road. See you tomorrow love.'

'Bye Mam. Night, night.'

'Lovely to meet you Mrs. Howard', said Caroline.

'Likewise, my dear. Please call me Eileen, there is no need for formalities,' trilled Eileen.

'Dad has missed a bigger night than he thought', observed Claire as she watched her brother and his trophy girlfriend walk into the night together. Martin was not going to be a free man for much longer, once the communication pothole in the road to matrimony was fixed. The ripe fruit was being plucked from the tree. Horrible thought, maybe her mother was right, and Claire had better get a move on herself before all the best men were gathered up by others. Were most mothers, at their core, similar to Mrs. Bennet in Jane Austen's novel 'Pride and Prejudice', eager for her daughter to marry a man with outstanding financial prospects, enabling her to enjoy a life of comfort and societal respectability? Was her own mother's dream of seeing her daughter married to a good, dependable man capable of earning a decent income a ridiculous outdated notion or a timeless aspiration of motherhood?

Luke Elliot was long gone, swept away with the tides of time to the other side of the Atlantic Ocean, in a fairy tale land far, far away. She did not want to be left with the pickings of the bruised and battered apples lining the bottom of the barrel. Perhaps she should heed her mother's firm advice to start searching for a worthy, kind, solid man of her own in the here and now, instead of dismissing her views as being old fashioned and insulting to the capabilities of women. There were many people around her age who were seeking commitments from their partners. Everlasting love was what Claire had once yearned for in her own relationship with Luke Elliot. It was hard for Claire to know if such uncomfortable deliberations rendered her an eminently sensible person or marked her out as being a pathetic disgrace to the sisterhood.

CHAPTER FOURTEEN

The next morning Martin joined his family members for breakfast at the hotel and it was such a splendid feast it could have filled an army's stomach for the day. Afterwards Eileen wanted them all to attend the Sunday Mass service together, but Martin and Claire opted instead to go for a stroll through the town, much to their long suffering mother's disapproval. Eileen went off to Mass with Ben, snorting that it was beyond her comprehension how she had reared a pair of heathens.

'You'll regret it if you give up on your religion. Good luck will follow you throughout your life if you keep close to the teachings and spirit of the scriptures. Your bit of religion is the only thing you'll have at the end of your days', she warned them darkly.

Her children laughed at her, refusing to listen seriously to her oft repeated words. They preferred to spend the limited time they had at their disposal in each others company, catching up with all their news. Claire was impressed with Sligo town as it had a shopping centre, a multiplex cinema, a theatre, an Institute of Technology, as well as plenty of hotels, restaurants and pubs. It offered a good place to live at more affordable prices than Dublin, encapsulating a sense of history mixed with modernity.

Martin took her for a spin in his car, so she could better appreciate the rich tapestry of the threads holding the fabric of the ancient countryside together. The Sligo countryside offered up an extensive playing ground for any intrepid soul ready to explore it. Claire surreptitiously glanced at her brother while he drove along in the full glare of the sun; she observed his tired red eyes and his pale skin indicated that he was spending most of his time indoors. This was not like her active brother at all, he who usually revelled in outdoor activities such as wind surfing, kayaking, hill climbing, tennis and golf. Caroline was right to be concerned about him, something was amiss for sure.

The brooding magnificence of Benbulbin, which forms part of the Darty Mountains, silenced Claire until her gaze fell on the shimmering blue of the sea, tossing and lapping onto wide stretches of golden sandy beeches, causing her to gasp with delight. The majesty of the mountain and the sea, the rolling green hillsides and the abundance of trees dotted on the landscape, brought to mind the celebrated poetry of W.B.Yeats, a man synonymous with Sligo. A line from one of his poems which she had learned in school whispered in her memory;

Tread softly because you tread on my dreams

Claire felt a stirring of her senses pulling her to the West and understood for the first time why her talented, cutting edge architect brother had chosen to leave the hustle and bustle of Dublin to make Sligo his home. She had considered it to be a temporary arrangement for him, always expecting him to return to live in Dublin or maybe travel forward afield to London or New York. Eileen too had expected him to return to the city of his birth and was forever spotting 'Houses for Sale' signs in their neighbourhood, perfect for Martin to buy and move into when he secured his ideal job in Dublin.

Claire felt guilty that she had not made more effort to keep in touch with her brother. She had only ever visited Martin once before in Sligo and that was when he had purchased a new build four bedroomed house in Strandhill. Ben had been a baby at the time and had howled the whole night through, upset by the unfamiliar settings and the absence of his wooden framed cot. Understandably, Claire had not been in the mood to explore Sligo the next day and had been fit only to congratulate Martin on his new house and high tail it back home to Dublin as quickly as possible, desperately willing her tiny lord and master to settle down and allow them both some shut eye. Five years on from her previous visit, Claire looked at the place with fresh eyes and liked what she saw. The sublime Caroline had grown up in Sligo and if she and Martin were to make a life together then they were likely to choose Sligo over Dublin as their permanent base. The realisation dropped that if their parents were ever to become infirm, or experience intense loneliness as many older people did, than it was going to be her responsibility to provide care and company for them. Martin would be living too far away to offer practical assistance on a weekly basis. Claire crushed down the thought, reflecting on the ruddy good health Tom and Eileen currently enjoyed for their age.

Martin and Claire entered into a cosy pub, the dimness of the interior causing them to blink after leaving the brightness of the world outside. The ceiling and every shelf in the place was decorated with stuffed animals, tins, containers, copper pots and pans, bronze ornaments, posters or countless relics of the past, giving it a charm of its own. There was a couple of hard drinkers at the bar, downing pints of Guinness. Martin ordered two cups of coffee and brought them over to an antique, drink stained table, positioned close to the open fire.

'Mam is worried about you because you haven't been home for four months. She thinks something is wrong', Claire blurted out the words.

'Nothing is wrong, everything is fine', replied Martin firmly but keeping his eyes averted.

'For some reason that just isn't ringing true Martin. Whenever the word 'fine' is used nowadays, it usually means the exact opposite', said Claire, shaking her head. 'Talk to me, I'm your sister.   If something is wrong then at least give your family the chance to help you', entreated Claire.

'Leave it out little sister, there is nothing you can do to help. In case you have not noticed, I'm old enough and big enough to take care of myself. As for Mam and Dad, they are too old to be worried about what I'm up to, they don't need my shit heaped on their grey heads. I'm coping with it and things will work out fine, given some time', said Martin.

'What things have to be worked out Martin?' asked Claire, refusing to back down. Her persistence was rewarded with the sound of silence.

 'Mam was wondering on the way down here if it was anything to do with Caroline', she stated baldly. Having met Caroline, Claire was willing to bet her favourite leather handbag that it was nothing to do with her but, she knew what buttons to press to get some reaction out of Martin, she had been winding her brother up since she was a kid.

'Caroline? What has she got to do with it?' asked Martin, startled.

'I don't know Martin, you tell me. Mam was afraid that you had hooked up with a girl who was making it difficult for you to maintain close contact with your family and that was the reason why you had not visited home for months', explained Claire.

Martin was looking at Claire as if she was crazy.

'It is true that some women are possessive and try to keep their men away from their family and friends, they don't want to share them with anybody. Mam was reading all about it in the problem pages of the newspapers and the issue of family separation is currently a hot topic of discussion on the radio', said Claire defensively. She was usually the first one to say that you cannot believe everything you read in the newspapers or online, beware of the fake news.

'That is ridiculous, Caroline is not like that at all and she is certainly not a problem', said Martin. 'She is close to her own family and has a cousin who is like a sister to her. Besides, we're not even engaged, let alone married. In fact, I don't know why she is still going out with me, I've been a real boor lately and she is way too good for me.'

Martin looked down and swirled his coffee in his cup.

'Why do you think Caroline is too good for you?' probed Claire.

'You've seen her, she is stunningly beautiful. Even if she was ordinary looking, which she is most definitely not, she'd still be too good for me in many ways. But frankly Claire, it is none of your damn business. It is not the parents' business either. Like I've said, I'm dealing with it', said Martin, trying to control his rising emotion.

Claire was struck again by the likeness between Martin and Tom and it was a similarity which went beyond the physical, for they were both proud, decent men. She felt a dart of love for her brother in that moment of recognition. She quickly reasoned that a single man could either be having girlfriend trouble, money difficulties, health problems, job stress, alcohol or gambling addictions or sexuality issues. Given that Martin looked wan but healthy and had denied having girlfriend trouble, the next most likely possibility for the root cause of his distress was money problems. The economy had grown in Dublin and in the bigger cities in recent years, but local enterprise and employment opportunities were still spluttering in whole tracts of the countryside.

'You are experiencing money difficulties, aren't you Martin? If so, you have plenty of company, levels of debt in the country are high. Countless people are financially stretched and spend all their monthly income to get by', Claire said gently.

'Okay, I admit it, I am having cash flow problems at the moment', said Martin.

'That is normal in business Martin, especially when an organisation is growing. Can't the banks lend you extra money to tide you over?' asked Claire.

'That's a laugh, the bloody banks will drown me rather than tide me over. They want cast iron guarantees that they will get their money back or they are not interested. You have a chance of finance if you are an export based food company but if you are a small, indigenous business linked to the construction sector they will laugh in your face if you dare to approach them. The local bank manager is useless because the decisions are made by the dictates of a centralised computer reporting system in Dublin. It used to be that the bank manager knew the reputation for loan repayments of whole generations of families in the locality and that counted for something but, no more. Banks, don't get me started! Dad always said they throw money at you when you don't need it and won't give you a red cent when you are desperate for it. The old man was right. I should have listened to him, he has been around long enough to know the score', said Martin vehemently.

'You are a brilliant architect Martin, you were at the top of your class in college for a reason. The economy is growing. Why has your money disappeared when the economy is on the up?' Claire knew that money disappeared the world over all of the time, but it was not usually Howard money. Their own money was too hard earned to be allowed to disappear lightly without trace.

'There are more jobs around but the wages outside Dublin are stagnating. The price of everything is going up, even simple things like going out for a meal with my girlfriend. Rural Ireland is struggling, you can see it in the closure of banks and post offices in the country towns and small houses are left vacant and decaying in the countryside. There is plenty of planning going on in the West but hardly any construction. My friends boarded planes to London, Australia and Canada and they have not returned. The taxes and cost of living here is too high relative to what they can afford with their disposable income in the other countries. They don't trust the economy here; it crashes, then goes into recovery but, people still hold their breaths, expecting the next recession to rain down on top of them. In Ireland, you always need to save for the expected rainy day, but my savings are gone, the money has dried up.'

Martin's face was tight and tense as he leaned forward in his chair to explain what had happened.

'I lease out a big office in town and the rent only goes upwards. Staff have to be paid, expenses and bills mount up. I spend a lot of time out of the office, meeting clients. I get plenty of promises but not much hard cash. The people with the money are not willing to part with it. But a lot of people do not have real money, you see them driving around town in new cars which they will never own. A big construction firm crashed recently owing me tens of thousands of euro and I have not got the cash reserves to chase non-payment through the courts. The one thing that has kept the business going has been house extensions for kitchen diners. What a wonderful use that has been for my first class architectural degree. I'd be embarrassed to meet my college lecturers.'

Martin looked gloomily into space for a moment before continuing his grim tale.

'The big developers are alright, they secreted away millions in offshore accounts and gifts to their wives, before declaring themselves bankrupt in the London courts and then merrily starting up again with a clean slate. Through NAMA and tax legislation, the government has aided and abetted foreign vulture funds to clean up, exempting them from corporation and capital gains tax, while decent lads with young families who are doing trojan work are being taxed and squeezed till the pips squeak. Reit corporations have paid damn all tax on billions worth of capital assets in the last ten years. Tax is for the little people, the workers and renters, not the institutional landlords. We are the prize clowns', said Martin with disgust.

'You are being too hard on yourself, you are not to blame for the policy decisions taken by government', said Claire, stricken by the bitterness in her brother's voice.

'My business is in trouble because economic activity and credit have been restricted for too long, sucking the life blood of cash out of the business. I know things are picking up, but it is too late for me,' he replied. 'To my eternal regret, shame even, I've let my employees down. I feel like I'm in the final stages of a marathon run and I haven't enough in my legs to power me pass the finishing line. To I'm too tired. I'm done.'

'You can get through this Martin, you are smart and can find a way. It must be in the bank's interest to keep faith with you while you collect the outstanding debt,' asked Claire.

'The banks are screaming blue murder about it. Their officials are obnoxious to deal with. My loans are peanuts to them, which makes it my problem, not their problem. They cut a deal with the big developers but consider it to be a 'moral hazard' to help out the small guy.'

Martin looked bleakly at Claire.

'I'm totally downsizing the business. I am going to work completely on my own, out of a room in my house, until I figure out where my future lies. I told my secretary last week that I had to let her go and she cried. Then I broke the news to Eric, the other architect, and he was crushed. He has a wife and three young children to support, with a big house in the countryside. The jobs are centralised in Dublin, which means he will probably have to live away from home. They won't move the kids out of their school and Eric can't afford to rent in Dublin and keep paying a mortgage on the family home in Sligo. I hate doing it to my staff, they are good people who trusted in me to make the business succeed. But I have to draw a line in the sand and admit the business has failed. Overheads are too high; the rates and taxes alone make me shudder. God only knows what will happen about the blasted lease on the premises, that still has to be sorted out'.

'I know it is hard Martin, but you cannot blame yourself for this', said Claire, trying to comfort her brother. 'Economic growth has been slow in many parts of the country, that is why people are migrating to the main cities. In Dublin, the word is that wage growth has been strong in the IT and financial services sectors but in other sectors the pay is low for the level of productivity being demanded. Pay levels have certainly picked up for architectural services, which is good news for you. There are cranes in the city skyline.'

'I do blame myself Claire, I should have made better decisions. I should have emigrated to Australia or Canada when everybody else was heading over there. I could lose everything before this is all over, the house as well as the business. I might be moving back to live with the folks in Dublin yet, clocking into a nine to five job. So much for being a multi-millionaire at forty', scoffed Martin.

'You will work through this Martin, I know you, and you will come out of it stronger and wiser and more successful than ever before. What has happened is not your fault. You are a hardworking, honest man, full of integrity. You have been shouldering an onerous burden alone for a long time. You did not turn to drink or use drugs; instead you put on a brave face and went out jogging to keep well. I am very proud of you,' insisted Claire.

'Thanks little sister, but I am not proud of myself. It is gut wrenching to know that all my hard work and effort has come to nothing. I'd have been far better off with a regular job rather than becoming self employed, this country does not reward enterprise. But please do me a favour and don't say anything to the folks. Let them enjoy their retirement. I don't want them to be worrying about me.'

'I won't say anything Martin, I promise. But if you are serious about your relationship with Caroline, you must be honest with her and explain your work situation to her. She might resemble a delicate fairy, likely to flutter into a faint upon being presented with bad news but, I suspect she has steel in her spine. If she loves you, she will support you. Mam also knows something is wrong, you have to set her mind at ease somehow, otherwise she will worry herself to death,' said Claire.

Martin considered her sister's words carefully before suddenly flashing her a smile.

'We'll blame it on the fallout from the economic uncertainties created by Brexit, which is what the leaders and dealers in the country are doing', he replied good humouredly. 'Brexit is causing us to retrench our business. That is not a lie, it is an interpretation. It will be boom times again for everybody on the island of Ireland, if only the great unknown of Brexit does not mess everything up for us. On a macro level, unexpected global events always have the potential to wreak havoc across the world, given the way air travel and international financial markets connect populations, employment and funds together. On a micro level, the best way to minimise Mam's concern is to be sparse on the detail, blame global events for causing bad business outcomes and, above all else, speak positively about the future. In time, the wheel will turn full circle, and all will be well with our world', proclaimed Martin dramatically.

'Excellent plan, agreed', giggled Claire, responding joyfully to the twinkle in his eye. She hesitated, gnawing her lip. There was something she had wanted to ask Martin about for five long years, but she had always chickened out of it because she was terrified of getting the wrong answer. She took heart from the intimacy and frankness of their conversation to finally pose the question.

'Martin, I never asked you how you felt about Mam and Dad gifting me Gran's house after Ben was born,' Claire asked earnestly. 'Do you mind that they signed it over to me and not to you? You are the oldest and I know that Gran adored you. Do you feel cheated out of your inheritance?'

Martin was totally startled.

'Of course not Claire. You needed a home for yourself and Ben, it was the best thing the parents could have done with it', said Martin emphatically.

'If it wasn't for Ben, I would never have taken it Martin, I swear. I'd have left it with Mam and Dad to rent it out for themselves'. Claire started to cry, for the thought of indirectly stealing from her brother had laid heavily on her conscience.

Martin hugged her tightly to him.

'There is no need to cry. Why do women always cry? When Mam and Dad gave it to you, I was fully convinced I was going to make my millions and a little two- up, two-down townhouse in Donnycarney held no interest for me. The house gives you and Ben security. Can you imagine the nightmare of renting in Dublin or living with the parents, good as they are? You need the house for youself and Ben and that is the way it is. I'm a fully grown man, well able to take care of myself. Ben is six years old and needs his mother to take care of him. Give yourself a break for once'.

'I'm sorry Martin, here you are all upset, and I've brought the talk around to me and my troubles. I'm such a selfish whinger,' said Claire, wringing her hands.

'You are not, you are a lovely person Claire. In a funny way, just thinking and talking about Ben, even for a second, puts my troubles into perspective. We have to look after the children, before we do anything else. I am also well aware that it is very convenient for me to have you living in such close proximity to Mam and Dad. They can concentrate their attention on you and not me. It also means I don't have to feel so bad about not visiting them as often as I should. Come on, blow your nose and let's go. It is time for us to meet up with Mam and your little man' suggested Martin.

Claire looked in sudden panic at the time and shrieked. Martin laughed and they both dashed out of the pub together like naughty children, heading like homing pigeons into the car and driving speedily but safely to the meeting place at the Weir. They spied Ben throwing pebbles and stones into the river, careful not to hit any of the ducks and swans swimming by but delighted at the distance the stones were covering before they splashed down into the water.

'It's a fine thing when I'm better at using my mobile phone than my children, who are supposed to be bright', chided Eileen, irritated by their tardiness.

Her children were full of apologies and swore they would treat her like a queen for the rest of the day. True to his word, Martin brought them to a renowned seafood restaurant for lunch, which had the extra comfort of a burning fire in a huge hearth. Martin succeeded in calming Eileen's fears, not so much by what he said but rather by his genial and relaxed demeanour. He reassured Eileen that although business was slow, he was working to a plan, which enabled him to gather his resources together, better placing him to avail of emerging, future economic opportunities in the aftermath of Brexit. He knew he was lucky to have his family, his girlfriend and his good health. His words were music to Eileen's ears, and she took comfort in the belief that it had done her son good to see his family and to know how much they cared about him. Meeting that lovely girl Caroline had been the icing on the cake for her. Claire mused that it was a good weekend when it ended with people feeling brighter, happier and lighter than they had at the beginning. Unless of course you were the divine Caroline, who did not need to feel an ounce lighter, let alone a dreaded pound!

CHAPTER FIFTEEN

A typical morning in the office began with Claire making a list of all the things she needed to accomplish that day. She worked methodically down through the list, ticking off the tasks one by one as she completed them. It was going according to plan, Claire noted with satisfaction. She had made a mental promise to herself that she would not complain about Ashley or her workload to any of her colleagues in the department. She intended to come in and focus on her job, be pleasant to everybody and go home at 5pm. That was the plan and, if she kept to it, all should be well.

When Claire left her office to fetch folders from the stationery room, Ashley came up behind her at break neck speed, waving a piece of paper held up high in her hand. Her face was twisted as if she had been forced to swallow a jug of bitter lemon mixed up with unripe grapefruit. Claire was in her line of fire.

'Claire, what is the meaning of this complete rubbish? It's the shoddiest piece of work I've ever had to read. I cannot believe we are paying you money to produce such trash. Don't ever put such a useless report on my desk again or I'll be taking it further, much further,' threatened Ashley.

Ashley was purple in the face, but Claire was completely bemused. She had no idea what Ashley was going on about.

'What figures are you talking about Ashley?', she asked calmly. 'I did not leave anything on your desk. I email my reports.'

Her manager stamped her foot with rage.

'Don't you dare lie to me. I'm referring to the Northern Ireland inter-charge figures of course. The calculations are crazy, completely off the scale. We would by fined by Revenue if we relied on these figures. Anybody with half a brain in their head can see that they are wrong. I know I have a different view of your abilities than you have of yourself but even I am finding it difficult to acknowledge the extent of your incompetence'.

'But I didn't work on the Northern Ireland inter-charge figures this year. I did produce the report last year and it was fine, but since nobody instructed me to do it this year, I did not go near it. You've got the wrong person', said Claire pointedly.

Ashley surveyed Claire with deep suspicion, unwilling to believe her. She drew in a deep breath and steadied herself before speaking in more even tones:

'Well, somebody calculated the Northern Ireland charge and, if it wasn't you, then who did?'

'I don't know, it is not my business. You'll have to check with Daniel, the instruction must have come from him', said Claire, shaking her head.

Karen Woods happened to walk towards them, on her way back to the office she shared with Ashley. Enough minutes had passed by for Ashley's face to return to its normal, deadly white pallor. Karen caught the tail end of the conversation but not the beginning and thus did not realise Ashley's dissatisfaction with the report.

'It looks like you have the Northern Ireland inter- charge report which I left on your desk Ashley. Do you want to discuss it with me?' asked Karen coolly.

Claire acknowledged that Karen immediately took ownership of the report which was under discussion. Was it possible that Karen had a hidden ring of steel in her which was mightier and tougher than Ashley's more visible blade? Or was she fearless because she was under the impression her report was correct?

Claire waited for Ashley to explode again, scorching Karen with fiery words of destruction, branding her a huge disappointment to the team but, to her astonishment, the opposite happened. Ashley swung around to face Karen with a wide beam stretched across her narrow face and spoke in her most pleasant voice.

'I did not realise you were working on the report Karen. A complex procedure has to be followed in order to arrive at the right figures and it is unfair to expect you to be able to do it on your own for the first time. Let me know when you have some free time and we will go through it together'.

Claire could not believe her eyes or her ears. Ashley had no compunction about ripping Claire to pieces when she had thought her responsible for producing the report but, here she was, now proffering Karen a helping hand, sounding supportive and reasonable. The report was not that difficult for an accountant to produce provided the steps, procedures and calculations set down in the Northern Ireland folder were followed when updating the spreadsheet. Nobody had talked Claire though it the year before, she had been given the folder and got on with the calculation herself. Nobody had held her hand.

Ashley had gone from verbally abusing Claire to adopting an attitude of sweetness and light with Karen in a blink of an eye. Her attitude was determined by the people involved, not by the actual content of the report itself. She wanted to attack Claire whereas she preferred to protect Karen and that lay at the core of the incident. Claire was no doctor and she knew nothing about psychiatric disorders but, standing there, up close and personal to Ashley in the constricted space of the corridor, she did find herself wondering if her boss was mentally unbalanced in some way. Ashley's reactions did not strike her as normal behaviour.

She relayed the 'Jackal and Hyde' story to Anna when she got back into her own office.

'Doesn't surprise me, Madam has one set of rules for her groupies and another for the rest of us. There is no hope of you or me ever satisfying or pleasing her so don't bother trying. I'm telling you Claire, that one would have me standing on my head, doing a dance upside down with no knickers on, and still not be satisfied that she had humiliated me enough'.

Claire laughed in spite of herself.

'Did anybody ever tell you that you can be very dramatic at times Anna?', she teased.

'It's no laughing matter Claire, her nibs sure is one mean minded bitch', sniffed Anna.

'She told me I had a different view of my abilities than she had', said Claire in a hurt voice. Thinking about the barb upset her, it hit a nerve and rocked her self esteem, causing her to question her capabilities.

'It's a good job you have too, otherwise you could become a down and out if you thought as little of yourself as she thinks of you. And mi'lady wouldn't throw a copper in your tin, for having turned you to drink, she wouldn't be held responsible for indulging your bad habit. Claire, you are a conscientious worker who would sooner refuse payment than turn in a mediocre job. I have more respect for poo stuck to the sole of my shoe than I have for Lady Muck'.

Those were strong words of intense dislike, but Anna had made up her mind about Ashley and there was no turning back for her. Claire was secretly not as fully convinced. Certainly, Ashley was a bad manager but, she had a difficult job to do, and maybe when she adjusted to the pressures of her role, things would settle down and get better. Claire reassured herself that nobody, including Ashley, could be that bad. Most people did the best they could in the environment they found themselves in. Anna and herself could be over reacting and reading the situation wrongly, tucked away from the others in their tiny claustrophobic office. Claire worried that they were feeding into each other's negativity, the darkness of their thoughts about Ashley constantly bringing their moods down. It did not help that Ashley was based in the adjoining office, her malignant presence lingering close by. Thoughts of Ashley were beginning to infiltrate Claire's dreams at night, causing her to turn restlessly in her bed, grasping her head to try to wrench out the jeering voice which tormented her.

Claire's attempt at maintaining a positive attitude was shredded into tiny pieces when she opened an email from Ashley;

Claire

You are to take over the responsibility of maintaining the Fixed Asset Register from Orla as from today. Orla will liaise with you to facilitate the smooth transfer of responsibilities.

Rgds
Ashley

Claire was shocked when she read the email and sat there trying to decipher its meaning. Maintaining the Fixed Asset Register was an administrative task as opposed to an accounting activity. Was her job been downgraded from business analyst to administrator? Where would she get the time to concentrate on her financial projects if half of her day was taken up with recording all the assets in a company the size of Leictreach?

Most big companies employed a person whose sole responsibility was to maintain the Fixed Asset Register and do nothing else other than track the movement of computers, printers, furniture, cars and equipment etc. The work was not in any way complex, but it ate up time daily. Claire's mind leaped ahead, and she realised that while she had worked in the company nobody had carried out an audit of the fixed assets and that task would probably be put on the agenda sooner rather than later. If she had to carry out an audit of all the fixed assets in the entire company, it would leave her with no time for any accounting work for months. She would be busy crawling under desks putting numbered stickers on people's hard drives, getting to know who polished their shoes and who chewed gum.

Claire groaned, putting her hand up to twist her hair. This was terrible news for her, just terrible. After all her hard work she was going to take a giant step backwards. She was taking over the job from Orla, a person who had never gone to college or tried to further her educational qualifications. Claire had to fight against this happening because taking over the responsibility for the Fixed Asset register had too many negative implications for her career development in the company. She typed an email to Daniel, deciding against copying it to Ashley.

> **Daniel**
>
> **Ashley has informed me that I am to take over the responsibility of the Fixed Asset Register. Although I fully appreciate the fact that it is important for the company to maintain the Register, it does not need the attention of a qualified Accountant. A clerical administrator can fulfil the function admirably.**
>
> **I believe I can add more value to the company through concentrating my time and energies on financial analysis work. I therefore am asking you to reallocate the task of maintaining the Fixed Asset register to somebody more suitable for the role.**
>
> **I am interested in further developing my knowledge base in cost centre analysis, the Treasury function and products/services revenue, costing and profitability analysis for both established and developing market segments.**
>
> **Regards,**
> **Claire**

She had to wait on tender hooks until the next day to receive Daniel's curt reply, which was copied to Ashley.

> **Claire,**

The allocation of duties and responsibilities for the 33 people working in the Finance department lie with the senior management team. Orla is giving accounting support to the Magino division and no longer has the time to maintain the Fixed Asset Register, a task she has performed excellently during the past two years. The maintenance of the FA Register is a Finance function. As a member of the Finance team you are expected to undertake any of the financial responsibilities which, in the opinion of your managers, you have the time and the ability to perform successfully, for the good of the department.

Regards,

Daniel

Claire felt sick when she read Daniel's unfriendly reply. He had put her firmly back in her box. There was no mention of any challenging, interesting future projects. Ashley must be laughing her head off with glee. Whether he realised it or not, Daniel was joining forces with Ashley in slapping her down. The managers were sticking together. This was only the second time Claire had ever asked Daniel for anything and he had once again given her a resounding NO, even though she had always given him a hundred and ten percent. He had not got her back, at a time she knew she was under attack. He had hung her out to dry.

It was going to be difficult to balance the volume of the Fixed Asset Register load with her accounting and budgeting work, but she had to try. Claire had studied and worked too hard for too long to be relegated easily and mutely into the ranks of clerical assistant. Being given the responsibility of the Fixed Asset Register sowed the seeds of bitter disappointment in Claire about the manner in which her career was stalling in Leictreach. She could not rely on Daniel for support. Claire blinked back tears, resolving not to cry, no matter how alone, angry and sad she simultaneously felt. She had done what she could and tried to make a stand against the direction her job was taking but to no avail. Her immediate options were limited, forcing her to get on with it and to perform as best she could with the cards she had been crookedly dealt.

CHAPTER SIXTEEN

The allocation of the unwelcome Fixed Asset Register to Claire brought her more under Ashley's tight control and made each day at work a disagreeable experience. Claire's stomach began to tighten every morning as she got ready for work. Her mind raced with a list of the tasks she had to accomplish that day, but she was very aware that, as the volume increased, the intrinsic interest she had in the work itself diminished. In simple parlance, the buzz was gone, it could no longer be described as a happy busyness. She used to get energy back from her work but now the tasks were draining her. Even though the individual tasks were easy enough in themselves for her to carry out, collectively they were onerous, and it was a constant challenge to meet the deadlines. Every task had a deadline and Claire was juggling multiples of them.

It weighed down heavily on her spirit, a burden she had to shoulder to collect her wage packet at the end of the month. She began fantasising about winning the Lotto, picturing herself getting out of Leictreach fast, kicking up the dust from her shoes. Her fighting spirit was down but not dead, making her try to see ways whereby she could position herself to be in a better bargaining situation. She began to suffer from inflamed sinuses, ingesting over the counter pills to clear her fuzzy head and blocked nose. People sympathised, saying it was caused by the high pollen count, but Claire had never suffered from this wretched sinusitis before and she linked it to sheer tiredness. It helped matters if she managed to get a good night's sleep but even that simple pleasure was becoming a hit and miss experience.

Work was on her mind more and more and it was beginning to make her less patient with Ben at home, especially in the mornings. Getting the little boy out the door for the morning drive to her parents' house was becoming quite the challenge. Each morning there was a different delaying tactic:-

'Mommy, I want warm milk, not cold.'

'I don't like those trousers, they're too tight. And where's my Star Wars top?'

'Those shoes are hurting me, they don't fit anymore. I've grown too big for them. I'll wear my boots instead. Where are my boots? They're dirty. You need to clean them Mommy.'

'I don't want the black coat, where's my blue coat?'

Howls when he hears the coat has been washed and is still wet.

'Why didn't you wash it at the weekend? It's my favourite. I'm not wearing the black coat, it's horrible.'

'I'm not ready to go, I have to finish playing with my cars, they're in a race.'

Claire would grit her teeth, attempt to get some food in his tummy before they went out the door, try to dress him to his liking and tell him he could bring his trains/cars/trucks with him in the car to Granny's house. Given that she had a strong belief that the family home was the one place a child should always feel happy and secure to be in, she strove to keep a harmonious atmosphere within the house. Because she loved her small son with her whole heart, she tried her best to keep calm and smiling, even if making soothing sounds half killed her on occasion.

Matters came to a head one blustery Monday morning when Ben spied a favourite transformer truck wedged beneath his bed and he managed to get it unstuck, using a toy sword to whack it sideways. Nothing would do the child but to hunker down in the hall to play with the long lost truck. Claire knew they had to get out of the house quickly, to avoid getting caught up with heavy traffic on the drop off to her parents' house. She decided to make a stand with her dawdling son, there was no time to humour him along.

'Come along Ben, we are running late. We have to go', said Claire briskly.

'I don't want to go yet Mommy, I need to stay here and play with my truck,'

Claire's heart sank when she heard the equally cool and amiable tone of her son's voice. She did not relish confrontations with her little man. Claire was skilled and practised at distracting Ben's attention away from things he wanted to do onto activities and conversation she favoured instead, and she could usually get around him without too much dissent being expressed. But Ben was capable of digging his heels in and proving that he could be as stubborn as any other six year old of his acquaintance.

'Pick it up and bring it with you Ben, you can show it to Granddad. I want you to put on your coat, it's raining cats and dogs outside.'

'I don't think so Mom. I'll just stay here and play with my truck a bit longer.' Ben turned his head around, his pink lips curved upwards as he smiled sweetly at Claire, his blue eyes reminiscent of the shimmer of the ocean waters under the hot summer sun.

'I don't have time for this Ben. Please put on your coat now. I have to go to work.'

Claire's voice was louder and sharper than the norm. She grabbed his coat off the peg on the wall and marched towards the child, who backed away from her.

'No! I don't want to put my coat on, and you don't have to go to work'.

'I do have to go to work', said Claire emphatically. If there was one thing she was sure of, it was that she had to go out and work for a living.

'You don't have to go to work. Why do you always have to go to work?' shouted Ben.

'I told you before, I have to go to work to earn money. I mean it Ben, put on your coat.'

Her son was not convinced by her argument.

'But I have no money', said Ben. He stretched his arms out towards Claire, before cupping his hands upwards together. 'See, I have no money'.

For a split second Claire did not know whether to laugh or cry. Here was her little boy telling her that he had no money, implying that he got along fine without it. He did not understand the importance of her going out to earn money and how could he be expected to, at his age? In Ben's opinion he was being rushed and bossed about for no good reason and anyway, he did not like his mother leaving him every day to go out to this mysterious workplace which she did not even like. Who knew what exactly went on in a small child's head?

Claire was conscious of the fact that she had to get Ben out the door and into the car or she would be late for work and then Ashley would chew her ear off for tardiness, on top of her other alleged shortcomings. Ashley had no concept of what it was like to juggle a full time job with parenting duties. She advanced on Ben, grabbed hold of his arm and tried to ram it into the sleeve of his coat.

'I don't want my coat on! No! I don't want it!' yelled Ben.

'Mommy has to go to work Ben', answered Claire, in much the same pitch.

Ben struggled and twisted and kicked against her determined attempts to force his upper body into the coat. Claire was about to call it quits on the coat and haul him bodily off into the car, when the fight was ended by Ben banging his head hard against the wooden stair frame. Claire immediately let him go.

'I banged my head. You hurt me. It's sore. It hurts. You hurt me,' screamed Ben, tears streaming down his face.

'I'm sorry Ben. It was an accident. I didn't mean to hurt you. Here, let me see,' said Claire, totally contrite.

'No, you hurt me. I want Granny! I want Granddad! I don't want you! You hurt me. I want my Granny, not you', said Ben, rejecting her attempts to comfort him, still outraged by the hurt she had caused him.

Tears flooded Claire's eyes. She was a miserable failure of a mother who had hurt her own child. She did not want to cause him more distress. Should she ring in sick for today and make amends with Ben? She could not do anything with him in this state. But it would be irresponsible to ring in sick when she had a tonne of work to get through and deadlines to meet. She went to the telephone and dialled her parents' home phone number.

'Mam, can Dad call around here to pick up Ben this morning? Yes, I know he's in bed, I'll wait till he gets here. No, I'm not sick. I was trying to get Ben to put his coat on and he banged his head hard against the stairway. No, he does not need a doctor, his head is not split open. No, he does not have concussion. Yes, he is very upset, we both are. I'd really appreciate you calling around for him and then I'll go into work. You will. Thanks a million. I'll phone work and let them know I'll be in late.'

Relief flooded through her, thank God for her wonderful parents, they never let her down. Claire turned around to her sobbing child, curled up on the floor. She was glad to see he was quietening down. Why had she made such a fuss about him needing to wear the coat to the car? It was parked in front of the house, he would not have melted in the rain. She had wanted to force her will on him, to make him obey her because she was the adult in the relationship and the one who was meant to be in charge. But she knew her son well and, in that mood, even if she had given in to him about the coat, Ben was likely to have refused to put on his seat belt in the car, making it unsafe to drive him anywhere. Claire needed him to do as he was told when she was in a hurry, otherwise she got completely stressed.

'Granny and Granddad are coming around to our house to see you this morning Ben. I'm very sorry for hurting your head, I didn't mean to. It was an accident.'

She went into the bathroom and ran tepid water from the tap onto a clean face cloth.

'Here, will you let me put this on the sore part of your forehead love? It might make it feel better' she asked Ben's permission. He was a person in his own right, not an appendage to her.

'It's still sore', he sniffed. Ben allowed Claire to put her arms around him and lead him into the sitting room. She settled down onto the sofa, Ben on her knee, hugging him close.

'It was an accident, darling. I wouldn't hurt you for the world. I love you very much. The pain will go away soon, I promise,' she said gently.

'You were very rough Mommy. I only wanted to play with my truck,' said Ben, crying again.

'I know honey. I'm truly sorry. You are such a good boy. I will try never to hurt you like that again. I made a mistake. Will you forgive me?' she asked.

Ben's tear strained face looked up at her and she realised how young and little he still was, his toddler years not long left behind him.

'I forgive you Mommy. I love you too,' he declared solemnly.

They were friends again. Claire put on that wonderful invention called television, saviour to all harried parents of small children and it helped to calm Ben down completely. Claire marvelled at how naturally young boys cried and it was incredible to think that fully grown up men tried their hardest to suppress their tears. Mother and son cuddled together on the sofa, waiting for Eileen and Tom to arrive. Claire realised that she was beginning to bring her work troubles home and it had the potential to adversely effect her son's health and happiness. Spurred on by her anxiety not to be late for work and give Ashley yet another reason to criticise her, Claire had been too impatient and rough with Ben and she felt terrible about it. It was too easy to frighten a child, to threaten their sense of security. If she was not careful, her difficult work environment would pollute her relationships with family and friends, going way beyond her work colleagues. She could not allow that to happen, she owed it to her son to do better and to be better than that. Let what happens in Leictreach, stay in Leictreach.

When Claire arrived into the office later on in the morning, she compiled a written list of the tasks she was scheduled to do that week and the average amount of time it took to complete each one. After reading through the list, she knew that, with the best goodwill and energy in the world, she had not a hope in hell of getting through all the assignments demanded of her in her standard contracted hours.

A mental image of Emmet drifted into her mind's eye.

'Where's the fire in your belly?' the Emmet of her imagination quizzed encouragingly.

The only substance coming out of her belly during the last month was green vomit. It could not go on, Claire had to learn how to deal with Ashley in a more constructive manner. It was essential for her physical and mental good health.

Claire propelled herself out of her chair and went to knock purposefully on Ashley's door. She was thankful to see that Karen was not in the room as she wanted to talk to Ashley privately. Ashley tilted her head to her left shoulder, a gesture she often made, and stared at Claire unwelcomingly, surprised at her impromptu visit to her office.

'You managed to find your way into work after all, congratulations', Ashley drawled caustically. 'It may turn out to be your main accomplishment today. Have you finished the analysis of payroll against budget in the central control departments?' she shot out the question in her customary rapid fire manner.

'No, I haven't got near it yet', replied Claire.

'You have to have it completed tomorrow by the latest', Ashley asserted.

'She's a cold fish, as lifeless as a dead eel in the river. She debases everything fresh she comes in contact with', thought Claire, dropping the list she had prepared onto Ashley's desk.

'Ashley, here is the list of jobs I have been asked to finish this week. There are nine separate tasks and the time estimation comes to forty seven hours. I'm conscious that the preparation for the annual budget should have been started last week as well and I have not had the chance to get near it yet. It is not possible to get all these things done in the standard working week. Can you tell me please which jobs you would like me to prioritise this week?'

Ashley scanned the document.

'You have given yourself plenty of time padding, haven't you?' she sneered.

'I certainly have not. Orla told me it took her the full morning every day of the week to update the fixed asset register and I have shaved a third of the time off it. Administrative tasks are taking up at least twenty hours of my working week. Can this administrative work not be redistributed to an accounts clerk, allowing me time as an accountant to focus on accounting tasks and projects?' said Claire, trying to reason with her boss.

'Those tasks are part of your responsibilities and you will have to find time to do them all. If you got into work on time, it might help you to meet your deadlines', said Ashley sarcastically.

'I put in an average of ten hours of unpaid overtime every week. One morning's late arrival is hardly going to put a dent in it. Can we focus on my question please, which concerns the need to prioritise my workload? It is not possible for me to get through all of these tasks in a thirty- seven and a half hour week, especially if you want reliable figures,' said Claire, determined to stand her ground for once.

'Obviously the figures must be reliable Claire, otherwise they are useless, and, by extension, your work is worthless. You are being paid to produce reliable figures in a timely manner,' said Ashley, serving up ice, not nice.

'Ashley, I am being paid a wage for a thirty seven and a half hour week and I am telling you, as my manager, that it is not possible for me to cover everything on that list working only my contracted hours. I have other responsibilities when I leave here in the evening. I need you to tell me what tasks you want me to prioritise,' insisted Claire.

'You are having trouble understanding Claire; everything on your list is part of your duties and responsibilities and it is all important and must be done this week. You are obviously failing to manage your own workload by yourself. I'll help you. On a daily basis, please record the time of every log on or log off on your computer, including any time you take off for breaks. Divide your day into fifteen minute segments, listing the activity you focus on in each of the time slots. I sometimes see you talking with people in the general office, instead of being seated at your own desk. Please record all meetings and phone calls which involve discussion concerning Leictreach business; any other types of conversation is time wasting. Keep a detailed diary of your work processes and outputs. This will yield information on the problems you are having with time management and provide us with insight into how best to manage and boost your lower than expected productivity level. We can review your performance together at the start of each day,' stated Ashley.

Claire studied Ashley's feral face and she swore she detected a smirk tugging at the corner of her compressed mouth. Ashley face was usually a cold, tightly controlled mask but it had slipped when she uttered her last suggestion. Ashley wanted to micro manage Claire, to take away all autonomy from her and to make her appear slow and inefficient. Every fifteen minute segment of time would be scrutinised and commented on. Claire was aware that many solicitors working in law firms had to divide their work output into time segments on a daily basis and this record was used as the basis for billing purposes. The difference was that this time recording system was not the norm in Leictreach and it would set Claire apart from the way everybody else in the department was supervised. Supervision over and above the norm screeched performance difficulties whereas the problem for Claire was the volume of work, not the complexity of it. The kindest thing to say about Ashley was that she had an inadequate personality.

'I'm not agreeing to being micro managed Ashley, not when it is not common policy in the department. Not one person in Finance records their work in the manner you are suggesting to me. Be reasonable, nobody here could produce my volume of work in the standard working week and stand over it as being right. It is even questionable if others are bothering to read some of the reports I am required to produce; if nobody is interested in a cyclical report then it should be discontinued. I am not paid enough to do the number of hours it takes to produce the body of work you are asking of me. There is no let up either, one week is busier than the next. I am well aware that there are secretaries working here who receive a higher rate of basic pay than me and who are paid overtime for the extra hours they put in, as well as annual bonuses. Even babysitters are paid extra for working more hours. How about paying me overtime for the extra hours I put in to get the various jobs done on time?', asked Claire, determined to remain calm and firm. She was not sure where she could find the time to do the extra hours, even if Ashley agreed to her proposal. What she really wanted was to be able to work her contracted hours, then go home and not give the organisation a thought until she arrived back in the office for another day, another dollar.

'Accountants are not paid overtime. You are paid to do a job, not to put in a certain number of hours. Do you expect a medal for coming to work? Everybody has to become more productive, including you. You have to be better and produce more to earn your money. There would be a queue of people out the door, all wanting your job, if you left today and it was advertised. Many people in their twenties are willing to do your job for your current salary and do not expect overtime payments. People are glad to work for a prestigious company like Leictreach because it improves their future employment prospects in the marketplace. I suggest that you stop your constant complaints and go back to your office and start doing the job you are paid to do, especially if you are feeling so pressed for time.'

As far as Ashley was concerned the meeting was over and she turned her attention away from Claire, cold shouldering her. Claire was loath to let the battle-axe have the last word.

'To recap Ashley, the balance of my workload has switched away from accounting projects to administrative functions, which is a big part of the problem and it would help a lot if the admin aspects to my job were reallocated to an administrative member of staff. I am good at my job, but I can only do what it is possible for any reasonably competent person to accomplish in the given timeframe. A good manager should be able to prioritise workloads for their staff and provide back-up when it is needed,' said Claire. A stony silence ensured as Claire made her way to the door, giving it a good bang behind her, guessing her parting barb was water off a duck's back. Claire might consider Ashley to be a lousy manager but to paraphrase her impossible to reason with boss, Ashley had a different opinion of herself compared to Claire's opinion of her. Ashley was probably under the delusion that she was doing a terrific job managing the awkward people in the department and, if there was a problem, then it must be the other person at fault. There was no talking to the implacable woman, her mind was made up and it was absolutely unchangeable.

Claire was still in the dilemma she had been in before her unhelpful conversation with Ashley. Should she slave away all hours of the day to ensure her work was completed or should she work a standard hour week and let her work pile up? Was it the manager's problem if the work did not get done or was it hers? There was a high risk of Claire having to shoulder the blame and being accused of laziness and inefficiency. Claire had always worked extra hours free of charge but at least she had the satisfaction of feeling she was learning and progressing in a job she enjoyed. As time went on, it was harder to galvanise her intrinsic sense of motivation, when she knew the work she produced, would be either unacknowledged or criticised.

Claire might have been better off saying nothing at all, for all the good her attempt to reason with the callous Ashley had done her. People seemed to like people more when they smiled, hummed, nodded and said nothing. Talking openly and honestly about her difficult relationship with Ashley was not doing Claire any favours in the company. She was increasingly being perceived as the problem, not Ashley. Perception was reality. Maybe she cared too much and the people who cared less about their jobs might actually get on better in them. But she owed it to Ben to have at least tried to reason with her manager, even if the attempt had failed. Ashley had been quick to remind her that there was no shortage of people who would jump at the chance of taking over her job, happy to be paid peanuts for the privilege of working in a blue chip multinational company. There was a big, fat zero chance of a pay rise or bonus this year, despite the volume of work she was expected to get through. Claire was fast coming to the conclusion that Ashley was intent on turning her into a busy fool.

To be 'liked' by everybody was not a prerequisite part of a job description because nobody liked everybody all of the time. Claire was unsure of what coping strategy she should utilise next because Ashley's malevolent behaviour towards her was impossible for her to understand. It was alien to her own gentle nature. Ashley was either an unbelievably terrible manager or was deliberately using the managerial structures in the organisation to 'manage' Claire out of her job, for no better reason than she did not like her.

There was a world of difference from knowing she was being bullied and from proving it. Employment law was there to protect against constructive dismissal but unfortunately putting up a legal defence tended to be a lengthy and costly process. Claire felt very angry, very helpless and very poor as she reflected on Ashley's poisonous words, in her boxed in cell of an office.

CHAPTER SEVENTEEN

Claire and Ben were having a fun time at the local playground in St. Anne's Park in Raheny on a bright Saturday morning. She had fond memories of Martin and herself spending hours there as children, going for runs up and down the slopes and leaping upon the fallen tree trunks. Martin used to climb adventurously to heights she never reached but always admired. The opening of a restaurant and market stalls close to the entrance of the upgraded playground enhanced the amenities in the area, making the park and its natural beauty irresistible to those lucky enough to have discovered its many pleasures. Since the playground was a beacon to the local children, it was unsurprising for Claire to see a school friend of Ben's being half heartedly pushed on a swing by his bored mother. The two mothers were chatting easily to each other about how great their children were getting on in school (any problems children have in school are only admitted to close friends) when Claire received a text on her mobile phone from Andrew.

'Doing anything? Want to meet up?'

As if on cue, Ben's classmate Sam ran up to her.

'Ben's Mom, can Ben come to my house to jump on my trampoline? Daddy put it up in the garden for me. Please, please ? You can jump really high on it, even my Mommy can. Daddy won't, he says he's too heavy. But we won't break it, it's very big for us.'

Sam's mother Mary laughed.

'It is good fun and great exercise for the legs, although I'd say the next door neighbours are fit to be tied. They keep on seeing my head bob over their wall, giving me a great view of their garden. It's been ages since Ben's been over to our house for a play date and we'd love to have him visit.'

'Please Mom? I want to go on the trampoline an' Sam's got the new Mario game an' he says we can play it together,' beseeched Ben.

'He will be no trouble at all. I will feed them chicken and chips for lunch, no bother, and they can have ice cream lollies for desert on condition they eat some fruit. Sam is lost by himself with no brothers or sisters and he is always talking about Ben', urged Mary.

Claire was familiar and comfortable with Sam's house and home setup and was happy to agree to the impromptu playdate. Mary was a friendly person and Claire thought that they could become friends if they saw more of each other. But it was as much as Claire could do to find the time to keep hold of the friendships she had already made. She had not seen Andrew for a few weeks and it would be good to catch up with him without having to check the time on the clock every ten minutes. Their lunch meetings had become more rushed and infrequent since she had begun reporting directly to Ashley.

'Will we set a time for me to pick him up or would you prefer to ring me later on, when the boys are getting tired and it is time to go?' asked Claire.

'We will play it by ear and I'll give you a ring when Ben wants to go home', decided Mary.

'Hey, I can go', shouted Ben. 'I'll race you to the climber Sam, the big boys have gone'. The two boys were off with the speed of formula one racing cars. Claire texted Andrew a message back.

Am in St.Anne's park. Meet me at main entrance near playground. Ben going on playdate, we too can play.

She lifted her face up to the warm breeze which caressed her cheeks, heartened to be outside enjoying the arrival of the sunshine, after tolerating months of cold and damp weather. She wanted to relax and allow the good aspects of her life envelop and soothe her troubled spirit. She resolved that she was not going to spoil the peace and tranquillity by mentioning one word about work to Andrew today. She was looking forward to spending some quality time with her closest friend.

Sam's house was conveniently only a walk away from the playground. She was hugging Ben goodbye at the gate when Andrew approached them. The child broke away and ran up to Andrew, shrieking in delight when the man responded by hoisting him up high in the air and spinning him around.

'Do it again', the dizzy boy entreated.

Andrew flung Ben over his shoulder in a fireman's lift and made his way over to Claire, depositing the child gently down onto the ground beside her. He ruffled Ben's hair affectionately.

'Look how big and strong you are getting, little man. High five', said

Andrew, making sure not to strike the child's hand too hard.

'Andrew you've forgotten your glasses', observed Ben. 'You shouldn't drive your car without glasses. You might crash. Look Mommy, Andrew hasn't got his glasses on'.

Andrew's hazel eyes twinkled down at her in his open face, enjoying her confusion.

'I got eye laser treatment two weeks ago. I'm told it went well', he confessed bashfully.

'You never said a word about it', remarked Claire.

'I wanted it to be a surprise', he admitted. 'It is not something you get done every day of the week'.

'I like you without glasses Andrew', remarked Ben. 'I can see your face better. You're strong too. Mommy, Andrew without his glasses is like Superman.'

'Superman, mmmm….. well you are super and you are a man, which I guess does qualify you to be Superman. I cannot argue with my perceptive son', teased Claire. Andrew flexed his arm muscles and struck a pose.

'Man of steel…..Up, up and away------yabba dabba doo……'

'Andrew sounds silly Mommy', giggled Ben.

'Super silly', agreed Andrew.

'Man of steel, means balls of steel', he muttered in Claire's ear, making sure only she could hear and causing her to splutter with laughter.

Mary was looking on with interest, observing the easy familiarity which existed between the threesome.

'Hello, I'm Mary, Sam's mother. And you are…?' she eyed him speculatively.

'Andrew Kennedy, a friend of the family'.

Mary looked disappointed.

'I saw you at Ben's party and I was wondering if you were a relative of his, even though I guess you don't look anything alike. It was a wonderful party, Sam said the best one ever. We'd better go now, lovely to have met you. See you later Claire.'

It was delightful to be alone together. Andrew and Claire were only a skip and a hop away from Dollymount Strand and they decided to go for a walk along the sea shore. They had not known each other as children but since they were both reared in the same locality, they had enjoyed similar experiences. Both had grown up with the beach on their doorstep and it was as familiar to them as her parents' back gardens. They had spent the long summer days of their childhood riding their bicycles along the seafront and over Bull Island bridge, onto the compressed sand of the Strand. In those days the beach was usually not too crowded, unless it was a roasting hot day. A lot of people living in North County Dublin preferred to seek out the beaches in Portmarnock and Donabate or head out to the coastal towns of Howth and Malahide in their cars for a day trip, rating them higher on the scenic scale. Those spots were further away and Dollymount Strand was much more accessible to the teenagers living in Raheny, confined to walking or bicycle trips for their daily meanderings between meal times.

Claire had always appreciated the fact that the natural beauty of Dollymount Strand was right on her family's door step, particularly since her father Tom had never been one for driving his children all over the place. Tom and Eileen had not worried unduly about any harm befalling their teenage children as they went out and about the environs of Raheny village. Martin and Claire had enjoyed a carefree childhood, with freedoms given to them that Ben was unlikely to experience in a more crime conscious world. Tom was thankful that the poverty which had afflicted much of the Dublin of his youth was reduced but he sorrowed over the increase in burglaries and gun and knife attacks reported in the city. He blamed the plentiful supply of hard drugs which flooded the city, eating into people's flesh and spirits, for destroying the strong bonds which had held poor neighbourhoods together in times of great hardship. It did not have to be this way. Ireland could be the best little country in the world to live in, with its plentiful supply of food and water, endowed with the stunning beauty of its countryside and seas.

Societal changes were far from Claire's mind as she splashed along the edge of the lapping waves, loving the feel of the water and sand beneath her feet and the kiss of the breeze tingling her skin, drawing strength and solace from her contact with the natural world. She bent down on her hunkers to scoop up a handful of sand, savouring the feel of the grains running through her fingers. Claire was pleased that the tide was in. When it was out, it left her with a yearning feeling, as if she must wait for it to turn back towards the land until she could feel settled again. Maybe it was to do with the fact that when the tide was out in Dollymount Strand, the water level remained knee deep for miles and, although Claire wanted to wade out amongst the waves until she could swim easily in its depths, she was too fearful of dropping off a deep under water ridge or being swallowed up by the turning tide as she tried to out race it back to the shore. She loved the sea but did not trust it. Claire stretched out her arms and reached up to the sky, twirling around and around in delight, imitating the dance small girls perform to imaginary music. Her mind and body began to relax for the first time in an age and she was glad. She did not want to lose the ability to feel happiness in the moment, for bitterness and resentment to be always there lurking in the shadows of her mind. She did not want to be the person who was always moaning about something. She wanted to be a person who thought the best of others and who treasured every day as meaningful. She wanted to find the silver lining in every cloud and find happiness in holding a grain of sand. Claire let go of the tension which had shackled her for weeks and laughingly kicked water over Andrew, not too much but enough for him to want to retaliate, and to send them both chasing each other along the shore.

Andrew grabbed her easily enough and poured a handful of sand down the collar of her jacket. This was an unusual thing for him to do but, it was fun.

'No Andrew, I'm sorry, I'm sorry, please, no more', she squealed.

He threw his arm over her shoulders and beamed down at her.

'Truce', he offered good humouredly.

When he continued to hold her in the crook of his arm, the expression on his friendly, open face changed to one of earnest intent. The unspoken attitude of 'this is my space, this is your space', which normally held true between them was about to get blasted into space.

'Claire, I don't want to pressurise you, but we have been great friends for years now. Susie and I have broken up, we are finished as a couple. I know she is not the right girl for me. I know this because I cannot stop thinking about you', proclaimed Andrew.

'Andrew, are you sure you want to say this?', interrupted Claire hurriedly. 'It will change things between us'.

He blanched at her words but stayed resolute.

'I have to say it; if I don't, I will regret it always, no matter what your answer is. I think you are gorgeous, I've always thought it, from the first time I saw you in college. I could draw your face blindfolded, I know it so well. I know you so well. I want to be much more than a friend to you, if you'll let me. Do you think we could try going out properly together and see what happens? Please Claire, is it not worth a shot? It could turn out to be the best thing ever,' beseeched Andrew.

Andrew's declaration was not a total surprise to Claire; she had always sensed the day would come when he had the courage and honesty to express his real feelings for her, provided she was not attached to another. In her hearts of hearts, Claire knew Andrew loved her. Other people had noticed their friendship and wondered why they had not got together as a couple. He had demonstrated his love for her in a thousand different ways over the years. Timing in matters of the heart was often crucial. Claire had been mad about Luke Elliott in college and that had knocked Andrew out of the picture. He had given her time to recover from the heartbreak she had experienced over Luke's callous abandonment of her and Ben. Then Susie had come along to sweep Andrew away into a new relationship. But now Luke and Susie belonged to the past and Andrew had gambled that the time was finally right for Claire and himself to come together as one.

Claire saw the mixture of anxiety and hope written large on Andrew's dear face and her heart sank. Although Claire had sensed that Andrew might profess his love to her one day, she did not have her answer ready. She genuinely did not know what her exact feelings for Andrew were, other then that she loved him as a friend, and she did not want him to go out of her life. Rejecting him could turn out to be a knock out blow to their close friendship. Claire always felt very comfortable in her relationship with him, and no matter what dark thoughts she confided in him, he never judged her. Andrew was the least judgmental person she had ever encountered. While her romantic endeavours for years centred on capturing the attention of the devilish handsome Luke Elliott, she came to value Andrew as the best male friend she had ever had. The only way their bond could be stronger was if they experienced physical intimacy together and Andrew was making it clear that he was looking for this sexual dimension to be added to their relationship. He was beginning this momentous change by holding her hand, which really signalled 'I want to have sex with you, over and over, through the long, lust filled, sweaty night'. The key question was whether or not Claire should go out with Andrew and give them a real chance of establishing a deep, sexual relationship together?

How much stronger could the bond connecting Claire and Andrew become if they shared a committed physical and mental partnership? It was a tantalising scenario.

What to do, what to do? There was the risk of losing Andrew's friendship whatever way she chose. Claire might lose his trust and friendship if she rejected outright his offer to be her boyfriend, without giving them the chance of exploring new experiences with each other. There were many possible ways to lose a person precious to you. If Claire did not agree to be Andrew's girlfriend, another girl would set her sights on him and eat him up for breakfast. He was by any standard reasonably good looking and he had shed the awful shyness that had crippled him in his teenage years and early twenties. Andrew would not be hers for the taking forever. How would Claire feel then? Jealous, wretched or indifferent? Claire had not paid much heed to Susie but then again, Susie had never threatened her best friend status. Susie had actually been quite an easy going character until Andrew had announced he was moving back home to his mother. Andrew's next girlfriend could turn out to be a possessive madam once the relationship was bedded down, insisting Andrew sever his close ties with Claire if he wanted to continue going out with her. Possessive partners had ruined countless friendships between men and women. It was women who tended to organise the social activity calendar for couples, unless it was for golf outings. Amazing all the wives who let those outings go without question, reasoning they were good for business. For any other social event, the wives/girlfriends were onto it like bears to treacle pots. It was nearly enough to make Claire wish Andrew was gay, then he could have remained forever the perfect male friend.

Deep down, Claire had been aware that Andrew had long been besotted with her, he loved only her. He had quietly adored her right through college, sometimes having a brief fling with some random girl, more often enjoying single status and being one of the gang. It would have been the easy option for Andrew to have stayed quiet about it and let the moments and years continue to slip by, until eventually they drifted away to different partners. She admired the brave manner in which he put himself on the line to ask her out. There was much to admire in this honourable man and yet…...did she really want him? Would she ever have wanted him badly enough to put herself out there on the line, in the same way Andrew had just done for her? What if they did go out together and it turned out they were incompatible in bed? The awkwardness would most likely be excruciating embarrassing or, admittedly much less likely, funny enough to laugh about. On the other hand, there was always the possibility that sex with Andrew could turn out to be mind-blowing brilliant, he could be the best kept secret sex bomb in the whole country for all she knew.

There was a lot to gain if the potential new romance between them deepened and endured but there was a lot at stake if the wrong decision resulted in their stalwart friendship being ruined. Claire realised that she did not want to make such a significant decision on the spot, she felt caught between a rock and a hard place. She knew she was being unreasonable and selfish in wishing that Andrew could have been content to wait around for another year while she sorted her life out. In spite of her dilemma she had to respect the fact that he had called her out on the big issue and that he considered the time for prevarication to be past.

'I don't know Andrew', she replied, after taking too long of a pause. He took a step backwards from her, but she clung onto his hand. She was nothing if not honest.

'Andrew, you know I love you. Ben and I both love you. You are my dear friend, my best friend. I count you as my closest friend in all the world. I don't want to lose you. I'm not saying no, but you have sprung this on me, and I need time to think before I can say yes. We have to talk this through. What if we go out together and it does not work out and I end up hurting you? Our friendship might never recover,' blurted out Claire.
'The possibility of getting hurt is a risk that has to be taken in all relationships Claire. I'm a big boy, I can take it. You learn it on the playing fields, where there is no pain, there is no gain. Besides, I don't believe you would hurt me if we went out together, you are not that type of person. It may not sound romantic, but I think we'd be fine together. We'd pull in the same direction and have each other's backs and be a good team, great even. God, that sounds terrible, I'm useless at this'.

Andrew raked his fingers through his hair and tried to find the right words to press his case again.

'Claire, you say you love me, but I love you more and I'm okay with that. I think the world of you, and I would give you the world if I could. I promise I will always give you everything I have to give. I want you to trust me and let me take care of you and Ben. Life is better with two people pulling together in the same direction, that is what I was trying to say before. I saw how tough it was for Mam, bringing me up alone, coping with jobs and bills and sickness all on her own. I promise I won't let you down. We are not kids anymore. Give the two of us a chance Claire, I honestly believe we can be happy together,' entreated Andrew persuasively, laying his heart bare.

Still she said nothing, still she held onto his hand as if for dear life.

'I'll shut up now', he said, embarrassed by his candour, a red blush flooding his face, making him suddenly look ridiculously young.

It was very difficult to rebuff such a loving, eloquent proposal from such a good person.   Claire appraised Andrew with fresh eyes as he stood before her on the sandy beach, every feature thrown into sharp relief by the rays of the clear sun set high in the sky, seeing him for a first time as a potential boyfriend. How well he looked. She had always described Andrew to be 'not bad looking' but she saw now that he had evolved into a good looking man. His hazel eyes were no longer obscured behind the heavy rimmed glasses and they gleamed down at her. Long distance running kept his body fit and toned, without any spare fat on his frame, and his faded Levi jeans were worn loose on his lean flanks and trim buttocks. His fair skin still made him appear younger than his actual years and he had let his sandy coloured wavy hair grow slightly longer. Claire had always considered the freckles on the bridge of his nose to be cute. The revelation that Andrew was growing more attractive as he got older struck her forcibly. He had matured from a thin, geeky, slight boned youth into a refined, fit, pleasant featured man. He was also blessed with a kind disposition and a sense of humour, and those qualities were there to see on his open, honest face. He had good job prospect, working as an accountant in a bank. Banks were a powerful enough force in the economy to ensure that in both good times and bad, their professional staff were paid comparatively well. Her mother was right, it would not be long before lots of women realised what perfect husband and father material Andrew Kennedy was cut out to be and more than one of them would set their determined sights on him. She had already seen it happen.

Perhaps it was not crazy to give Andrew and herself a chance of making it as a couple. She thought back to the speed dating night and how none of the many men she had met there measured up to Andrew. It was on the tip of her tongue to smile and shout out 'YES', they would give it a go and see what happened and what fun they would have finding out. Then an image of Luke Elliot flashed through her mind and she recalled her face red raw from crying as she buried it into her pillow night after night after he deserted her. She knew Andrew would never abandon her in the same callous fashion but the pain of her past experience with Luke had broken her heart and it had knitted back together in a more cautious, timid way in the intervening years. Claire had to be sure about her feelings for Andrew before she could risk changing the nature of her friendship with him. But was their friendship irrevocably changed from this day forth anyway, because of his declaration of loving intent? True, it would be disastrous if the attempt of romance between them failed, leaving them feeling awkward and stilted together But why should it fail, when Andrew was a fit, attractive and attentive male who seemed to find her attractive? She was not Dracula's bride and somewhere in her veins ran hot blood and strong passions.

The crux of the matter was that Andrew was an attractive guy but was Claire attracted to him? From the first hello, Claire had been irresistibly physically drawn to Luke Elliott and that had turned out to be an unmitigated disaster, except for giving her the gift of her beautiful boy. If she had been capable of such burning passion and obsession for Luke, could she not summon up the necessary quota of physical desire for Andrew to make their relationship succeed? How deep were her sex hormones buried? It had been so long since she had sex with Luke Elliott that they had become dormant, or perhaps, had even dried up altogether. She had not kissed a man passionately for years. She needed to have a lip locking first kiss with Andrew to discover if her body could still tingle, wiggle and jiggle.

The two of them had always been careful to respect the physical boundaries commonly accepted as delineating platonic friendship. They had never kissed on the lips. Claire did not know what Andrew felt like to hold and caress. It was not Andrew's fault that she had never felt the urge to rip off his clothes and have wild sex, Claire thought in panic. It was her fault, she had become a sexless thing through lack of use. Unbidden, the thought whispered through the recesses of her mind that one kiss shared between a man and a woman forever changed their relationship. She had to speak up and say something, she had never stayed this quiet for so long in Andrew's company.

'Andrew, I want to keep you as a friend, more than anything', she said hesitantly.

Not surprisingly Andrew's face twisted into a grimace when he heard the word 'friend'. It was not for the cause of friendship that he had laid bare his soul and secret desires. Claire hastened to have her say before he switched off from listening to her.

'Honestly Andrew, I'm not saying no to you, you must believe me. Give me a little more time to consider us changing our relationship. I want to be sure, for both our sakes. It affects Ben as well. I know it is a lot to ask but can you please wait a little longer for my answer Andrew?' she beseeched him.

Golden streaked, red strands of hair blew across her blue eyes and he gently brushed them back from her forehead, winding a thick curl around his finger.

'You have incredible hair, I have never seen anything like it', he said. 'Stop panicking Claire. I guess I owe you time to mull it over, it is not as if we have spoken about it before. But don't think on it too hard Claire, it is really not that complicated.'

'Ya think?' smiled Claire weakly.

'It is a good thing we are discussing it, not a bad thing. We cannot go on like this. If we can't be together as a proper couple, then perhaps we should see less of each other. I'm no psychologist but I reckon we are fulfilling some need in each other which shuts us off from other people.'

Andrew was an intelligent man who spoke nothing but the truth. The winds of change caused a shiver to go down Claire's spine. For the first time in years she had a sudden impulse to throw caution to the winds, if only for a minute. If the relationship between herself and Andrew was to imperceptibly change forever regardless because of the decision she made, Claire might as well have her kiss.

'Do me a favour Andrew', she suddenly piped up, curly head slightly tilted and a big smile on her lips. 'Kiss me please'.

He looked at her in disbelief.

'Really? You mean it?'

'Yes, I mean it. Just one kiss. No promises. In the name of research, you understand', she teased.

Andrew snorted with laughter.

'You can still surprise me. Right, I had better give it my best, there's a lot riding on it'.

'Kissing Andrew, no riding yet', said Claire giggling. She pressed her hands against his chest, looking fully up at him. 'We can still be friends Andrew, either way, that isn't going to change, is it?'

'Of course we will remain friends, the best of friends', replied Andrew. 'Now I do believe you promised me a kiss.'

He eagerly lowered his head and tightened his arms around her waist. His lips lightly touched hers, gentle and exploratory, before he applied the slightest of pressure, enough to encourage Claire to open her mouth and respond back, allowing nerve ends to activate and tingle. When the inside of their mouths became moist and fluid, Andrew's tongue flicked out to probe her lips, teasing and tantalising, causing her to curve her body closer to his, feeling the satisfying hardness of his body complimenting the softness of hers. It was all very satisfying and held the promise of much, much more. Claire was also pleased to discover that Andrew led first with his lips and then followed gently with his tongue; she had always disliked it when a guy on a first kiss tried to ram her mouth open with his tongue. It would have been the easiest thing in the world to fall down on the sand and roll on top of each other.

When they drew breath, they grinned at each other, both conscious of their bodies hot response to their first kiss.

'Well, did I pass?' asked Andrew, trying not to sound jubilant.

'With flying colours.'

'The is a lot more ground I can cover, if you let me', teased Andrew.

'I don't doubt it. I promise to give you my answer soon. Will you promise me that you won't rush off to be with anybody else till then Andrew? Otherwise I'll have to say yes to you right now!' Claire did not know what she would do without Andrew She relied on his sound judgment and support, she found comfort in his friendship and kindness, she needed him as a bedrock of protection against the malign forces battering her down. She was slowly realising that he was too important a presence in her life for her to lose and therefore she was most likely to agree to go out with him. She had thoroughly enjoyed the kiss they had shared, which was a big relief as well as a most pleasant surprise. There had been nothing platonic about their kiss.

He gave her an affectionate hug.

'Relax, I am not trying to bulldoze you Claire. I had hoped I was making you an offer you could not refuse, considering my alter ego today is Superman', he jested. 'I'm going nowhere for now, except perhaps to lunch'.

'A man and his stomach. Mam says never to tell a man bad news on an empty stomach", said Claire, smiling weakly.

'A wise woman, your mother. She also prepares food fit for serving up to royalty, making your father a very lucky man. My mother excels at burning sausages. No wonder Dad went off to an early grave,' joked Andrew, marking a return to their easy banter.

A fundamental change had occurred in Andrew and Claire's relationship with each other during their close encounter on Dollymount Strand, against the background of the dazzling waters of the Irish Sea. Once words are spoken, they cannot be unsaid. An action can be reversed out but cannot be undone. Her judgment had to be sound, uniting her head and her heart, because she could not afford to make another wrong, big decision. Claire had to make up her mind about something which could turn out to be either the best decision or worst mistake of her life.

CHAPTER EIGHTEEN

Claire's phone rang and she was surprised to hear Daniel's voice on the other end of it, asking her to call into his office to see him. Claire had few dealings with Daniel these days and so she had no idea what he wanted to speak to her about. She was glad he had made contact with her, even though the last time they had spoken he had unfairly criticised her report. She badly needed an upgrade to the quality of her work content and he was the only person in the department who might make the change happen for her. Last year she had relished her job and had perceived Leictreach to be a fine company to work for but nowadays her job satisfaction level had fallen through the floor. But as soon as she opened the door of Daniel's office, she knew immediately by his face that trouble was brewing.

'Come in and close the door Claire. I have to talk to you privately', he directed unsmilingly. Claire immediately felt nervous and her stomach tightened into knots.

'Relax, you have done nothing wrong', she mentally told herself, taking a deep breath.

'There is no easy way to say this Claire, therefore I am going to come straight out with it. A complaint has been made to me by one of your colleagues about your behaviour', said Daniel.

Claire felt an electric current flood through her system, putting her in fight or flight mode. Of course, the complaint could have come from Ashley, but she sensed that this matter was about something else entirely or else Daniel would have worded his statement differently.

'Who has made the complaint?' she asked.

Daniel shook his head.

'I cannot tell you that because the person came to me in confidence. She was very upset. I will say that it concerns the team put together to sort through the disarray which arose in the payroll office following the departure of Paula Dobson from the company. This person alleges that you have undermined and criticised your Finance colleagues to HR and payroll personnel during the team's investigation into the procedures in place in the payroll office, such as in regard to salary advances. The complainant is of the opinion that this resulted in heightened resentment from the two payroll assistants, which in turn slowed down the speed at which their work could be completed and corrective measures actioned. The person believes your negative commentary damaged her reputation in the company. Is this accusation true Claire?'

'No Daniel, it is absolutely not true', she replied vehemently. 'I'm shocked somebody has made this complaint about me.'

Claire was completely thrown off guard by the accusation. Paula Dobson had been a qualified accountant who had been employed in the company for years and knew everything there was to know about the payroll function. When she left, she was replaced by two clerks who considered it to be their job to run the payroll and to make sure everybody got paid. The payroll clerks were totally unconcerned about any 'complicated stuff' like reconciliation work. They did not reconcile payments made through payroll with anything, such as bank, salary advance accounts, pensions. Matters had further deteriorated when the payroll office was relocated out of the Finance office block to the building which housed the Human Resources department. Daniel had put together a team of four people, comprising of Claire, Anna, Joan and Sandra, to blitz through all the payroll records. He wanted to make sure everything in the payroll office met the regulatory standards of Revenue and the company auditors and also that recipients of salary advances paid back the money due to the company. Claire could not believe Daniel was telling her that one of the other girls in the team thought that Claire had been bitching about them to people working outside the finance department.

The only person Claire had let off steam about within the organisation was Ashley and that had only been to Anna in the privacy of their office; since Anna detested Ashley even more than she did she was on safe territory there. She certainly had not criticised any of her other colleagues in Finance to people in the wider organisation. She kept herself quietly to herself as much as possible. Claire tried to find the right words to exonerate herself from the unfair situation she unwittingly found herself in.

'It never entered my head to say anything negative about my team members at all. I never thought it, so I certainly never said it. I have worked with the payroll people before on my own and I know better than anybody that it can be difficult to get the information we need from them. They do not understand what we need the information for. Their focus is ensuring people get paid their salaries on time. I certainly have never criticised any colleague in their dealings with them. I know the clean up project took longer to complete than originally planned but everybody worked hard on it and the goals were accomplished. I don't understand where this is coming from at all'.

'Are you sure you said nothing to anyone Claire, nothing that could perhaps have been misconstrued? As I've said before, this person was extremely upset when she came to me' probed Daniel.

'Daniel. I said nothing, nothing at all. I did not have a negative thought in my head about the work the others were doing. I have a lot of respect for Anna, Sandra and Joan. I work with them, not against them. There is no basis for this complaint. Who am I meant to have said anything to? Has anybody in HR or the payroll office substantiated this accusation? The answer has to be no because I said nothing to nobody. Where is the back up to this complaint about me?' commented Claire, totally perplexed.

'Okay Claire, I had to ask. There must have been crossed wires somewhere. On a more positive note, I want you to know that I was pleased with the end result of the teams' work. Going forward, we might have to look at getting somebody more senior in the payroll office, somebody who possesses the same skills set as Paula', said Daniel, finishing off the conversation.

Claire left the room, feeling dazed and upset. The complaint against her had come like a bolt from the blue. Who had said such a thing about her? It was such a lie. She had simply been sitting there trawling through the books, trying to do a good job and keeping her mouth well and truly shut. It was tedious work, untangling a web of incorrect entries and omissions in the records. There were no short cuts putting a jigsaw piece together. Which of the three people in the team had spoken out against her to Daniel? Not Anna or Sandra, she simply could not believe that they would do such a malicious thing. That left Joan as the person responsible for shoving Claire's head down onto the guillotine, the very person whom Claire had helped the most. She had certainly never done any harm to Joan. Claire had not missed the fact that Daniel had passed over her query on what backup to the complaint existed, which was not surprising given there was none.

Yes, Claire concluded, Joan was the most likely culprit in the grubby affair. She had been appointed by Daniel to head the team and the progress had been slower than she had expected. Dealing with the payroll girls was like painfully pulling teeth because they interpreted questions as placing blame on them for the payroll accounts being in a mess. The clerks had been thrown in at the deep end without proper training and supervision. Joan as team leader had obviously become frustrated and worried that Daniel would hold her responsible for the length of time it was taking to rectify the payroll accounts. She had never been team leader before and she valued the added status the role gave her. Joan must have been afraid that Daniel might not appoint her to a leadership role again because the project had gone over time and had therefore decided to deflect any blame away from herself and onto Claire. It was an unpleasant tactic but had proved effective. Joan had succeeded in fully convincing Daniel of Claire's supposed guilt before the latter was able to deny any wrongdoing. Daniel's face had been thunderous when the unsuspecting Claire had entered his den. Claire had no chance beforehand to construct detailed arguments in her own defence and she did not know if her on the spur of the moment denials were strong enough to truly sway Daniel from his original belief that she was guilty as charged.

Was there any point saying anything to Joan about what had just happened? The woman had shown herself to be neither honest nor trustworthy. There was every chance that she would deny saying anything negative about Claire to Daniel. Worst still, she could twist Claire's words any way she wanted and go running back to Daniel with more unfounded complaints and whinges.

There was an old saying of *'least said, soonest mended'*, but what trouble Claire had gotten into, without even opening her mouth. Claire was sick to her stomach at how despicable a person Joan had shown herself up to be. The number of people she could trust in the finance department was getting smaller by the day. Joan had tried to damage Claire's reputation, ironically by claiming that Claire was the person responsible for tarnishing her own. Claire would say nothing about what had happened in Daniel's office today to anybody, not even Anna. Anna had been a member of the team and she could go off gunning for Joan and then the whole department would hear about it and take sides. Good rarely came out of a bad thing.

CHAPTER NINETEEN

Claire was no clearer in her mind about what to do about Andrew. It was not fair to keep him waiting long for her response. She twisted and turned at night, her sleep either disturbed by thoughts of Joan's machinations with Daniel or fretting about whether or not she should become Andrew's girlfriend. By Thursday she was bone-tired with all the stresses and shenanigans and the sleep deprivation she was experiencing. She was surprised and not very pleased to get a text from Andrew at 10pm, asking her to open the door as he was standing on her doorstep. He had promised to give her time and space to consider his proposal. Surely he was not here to press her to give him an answer tonight?

Claire opened the door quietly, finger to her lips until she brought Andrew into the living room. She did not want Ben to hear a noise and wake up, for if that happened, he could be up for hours before going back to sleep and he had to go to school the next day. She was cross with Andrew for calling around unannounced at such a late hour during the working week.

'I'm tired Andrew. What is so urgent that it cannot wait until tomorrow?' she asked unwelcomingly.

Andrew looked white around the gills, his face taut.

'I did not want to tell you over the phone, it is best to tell you face to face. I did think about waiting but...... it is important news for you', replied Andrew.

'Nobody's dead, are they? There is no need for you to be a drama queen because you have taken up amateur theatrics. Sit down and tell me what is so important that it has you dashing over here as if the world is about to end,' said Claire, using sharpness to mask her mounting concern.

Andrew was not family or a neighbour, which meant that he was unlikely to be imparting bad news to her about Tom and Eileen. What on earth could it be? The name 'Luke Elliott' suddenly flashed through her mind, like a bolt of lightning slashing though a dark sky. The two men had hung around together in college and therefore had known each other well. After all these years, had Luke decided to get in touch with her through Andrew, turning her friend into a messenger boy?
Go on, tell me', said Claire wearily, surrendering to the inevitable, sure her

premonition was right. Her mouth quivered as she dropped down onto the sofa, placing the palm of one hand under her chin and three fingers into her mouth, reminiscent of a small child's anxious gestures.

'There is no easy way to say it, except straight out. Luke rang me today while I was at work. He was able to trace my whereabouts through my linked in profile. I was stunned, totally not expecting it. He wants to see Ben and he wants to be part of his life.'

Claire felt as if she had been kicked in the stomach and she had to breathe in deeply to stop herself from hyperventilating. Hearing Andrew say the words aloud made it real. Luke Elliott wanted to re-enter her life, he could no longer be considered a ghost like figure from the past. The world which she had constructed carefully around herself, Ben and her parents spun around on its axis. It was too much, too much on top of everything else she was trying to cope with.

'He's a bit bloody late about that, isn't he, six years too late? ', Claire exploded. 'I've not heard a peep out of him for years, absolutely nothing. He has never attempted to access me through social media and he obviously uses it. I know he does, that's why I have avoided it like the plague all these years. His absence from our lives has been so absolute he might as well have vanished off the face of the earth, not just taken an airline ticket to America. He wanted nothing to do with us when we needed him most. I was scared stiff at having to cope with a tiny baby on my own. I'd have been in a fine mess if Mam and Dad had not stepped in to support me.'

Andrew looked nearly as upset as Claire felt. She steadied herself, needing to be calm and rational.

'Did he mention me at all? How can he have a relationship with Ben but not with me?' wondered Claire.

It was an important point to clarify. Andrew hesitated, unsure as to the best way to word Luke's intentions towards Claire but, determined not to misrepresent the situation to her.

'It is my understanding from the conversation I had with Luke, that he thinks of you only in terms of you being Ben's mother. He intends to base any future relationship with you on that foundation', said Andrew carefully.

'Wonderful the way he can use you to reject me all over again. He does have a certain style about him,' said Claire tartly.

'Don't be hurt Claire, bear in mind Luke has not seen you for more than six years. Everything will change again, if you decide to see him and talk together. You are a different person from the carefree girl he mostly remembers from college.'

'I was not carefree when I told him I was pregnant. He wanted to know if I would consider going over to England to have an abortion. He wanted me to kill our child. That is how much regard he had for me and our defenceless little baby,' recalled a distraught Claire.

'Claire, Luke would never have wanted to kill any baby and especially not your baby. A lot of men do not have strong feelings for a foetus. Often their protective instinct only kicks in after the baby is born', pointed out Andrew reasonably. 'I know it is very different for many women, who can be fiercely protective of the foetus they are carrying. But no decent, civilised person wants to hurt a living child in any way. I honestly believe that Luke is well intentioned towards Ben and he certainly means him no harm. He simply wants to get to know his son and to help out if he can.'

There was nothing simple about the situation. Claire was not able to forget or forgive the years of hurt and loneliness she had experienced after Luke rushed to board a flight out of the country, taking him far away from her and his paternal responsibilities. She might not have felt as bad if he had remained within touching distance but, the manner in which he had removed himself was very deliberate and wounding. Timing was everything and the silent Luke Elliott had waited too long. He was the man who had stalked her dreams, causing her back to arch and her body to twist in frustrated passion as she lay alone in her bed. Luke had been her heart's desire and he had carelessly ripped it apart when he had chosen to fly away from her and their unborn child.

The fragments of her heart knitted together again when she held her baby boy in her arms, making him the chief recipient of her love and attention. She was able to live in the moment when she was with Ben. It would be impossible for Claire to be ever truly happy again if anything bad happened to her little boy. She had a recurrent nightmare where Ben died and, as they were lowering his white coffin into a hole in the ground, she flung her body on top of it and hugged onto it frantically until her own heart stopped beating and they were buried together. She had lost the father of her child through desertion but, she had adjusted and got on with her life. She could get over the loss of any man, but she interpreted her dark dream to mean that she was incapable of surviving the loss of her child.

Her child must come first. This searing thought burned its way though the fog of confusion in her mind. She did not matter in all of this, Ben and his well-being must take priority above everything else. The focus of the decision to be taken must remain on Ben and on what was best for him. Luke was part of the past but, he wanted to be part of her son's present and future life. Andrew was trying to put it as diplomatically as possible but, Luke was back on the scene because of Ben and not for her. In order to do the right thing by her son, Claire realised that she needed more information about Luke.

'Why did Luke get in touch with you instead of me about seeing Ben? Has he been in contact with you during all these years and you did not tell me about it? When you asked me out last weekend, were you aware that Luke wanted to re-enter our lives?' questioned Claire in rapid gun fire shots. She was in 'shoot the messenger' mode, full of distrust and unease.

She knew her questions were unfair, but the situation felt all wrong to her and she was not yet able to face it in a calm, cool and collected manner. Not surprisingly, Andrew winced and was hurt by her suggestion of double dealing.

'Claire I swear to you that I have not seen or heard from Luke for years, not since before Ben was born. You do not have a social media presence and he had no idea of how to contact you, other than through your parents. He has a record of their home address and phone number, but he also realised that they are likely to be as mad as hell with him and unlikely to entertain his request for the two of you to meet up to discuss Ben. He knew we were good friends in college, and he reached out to me because he reckoned we could still be in contact with each other, and I could pass on his message to you.'

Luke's charm offensive would have been totally wasted on her parents. He must have been very convincing to persuade Andrew to break the ice with her on his behalf.

'What is this message which is meant to be of importance to me but probably is not?' queried Claire acerbically.

'Luke wants to fly over from the States to meet up with you and Ben. I told him I would only give him your mobile number if you agreed that he could have it. He has left his contact number for you to use, if you choose to do so. He is very anxious to see Ben. He says his biggest mistake was in not living up to his responsibilities as a father. It bothers him that Ben is growing up without him in his life. He will get on a plane and come over here straightway, if you give him the nod.'

'Are pigs flying alongside that plane?' Claire said, emitting a snort of derision.

'He is aware that too much time has gone by without any contact between you and if he leaves it any longer it may be too late to fix it. He wants to see you and Ben and to try to make amends for past mistakes. It will be his first visit home to Ireland since he left for America', elaborated Andrew.

'Let me get this straight. Luke is planning to come over here for a few days to see us ? His life is still in America, not Ireland? He thinks he can fly in here, turn our lives upside down and then bugger off back to the States for another six years before we hear of his existence again? Is he crazy or just the most selfish man living on the planet?' Claire was so angry with his presumptuous behaviour that she wanted to howl with rage.

'Luke does intend to stay living in America, he made that quite clear. He loves it there', confirmed Andrew. 'He wants to meet Ben and tell him he is his father and set up some type of on-going contact with him. Obviously that can only happen with your agreement'.

'Obviously! With his type of egotistical arrogance, it's a miracle he recognises that hc has to consult me at all.'

Andrew did not let her sniping distract him from the main issue.

'The bottom line is that Luke wants to meet up with you to talk about seeing Ben. I'm forwarding his number to your phone and you can contact him at any time if you choose to make arrangements. Or if you prefer it, you can give me permission to pass your phone number onto him and he can ring you instead. After that, I'm done, it will be up to the two of you to sort things out between you.'

'Very convenient for you, I'm sure. Nothing like dropping a bomb and then running for cover. What if I am done with Luke too? I'm inclined to delete his number and not give him another thought. It would serve him right after his lack of contact over the last six years. Why are you helping him

Andrew? You asked me out and it would be easier for us if Luke was not in the picture. He has treated us all badly, you included. We were all dropped as fast as hot potatoes when it suited Mr. Big. This country was too small for him. We were the little people to be ignored and disregarded. He cast your friendship aside as surely as he cut himself off from Ben and me. You owe him nothing. So why are you doing his dirty work for him?' challenged Claire.

No man likes to be accused of being a lap dog and Andrew bristled visibly.

'I did not get involved to help Luke out, I don't give a damn about him. I'm doing it for you and Ben. My Dad died when I was near Ben's age. I remember it as clearly as if it happened yesterday. I always missed him and wanted him back. I believe it is better for a child to have contact with his father, on condition that the father is not abusive in any way. Luke was a good bloke to be around in college, he was never mean tempered and he did not get involved in fights. After you calm down and get over the shock, you might decide that it is better for Ben in the long term to get to know his father while he is still growing up. Otherwise he might always wonder about him and feel rejected by him or maybe feel there is something wrong with him because his father could not be bothered with him. I am doing this for Ben's sake, not to help out Luke'.

As Claire looked daggers at him and opened her mouth to protest, Andrew held his hand up in the air, as if to ward her off.

'I am just the bearer of news here Claire, remember, I am your friend and not the enemy. It is your decision and only you can make the call'.

'How can I make the call Andrew?' agonised Claire. 'I feel I don't know the first thing about Luke, the real man. It is as if the guy I fell in love with in college was somebody I conjured up from my imagination and made him into the person I wanted him to be. How can I introduce a stranger to my son and in the same breath announce that he is actually his father? I can't do it, I won't do it.'

'I am not telling you what to do Claire but I am suggesting there is the possibility that something positive may emerge from you and Luke meeting up to talk. It might never go further than you having one face to face conversation together and that is your right to choose. Luke forced his decision to leave the country onto you to bear but, this time, you have the power to decide whether or not Luke is worthy of the introduction he seeks with Ben. You can observe the man he has become, for he is just a man

Claire, like any other, he is not a fantasy figure. Luke is Ben's father and he wants to see him. It is a proposition worth considering. You might even feel better about everything that has happened if you meet up with him and clear the air,' said Luke calmly.

Claire sank down despondently on the sofa, the fight and anger draining away from her body. She felt sick at the thought of meeting Luke.

'I don't feel like I will ever feel good again', she whispered. 'Life can be very hard Andrew.'

'I know honey. The last few years have been rough on you, you've had to cope with a lot, navigating between Ben and your parents, the years full of study followed by work. It must be exhausting at times. The hardest thing that has ever happened to me was my Dad dying when I was a kid and I've had time to get over that one. Ma says that life has its ups and downs and somewhere along the way everyone takes a hit.'

'I know I am lucky to have you as my friend Andrew. I'm sorry I was mean to you, I didn't intend to be', sniffed Claire.

'You are not mean, you are very tired and in shock. Like you, I am not thrilled by the timing of Luke's resurfacing but we have to deal the cards we are given as best we can. As your friend, I'm going to get you a glass of hot whiskey and send you off to bed. Tomorrow morning, I will ring that bad boss of yours and be very charming when I tell her that unfortunately you are too sick to come into work. I'll put on a macho American accent and make her curious.'

'She won't have a clue who you are, she thinks I'm a machine, not a woman. I should go into work Andrew, I have tons to do and there's nobody else to do it if I'm not there. I don't like ringing in sick. Mam and Dad would not approve', protested Claire half heartedly. She felt sick to the pit of her stomach at the moment but it was possible that she would feel better in the morning and be able to face into a day's work.

Claire had absorbed her parents' work ethic, which was if a person was able to walk and talk and had no temperature then they were capable of doing a day's work. The concept of people counting an allowable number of uncertified sick days as an extra holiday entitlement was outrageous to them. When Claire had first started working in the office she was surprised to learn that her colleagues resented anybody coming in with a bad cold or flu, fearing that the virus would spread amongst all the workers in the confined office space. People would vociferously urge the person feeling under the weather to go home to bed. Tom and Eileen were incredulous to think that a person should stay out of work because of a sniffle or a cold. Andrew was having none of it.

'You don't have to tell your parents everything Claire, you don't have to hand them over a big stick to beat you with. Tell them you have a day off. Besides, you are not ringing in sick, I am doing it for you. You've had a big shock, you're exhausted and you need to rest up. Leictreach are not paying you enough for all the effort you put in and at the very least they owe you time in lieu. If senior management can swan off to a luxury hotel with a golf course and a spa for three days to discuss 'strategic planning' then you can rest in bed to recover your strength. Prioritise taking care of yourself for once. The decision is made, I'm going to make the call for you tomorrow', asserted Andrew.

'Thanks Andrew' said Claire capitulating. 'You are my best friend in the whole world.'

'Well, you are the only friend I have who I'd send to bed, alone I might add. Now where is the whiskey bottle? I know you keep one tucked away for medicinal purposes and the odd visitor. It will help you sleep once you skedaddle off to bed.'

Claire went upstairs to bed and minutes later she was all cosy, tucked up under the duvet. Andrew knocked lightly on the door before he entered the room and handed her over the hot toddy. The unsung hero then quietly slipped out of the house as the clock struck midnight, a solitary figure striding forth into the crisp night, his absolute goodness and unselfishness unknown to the casual passer by.

CHAPTER TWENTY

Claire took Andrew's advice about staying away from work the following morning and not mentioning to her mother that she had pulled a sickie. Even on a normal day at work her stomach tended to be tied up in anxiety knots and the events of last night had added to her stress levels. Rest and a walk along the beach was more akin to what a doctor would prescribe for her in the circumstances; the other option was stuffing a fist full of Valium into her mouth but, she was reluctant to go the drugs route for help in calming her mind. If she started to take antidepressants she feared she might never summon up the will power to get off them again.

The seaside was always there for her as a back drop to her life, mused Claire. A walk along the waters' edge, observing the rhythmic flow of the waves, soothed her soul when she was sad and the sandy beach was a never ending source of recreation with Ben. The ever changing colour of the water had fascinated her ever since she was a little girl, scanning its surfaces in the hopes of catching sight of a beautiful mermaid playing in the surf. She had discovered long ago that Dollymount Strand was the perfect place for her to seek inner harmony. She was pleased to see that the tide was coming in and on impulse she took off her shoes and socks to paddle in the cold sea water. She strained her eyes to make out the horizon line which divided sea from sky, marvelling at the sameness of their blue hue which dazzled the eye. She let the ebb and flow of the sand and waves tease her feet and send tingles up her body, wanting to feel fully alive and connected to nature. It consoled Claire in times of uncertainty to know that the tidal waves rolled in and out of the shore with the regularity of night following day, as the moon revealed itself when the sun faced away. She admired the sea for its majestic beauty, its ability to guard its many secrets and its powerful refusal to be tamed by man's best efforts to control it.

One of the main reasons Claire came to spend time by the sea during a period of trial and tribulation was that it was a place where she could be honest with herself. As she strolled slowly through the shallow waters, she acknowledged the hurt she felt deep inside her due to being firmly rejected one more time by her ex lover. It had been made crystal clear to her, by a true friend, that Luke Elliott wanted to make contact with her solely because he wanted to build up a relationship with Ben and not because he wanted to see her again.

How could she have meant so little to him when she had totally adored him? It was a mystery to Claire how it was possible for an intelligent woman like herself to crave a lover who did not place any value on her devotion to him. It was possible that Luke Elliott might not respect Claire as a person in her own right. He could view her as a plaything, a nonentity. She had been consumed by thoughts of him while he scorned her. Maybe she had bored him. It was one of the tough lessons of life but she had to get over being discarded, she had to put it behind her and move forward. There were men and women who were rejected by their partners in every corner of the world every day of the year and they got over it.

Claire had fallen deeply in love with Luke, so much so that she had craved him as a drug, wanting to get closer and ever closer to him, to literally get under his skin. She had been devastated and humiliated by his absolute rejection of her. If Ben did not exist Claire would have preferred never to have set eyes on Luke again. She felt ashamed of how deeply she had felt about him when he cared little for her. If she had come across Luke by chance walking down one of the main city centre streets she would have dived into the nearest shop entrance to avoid him. Claire had given Luke her heart and he had no regard for it, he had swept her aside as if she was an inconsequential nothing. Piece by painful piece, she had put herself back together and forced her mind not to dwell on him, telling herself he was not worth the trouble. She would have gotten over Luke Elliott years ago except that she gave birth to his son.

There was the rub of it, she was never able to mentally say goodbye to Luke Elliott because he was the father of her child. Ben and Luke did not look alike but they shared the same cobalt coloured eyes which mirrored the brilliant tint of the ocean she admired so much. In all other respects her son looked like a Howard and people could easily mistake him for her brother Martin's boy. From time to time Ben would do something which was unlike anything her brother had ever done at the same age and seemed to be more indicative of Luke Elliott's maverick spirit. For instance, even at his tender age Ben was coming up with ideas for making money, such as when he bought a big bag of lollipops for €3 in the local supermarket from his stash of birthday money and he started to exchange the lollipops for match attack cards. The teacher went mad when she found out about it and read him the riot act but Claire had recognised Luke Elliott's entrepreneurial spirit coming through in Ben. Recently Ben had placed a table and chair in the middle of the road with a bold sign stating 'Toll Road, €2 to Pass' attached to a broom handle. He literally stopped the traffic and caused one lady motorist to press her horn incessantly until Claire came out and dragged Ben and his furniture out of harm's way. Part of her wanted to laugh at his ingenuity, even as she scolded him for pulling off a dangerous stunt.

Like father, like son. Claire had never played an instrument but a guitar had usually been only arm distance away from Luke Elliott. Ben was musical and loved to sing and dance. Claire had bought him a wooden recorder and he was trying to teach himself by ear to play tunes on it. Ben enjoyed playing board games with his Granddad and he quickly set out to understand the rules. Once he understood the game and had mastered the methodology of playing it, he might try to put his own take on it, for instance, using two dices simultaneously instead of one. Tom had considered Ben too young to learn chess but his grandson pestered him to teach him the game until he gave in and did so, with the happy outcome that the two of them regularly played quite competitively with each other. Claire believed that Ben's interest in chess was the mathematical brain of his biological father coming through. The whole family often spent hours playing cards. Claire knew Ben possessed the ability to become a proper card shark and therefore she was already brainwashing him about the dangers of gambling and being careless with money. Tom encouraged the child to play card games with him because they both enjoyed the pastime and he reckoned Ben had the makings of an astute share investor in him. Learning how to play cards was a social activity and the skills a person picked up while mastering the various games could be put to good use in the world of business. Tom fondly imagined that Ben was the reincarnation of himself as a young lad but, with education, the boy would have greater career opportunities than he ever had and the sky was the limit for him. Claire suspected that the stamp of Luke Elliott's genes left a deeper mark on the boy than had ever been admitted within the Howard clan. Their boy Ben was a Howard but he could never be all Howard. It was this truth that sent Claire round and around in circles as she considered her dilemma; was she to allow Luke to be an active presence in Ben's life or not to be? Regardless of her complicated feelings for Luke, Claire had to do the right thing by Ben.

Her initial reaction on hearing that Luke intended to remain living in America instead of coming home to Ireland was to dismiss the idea of introducing him to Ben. Why disturb her little boy's happy equilibrium by bringing in a potentially influential, but rarely seen, father into his life? Everything was fine as it was. Ben's grandfather was the dominant male in his life and the unconditional love which bonded the old man and young boy together was wondrous to behold. Ben had good relationships with Martin and Andrew and also had positive feelings about the other male figures he was familiar with, such as his sport coach or the fathers of his little friends. There was no problem with Ben, he was a happy, well adjusted little boy, who got on well with everybody. Young as he was, it was evident that he was a smart, active child who had the capability to excel at school and in sport. Why introduce Luke into Ben's world, exposing the boy to the risk of bonding with a father who could later decide to abandon him for a second time? Out of sight, out of mind and Luke was far away from them in his abode in America.

Would her son have a better life with his father in it? Claire was no expert but she did not need a psychology degree to know that a father normally played a key role in a child's life, particularly for a boy. Andrew had hit a nerve when he confessed he had never stopped missing his long deceased father. Every time Claire was out and about in the park or playground with Ben, she spotted a boy's face lighting up as he ran towards his Daddy. How many times had Claire's heart ached a smidgeon when she heard an excited child's cry of 'Daddy, my Daddy' float through the air, knowing that Ben was unable to utter the call?

Fathers were impossible to ignore but Claire tried to minimise the non existence of a father in Ben's life by telling him that lots of children had a Daddy but not many were lucky enough to have a great Granddad like he did. She was on shaky ground because in books, television programmes and family event days, Dads featured much more prominently than Granddads. If Luke Elliott's message proved true, then Ben could lay claim to two parents instead of one, for better or worse. If Claire waited until Ben was a young adult to make the decision himself as to whether or not he wanted to seek out his biological father, too much time might have elapsed for them to develop a meaningful relationship. By then there was a high probability that Luke would have other children, through new relationships, who would take priority over Ben.

Was Luke Elliott capable of loving his son? He was undoubtedly a selfish man. Through his personal choices, Luke had missed out on all the influential mile stones of Ben's early childhood. Looking after a baby was hard work but the reward was there in the bright eyes gazing intently up at you and the feel of the light bundle of flesh and bones trustingly cuddled up in your arms. The welfare of a totally helpless, vulnerable human being depended on you. Since Luke had not experienced any of Ben's babyhood, Claire questioned whether he had the capacity to truly connect with the active six year old boy, demonstrating parental feelings of tenderness and protectiveness, including a reservoir of patience and acceptance which was usually only there for your own child. Then again, these theories on parent-child bonding were relatively new and might be overstated. Each generation had their own set of beliefs. In Victorian England, many parents in the higher echelons of society only developed an interest in their children when they grew older and became more interesting. Nothing changed more frequently in society than the best theory for raising a child.

For a full two years after Ben was born, Claire had hoped feverishly for Luke to return home to them, stoking up a fire in her dreams. Her attitude towards Luke changed and hardened when Ben turned two, after he had missed out on Ben's infancy. Cold water was resolutely poured on the flame of hope she had kept alive. Claire began to build a wall around her heart, with each brick reinforcing the belief that Luke was never going to come home to them. If Luke Elliott returned, there was a danger that the wall which she had painstakingly erected through the years, for her own protection, was going to be blasted apart. Luke had become the more formal 'Luke Elliott' in her mind, in an attempt to create distance between the man and the pain he had inflicted on her life.

Claire was a mother and as such she must put her child's needs before her own. She had to do right by her son. She had made a mess of her relationship with Luke Elliott and there was a real possibility that she was going to spoil the close friendship she had enjoyed for many years with Andrew Kennedy. Her work situation was going from bad to worse. The one thing she was proud of was Ben, who was a complete credit to her in all respects. Her parents gave her huge help in rearing Ben but Claire cut herself some flack by realising that a good part of the reason Ben was such a terrific, happy boy was because she was a good mother to him. As a loving mother, she owed her darling son a duty of care, even if it necessitated putting aside her own doubts and insecurities. Her instinct was nudging her to the conclusion that the right course of action to take, even after all this wasted time, was for her to meet up with Luke and start a conversation with him.

Claire felt relieved that she had made the first part of the decision but she shrank at its implications. She needed to see Luke in order to judge whether or not she should introduce him in a real way into Ben's life. But she was not going to make the call yet; she had to take time out to get accustomed to the idea. She also felt she had a moral obligation to inform her parents of the development and that was surely not going to be an easy conversation. How would Ben react to the news? Perhaps she had better try to find out, or at least prepare the ground with him.

Claire stared out at the surf flecked sea, her eyes drifting upwards to the snow white clouds skittishly chasing each other high up in the sky. The deep blue sky- the same colour as the sapphire ray which sparked life in Luke and Ben's eyes. It was as if nature was calling out to her, reminding her of the power of the elements and inherited DNA. She turned away and headed for home.

What will be, will be.

That evening, when the homework and games were over and done with, Ben flopped down beside her on the sofa and she affectionately reached out to tousle his hair.

'I have been wanting to ask you something for a while Ben. Do you ever think about your Daddy?'

The child's cobalt eyes, the visible physical mark of his biological father, swung towards her in bemusement.

'I haven't got a Daddy, Mommy. You know that,' he chided her.

'Ben darling, you do have a Daddy. We don't see him because he lives far away, in America,' Claire reminded him. She had told her son that part of the story before but had not mentioned it in a long time.

'Oh, that's right Mommy, he lives far, far away. We'd have to go to see him on an aeroplane,' said Ben. He was already looking around for the next toy to play with.

'If your father came here for a short visit Ben, would you like to see him?' asked Claire, trying to sound casual.

'I don't know Mommy. What do you think?' he queried, his eyes big and innocent.

Ben was still very young and he was usually ready and willing to be guided by the wisdom of his mother, who he considered to have almost, but not quite, as much knowledge as his teacher. He was not to know that Claire was grasping around in the dark for the right answer to this particular question.

'I think perhaps it could be a good idea,' she breathed out the words softly.

'Yes Mommy, it's a good idea', Ben beamed up at her. 'And then we can go on an aeroplane to America. I've never been in an aeroplane before.' He raced around the room with his arms stretched out, noisily imitating a plane, all thoughts of a mysterious Daddy already out of his mind. A Daddy was not part of his present reality and Ben was busy living in the moment.

Claire decided to follow her son's lead and push Luke Elliott out of her mind until the time for meeting him suited her better. Luke probably had a fantastic job and she preferred her own career to be back on track before seeing him in the flesh; she certainly did not want to come across as a dissatisfied loser. She also did not want Luke to think he only had to click his fingers after six long years to have her come running to him to do his bidding. Besides, she did not appreciate the way in which Luke had dragged Andrew into the mix, she preferred to keep those two men in separate mental compartments. She needed to discover how deeply she felt about Andrew, before she came face to face with Luke and his smart aleck comments. She was not about to make big decisions in her life in haste. If you did nothing, you did nothing wrong. This time around she was going to call the shots with Luke, it was her way or the highway, yes sir, he could like it or lump it. There was going to be no more turning herself inside out in order to meet with his approval. This time it was going to be different because she was different. Luke Elliott must understand that fact, if he was ever to get within whistling distance of Ben.

CHAPTER TWENTY ONE

Back in Leictreach the following Monday morning, Claire's resolution to stay focused on the tasks and not on the personalities at work was tested when Ashley paid her an unwanted visit.

'What was wrong with you last Friday?' asked Ashley.

'I had a stomach bug', said Claire. Her manager was not impressed.

'Hmm, it's always a stomach bug or a sore back or a sore throat to explain away uncertified sick leave. Or how about a migraine? That's a good one to have on the list too, as I'm sure you already know', snorted Ashley. 'All sick leave should be certified, otherwise it is open to abuse. I have never been out of work without a sick certificate, issued by my doctor'.

'You must have a very accommodating doctor Ashley. Pay him well, do you?', sniped Anna, staying loyal to Claire. 'As a manager you should know it is company policy to allow every employee five days uncertified sick leave in a year. It saves clogging up doctors' clinics. Friday was Claire's first sick day this year. She does not have to explain herself further to you.'

'Careful, you are on thin ice Anna. Perhaps you had better turn your attention to finishing today's bank reconciliation. I will not authorise the day's holiday you have requested, unless I am sure all your work is fully and accurately completed.'

'She is unbelievable,' said Anna, when they had the office to themselves again. 'She wants us to beg for our holidays. It kills her if we are off work for a day. She practically called you a liar for ringing in sick. A manager who was concerned for the well being of her staff might pass a comment like *I am glad to see that you are feeling better and have recovered enough to return to work today*'. And I can't remember the last time you called in sick, you are never sick. It's the stress of working in this bloody place, with the likes of her on our backs. I wish she'd fall into a nest of wasps and be stung to death. No such luck, they'd welcome her in as the new queen.'

'She is not going anywhere Anna, she has got too good a thing going on for herself here', said Claire. 'Leictreach is a blue chip company. Daniel has made her the de facto boss. She must be on a good salary. We were all well trained in our jobs before she got here, which means she has inherited a good team around her, who delivers the goods on target. A reliable, experienced team can make the worst manager look good. We will have to find a better way of dealing with her pettiness'

'Unfortunately, there is no better way of dealing with her', replied Anna heatedly. 'She has no sense of right and wrong and she is oblivious to the fact that she treats people badly. She believes any problem is caused by us, not her. She thinks she is the bees' knees, a manager who has to stand firm to get the lazy, untrustworthy drones to do an honest day's work'.

Claire recognised the truth in Anna's words but she still had to find methods of coping with Ashley's constant criticism and micro managing. Her main tactic of dealing with Ashley had always been to stay as far away from her as possible but that was getting harder to manage since she had to report into her for everything except the budgeting. Claire's guarded manner towards Ashley deadened her mood and her open, sunny smile was rarely seen around the office. Deirdre remarked on it when she dropped invoices into Claire's office one of the days.

'Your sparkle is gone Claire, do try and get it back', the older woman urged her bracingly.

Deirdre was an older, self-sufficient lady who did not believe in depression and thought that busy people had no time to be depressed. Claire was unimpressed by the woman's advice; being sparkly was the least of her concerns when she was trying to keep her head above water in the department, she was close to drowning here. She could sparkle like a gem when she was away from this place on holidays. Her family had not seen much sparkle from her lately either and they deserved to witness it far more than her unsupportive colleagues.

Claire tried to analyse the tactics Ashley used to manage her. Ashley was like a strict, unreasonable teacher who yielded all the power in the classroom, expecting the pupil Claire to toe the line or risk being punished or expelled. There was no sense of give and take. The emphasis was always on the negative, on what was not done, rather than on the positive outputs and good results. Ashley took all of Claire's information and sucked it upwards, giving no knowledge back in return. Claire learned nothing new from Ashley, nor did the manager ever help her solve a problem or give her an explanation on how certain calculations were made. The information channel was always a one way traffic flow, defying gravity as it was propelled upwards from the lower echelons. Claire felt as if a vampire was bleeding her dry, leaving her weakened over time.

There was no new learning or development occurring to give her a rush of fresh energy. Daniel had been in the habit of allowing his accountants read some of the senior management reports for information purposes as he believed they should be kept informed of developments within the wider organisation but Ashley had cut off their distribution. She was not invited to meetings and as time went by, she received far fewer emails from colleagues in the wider organisation. Her email flow was concentrated between Ashley and herself.

Ashley employed more than one weapon in her armament and they were each effective in their own way of belittling a subordinate. Her most obvious tactic was to pile on the work without giving Claire the necessary time to execute it properly. Ashley always asked via email, at least one day too early, if a task was finished, forcing Claire to acknowledge that she was still in the process of completing it. As Ashley was the ultimate micro manager, she knew exactly when it was still a work in progress and her tactic built up an impression that Claire struggled to get tasks done on time.

Claire had begun to dread opening her email 'In box' message folder, for here there was no escape from Ashley. Ashley sent her messages constantly throughout the day, typically asking her if she had done one thing, while knowing full well that Claire was working on something else altogether. If Claire had a conversation with Ashley on a Tuesday, telling her that she planned to schedule a piece of work for completion on the Thursday, she was sure to get an email from Ashley on the Wednesday in between, asking her if it was done and if not, why not? Raging at the woman's duplicity, Claire then had to reply in email that no (as already mentioned) the job would not be completed until the next day because of X, Y and Z. Claire feared that Ashley was using the email system as a tool to trip her up and make her appear inefficient. She was convinced that Ashley was building up a file to use against her if she ever had the temerity to lodge an official complaint about the way she was being treated with the Human Resources department.

Another trick was to give Claire loads of itsy bitsy administrative jobs to perform; these were not part of her formal job description and fell below the managerial radar but when combined together they left her with much less time to perform her substantive analyst role, upon which her performance was to be evaluated. Requests for her to do extra tasks were phrased in polite one line emails and made to seem as if it was a handy little number, not substantive enough in itself to warrant official protest. Ashley never called on Claire to deal with the higher level, interesting financial analysis exercises; on the contrary, the task was always administrative, a downgrading of her role as business analyst. Claire gritted her teeth and got on with it, her pride making her reluctant to admit how much of her day was being taken up with administration duties.

'Ring Revenue about the tax clearance certificate, we need one to be issued to us urgently. It should only take you a couple of minutes to sort out', Ashley had instructed her yesterday. There was a phone queuing system to go through before being connected to the relevant section, only for Claire to be informed that Revenue needed further information before they were able to issue a tax clearance certificate to Leictreach, which she then had to search out and send onto them. Far from taking a few minutes, the exercise took up an hour of her time. Ashley always underestimated the time it took to complete a given task, no matter what it was.

Claire often broke sweat to meet unnecessarily tight deadlines but any satisfaction she felt was wiped out by Ashley immediately shooting back an email outlining the next task she wanted done. It was relentless stuff, with no let up and no thanks. Ashley never, ever thanked her for her work. It was next to impossible for Claire to plan out her work schedule for the week in any meaningful way. She was always fire fighting. One week, she was given the tax saver travel tickets to administer for the whole company, the next it was the bike to work scheme. Behind every task, there were ten more lined up. Claire felt like she was a moving target for Ashley to take swipes at for her own amusement, a little wooden puppet doll with dangling legs whose strings were pulled and controlled by a malicious puppeteer.

'Are you bringing work home with you?' asked Anna.

'Sometimes', replied Claire, trying not to blush.

'Don't do it Claire, it's a bad habit to get into. You'll get no thanks for it either, not from the likes of her', said Anna, nodding her head in the direction of Ashley's office. 'You can only do so much in the time. Me, I leave on the dot of five, they get what they pay me for and not a minute more. I'm not killing myself to earn Ashley a big bonus. It will be money in her pocket, not mine. Go home and spend the time with your child. He'll be grown up before you know it.'

It was a sensitive subject because Claire was remotely accessing her files at home, after Ben went to bed. It was the only way she could get through all the work she was responsible for doing. She was beginning to question her job proficiency and the speed at which she was able to compute and compile her figures reliably. If truth be told, she felt ashamed that she needed to put in additional hours at home in order to meet her work targets and she did not want to advertise this fact around the place. Claire's confidence in her own ability was taking a hammering. Had she passed her accountancy exams with flying colours by some fluke? What if Ashley's evaluation of Claire's performance was correct and she was rubbish at her job? Perhaps a similarly qualified person could do it better? Claire was slowly acknowledging her secret deep fear, which was that she was not good enough at her job to truly deserve to hold it. Maybe she should be brighter, faster and impressive enough to cause Ashley to both respect and fear her enough to back the hell away.

Ashley was scathing if she detected any error.

'The revenue figure on page 3 of the report is wrong, I can't trust you with the data Claire', snapped Ashley.

It turned out the figure was only wrong because Claire had not been informed or given access to information about a new category of product which had come on stream. Ashley told her nothing about what was going on in the wider organisation. It was becoming increasingly difficult for Claire to access information because she was never invited to meetings. Her name was no longer copied on any emails sent by the heads of departments as she was out of the information loop. It was a big part of Ashley's job to review the work her team prepared and she tore into Claire on the few occasions she noticed an error in her figures. Claire had got into the habit of scrutinising her spreadsheets very closely before submitting them to Ashley. The exhaustive rechecking of her work took up time Claire could ill afford to spare but it was necessary to avoid Ashley's withering criticism.

Claire was aware that the manager treated people differently, depending on whether or not she perceived them to be members of the support group she was building up for herself in the department. When Isabella, the quiet Spanish girl who had recently started work in accounts payable, made a mistake which resulted in a creditor overpayment, Ashley had reassured the agitated girl.

'These things happen from time to time. Don't worry, we will get the money back, that is the main thing.'

The mouse like Isabella flashed Ashley a smile every time she saw her after that encounter. If Claire or Anna had been responsible for an overpayment Ashley would have had their guts for garters.

As a result of Ashley's dichotomy of attitude and behaviour, two camps were building up within the department, the *'In with Ashley'* and the *'Can't Stand Ashley'* opposing sides. Deirdre had no problem with her because Ashley treated the older, strong minded Deirdre with respect and the two benefited from fostering a cordial relationship. Deirdre was a single lady who had worked with great dedication and diligence in Leictreach for years and Daniel held her in high regard. As the months went by, the groupie Ashley crowd grew in size, due to people appreciating the fact that their bread was better buttered by being part of the 'In' crowd and by her adopting a reasonable managerial approach to them. Daniel had handed over the interviewing and selection of new staff into the department to her and naturally enough Ashley only recruited people she thought she could control. She favoured the new starters over people like Claire, who she had inherited when she took on the job as manager in the finance department. The new recruits quickly sensed that Claire and Anna were out of favour with the powerful people in the department and therefore kept their distance from them, wary of being caught in 'bad' company and eager to affiliate themselves with the more popular 'people who matter' group. A sense of integrity did not come into it for the new recruits, it was too early for them to have skin in the game.

What was Ashley's problem anyway? Why was she intent on inflicting injury and discord? Claire did not understand it at all. Was she miserable as hell with her life? But why? To a casual outsider Ashley was reasonably attractive, she had long legs and her short blonde hair was in good condition, her ash white skin was clear and although her face was thin (like the rest of her rail thin body) some men were quite taken with the horsey look. She was a qualified accountant and undeniably smart. She did not need to harass anybody to progress ahead in the organisation, which meant she must be doing it for kicks.

Anna and Claire were experiencing the same problems with Ashley, tucked away out of sight from the general office in their shoe box sized office. In some ways it was worse for Anna than it was for Claire since all her work fell directly under Ashley's supervision. Anna was in a perpetual state of outrage at Ashley's arrogance but, with no formal business qualifications, four children and a husband out of work, her hands were tied behind her back and she felt she had nowhere else to go. At least Claire still did the accounting and budget work for the central departments and this still fell under Daniel's remit, since he wanted to keep all the month end, planning and forecasting reporting under his direct control. Ashley controlled the balance sheet reporting.

There was no doubt that Ashley was intent on eroding the quality of the job assignments allocated to Claire. One day she appeared in Claire's office with a box full of food vouchers and catering invoices and dropped them unceremoniously on top of her desk. Claire was not one of the people in the organisation entitled to a food voucher booklet and she wondered why on earth was Ashley giving them to her?

'The catering manager says that he is not taking charge of the administration of the food voucher booklets to staff members any more. According to him, it is a money substitute and therefore should be a function of the finance department. I want you to make sure that everyone in the company who is entitled to one gets it distributed to them every month. Be warned, the mob will beat down your door for the food vouchers if the delivery is late. Check the invoices are correct before authorising them for payment', dictated Ashley.

'I am employed as a business analyst Ashley. Handing out food vouchers is not part of my brief', protested Claire, trying to gather her startled wits around her.

'For heaven's sake Claire, you won't find '*distribution of food vouchers*' in anybody's job description, that's why they have been dumped here with us. Everybody has to carry out work which is not in their strict job description. It is a small administrative task that takes half an hour once a month, just get on with it and it will be done before you know it. You can check up on the issuance of free newspapers around the company while you're at it, I'm sure some people are appropriating them instead of buying their own, the free loaders', snapped Ashley.

Only senior executives were entitled to pick up a company purchased newspaper from the reception desk and bring it to their office. Claire blanched at the thought of telling managers to hand over their daily newspaper, which they loved to read over their morning coffee. She was not going to go near that one! But the lunch vouchers booklets were given to about three hundred workers and if they were not distributed people would certainly come looking for them. By the time the lunch vouchers were checked for order changes, counted out, packed and distributed around the company, five precious hours out of her day had passed by. So much for Ashley suggesting it to be a half hour task, it had turned out to be another example of an administrative task that ate up her time. Nobody was going to volunteer to take the thankless task away from her either.

The biggest bust up between Ashley and Claire during this painful period of attrition centred around the issue of holiday leave.

'You have forgotten to sign off the holiday request I put in months ago for two weeks off covering the end of August and the beginning of September. I need a copy for my personal records', said Claire.

'I have not forgotten to sign them off, I did not agree to your request. Karen and I are both going on a training course in the first week of September and Joan has booked time off to go to a family wedding. When I consider whether or not to sanction a holiday request, I must consider if somebody in a related job has also booked the time off. I do not want multiple staff to take leave or be out of the office at the same time, that is no way to run a department', said Ashley.

Claire was gobsmacked by Ashley's announcement, it had not occurred to her that there was a problem with her taking the two weeks leave, given she had requested the time off ages ago and had not taken any summer leave. Besides, her work area boundaries were clearly defined and did not overlap with the other three, none of whom provided holiday cover for her. Karen had become Ashley's de facto deputy, hence, if any two accountants should not be out of the office at the same time then it was the two of them, not her.

'Last year, Daniel permitted me to have the first week off in September because Ben was starting school, he did not view it as a problem. I have holiday days to take and the company policy is 'use them or lose them' in the calendar year. Me taking holidays in September will not interfere with anybody else's workload,' pointed out Claire.

Ashley shrugged her shoulders.

'For some reason I don't understand, it is considered a big deal when kids start school. We all had to do it. Kids are fine starting school, it is the parents who make a song and dance about it. In regard to your holidays, you can have the last week off in August and another week off towards the end of November. That is my best and final offer to you, take it or leave it.'

'But I don't want to take a week off in November. Holiday time is precious and has to serve a purpose. For instance, the school midterm break is in October and it would be much more useful to me to be at home with my son then, as compared to November', protested Claire.

'That's not going to happen. October is a very busy month in the department because we will be finalising budgets. It's out of the question for you to be absent at such a crucial time for the finance team', said Ashley, quick to quash the idea of Claire taking holidays in October.

'Ashley, please try to see it from my viewpoint. Can we not reach a compromise regarding my holidays? Give me the week off in September and I will forget about the October midterm break. My parents are going to be in Italy during the first week of September and I need to be at home to look after my son while they are away. There is even more to it than that, I feel I should be at home to settle Ben back at school. There is pressure on the school to increase its pupil intake and his year is going from two classes to three. This means his class is going to be split up and he will probably be separated from some of his friends, which will be upsetting for him'.

'He'll be fine, kids adjust', replied Ashley, unmoved.

'My routine work does not overlap with Karen or Joan's responsibilities. Please let me have the two weeks off Ashley', beseeched Claire.

'No.'

'It is too late for my parents to cancel; my mother has practically packed her suitcase. My parents have paid for this holiday already and have been looking forward to it for months. Don't you understand, I have nobody else to look after Ben when they go away', said Claire, trying to explain the situation fully to Ashley.

'Your childcare arrangements are irrelevant to me. Keeping the department adequately staffed is my concern. You can probably arrange for somebody else to mind the kid, if it is that important to you. If not, I am sure your parents can reschedule their holiday. People their age always take out holiday travel insurance'.

'I can link into the systems remotely and work from home in the first week of September Ashley, I do not have to be physically on the premises to work on the reports,' suggested Claire, trying to negotiate with Ashley in her search for a resolution to the impasse.

'I said no Claire. I do not want my people working from home, I prefer them to be here in the office. I don't believe people work as diligently at home compared to being in the office, where managers can keep an eye on them. It is the manager's prerogative to agree holiday dates, bearing in mind the needs and responsibilities of the department.'

Ashley pursed up her lips as if she was sucking on sour lemons.

'Fill in the holiday form to take off the last week of August and a week in November and I will sign it. You can go now', she directed majestically.

Clare had to breathe in deeply to calm herself when she got back into her office. She had to make a phone call.

'Mam? I have just been told by my manager that I can only take holidays for the last week in August but not the following first week in September.'

'But we are going for the two weeks, not one, dear', replied Eileen.

'I know Mam. I will try to see if I can get Martin or Andrew to mind Ben for the week in September', said Claire.

'Don't do that, poor Ben will be going from pillar to post, not knowing who is looking after him. Neither Martin nor Andrew have ever looked after a young boy for a week. Ben will be starting back at school as well, which is a big event for any child. No, I won't have it. We must rearrange our trip for another time. It is lucky your father and I took out insurance. It is such a pity though, especially as it has been arranged for quite a long time. Your manager is very late telling you that you can't go Claire. Before I cancel the arrangements, are you sure you definitely cannot get the two weeks off?'

'Not unless I go out sick,' said Claire gloomily, feeling horribly guilty.

'Oh, don't do that, Claire, you know neither your father nor I approve of that sort of thing. You have to look after your job. Don't worry, we can re-arrange it for another time, Italy is not going anywhere. Obviously, Ben must be looked after, he comes first. We might see about going away for the August week only', said Eileen.

Her mother was so good. A stab of pure hatred for Ashley shoot through Claire. Eileen was extremely disappointed to hear that her plans for a dream holiday were dashed and for what reason? Claire could have worked up extra hours, when she was office based during the remainder of the month of September, to ensure all essential reports were completed. She had the ability to remotely work from home due to technology advances. If she were sick, they would have to cope without her. Ashley was using her power of decision making over the sanctioning of holidays as a controlling tool. It was a power tool which directly affected her subordinates' lives and relationships outside the organisation and in this instance, the manager had wielded it to negative effect.

Ashley was making Claire's life much more difficult than it needed to be. Deirdre had ordered her to find her sparkle; Claire felt like a Chrysanthemum firework ready to explode.

CHAPTER TWENTY TWO

The annual budgeting and reforecasting was the only higher level business reporting Claire was currently involved in and she was determined to guard it. Even though Daniel was away working on the ICT project most of the time, he was determined to keep control of the planning and budgeting processes within the company. The main budget figures were prepared annually and, once the senior management team approved the figures, they were cast in stone for the set period. The annual budgets anchored financial evaluations, while the reforecasting exercise amended the figures to take into consideration changed circumstances in the external environment or in the internal decision making priorities of senior management. If Finance got the budget figures wrong, it gradually became visible throughout the year to the report readers, since variances between budgets compared to actuals built up. Daniel had an instinctive feel for the company's numbers and it had been a long time since a material error in the company's budget had slipped by his eagle eye.

The Facilities department for a company the size of Leictreach had an annual budget of millions and it was Claire's job to estimate the proposed capital and current expenditure with the Facilities manager, incorporating new upcoming project costs. The Facilities manager, David Maguire, kept the buildings in a good state of repair and maintenance but he was an electrician by trade and he needed the input of somebody with business training to help him prepare a realistic annual budget. Claire had to work closely with him to build accurate figures into the budget, making it essential for her to push all her other work aside for a week, a fact she had flagged well in advance to Ashley. Claire assumed Ashley appreciated the importance heads of departments attached to budgets and she expected Ashley to leave her alone for the duration of the compilation process, if only for the greater good of the department's reputation. But Claire could not have been more wrong; she was not left in peace to concentrate on putting the budget together at all, in fact the opposite occurred. Ashley issued her with a flurry of dictates: -

'The fixed assets register has to be updated every day. New computers have been purchased for the SMU division and they have to be entered into the system right now'.

'The production statistics report for the Central Statistics office has to be in to them by the end of the week, otherwise it will be late. Do it now, it won't take long.'

'The stock levels in the MDI department are higher than normal. Give them a ring and find out what is going on over there.'

'Since Anna is out sick today, I want you to update the bank reconciliation. We can't let it slip,' instructed Ashley.

Although Anna had no formal accountancy training, she was intelligent and highly skilled in reconciliation work through years of experience. Ashley knew full well that the bank reconciliation in a company the size of Leictreach was a humdinger of a job and that a person needed to be familiar with it to get it completed in a reasonable time. It was unbelievable, the way the list of queries and requests went on and on. At the beginning of the week Claire tried to facilitate some of Ashley's requests, but she quickly realised that if she capitulated to the bulk of them, she would never get near the budgeting. She did not want to refuse Ashley's instructions outright but could commit to doing them only after the budgeting was completed, much to Ashley's displeasure. Claire's nerves were stretched to breaking point, as she came around to believing that Ashley was trying to sabotage her work on the budget. The budgets were part of Daniel's remit in Leictreach, not Ashley's, and she did not give a monkey's curse about them being done, since they had no impact on her own performance appraisal. However, budgets were very important to Daniel and it certainly appeared to Claire that Ashley was intent on making her appear incapable, inefficient and unreliable to him.

'I can't do it this week Ashley, I have to concentrate on the budgeting. The deadline is Friday and everything else will have to wait. I'll turn my attention to your requests next week, no problem, but I simply have not the time this week', said Claire, anxious to be let alone.

'The world does not stop because you have budgeting to do Claire, you have not the luxury of only doing one thing. You have other responsibilities as well. You are expected to have the ability to multi- task', said Ashley.

'I'm employed as a business analyst Ashley, and right now I am estimating and analysing the budget figures, If you have a problem with that, take it up with Daniel', retorted Claire, at the end of her tether.

A disdainful smile briefly appeared on Ashley's narrow face.

'I will certainly bring your obdurate attitude to Daniel's attention and when

I do, remember, it was your idea', retorted Ashley.

Claire watched her leave with trepidation, knowing that more trouble was to follow. Sure enough, about ten minutes after the conversation with Ashley, Claire took a phone call from the big boss himself.

'Ashley tells me that you are having difficulty handling all your work responsibilities. The budgeting is too important to take chances with Claire. It has to be completed by Friday of this week. We are a multinational company and we have no flexibility with deadlines. Do you want me to take it away from you or can you handle it?' queried Daniel, getting straight to the point.

Claire had an eerie sense that her career in Leictreach was on the line.

'I can handle it Daniel', replied Claire vehemently. 'I have the bulk of the work done. I just need to be allowed to concentrate on it for the next two days and to be able to put my other work aside until then. Can you please tell Ashley to let me prioritise the budgeting work over everything else until Friday?'

'Ashley already knows that the budgeting work takes priority over everything else this week. I need it completed and sent to me by 12pm on Friday Claire. All the departmental budgets have to be entered into the system this week, so I can get started on the sensitivity analysis. Do I have your word that the Facilities budget will be sent to me by the Friday deadline? '

'Yes Daniel, you do', asserted Claire firmly.

'Fine, I'll leave you to it then', said Daniel.

Claire felt upset as she put down the phone receiver. Ashley had complained about her to Daniel and now he wanted to take the most valued part of her job away from her. She might as well call herself an accounts clerk or data processor if they took the budgeting away from her. Daniel had completely missed the elephant in the room, which was that Ashley was prioritising everything but the budget as far as Claire was concerned. As financial controller, Daniel assumed that all the divisional managers in the company understood the importance of formulating a reliable budget in a timely manner. It was actually beyond his comprehension that one of his trusted managers in Finance could intentionally sabotage part of his prized budget, out of nothing but sheer spite for the unfortunate person charged with drawing it up.

Claire's phone rang again.

'Claire have you completed the analysis of the canteen costs? We have to make a decision on whether or not we should increase its subsidy,' Ashley's shrill voice assaulted Claire's ears again. Not content with landing Claire in hot water with Daniel, the malevolent woman had returned to taunt and tease, relishing her ability to make life uncomfortable for the underling.

'Daniel told me to prioritise the budgeting till Friday, everything else has to be put on the back boiler. I'm glad the issue has been clarified. I'll get back to you about the canteen costings next week. I'm sure you understand,', said Claire sweetly, hanging up. She was going to put her phone on voicemail and, if necessary, barricade the door. The sight and sound of Ashley was stomach churning.

Claire possessed her own determined streak and she worked like a demon to piece together a credible budget in the limited time available to her. She was not finished by departure time Thursday evening but she emailed the files to herself, thanking God she had excellent broadband internet connection at home. She intended to work late into the night to complete the budget, after she put Ben to bed. She tucked the documents she needed as reference points for the budgeting into her bag, realising guiltily she was glad Anna was not there to see her do it. She might as well resign her job tomorrow if she missed the deadline, as her credibility with Daniel would be shot to pieces.

Anna had been out sick from work all week and it had been brilliant timing for Claire; it meant the office was quiet and she had space to spread her folders out on Anna's desk as well as her own, which was helpful for finding documents quickly. Claire did not wish Anna ill because she did like her and her heart was in the right place. The woman was draining to deal with sometimes, due to her constant chatter and negative commentary about people and operations in Leictreach. It also came back to the fact that the office was too small to accommodate two people at work comfortably. For now, Claire had to get to her parent's house as quickly as possible and spend time with Ben before sending him off to bed early. She had lots of work to do as soon as he fell asleep.

Her mother's welcoming words as she entered the house caught her like a blow.

'I'm glad you're home dear, Ben's been waiting for you. The little dear is not feeling himself at all and he only picked at his food. I'm afraid he's coming down with something, the poor child'.

Ben was sitting quietly on the sofa, watching one of his favourite programmes on the television. He turned big, tearful eyes towards Claire, but did not get up to run and greet her as was his custom.

'I'm not feeling well Mommy. My tummy hurts', he said.

Claire went over to him and hugged him tightly.

'I'm sorry to hear that you're feeling bad, darling. We'll get you home and take it easy. Hopefully you'll feel better in a little time', she said gently.

Claire was more than sorry to hear that her little boy was feeling sick, she secretly felt panicked about it. What lousy timing, she had so much work to do that she simply could not get through it all and meet Daniel's mid day deadline for the budget tomorrow if she was up all night tending to Ben, instead of sweating over her computer. Could Claire ask her parents to let Ben stay at their house tonight and watch over him for her? They could ring her if Ben got worse and she would come around straight away. She could not stay the night in their house because they did not have high speed broadband connection. Nearly as soon as the idea came to her, she shook it away. No, she could not ask Tom and Eileen to look after Ben while she slunk away into the night. Eileen would be appalled that Claire was putting work (which should have been completed in good time at the office) ahead of her sick child and be tempted to label her that most dreadful of things, an uncaring mother. Her parents were not getting any younger either, they needed their sleep, especially after minding Ben all day. She must calm down and hope for the best, which was that there was nothing much wrong with her child that a good night's sleep could not cure.

When they got home, Claire tried to be a good mother and concentrated all her attention on Ben, determined to push all thoughts of the budgeting to the back of her mind until she got him to bed. She gave him two spoonfuls of medicine but it took her ages to get him settled in bed. She read him a bedtime story and then he wanted to be hugged tightly in bed until he fell asleep in her arms.

'I don't want you to go Mommy, stay with me all night, please', he entreated.

Claire lay down beside Ben on the bed and stroked his hair until he fell into a restless sleep. It was as if subliminally the child knew that part of Claire was anxious to be away from him, although he did not know the reason why, and he clung to her all the more fiercely, fighting sleep until he could not keep his eyes open no longer. At 10.40 pm she was able to move cautiously off his bed and tiptoe quietly downstairs to put on the computer. She held her breath as the internet made the connection to her files. She had so much work to do, it wasn't funny.

Three quarters of an hour later, when Claire was getting into the detail of her budgeting plan, she heard Ben cry out urgently for her.

'Mommy I'm sick. Mommy, come here, I'm sick.'

Claire rushed upstairs and put on the light in Ben's bedroom. The child was standing beside his bed and he was all big eyes and trembles, drenched with the vomit he had forcefully spewed over his pyjamas, the floor, the bedclothes and pillow. His skin was as white as a starched sheet.

'Look, Mommy, sick', said the little boy pointing to the mess surrounding him, looking too shocked for tears.

'It's alright, my baby, it's going to be alright. Mommy will make it better. Don't worry my love, we'll fix everything up and it will all be fine.'

Claire swept the child up into her arms and carried him into the bathroom, where she quickly stripped the offending pyjamas off him, wiping him down with a warm, damp towel. She swaddled him in another large dry towel and felt his frame quiver under her gentle hands. He felt small and fragile without his clothes on. How could any adult ever hurt a helpless child? It was wicked beyond forgiveness. Claire quickly pulled out clean underwear and pyjamas from the chest of drawers and dressed Ben in them. She was relieved when Ben began to sob loudly because she knew from bitter experience that when Ben was seriously ill with a high temperature, he became silent and doll like, passive and non protesting.

With difficulty, Claire carried the child downstairs into the sitting room and placed him on the sofa, all the time murmuring words of comfort. Her speech reverted to the words and tones she had used to soothe him with when he was a toddler.

'You've had a fright but you will be all better soon, my darling. Ben is such a good boy, Ben is the best boy in the whole world. Rest now angel, everything is alright, everything can be fixed', she crooned.

Ben's tense body gradually began to relax and calm. She got out the digital thermometer to take his temperature and was heartened to see it read 101°F, higher than normal but manageable. He was such an active boy that when he got sick it took a few days of quietness for him to fully recover his energy levels. Claire dipped a folded face cloth into a bowl of tepid water and pressed it onto his forehead and to the back of his neck. She gave him more medicine once four hours had elapsed after the previous dosage.

'Sing me a song Mommy, sing me *Daisy, Daisy*', Ben murmured.

Claire sang every song in their repertoire before falling silent. Ben clung close to her, his eyelids fluttering down over his brilliant blue eyes. Claire could see the effect of the medicine kick in and Ben's rapid breathing slowed down, allowing him to rest. After two hours had elapsed, his temperature thankfully fell below the hundred Fahrenheit mark. Claire considered it safe to leave the sleeping child alone on the sofa while she went upstairs to change the sheets and duvet on his bed. She scrubbed out the vomit droppings on the carpet beside his bed as well. She came back downstairs to the sitting room and touched his forehead with her hand, relieved that it felt more normal and his breathing was easier. She carried him upstairs, step by careful step, anxious not to drop him or bang his body against the banister, praying he would not wake up. He instinctively flung his arms around her shoulders, which was a help, but she still had to brace the whole strength in her body to carry him upstairs to his bed, without either of them coming to harm. She placed the bed clothes loosely around him and kissed his cheek.

'I love you, Ben darling', Claire whispered as she looked down at her small child, still so dependent on her to meet his basic needs. 'You are everything to me.'

Which was just as well, she thought wryly, because caring for him that night meant that she might not complete her project on time, jeopardising her career in Leictreach. So be it. What else could she do? She felt upset and guilty that her focus earlier on in the evening was on getting Ben into bed as early as possible rather than gauging if he was well enough to leave alone. Her innocent boy should not be negatively affected by her problems at work. She could not recall her own father ever bringing any work home with him. It had been his habit to arrive home, change out of his work clothes and go into the garden for half an hour to unwind before dinner, rarely talking about anything that happened at work unless he had a funny story to share. Tom had always appeared to be unfazed by his job, although he certainly had put in long, hard hours when the occasion demanded. When Claire left Leictreach that evening, she had been thankful that technology gave her the ability to access her files, enabling her to work from home. She wondered how many people found that the lines between work and home life had become too blurred, with professionals slaving away the hours at home, boosting the productivity and profitability of the company but taking away from the quality of family life.

Claire went into the kitchen to make herself a much needed cup of coffee and a toasted ham and cheese sandwich. She knew she was going to have to work right through the long night, in order to keep her promise to Daniel. He was finished with her if she let him down. 'Please God, let Ben recover and sleep through the night so I can get the budget done. I have to get it done', she prayed, stretching her aching shoulders. Claire was not in the habit of regularly praying to God but in times of true need she did call upon the Almighty for assistance. She was not her mother's daughter for nothing.

Somebody up there must have heard her prayers because Ben remained asleep, allowing Claire to work frantically through the reminder of the night, racing against the clock. At precisely 6.30am she saved the completed facilities budget to the shared drive and for good measure she emailed it to herself. A wave of relief and satisfaction washed over her. Some people climbed mountains for fun, other people had to make deadlines for survival in the workplace. Claire knew that she had risen to meet a challenge in trying circumstances, but her efforts would not merit praise. There was only hell to pay if she had not delivered on time.

Claire went upstairs to check on Ben and was pleased to discover that his temperature had fallen back to normal. Ben must have picked up one of those twenty four hour bugs that children specialise in catching to inconvenience their parents. She had a rejuvenating hot shower and dressed in a business suit, feeling much better. Claire re-entered Ben's bedroom, urging him in soft tones to wake up. There was no need for him to get dressed, she was going to wrap him in a blanket and pop him in the car. He was going to stay with his grandparents and have the day off school. She had a bag with his clothes and toys all packed for him.

'Don't go to work today Mommy. I need you. I don't want you to go. I want us to stay here,' said Ben, tears welling up in his eyes.

'I know baby. I have to go to work but I promise you, I'll be home early today'.

'Don't go Mommy, say you're sick. You look sad,' he entreated.

Claire thought she had better lash on the makeup, she was exhausted after the all nighter she had pulled. No wonder high achievers were reputed to snort cocaine to stay awake and pump up the adrenaline.

'I'm only going in for a short time Ben. You will have a lovely time today watching all your favourite programmes with Granddad. It's Friday, so we will have the weekend together. As a special treat we will go to the cinema tomorrow'.

The promise of a trip to the cinema worked its magic and Ben immediately brightened up.

If only life stayed that simple, mused Claire as she drove Ben to her parents' house in Raheny. The budgeting was the only piece of work Claire much cared about in her current job. She intended to make sure Daniel knew she had completed the Facilities budget, on time as agreed, and it was ready for his attention. Then she was going home because she desperately needed rest. If Ashley insisted on having a sick certificate for her records, then she would get her one, but it would be for more than one day off work. There was nothing urgent or interesting to do at work for the foreseeable future and a week at home would do her the world of good. It might help her gain a new perspective about what was happening in Leictreach. A person could work to live or live to work. She was living for work at the moment, but it was not worth it unless her salary and career prospects improved considerably. Maybe it was worth it only if you truly loved your job.

Eileen hugged Ben in the manner of a mother hen gathering up her chick to tuck under her wing.

'My little Ben is not well? You poor child, come to Granny......you will have anything you want today, anything at all'.

Eileen scanned her daughter's face searchingly.

'Gracious Claire, you look terrible child. You must have picked up the same bug Ben has. Come in and go to bed and I'll ring them at work to let them know you are not coming in today', suggested Eileen concerned.

'I have to go in to finish something off Mam, but then I will come home as soon as I can to rest. There is nothing wrong with me that a few hours in bed won't cure', said Claire wryly. She must look like she was at death's door for Eileen to suggest that she should skip a day's labour.

When Claire arrived into her office, she accessed the budget files from the shared drive and emailed them to Daniel. For good measure she left a voicemail on his phone, telling him the file was saved, sent and ready for him to review. She breathed a sigh of relief, her project was complete and she was running on empty. Claire did not care about any of the work Ashley was screaming for, none of it was really important and could easily be put aside for a few days. She knocked on Ashley's door.

'I'm going home Ashley, I don't feel well', she said.

Ashley looked at her suspiciously.

'But you've just come in. You look fine to me. Taking a Friday off work is getting to be quite the habit with you.'

'I hardly think my taking two days sick leave in two years working for the company constitutes a habit. I am not feeling well and I intend to go and see the doctor. If she writes me a sick cert, I will send it to you,' Claire retorted with spirit.

'There is a lot of work to be done here and you are behind schedule. It took you forever to do the budgeting, you made it a mountain out of a mole hole. You may as well come back as soon as you can, because nobody is going to do your work for you while you are away', said Ashley nastily.

'Thank you for your concern. I will let you know the date of my return to work, as per the doctor's instruction', replied Claire distantly, leaving the room with dignity.

Did Ashley ever consider there was something wrong with the targets and schedules she set? She was such a bad manager, it was unreal. When Claire returned to her office, she spotted a new email from Ashley in her Inbox. Even though Claire told herself to leave it alone and just go, that no good would come out of reading it, she opened it out of a sense of morbid curiosity.

Claire,

Please send in any medical sick certificates you may receive, marked for the attention of Karen Woods, from this date onwards.

Regards,
Ashley

Claire bit her lip in fiery indignation. Like most of Ashley's emails to Claire, an unknowing outsider could read it and not spot the inevitable sting in its tail. Up to this point Claire and Karen had been placed on the same horizontal rung of the ladder in the finance department. The instruction for her to send sick certificates directly to Karen Woods simultaneously put Karen in a supervisory position over Claire and pushed Claire one step down in the organisational chart's chain of command.

'Did Daniel know about Ashley's attempt to elevate Karen above Claire in the department's hierarchy of command? Had he sanctioned it?', mused a wounded Claire.

Ashley could take a flying leap. Claire had no inclination to report into Karen Woods, "she who had failed her accountancy exams a zillion times before passing them". She would not accept being demoted by stealth, even if it had the advantage of getting her away from the poisonous Ashley. Claire made up her mind that she would not follow Ashley's implicit instruction to report to Karen, unless Daniel told her she had to do it.

Claire shut down her computer, put on her coat and grabbed her bag. She was not going to dignify the latest email with a response today, she was too tired and upset and she needed to think through the phraseology of her reply. She felt her stomach lurch and she raced into the ladies restroom, diving into a cubicle just in time to vomit unceremoniously down the inside bowl of the white porcelain toilet. The vomit seemed to pour out from every cell in her body, foul smelling and putrid, culminating in an eruption of her throat, mouth and nose, not able to stop. When her muscles finally squeezed out the last drip of bile from her stomach, Claire slumped down holding her head limply in her hands, supporting her back against the side of the toilet. She was a spent force. She heaved in huge breaths, knowing she had to put her energy back together again and get her the hell out of here before the others came in to use the restroom during the morning coffee break. She did not want anybody to see her in such a weakened, vulnerable state. Claire blew her nose vigorously, spat and wiped her mouth with tissue and then forced herself to stand upright.

Before she knew it, her body was gathering speed and momentum and she was able to walk out of the building with a steady step. Her mind was amazed at the ability of parts of the human body to function normally while under duress. Another rational part of her brain recognised that what was happening to her was not good, that mental stress coupled with exhaustion was making her physically ill. A sick mother was no good to her child. She had to go to the doctor and she was going to ask for a sick certificate to cover her for the full week off work. Claire was going to ignore Ashley's instruction for her to send the sick cert to Karen and instead forward it on to Ashley herself, because she was the person who held the official supervisory post. There was a possibility that Ashley's own mother loved her but Claire doubted she could actually like her daughter, given she was such a deliberate, malicious bitch.

CHAPTER TWENTY THREE

The doctor was concerned about Claire's well being and gave her a sick certificate stating that she was 'Unfit for Work' for a week, giving the employer no further details of her patient's complaint.

'I understand that you are exhausted. We are not machines. It is not easy for a single parent to juggle child care with a full time job. Between you and me, there is a stream of burnt out people coming in my door, completely stressed out because they have to deal with an unreasonable boss. There definitely seems to be a particular problem with female managers, although I can't say why. I just know it is a problem which is making people sick', said the doctor.

She prescribed rest, vitamins and gentle exercise for Claire, as well as giving her the name of a recommended counsellor.

'If you begin to feel seriously depressed and are not able to throw off the sensation come back to see me again and we will reassess the medication you might need. I'm reluctant to prescribe anti-depressants for the moment, they can be difficult to come off. Please consider the counselling option,' advised the doctor.

'How much does a counselling session cost?' enquired Claire.

'About €70 per hourly session. You might only need to attend a few though before you start to feel better'.

€70 a session for talking about her problems! Claire could buy Ben a new pair of shoes for that amount of money. She had heard that counsellors listen to the service user (they are not called patients anymore) but did not advise on the best course of action to take. It could take hours to analyse and understand where her relationship with Ashley went drastically wrong and what was the point of paying over a fortune of money for that? What was done, was done. If it came to it, she would prefer to take the drugs, at least that way she could claim money back from the drug refund scheme.

Claire had no intention of either taking drugs or attending a counsellor. There were countless people dealing with difficult situations by staying healthy and chatting to friends and family and that was the route she preferred to follow. She took it easy for the whole week, revelling in the extra time she got to spend with Ben, and felt refreshed when she went back to the office on the Monday. She was surprised to discover that Anna had not returned to work during her absence, meaning there must be something seriously wrong with her after all. Blast, she had meant to make contact with her before now, but the thought kept going out of her head.

'Sorry U sick. What's wrong? I was out sick for week too. Claire', she texted Anna. There was no answering bleep back, which was unusual as Anna lived with her mobile phone attached to her hip.

The phone did ring but it was Ashley, not Anna, on the other end of the line.

'So, you're back. I have meetings all morning. I have sent you a list of the jobs that are outstanding from last week. Get working on them. I have a meeting scheduled for 2pm but I can meet up with you afterwards to review your progress', directed Ashley.

At least that gave Claire time to settle down to her tasks in peace and she was gratified by the amount she was able to tick off her 'Items To Do' list before her meeting with Ashley. There were times when Claire impressed herself with the volume of work she was able to produce in a given time frame, but she would be waiting till hell froze over before Ashley acknowledged it. Later on in the afternoon, it was all she could do to refrain from rolling her eyes in her head as she watched Ashley silently flick through the pages she had handed over to her.

'You are unlikely to meet your targets this month Claire. You must improve your performance level'.

'Your schedule did not factor in time for the budgeting process Ashley. It also did not take account of the fact that I was out of the office being sick for the week. Once those two factors are considered in, my output for the month is more than fine', Claire defended herself, irritated by Ashley's unrelenting negativity towards her.

'It certainly is not', snapped Ashley. 'A junior from an agency could do more. There is another matter I want to talk to you about. It is about the fixed asset register. When we go live on the new IT system, I want you to register every component listed separately on the invoice as an individual asset.'

Claire looked at Ashley as if she had gone mad.

'But that means that instead of one computer registered as one asset, it will have to be broken up and registered separately as a monitor, workstation, cables etc. There is no added value to the method you are proposing. It will take forever, I won't be able to do any other work,' protested Claire.

'Of course you will Claire', said Ashley, with a dismissive wave of her hand.

'A company the size of Leictreach purchases large quantities of computers and laptops every year. What you are proposing will significantly increase the time required to register the asset on the system. You are asking me to go way beyond the level of input required of previous administrators of the fixed assets register, for no good reason.'

'We are introducing a new IT system, naturally things will be done differently from before,' said Ashley primly.

'The costs involved in breaking one whole asset up into its constituent parts for processing in the system far outweighs any benefits Ashley. I cannot agree to process the assets in such a nonsensical manner,' said Claire, aghast at the proposal.

'We will see about that. You may go Claire', said Ashley unfazed.

Back in her own office, Claire immediately put a call through to Katherine, the girl in the ICT department who would have to generate the purchase order requests on the system when it went live. It was obviously Ashley's intention to multiply the work involved in the administration of the fixed asset register and to box Claire into this role. Claire needed allies outside the department to win this battle. Katherine snorted in disbelief when Claire told her that if Ashley had her way, she would probably have to issue at least four POs for every computer which was purchased.

'Separate out a monitor from the hard drive and keyboard? Get out of here, the woman is mad. Does she have any idea of how busy we are down here? Can't be done, simple as that. Ken will have no problem setting her to rights on that one.' Ken was head of the ICT department.

Claire wanted to hug Katherine.

'Can you or Ken email Ashley to that effect, and copy Daniel on the email?'

'I'll do it, no problem. I'll copy you on it too. I'll do it straight away before it goes out of my head. Don't worry about it Claire, it won't happen. I don't know how you work for Ashley, I couldn't do it. I heard she was difficult, but I never figured her out to be stupid,' said Katherine.

Claire would have liked to attribute Ashley's actions to stupidity, because that made them more excusable. Unfortunately, Claire had a healthy respect for Ashley's intellect and guessed that her actions were not powered by foolhardiness but by an intention to sabotage Claire's career development in Leictreach. Ashley drove along efficiency and performance measures with the team players she favoured, winning kudos with Daniel along the way. When she wanted rid of somebody, she was more than willing to sacrifice what was considered to be good practice in the department, in favour of pushing the undesirable minion out through the door.

The emails went flying between Ashley, Claire and Katherine about the proposed changes to the registration of the fixed assets, with Daniel copied on them all. It was apparent to the most disinterested onlooker that war had been openly declared between Ashley and Claire.

Ashley dropped into Claire's office for an intimate one to one chat, facilitated by the fact that Anna was still out of the office on sick leave.

'You do not appear happy with your position here in Leictreach Claire', Ashley observed coolly. 'Everything I ask you to do is a problem. There are hundreds of well qualified people in this city who would be more than happy to have your job. I am not telling you to go but, for your own good, if you can't stand the heat, then get out of the kitchen. We don't want you to leave but perhaps it is time for you to consider a better use of your talents, one which you will find more fulfilling'.

Claire had been more than happy with her job in Leictreach until Ashley had joined the company and been appointed her manager.

'We don't want you to leave' What a lie.

Claire knew that Ashley was fully capable of lying without blushing or batting an eyelid. At least there was much more truth in the **'get out of the kitchen'** line. Ashley was careful to be pleasant and polite to Daniel and he might not believe Claire if she went to him and reported what Ashley had said to her in the privacy of the office. He was definitely reluctant to override any of Ashley's decisions. If Claire reported Ashley's threatening comments to Human Resources, she was likely to deny the charge. In a non-unionised workplace and with limited funds it was difficult for Claire to know who she could turn to for help. No wonder she was upset and needed countless cups of coffee to help her function during the day. It was miraculous she was able to stay away from pill popping.

Since the emails regarding the most recent dispute between herself and Ashley had been copied to Daniel, Claire was not too surprised to see Daniel standing framed in her doorway, the next time he happened to be based in his old office for the day.

'What is all this nonsense going on between you and Ashley?' he asked.

Claire noticed how tired and harassed he looked. She wondered how much she should say to him about the problems she was having in dealing with Ashley.

'Ashley wants me to register each of the component parts making up a PC as a separate asset on the new system. I can't do it Daniel', Claire explained.

'Do what has always been done Claire, register one computer as one asset. It is not rocket science. I'm too busy for this', Daniel snapped at her. Claire was taken aback by his curtness, as he was usually calm and measured in what he said and how he said it. He did not enter her office, but instead looked across at her in puzzlement from the doorway.

'Could I have been wrong about you? Three people can't be wrong', he muttered, more to himself than to Claire. With those words, he vanished quickly away.

Claire gasped in hurt disbelief at the empty space in the doorway. If her hearing served her right, Daniel was placing the blame for the dissension which had arisen on her shoulders, instead of identifying Ashley as the main culprit. Ashley was the person who had proposed the unnecessary, time wasting changes in registering the fixed assets, leaving Claire with no option but to fight back against its imposition. It was a good thing that Daniel had instructed Claire to ditch Ashley's proposal. It was a bad thing that he failed to understand that the blame for the discord lay with Ashley and not Claire.

Daniel's comment of *'three people can't be wrong'* bit deeply into Claire. Obviously three people had complained about her. Who were these three people? Ashley could safely be placed at the head of the queue, followed by the mysterious individual who had made malicious complaints to Daniel by falsely alleging that Claire was criticising her colleagues in Finance to people outside of the department. But who was the third person lurking in the shadows?

Claire realised that Daniel was an accountant by nature and training and he did not like it when his numbers did not balance up. He was a numbers person, not a people's person. He did not like people to rock the boat. He did not know or understand about groups forming in his department under his nose, he was too busy trying to make sense of technical, complicated spreadsheets.

'Three people can't be wrong'

How those words stung! But three people banded together could be wrong if they all thought and acted as one. There was a group dynamic operating here and Claire was standing apart from the group herd. One group was pitting itself against one person. Yes, in such circumstances, three people could be wrong and the solitary individual right.

Claire acknowledged that she was at war, with her opponent growing in strength and numbers. She had won a point against Ashley today, when Daniel had struck down the proposed change in registering the fixed assets but she had lost the main battle of keeping Daniel onside. The opposing troops were advancing. It might seem crazy to be thinking in terms of battle when there was no blood or guts or death involved but Claire was heavily invested in a series of fights, trying to preserve her sense of dignity, integrity, worthiness and personal perspective of a world filled with essentially good people, not bad. She faced bleakly into an uncomfortable truth, which was that one person on his own never won the war.

Claire definitely needed more allies. By chance, she fell into step and conversation with Elaine Higgins, a middle ranking human resource executive assistant with Leictreach, on her way to the train station that evening. Elaine informed her she was finishing up in the company at the end of the month to join her fiancé Josh in Sidney. After two years living on different continents it was time for them to either live together properly in the same country or break up their relationship.

'Can I ask you something off the record Elaine, seeing that you are leaving the company? I promise I won't repeat what you say to anybody,' asked Claire. Elaine hesitated, before nodding her head, her brown eyes wary.

'My manager Ashley Scanlon is bullying me. I'm having a terrible time with her. Without going into specifics, if I went ahead and lodged a bullying complaint against her with HR, what are the chances of my getting a fair hearing and the complaint being upheld against her?'

'Off the record? Promise not to quote me to anybody? I might want to come back and work here again one day. Never say, never,' said Elaine.

'Off the record, I swear,' confirmed Claire.

'Honestly, I cannot advise it Claire. If the complaint is a serious one and alleges a sustained pattern of bullying behaviour, the Dignity At Work complaint policy will be set in motion. This will involve bringing in an independent investigator who will speak to you and Ashley separately, with a person from HR keeping a written record of the meetings. Witnesses will be called in and they will have to sign their names to statements they make. These will be seen and read by both you and Ashley,' explained Elaine.

'Therefore, if anybody says anything negative about Ashley, she will be able to read it and trace it back to the individual witness? But that is no good, people will be afraid of saying anything negative about her because they report into her and she can turn around and make their lives a misery. They will be next on her hit list', said Claire, dismayed.

'That consideration is overwritten by a person's right to know what is being said about them and to be allowed to respond and make rebuttal in defence of their own good name. But you are right, most people keep their mouths shut rather than risk jeopardising their relationship with management. They know there is a high probability that the person making the complaint will leave the company and the manager will remain. Witnesses are not sent off to a different department while the investigation is going on, they have to remain working within their own department and therefore continue to have routine dealings with the manager in place. Usually the person making the complaint against management goes on sick leave during the dispute but this requires sign off from a doctor. Sometimes the complainant leaves the employ of the company after management agrees to give them a settlement, which varies in size depending on who and what is involved. Settlements used to be typically twice salary but nowadays a person is doing very well to get a settlement worth one and a half times salary. If management play hardball, the process can take years. Often a person is dismayed by the time it takes to settle the dispute and he or she may decide to leave the company without any payoff, preferring to have a fresh start in a new organisation, for mental health wellness reasons.'

'Is the independent investigator really independent, given his services are paid for by the company?' asked Claire.

'Hard to say, it depends on the individual. Some people doing it are not that interested in the rights or wrongs of the case, they are in the game to be paid. The Human Resource department supports managers in the organisation, its core purpose is there in the title. The HR representative taking notes is therefore normally on the side of management and can put a spin on the witness statements. The HR notetaker is a spy in the camp for the HR department to monitor proceedings and gather information about the case which they can use to protect the organisation, if need be, against claims or reputational damage at a future date. The spin can come from something as simple as including one half of a sentence in the written statement but omitting the second half, which can change the meaning or context of the original statement, for example, if the witness statement records that X behaved in a very controlled manner but omits to mention Y's reaction it is likely the reader can erroneously infer that Y's manner was less controlled than Xs. Most people don't spot the nuances. If management support Ashley, any adverse findings by the investigator will be brushed aside and excused.'

'You cannot be serious?' Claire was aghast.

'It is very difficult to win against the company Claire. There is a whole management team behind any one manager. When push comes to shove, HR will always support the management team. If Daniel as financial controller supports Ashley, he in turn will be supported by the finance director. The finance director is tightly connected to the CEO and the HR director is there to serve the wishes of the CEO and the senior management team. People in Finance are linked in closely to the top management tier and you will be taking them all on. It is not just you going up against Ashley, one against one, it does not work like that. They can easily string it along for two years and more, if they want to.'

'It can't take that long, the stress level of the person being bullied will go through the roof. Bear in mind that people have to earn a living,' said Claire disbelieving.

'A two year time span is not only possible but probable, especially if management want to quash the issues raised. Then there is the question of whether it turns into an industrial relation issue as opposed to a bullying complaint. If one person only is affected, then it could be bullying, if a group of people are affected then it becomes an IR issue, a collective grievance. The list goes on and on. It is all about people's perception. You are a professional in a two person dispute, working in a non-unionised workforce, hence the unionised WRC industrial relations mechanism does not suit you. Even if it did, it has a backlog of cases to get through before it gets anywhere near your individual case. If you choose to go the legal route, you need your own solicitor, who will start talking about junior and senior counsel to represent you in court. You need deep pockets to employ their services. If you go down the legal route, you must be sure you will win. That's very important. Ashley will not have to worry about funding her own legal defence, because the management team will act collectively in defending the company's reputation. Claire, you must understand that if Daniel decides to support Ashley then it is game over, the whole management team will row in behind him and, by default, her. You are either with management or against them. While the dispute is going on, it will consume your life. You have to be sure it is worthwhile going down that route. What happens if you spend all that money, time and worry and still end up losing? Look, I have to turn left here, I can see my bus approaching. Remember, we agreed that you won't say a word to anybody about this conversation?' said Eileen, anxious to hear Claire's promise.

'Not a word', agreed Claire, thoroughly shaken by the forthright frankness of Elaine's response. In normal circumstances, Elaine would have been discreetly noncommittal, but she had resigned her post to emigrate and she instinctively liked Claire and wished her well. Although the bullying policy and procedures were in place in the company and proudly displayed on the intranet as a model for best practice to maintain the dignity of staff, Elaine had warned her that it was not a fair fight. The system was rigged in management's favour, making it unlikely for the complainant to succeed in an action pitted against a manager. It appeared there was not a word she could say to HR about the bullying she was experiencing in Finance, without bringing the might of the whole establishment down on her shoulders. Claire had to either find another way to fight Ashley within Leictreach or find herself another job in a different company. To fight or to retreat? That was the question which tormented Claire every day, because although she was desperate to ditch Ashley as her manager, she was not mentally prepared to leave Leictreach. Claire wanted to leave the manager, not the company.

CHAPTER TWENTY FOUR

Claire was mulling over her difficulties with Ashley and Daniel, without any hope of recourse to HR, when she decided to get herself a comforting cup of coffee in the canteen to help her mood and concentration level. How could Daniel fail to realise that the atmosphere in the department had been much better before Ashley's arrival? She was totally bemused by his inability to identify Ashley as the root cause of the discord which was spreading throughout the finance department. She spotted Deirdre sitting down alone at a table and went over to join her.

'What's up with you Claire? Is it Ashley again?' the older lady eyed her shrewdly.

'Who else? We cannot stand to look at each other, let alone work together. But it is getting worse. Daniel is siding with her against me', Claire confided.

'For all his faults, Daniel is not a devious man and he is blind to Ashley's mischief making. She had better watch out though. Daniel has a mild demeanour, but his star sign is scorpion. If his blindfold ever drops off, he has it in his nature to give her a deadly sting,' nodded Deirdre sagely.

Although Claire had always admired and respected Daniel, she too had sensed that he was not a man to cross.

'I can only hope', said Claire, letting out a wistful sigh. 'What can I do in the meantime?'

'Ashley is a bully and like all bullies you have to stand up to her'.

'I do try, but it isn't working. She has an answer for everything. How do you get her to stay away from you Deirdre? You report directly into her and she seems to leave you alone.'

'My mother was a bully. I come from a large family and two of my sisters are bullies as well. I grew up in a household of bullies and somewhere along the way I learnt to deal with them. I possess a withering tone of voice when I'm annoyed. I'm not above making a biting sarcastic remark, aimed at a person's Achilles heal, if I deem it necessary to put somebody in their place. I just know that I've been around bullies since I was a baby in a cradle and I'm not afraid of them. Ashley does not try to bully me, never has. As a result, she and I can work reasonably well together.'

'You must be the only person in the department able to say that about Ashley', said Claire.

'There are people Ashley cultivates a positive liaison with, Karen Woods being the obvious example. Karen smiles at everybody and says absolutely nothing and Ashley thinks she can mould her anyway she likes. I'm as tough as old boots and I recognise the same traits in Karen. She is from the North and for centuries the women there have had to hold their families together as their men went off to find work in the UK. The women fight tooth and nail to hold onto what they have. Ashley does not appreciate that Karen is as resilient and sturdy as a mountain goat.'

Claire gave a weak laugh.

'With hard hitting horns and hooves?'

'Exactly. But remember Claire, you have the ability to hit back as well. Tell Ashley to fuck off. Stand up for yourself.' Deirdre had such a cultured voice that she could make the words 'fuck off' sound as polite as saying 'it is time for you to leave now'.

'I can't tell her to fuck off Deirdre, I'd be reported and told to leave. We are professional women working in an office environment, not men talking the lingo on a building site. Part of me would love to say it to her but it would backfire badly on me.'

'She won't leave you alone until you stand up to her. Don't let yourself be bullied. Look her directly in the eye. If she is standing, get up on your feet too so she is not looking down on you. Pitch your voice low, throw your shoulders back and be confident. Keep notes on everything. You have a child Claire, defend yourself as if you were protecting him.'

'Thanks for the advice Deirdre, I'll do my best. You are kind', said Claire.

If only it was as easy as Deirdre suggested to stop a bully in her tracks. Claire had tried to stay away from Ashley and when that did not work, she had attempted to reason with her. She worked hard every day, completing her tasks as efficiently as anybody else in the department. It was difficult for her to know which way to turn.

Claire knew that lots of girls in the office had gone to see a particular fortune teller who was located in a room over a nearby pub and they had tittered excitedly after their visits. Uncertainty as to what was the best way forward propelled Claire irresistibly towards the premises of this highly regarded fortune teller during her lunch hour. The rain whirled around her, but the weather suited her despondent mood. How could she go home after work feeling all stressed out again, knowing Ben was sensitive to her mood ? His anxious eyes would follow her as he tried to make her laugh, give her a comforting hug or bring her something he thought might cheer her up. He was quieter in the house these days and she hated that, wanting her carefree, mischievous boy back. But Claire was finding it harder to shut off her negative feelings about work when she was at home.

'Cop on, grow up, be the adult here, be the parent', Claire chided herself.

There were times when being the sole parent to a small child weighed heavily on Claire's spirit. For six years she had no choice in the matter but, since Luke Elliott had reached out to her through Andrew, she wondered if she had done the right thing by refusing to allow him to be an active presence in their lives. Perhaps destiny had brought the promise of Luke's presence back into their lives because Ben needed his father to support him while his mother struggled to sort out the mess she was in? How dare that dishonest, upstart Ashley come into Claire's pleasant world and deliberately make it a misery? Ashley had been put in charge of staff because she was technically proficient and had excellent qualifications but nobody had carried out a personality test to assess her integrity or her managerial ability. Ashley should not have been left in charge of a monkey, let alone other people. Far better to have put her in a room by herself, with only a computer for company, and leave her there alone with her spreadsheets. The system used to appoint a person to a managerial position in a large organisation was nothing but a bad joke.

A bully will always bully more than one person over time, it was the nature of the beast. The ironic thing was that Ashley was oblivious to the fact that she was actually a bully, she considered friction to be always the fault of the other person. She probably credited herself with being a tough but fair manager who got the job done. Claire knew that Ashley had bullied Tracey, Anna and herself. There was sure to be others joining the list over time. In the meantime, Ashley was being clever enough to build up her own supporter base, making it more difficult for her luckless victims to pin down the bad behaviour and make her accountable for her bullying behaviour. Ashley's words flamed in Claire's ear.

'If you can't stand the heat, get out of the kitchen.'

The thought milled around Claire's head that all too often the perpetrator of the bullying remains on as an employee of the organisation while the person who suffers harm is forced out. Organisations had put the squeeze on employees during the recession, forcing wages and pension entitlements downwards, especially for new starters. The economy was growing strongly but wages had not recovered to the level they had been 'at prior to the financial crash. Collages were turning out thousands of business graduates every year and there was strong migration of labour into Ireland from Eastern Europe, enabling employers to draw on a huge pool of skilled workers. She could not throw in her job and walk away, swapping what was once a promising career for a place on the dole queue. She was not even sure if she would qualify for welfare payment supports if she voluntarily left her job. The only way she could leave Leictreach was if she had another position to go to.

Claire nearly tripped over a solid placard jutting out at a right angle from an open side door.

'Mystic Meg
Fortune Teller

Tarot Cards, Crystal Ball, Tea Leaves, Palm Reading.
€30 a session
All Welcome

Come On In.

Claire paused, she had never gone to a fortune teller before in her life, she came from a household which did not believe in them.

'Superstitious nonsense', Tom snorted when the topic was aired on television. 'If a person needs help let them take themselves to the local Church and pray to God for guidance. Hard work, perseverance and making the right choices in life is the secret to a happy life, not listening to the opportunistic ramblings of a gypsy.'

Claire could buy a substantial amount of groceries for the week for €30. A tiny voice in her head whispered, go on, be extravagant just this once, you don't have to tell anybody. Her dad had said that making the right choices in life leads to happiness and, given that Claire was mystified as to what constituted the best course of action, perhaps the Fortune Teller could point her in its direction. If she was able to do that, the money spent could turn out to be the bargain of the century. Once the decision was made, Claire raced up the stairs before she could change her mind, eager to hear what Mystic Meg had to say.

There were four wooden chairs lined up on the landing outside the door, all of them empty, probably because of the rain. Claire knocked on the door and was told to enter. Her first reaction was one of surprised disappointment because Mystic Meg looked anything but Mystic. She was a small, round woman in her fifties, with no makeup on her face and her grey hair was tied back in a neat bun. She wore a plain black top covered with a fawn coloured cardigan and a knee length brown cord skirt, thick tights and laced up black shoes. Mystic Meg smiled pleasantly and questioned Claire about the type of reading she preferred. Claire opted for the crystal ball as opposed to the tarot cards.

As she handed over the money, Claire doubted if the taxman would see a cent of it. It was possible that Mystic Meg did a roaring trade and could afford a palatial pad in the suburbs, far from her dingy room. Claire's heart thumped when Meg lifted up the heavy black cloth to reveal the enticing crystal ball. She tried to look sceptical but in truth she was nursing an inner hope that Mystic Meg possessed the rare gift of psychic power.

'You have a child, a little boy', Mystic Meg pronounced with great seriousness.

'Yes', said Claire relieved. She was not wearing a wedding ring, it was not obvious she had a child. Meg could have guessed wrongly that she had a little girl or indeed no child at all. So far, so good. Ben was such an intrinsic part of her life that if Mystic Meg had gotten that part of her story wrong, she might as well demand her money back and walk out of here.

'He is a beautiful boy, a fine boy and a source of great happiness to you. I see a broken relationship with the father. There is another dominant male figure, he is older and is a strong influence on your life.'

'Must be Dad', Claire thought to herself, trying not to blink. Mystic Meg was off to an impressive start.

'What about the father of my little boy? Should I see him again? Should I let him become part of our lives?' asked Claire desperately. Tell me what to do, Claire all but wanted to scream at the fortune teller.

'There is a fork in the road, with two lines going in different directions.

One line is shorter than the other. The decision is yours to make. Trust in yourself and you will make the right one', was Mystic Meg's unhelpful reply.

'You will have another relationship. Two very different men will ask to marry you at the same time and you are not sure which one to choose. Choose carefully, for only one is right for you. You will be very strong together and nothing will break you up. You will learn to love this man very much'.

That did not sound like Claire's relationship with Luke, given that her pregnancy and his wanderlust had already broken them up.

'Is there any chance of a good relationship with the father of my son?' she asked, holding her breath for the answer.

'It is difficult, it is not a perfect match but all things are possible. I would have to read his fortune to know. He is there, swirling in and out'.

Mystic Meg paused again and looked intently at the crystal ball.

'You will have two more children, a girl first and then a boy. There are also two children, not of your own, who you will be very close to. There is deep sadness but it also brings closeness. You will collect beautiful memories. Do not despair as I see you at the end of your days surrounded by people, with much happiness, peace and laughter. '

'How will I know which man to choose? What does he look like? What if I pick the wrong man?' The words burst out of Claire's mouth.

'That I cannot tell you, other than to say that he does not stand apart from the crowd. You must not overlook him for he is very important to your future happiness. He has beautiful eyes, your husband to be, and is a very hard worker,' Mystic Meg looked directly at Claire.

'You must work harder to gain happiness, it is within your reach but you have to work harder to win it.'

Mystic Meg looked down at the ball again.

'You are in conflict with somebody. Don't worry about it, it will pass. I see a great change coming to the organisation you work for'.

'Do I have a future in it?

'I don't see a future for anybody in it, there will be many job losses, it will shut down.   You are not to worry about it. You will have another job, a better job, and you will be successful in it. I see a career change for you but not for a few years, perhaps something to do with more learning'.

'Treat your parents well. I see that one of your parents will become ill. Make sure you take care of them, they are good people.'

Mystic Meg looked up and smiled pleasantly.

'That is enough. You have many talents. Remember, happiness does not appear by itself, you must put more effort into being happy and all will be well.'

They shook hands and Claire felt her hand tingle as she exited the building. The rain had stopped in the time Claire had been inside conversing with Mystic Meg. What else had changed? Claire was suddenly furious with herself for having gone in to see the woman.

'People at work are knifing each other in the back to get a step ahead in an organisation which is going to be shutting up shop anyway, in all likelihood transferring its business to Eastern Europe. No advice on what to do about Luke. I've just been told that the easiest thing in the world for me would be to overlook the one man who could bring me happiness, that he is buried in a crowd. Great, bloody great. All I have to do is make the right choice. I've done a hunky dory job of that so far, haven't I? One of my parents will get sick. Wonderful, just wonderful! Maybe all I have to do is to spend a fortune finding a fortune teller who won't scare the living daylights out of me'.

She had been the bigger fool for going to see the fortune teller in the first place and she should have spent her hard earned money on a therapist, all ready to cite her positive reinforcements and mindfulness theory instead of listening to Mystic Megs half baked prophecies. Mystic Meg would drive her half mad if she paid too much heed to what she said. In future Claire would take her parents advice and stay away from a fortune teller's superstitious ramblings.

CHAPTER TWENTY FIVE

Claire stepped out for a walk around the block at lunch time and came across a young salesman called Tony Dempsey, looking the worst for wear. They had grown up in the same locality and she knew him well enough to have a friendly conversation with him.

'Rough night Tony?' she said with a grin, noting his unshaven face and the deep drag he took from the diminishing cigarette he held easily between slim fingers. He was leaning his bean pole body against the side of the wall but straightened up when Claire approached.

'Hiya Claire. Yeah, it was good night, and an even better morning. Better not come too near, I've already been slagged off for coming straight to work smelling like a brewery'.

'What was the occasion?'

'A bunch of us went out on the piss last night to celebrate being awarded a new government IT training contract. It's a big one. We wouldn't have made our bonuses without it.'

'That's great Tony, congratulations. Do you mind me asking if your bonuses are tied totally to your sales figures or are other considerations, like the costs of providing the service, factored in?'

'You've lost me, Claire. The only thing that matters is making the sale, nothing else counts. We do the deal and let other people worry about the details. Yesterday we landed the big fish in the small pond. Bill Anderson led the team and he's getting the big bucks so drinks on him last night. He's not made it in today but so what'.

'It's great that your team secured the deal. It is not easy to make sales these days, the competition is fierce. You were right to go out and celebrate.'

'Cheers Claire. How've you been? I never see you out and about in the pub scene. Want me to let you know the next time the gang is going out?'

'Thanks for the offer Tony but I have a six year old at home who keeps me away from pubs. Maybe in ten years time? Will you wait for me?' teased Claire.

'Course I will Claire, anything for you. It will give them time to upgrade my car to a BMW'.

'Ask for a Rolls or a yellow Mercedes, it will make you look like a VIP. In the meantime, have another ciggy.'

'You want one?' Tony offered.

Claire gave it serious consideration for a split moment, she could see the appeal of taking a cigarette drag.

'Thanks, but no thanks Tony'.

The light banter cheered Claire up and she was in better form when went back into the office. Her mind raced with the implications of what Tony had inadvertently let slip to her. The sales bonuses for the ICT training division were tied purely to sales revenue and did not take account of the salary, administration or facilities costs involved in providing the training services. Given the eagerness of the salesmen to close the deal it was more than likely that they were giving out deep discounts to customers in order to meet their sales targets.

When Claire got back to her computer, she typed out a proposal to Daniel which would involve her carrying out a cost benefit analysis of programmes run by the ICT training division and an evaluation of the sales technique employed therein. At the very least bonuses should be tied to the breakeven point of a contract, not to the overall sales figure, since the cost of providing the service could outweigh the price paid for it. At present, a salesperson could be given a huge bonus for bringing in a big budget revenue project which ate up so many resources it actually cost more money than it generated, and it should never have been undertaken in the first place. It was a gaping hole in the administration of the key performance indicator (KPI) measurement system used for bonus payments. That fact was blindingly obvious to Claire as was the advisability of looking closely at the regulation of the discount system operated by the salespeople. Claire felt quite excited as she emailed her proposal off to Daniel, hoping he would bite at the bait. She would love to get her teeth into a data analysis project again.

She did not have long to wait for his reply.

Claire,

Thank you for your proposal regarding the revenue/cost analysis of the ICT training division, it raises points worth discussing with the divisional manager Nick Thompson. However, given the issues that have arisen about your existing workload, I do not intend to ask you to work on more projects at the present time.

Regards
Daniel

Why not? Claire wanted to scream. Ad hoc projects were part of her job description and this one was right up her alley. She could do a great job on it, one which would add value to the organisation. Instead of letting her do the type of job she was naturally good at, her managers were burying her in administrative and reconciliation work.

Her phone rang later on in the day and she groaned as she saw Ashley's number flash on the panel screen.

'Deirdre is out sick today. There is a payment run going out on Thursday. I want you to go over to Accounts Payable and help prepare for it'.

'Is Karen not available to help out in Accounts Payable?'

Claire was not being awkward by asking this question because she had never worked directly in Accounts Payable whereas Karen Woods was familiar with it as she had recently taken up the position of supervisor there.

'No, she isn't', snapped Ashley. 'Not that it is any of your business but Daniel has called her over to discuss a new project. She doesn't have time to do processing in Accounts Payable. You're not doing much, get over there and help out or it will be next month before our suppliers are paid. If that happens, you can handle all the irate phone calls'.

Claire shuddered at the thought.

'I am busy with my own work but I will go over to Accounts Payable and do what I can to help', said Claire, forced into a corner.

Claire had to spend two days working in Accounts Payable because they were short staffed and of course it put her behind with her own job. Every day had the same gripe for her, which was that she was extremely busy doing routine tasks more suited to a person of lesser ability. She would not have minded doing some administration work, it was the sheer volume of it which bothered her so much. She could not voice this complaint out loud, for fear of causing offence to a listening colleague of lesser ability who was proud and happy to do the tasks Claire resented. They would interpret Claire's discontent as a direct criticism of their own output.

Claire felt like she was walking on egg shells with her colleagues in Leictreach. She tossed and turned in her bed at night, dreaming of her job and the people she worked with. Every morning her stomach lurched as she hauled herself out of bed, propelling her into the bathroom to vomit down the toilet. She tried to hide it from Ben but the little boy was not deaf and he often heard her retch in the bathroom. She made an effort to lock the door because she did not want him to witness her crouching face downwards over the toilet bowl.

'Minimise the mess, minimise the mess', she scolded herself as she lost control of her stomach muscles and spewed out its contents, trying to position herself so that it would not spray onto the floor. Young as he was, Claire knew that her son wanted to help her but was also frightened to see his mother get physically sick. There was no father in the house for him to run to for consolation. During the times when Ben heard his mother being sick, he ran to the hot press on the landing to get out a clean towel for her and he stood outside the bathroom door with it in his hands until Claire came out to face him.

'Are you all right Mommy? Are you finished being sick?' he asked her, eyes huge and apprehensive in his young face.

'I'm fine, darling. I just keep eating something which disagrees with me and it makes me a bit sick.'

'Stop eating it Mommy. I don't like you being sick', pleaded Ben, close to tears.

'I will once I know what food is causing it Ben, I guess I'm allergic but I haven't figured out what I'm allergic to', said Claire. An ugly picture of Ashley roaring with her mouth wide open flashed in her mind.

'Don't eat peanuts Mommy, Dylan in school says he will die if he eats a peanut. I don't want you to die', entreated Ben.

'I know I am not allergic to peanuts Ben. I guess I'm intolerant of some food, not allergic to it. Don't you worry, whatever it is only makes me feel sick for a little time, then I get over it. I certainly won't die. I'm fine now', comforted Claire, hugging the child.

'Go to the doctor Mommy, I don't like you being sick', cried Ben.

'I promise you, I will stop being sick once I know what food to avoid. This is only a temporary thing. See, I'm all better now, there is no need to worry about me', said Claire smiling weakly, doing her best to reassure and comfort him.

Ben allowed Claire to lead him gently away from the bathroom door and she tried her best by word and deed to show him that all was well with their world. She packed the shelf with his favourite sugary cereals to tempt a smile back on his face. Claire had hoped that Ben would get used to her being sick and that it would stop bothering him but, the opposite was happening. It was taking more time and effort to convince him that she was well again after having been sick. The other night he had cried for a full twenty minutes when she had come out of the bathroom after a bout of vomiting. Adults do not give children enough credit for being rational, logical creatures, mused Claire. She feared that Ben was close to recognising the truth of her distressed state of mind in a conscious way. Claire's skin was erupting into spots along her neckline and she had dropped two dress sizes. She knew that the constant vomiting was not good for her mental and physical wellness but the problem was that she did not know how she could stop the retching, it seemed to have a life of its own.

If Claire needed proof that things were getting worse at work instead of better, she had it when the training schedule for the soon to be introduced new IT system was posted on the shared drive. She scanned the schedule in disbelief; there must be some mistake. But there it was, the complete list of people in Finance, with details of the training courses each was authorised to undertake.

Claire counted the number of training days different people were allotted: Ashley 10, Peter 9, Karen 8, Joan 7, Mark 6, Niall 6, Deirdre 5, Orla 5, Susan 4 and so on until she came close to the bottom of the list to find her own name, Claire Howard 2 days of training. Anna and herself had both been assigned the minimum number of days training on the new computer system, alongside the most junior processing clerks in the department. It could not be right, and if it was for real, it showed how far she had fallen.

The number of training days allotted to each person showed the pecking order of the hierarchy of the finance department, with Ashley at the top and Claire amongst a small handful at the bottom. It was hard to believe but the proof was there before her very eyes. Her imagination had not been playing tricks on her and her private worst fears had been publicly confirmed. Not only was she being blocked from progression and training, she was being ruthlessly pushed aside and pulled down to the bottom rung of the department. People like Joan whom she had helped and imparted knowledge to in the past year had bypassed her in the race to the top. Claire admitted to herself wryly that it was a race to the top of a very small world but it was the world they all lived in all the same. She looked at the training schedule again and felt a red flush of humiliation surge through her cheeks. She knew that her co-workers were avidly reading down through the list in the same manner as she had done. She was officially a dead duck in the water and this circulated list meant everybody in Finance knew it.

What was Claire to do? Her fingers drummed nosily onto the desk. Firstly, she had to email her request to Daniel for extra training days. He might agree to her getting a bit more training but realistically Claire knew that Daniel must have sanctioned the number of days and type of training each person in his department was due to receive.

It was appalling management, regardless of the manner in which she was being treated. Leictreach had spent millions of euro on the development of an integrated ICT system and top management had decided to cut corners by giving their employees the minimum number of training days necessary for them to work competently on the new system. If ever the old saying of penny wise, pound foolish applied, this was surely the case. It was downright stupid to spend millions on a super, duper system and then not train people on how to use it properly, leaving the system under utilised, with many of its features and capabilities not being used at all. The training should be maximised while the consultants who designed and implemented it for the company were still around to show staff how to operate it efficiently.

The second thing she was going to do was to have lunch with Andrew, recount her tale of woe and calm herself down from her bitter disappointment. As always, Andrew was a source of comfort to Claire.

'I can't say how sorry I am that you are going through all this bullshit at work Claire. You are bright, conscientious and hardworking. You are the last person who deserves to be treated badly', said Andrew, reaching out across the table to squeeze her hand.

'They certainly don't see it that way', said Claire, a tear drop falling onto their entwined hands. Claire had a proud spirit and she felt her public humiliation deeply. All her good work in Leictreach had been forgotten by Daniel and counted for nought.

'I am not sure what to say, I have never come across this situation directly myself. Do you want me to have a word with this Ashley character? You can't tell her to fuck off, as Deirdre suggested, but I can', proffered Andrew.

'That is sweet of you Andrew, it really is, but I think it would only make things worse'.

'What are you going to do? You are miserable in that job Claire, it can't go on.'

'I know. It is bad for Ben as well as myself. The obvious thing to do is to find myself another job elsewhere but I hate the thought of Ashley driving me out of Leictreach. I was there first and the company has the reputation of being a great employer. I see people in other departments who are busy at their jobs but they are in good form and relaxed. I've decided the next step for me is to try to secure an internal transfer,' confided Claire.

'Leictreach is a big organisation. That might work alright,' Andrew nodded.

'Fingers crossed. Daniel is going off on a short holiday and I will put feelers out while he is away' said Claire.

'Daniel believes everything Ashley tells him?'

'Regretfully, yes, and that is the nub of the problem', replied Claire.

At least she had the makings of a plan, Clare mused, as she made her way back to work. She was passing the company car park when she spotted Tony Dempsey from the ICT sales division, having a smoke outside. He must easily be on twenty cigarettes a day, she thought in amusement. Tony waved her over to him with his arm.

'Hey Claire, what is the low down on this Karen Wood bird who works in your department?'

'Why do you ask?', asked Claire, surprised.

'She has come into ICT, asking loads of questions. Nobody wants to tell her a thing, we think she's sniffing around after our bonuses. Our manager has told us to cooperate with her. What's she like?'

'I really don't know her well Tony, I've had very few dealings with her. She is guarded and will say nothing rather than say anything wrong. She will smile with her mouth closed and nod a lot, say little and listen to everything', said Claire wryly. 'Don't worry, your team has been promised your bonuses and that means they can't take them away from you this year.'

'Wouldn't put anything past management, it's a cut throat world and they're reneging on things right, left and centre. They might want our bonuses next year, the sneaky bastards,' said Tony, dropping his cigarette butt on the ground while he drew his finger across his throat, making a strangled sound. 'Sure you don't want one Claire?' Before Claire could blink, he held another cigarette in his bony fingers.

'Thanks Tony, I will today', Claire put out her hand to join him in a smoke. One cigarette would not kill her. She had better not let on to the disgruntled Tony that she knew anything about Karen's project or he would be snatching the cigarette back off her. She was bitterly disappointed with Daniel. He had obviously allocated Claire's proposal to investigate the operations of the ICT sales team to Karen Woods as opposed to letting herself run with it. Claire knew she was fully capable of making fair recommendations to improve the workings of the ICT sales division, as well as identifying who were the real stars of the sales team contributing to the department's profitability margin. Karen got awarded the interesting project and the eight days training while Claire was assigned to processing data and the minimum two days training. She did not need a business degree to realise two plus two was no longer making four in the finance department of Leictreach plc.

CHAPTER TWENTY SIX

There was a great buzz of excitement in the Howard household one bright Saturday morning. Claire's brother Martin was due to walk through the doorway of his childhood home by lunchtime, accompanied by the ravishing Caroline. Eileen was quivering with nervous anticipation as she scrubbed and polished to get her house gleaming, determined to do her son proud. Claire backed hastily away from the kitchen door when she heard her mother take the nose off her father for daring to walk over her nice, clean floor with his big, muddy, garden shoes still on his feet. It did not surprise her when Tom headed out the front door with Ben attached to his side, saying the men of the house were going out for a couple of hours peace and they would leave the women to it. For the most part, Tom and Eileen knocked along together very well, unobtrusively devoted to each other, united in a common understanding of how they should live their lives. After forty years of marriage, Tom knew well that when his dear wife was on a mission, she was a force to be reckoned with and it was best to clear out of her way. Eileen kept a clean, tidy home as a matter of habit, but by the extra effort she was making to wash the crystal and lay out her best china, a person would be excused for thinking the Queen herself was arriving for afternoon tea. Claire had a suspicion that it was more the prospect of her mother greeting a potential future daughter- in -law in her home for the first time which put her in a frenzy of baking and cleaning. Eileen was never one to let the family side down.

Claire and Eileen shared the same instincts about Martin's relationship with Caroline, which was that they both expected Martin to marry the girl. Any warm blooded man could not be immune to Caroline's classical loveliness, he would be drawn to it as irresistibly and inevitably as a moth to a flame. Eileen was imagining the beautiful little Howard grandchildren Martin and Caroline would give her as she happily dusted and vacuumed. Sure look at Ben, the spitting image of his grandfather and uncle, excepting for his striking aquamarine eyes. Either way, Eileen and Tom were going to end their days blessed with beautiful grandchildren, something Eileen thanked God for on a regular basis, given she had remained childless herself for too many years.

Claire knew that it was Eileen's fierce love for Martin which had her pulsating from the top of her head to the tips of her toes on this clear Saturday morning. Eileen and Tom had been married ten years before Martin was born. To say he was a longed for baby was the understatement of the decade. At the time in vitro fertilisation treatment was not a viable option for a childless couple of modest means in Ireland and the best medical and spiritual advice offered to the married Tom and Eileen was to relax and try again or consider adoption. Eileen wore the path out between her house and the local Church, going there to light candle after candle, praying for a baby. Even the priest teased Eileen she must be a pyromaniac with the number of candles she was lighting up underneath the statue of Our Lady. Eileen had made no secret of the fact that the most traumatic event in her life occurred four years into her marriage, when she lost the baby, she had carried in her womb for fifteen weeks. She was inconsolable in her grief, and felt that nobody, even her loving Tom, could comprehend her despair. It was made more acute by the fact that she saw bouncy, smiling babies everywhere she turned or, what was even worse, she noticed all the thin, pale faced, neglected looking children roaming the streets.

Gradually she let herself be comforted by Tom telling her that the miscarriage was nature's way, that if the baby had gone to full term, the likelihood was that the poor child would have special needs and have experienced a life filled with physical pain. It was God's will to take the baby at fifteen weeks and save their little angel from suffering on earth. This belief helped Eileen to slowly came to terms with her loss and find the courage to try again for a baby of her own to hold in her arms. Finally, the miracle son Martin was born and three years later, when Eileen had turned forty years of age, they were doubly blessed to welcome their healthy baby girl Claire into the world. From the beginning, Martin was Eileen's little prince and Claire was the apple of Tom's eye. There was no need for Eileen to continue lighting a bonfire of candles in the Church, God had bequeathed upon Tom and herself a son and daughter and their hearts were full.

In a funny quirk of fate, it was Eileen's intimate knowledge of the heartbreak of desperately wanting a child and not being able to have one which had led her to come quickly around to accepting Claire's pregnancy with Ben. Given that Eileen had experienced difficulties in becoming pregnant and carrying a child in the womb, it was possible that whenever her daughter found herself a husband, the couple might find themselves struggling to have a child together. Many a daughter inherited her mother's biological problems, it ran in the genes. After having Ben, however unplanned his arrival into the world had been, Claire would never experience the heartbreak of being childless by circumstances and not by choice. A baby was a miracle, an innocent soul to be nurtured and treasured. Ever united on the big issues, Eileen and Tom both loved Ben as dearly as they cherished their own children, flesh of their flesh. They were both looking forward to Martin giving them more grandchildren while they still had the energy to enjoy them.

Eileen rushed to the door when the bell rang, arms open to embrace the people standing on the doorstep. She was stopped in her tracks by the sight of a beggar woman wrapped in a shawl, pushing two raggedy children upfront under her nose.

'Can you spare a copper or two Ma'am, for the childer? They're fierce hungry so they are', the plaintive voice rang out.

Eileen knew she was the only woman on the street to give food and provisions to the beggars who regularly called at her door but she could never bring herself to refuse them. She had so much and they looked like they had so little. She knew that the welfare state was good in Ireland and should be sufficient for anybody to get by on but still, she never sent the needy away empty handed from her door. She had bought two pillows from a man who called around to the house the other day, simply because he had a young boy with him and it reminded her of the men who went around selling encyclopaedias years ago, with their families' financial survival dependent on them making the sale. There was no harm in it, she reckoned that night as she plumped up the pillows, they were of good enough quality and Tom did not have to know how she came to buy them.

'Wait here a minute, I'll be back', said Eileen, closing the door. She was a charitable woman but not a fool, and she did not want one of the children darting inside to steal something while her back was turned. Eileen went into the kitchen and looked at the laden table, groaning from the weight of the goodies. She quickly filled a plastic bag with a selection of tins of soup, bread, beans and fruit, wrapped a home baked fruit cake in tinfoil and popped it into the bag and swept up some iced pink and white cup cakes into her other hand. She went back to the front door and handed the bulging bag to the woman and the cup cakes to the children, whose eyes lit up with surprised delight.

'God bless ye Ma'am, God bless ye. You're a good woman, I'll say a prayer for ye, so I will. It's for the children'.

'You're welcome, but please see that the children get it', directed Eileen.

The woman cast a wary eye at Tom, who was walking up the driveway with Ben, and took flight, her shawl swirling about her, fearful that he would seize her bounty. She was not to know that Tom was well used to his wife's generosity to strangers and accepted it as being part of her.

'You giving away our lunch again?' teased Tom, pecking Eileen on the cheek.

'Can I have one of those cakes please Granny?' piped up Ben, hungry after running the legs off himself in the park.

'They are on the table pet, yes, you can take one or two. You don't want to spoil your dinner. There is plenty for everyone, nobody is ever going to starve in this house', said Eileen.

'Why do you never say no to the travellers Mam?' asked Claire.

'Now that is a good question', said a smiling Tom.

'I'm not sure dear, I think it might be because my own mother never turned anybody away from the door, no matter how little we had. I do it in memory of her', replied Eileen. She laughed merrily when she saw Claire's face.

'Don't worry, when the time comes, you can do something else in memory of me.'

She spotted Martin's car pulling up on the kerb outside the house and her face lit up with joy.

'They are here Tom, Martin is home. Wait till you see her, she is a real beauty,' Eileen gasped, clutching Tom's arm tightly as her son and his girlfriend got out of the car.

Tom clapped his son on the back and shook Caroline's hand appreciatively.

'They did not lie to me, you're a bonny sight alright and no mistake about it. I reckon you've heard that said to you a time or two before,' he twinkled down at her.

'You could be right about that Mr. Howard, although it is always nice to hear a compliment. I always thought Martin was good looking but he did not tell me he clearly took after you', said Caroline, paying Tom back the compliment, much to his delight. She would be blind not to notice that Martin was the image of his father while Claire resembled Eileen, except for her trademark burnished red curly hair.

'You are as fresh as a sea breeze. None of that Mr. Howard nonsense please, my name is Tom and this is Eileen. We might as well be on first name terms from the start.'

'I am very pleased to meet you Tom, I have heard a lot about you. And of course, it is lovely to see Eileen, Claire and Ben again. Thank you for inviting me into your beautiful home', replied Caroline prettily.

'Not at all my dear, it is our pleasure', said Eileen, ushering the group inside with a high voltage smile.

Over the course of a banquet lunch Martin finally came clean with his parents about the fact that he had been experiencing business difficulties for years. Eileen gave a strangled gasp of horror but Claire was surprised at how calmly her father handled the news.

'It never has been easy to run your own business in Ireland, the grants and supports go to the multinationals and the indigenous firms focussed on export markets. At least you still have your house and you have no children to worry about. You are young and can pick yourself up and start over again. The economy is growing and the tide will lift all boats', said Tom pragmatically. 'Is there anything we can do to help you son? Dublin is powering ahead of the rest of the country. You can move back into your old room and find yourself a job in the city to get back up on your feet and up the ladder.'

'Thanks for the offer Dad but you wouldn't want me under your feet again after this length of time. My life is in Sligo now, not Dublin. I had a piece of good fortune when the company who held the lease on the office premises went bust and I was able to walk away from the contract without incurring a financial penalty,' replied Martin.

'Their bad luck turned out to be your good luck?'

'Exactly. I'm back working out of the house again but the good news is that I have picked up a contract for designing a big, new apartment block on the outskirts of the town. My reputation for quality design remains intact. I will remain self-employed for another year and see how it goes, taking on board the lessons learnt the hard way over the years. I will never again agree to defer payment for significant sums of money on submitted projects', elaborated Martin.

'Good man, you are picking yourself up well after the fall. Actions speak louder than words. Deal honestly with people and deliver on your side of the bargain and your reputation will spread over time. Nobody can ask more of you than that,' said Tom.

'This will always be your home Martin, we never took the key away from you. I'm not sure being self-employed is the right idea. Let somebody else do the worrying and take the risk. You father did very well having a steady job in a semi state company and he has a comfortable pension now. You might be better off coming back here to us in Dublin, to reboot your career in a big firm', said Eileen, with a tremor in her voice.

Martin went over to kiss Eileen's cheek gently before moving to stand by Caroline. He pulled out a ring from his trouser pocket and pushed it gently along her engagement finger.

'Thanks Mam but Caroline and I have something to tell you. We are engaged to be married. Caroline has done me the honour of agreeing to be my wife. Not only is she an incredibly beautiful woman but she has been fully supportive of me since she learned of my financial difficulties. It has brought us closer together. I am a very lucky man', announced Martin.

'I can't disagree with you there son. It's wonderful news. Congratulations. Welcome to the family Caroline, you certainly make a lovely addition to it', said a delighted Tom, getting up to hug Martin and Caroline. Eileen and Claire moved forward to share in the congratulations and celebrations, surprised by the speed of the engagement but not by the fact that Martin intended to marry Caroline. Claire did not try to analyse the feelings which were flooding through her, she just went with the flow of goodwill experienced in the moment.

'Welcome dear, we wish you every happiness in your life together', murmured Eileen.

'I've never had a sister', said Caroline to Claire. 'I hope we become great friends.'

Claire had a sudden urge to say 'I doubt that will ever happen', but squashed it down severely and instead uttered the sweet words of 'I'd like nothing more.' When the excitement died down, Eileen asked the happy couple if they planned to have a small or big wedding.

'We are not sure yet, since I am an only child my father wants to walk me down the aisle of our local Church and throw a party for the whole town. Martin and I might opt for a small wedding ceremony in Rome with close family and friends in attendance and honeymoon in Italy afterwards. We don't want the wedding to cost a fortune, even though Daddy insists he will pay for it all. The main thing is that we want to get married quickly, neither of us wants to wait long.'

'I've a few bob put aside that can be used to pay for your wedding', bristled Tom.

'Thank you Dad but we can pay for our own wedding', said Martin proudly.

It was on the tip of Tom's tongue to point out that Martin had just been telling them about his money problems but his wife gave him a glare and a dig in the ribs to stay quiet.

'Of course you can dear', she spoke soothingly. 'But tell me, where do you intend to live after you get married?' She held her breath, fearful of the answer. She had friends whose children had emigrated, too many for her liking. She would be devastated if Martin and Caroline were planning a fresh start in a country as far away as Australia. What was the point of belonging to the EU when young Irish people choose to go to live in England, Canada and Australia whenever jobs dried up in Ireland instead of mainland Europe? It made no sense to Eileen. They youngsters would be racing to America if they could only get their hands on impossibly scarce working visas.

'We are not sure Mam. Caroline and I will stay in Sligo for the immediate future but we are not ruling out having a little adventure once my finances are sorted out. A lot of people in my profession gain valuable work experience in Australia, Canada or the Middle East and get well paid for it. Caroline has a business degree and will find work wherever she goes. We will put out feelers about going away for a few years'.

'Oh my God, you are going to emigrate. I knew it, once you began talking about money matters. We'll never see you or our grandchildren', said Eileen, trying not to cry.

'Mam, we don't have any children. I'm sure we'll come back once we have children. Mam, don't cry, please don't cry. We might not even leave the country', said Martin, shaking his head in dismay when his distressed mother abruptly turned on her heel and headed out of the room to the sanctuary of her kitchen.

'Leave her to me son', said Tom, placing his hand on Martin's shoulder. 'Don't you worry, follow the path that is right for you and Caroline. You have your own lives to lead and will only get one shot at it. Your mother and me will be fine. We have Claire and Ben here as well as each other. The world is a smaller place now and you will be only a phone call away from us.'

'What's wrong with Granny?' asked Ben.

'Your granny is crying tears of happiness because Caroline and I are going to be married. Isn't that great? Come with me and I will show you a very special action figure. It stretches out the whole width of the car', said Martin, expertly distracting the boy's attention away from his grandmother by the prospect of playing with an alluring new toy.

'No way, Uncle Martin, you got me a cool new toy! Show me, show me', yelled Ben excitedly.

'Come this way, my boy', said Martin ushering the child out to the car, wishing adults were as easy to please as children.

'Where is the bathroom Claire?', said Caroline. 'I need to freshen up.'

As Claire directed Caroline to the bathroom, her eyes fixed upon the girl's enormous solitaire diamond engagement ring. The wild extravagance of the ring did not tie in with Martin's statement that Caroline had been understanding of his strapped for cash financial predicament. How could her broke brother have afforded to buy such an expensive solitaire ring? You could have furnished a house with the price of that ring. Should Caroline not have settled for a normal engagement ring of two or three small diamonds rather than one which could be added to the Crown Jewel collection?

'Your engagement ring is beautiful', commented Claire, hoping to coax out information about its purchase without causing offence.

'Isn't it! I love it', exclaimed Caroline gaily. 'Martin and I picked it out together. It was expensive but you have to pay for quality. Martin said that although he is short of cash for now, it is only a temporary thing and he wanted me to have a ring which I would want to wear forever. He was able to top up the mortgage to release funds to tide him over, thank goodness.

I'm so lucky to have Martin, he is wonderful and really understands me. But you know how thoughtful he is, you are his sister.'

'Yeah, Martin is great', said Claire. 'I'd better go and see how Mam is doing. She is upset, not about the engagement.... she is thrilled about that....we all are, it is just the emigrating part which has upset her'.

When Claire entered the kitchen, she found Eileen nestled into Tom's shoulder, with him stroking the back of her hair lovingly.

'They are young and adventurous Eileen. It is natural that they want to travel and see something of the world before they have children. It is a good thing we reared our son to be independent. The world is their oyster and they want to seize its opportunities and experience different cultures. But in time they will be back because there is no better place than Ireland for rearing children. Let them go and enjoy themselves while they can. Ah, there is no need for tears Eileen, he is marrying a grand girl, a princess', he said.

'Look around you Tom, we are not royalty', sniffed Eileen, lifting her head to look around the familiar kitchen. She immediately spotted Claire and straightened up. Claire was struck by lines etched on Eileen's face which she had never noticed before and thought that her mother had aged ten years in the last ten minutes.

'I know that love, but she is as good looking as Princess Grace of Monaco was, back in the day, and I can't pay her a bigger compliment than that', enthused Tom.

'Will she like us Tom?' asked Eileen anxiously.

Tom kissed the top of her head. 'She already does, my dear. Come back to the room and I'll pour us all a glass of the special fifty year old bottle of whiskey they presented me with on my retirement. I've been saving it for a special occasion and this is it. Come on dear, stop your crying, we are celebrating a happy event today.'

The family gathered in the sitting room and were soon all smiling and joking as if they had not a care in the world, toasting the health and happiness of Martin and his blushing bride to be. Claire joined in but was distracted; she wondered if she felt jealous of her future sister-in-law's film star looks or if there was something else bubbling beneath the surface of her emotions which was troubling her, like Caroline being prepared for

Martin to take on extra debt in order for her to acquire status jewellery. Claire actually felt glad that the constant vomiting of the last few months had resulted in her losing weight because otherwise she would have felt like ten tonne Tessie the elephant beside the willowy Caroline. She did not know what to make of Caroline but she expected she would have plenty of time to find out in the coming years. She sensed that with Caroline what you saw was not what you got. Claire looked across at Caroline's heart breaking loveliness and knew, in the pit of her sensitive stomach, that her future sister-in-law was going to be on the fringes of her own life according to the terms of the 'till death do us part' marriage vow taken by Martin. Her brother was cut from the same cloth as their father and the Howard men did not ever walk away from their wives, whatever the circumstances. It was do or die.

CHAPTER TWENTY SEVEN

Claire had the goal of getting a transfer to a different division within Leictreach but she had to carefully consider the best strategy for obtaining it. The obvious route to go would be to put in a transfer request to the Human Resource department. The HR director was not yet fully established in his position within the company and he held Daniel in the highest esteem. Daniel was the well liked, long serving financial controller of the company and he knew everybody there was to know. Claire believed that the HR director was the stooge of top management and as a relative newcomer, he was reliant on the goodwill of the CEO for his position, pay and bonus. Not a week went by without the CEO making contact with Daniel, he trusted him to steward the ship and rated him as highly as the finance director. Claire had met the HR director on a few occasions when she had gone over to the office block accommodating the payroll and HR offices and her instinct told her that he would not risk tangling with Daniel. Daniel was one of the three most powerful people in the organisation and Mr. HR man was not going to do anything to upset him. Claire could put in her transfer request to Human Resources but they would do nothing until Daniel returned from his holiday and they were able to check it out with him. Ideally, Claire would like her job transfer to be arranged before Daniel returned to work, needing only his sign off on her release. Since he obviously did not value her as a member of his team anymore, he should not stand in her way of working for somebody else within the company.

Claire had always got on well with two divisional managers, namely, Declan Carroll in Telecommunications and Robert Blake in Electronic Systems Installation (ESI). They were both worth talking to before she made any career changing decisions. She picked up the phone to ring Declan Carroll first. She asked him if she could speak confidentially to him. Declan wanted to know if Daniel was to be made aware of their conversation on his return from holiday. Claire said that no, she would prefer it if the conversation remained strictly between the two of them. With this agreement in place between them, Claire spoke frankly about her current work situation. It boiled down to the fact that she could no longer continue working in the finance department and in order to continue working for Leictreach she needed a transfer out to another division. Could she come to work for Declan in the Telecommunications Division?

The reply was disappointing.

'Our share in the telecommunications market has been contracting and it has become important for me to beef up my business support team to build up market share. When I brought this up at a recent management meeting, two names were mentioned, yours being one of them. I'm sorry Claire, but ultimately, I decided that I needed an accountant who had three to five years experience working directly in the telecommunications field. We advertised outside the company and a new accountant is due to start on the first of the month.'

'I understand Declan. Thanks for considering me anyway', said Claire.

'If it's any consolation Claire, I strongly preferred you over the other inhouse candidate. I think you have great potential. Just at this time I need somebody with more experience in telecommunications who can hit the ground running. I had no idea you were experiencing such difficulties. Whatever you decide, I wish you all the best in your future career'.

Claire thanked him and put down the phone. Nice man, but ultimately useless to her. Claire glanced doubtfully down at the phone. Declan Carroll had sounded sincere and he had been honest with her but he had known Daniel for years and she could not help wondering if he would relay their conversation back to her big boss. She shrugged her shoulders, in for a penny, in for a pound.

Claire dialled Robert Blake's number next. It was her lucky day and she got through to the head of the ESI Division, instead of it going to voice mail. Claire went through the same opening piece with Robert as she had with Declan, but this time was asked to come on down to his office in order for them to have a proper talk together.

Unlike the telecommunications' business arm of Leictreach, the ESI division was to be found in the same building as the finance department. Robert and Claire had often greeted each other with a smiling hello as they walked the corridors. She made her way to Robert's office on the ground floor, urging herself to be calm, cool and collected. The office was large, with light streaming through the high windows, hitting off a big, rectangular table standing at the far right of the room. It would be perfect for holding meetings to accommodate a group of up to six. Robert was seated behind his own desk, which was set at a perpendicular angle to the other table and was half covered with booklets and folders. He was a tall rangy man in his late forties, with a prominent broken nose, light coloured hair and high cheekbones. He welcomed Claire into the room with real warmth in his voice and a twinkle in his green eyes.

'There seems to be cloak and dagger drama going on in Finance. Let's see if we can sort something out.'

The divisional manager listened sympathetically to her story, without interruption.

'I'd guessed something was wrong Claire, I'd noticed you have not been your usual cheerful self for some time', he said. He paused, drumming his fingers on the desk.

'Are you good at your job Claire?' he asked her bluntly.

'Yes', responded Claire without hesitation.. 'Last year I was awarded a 15% pay rise, at a time when most other people in the department got at most 3%. Daniel actually asked me to keep quiet about the size of my salary increase, because it would upset other people in the department. I've always done a good job and earned my money.'

'It was only when Ashley started working in Finance that the trouble began? You never had a falling out with Daniel before then?', probed Robert.

'No. I had a good relationship with Daniel before Ashley joined the company. It is only since Ashley started to work in Finance that the real trouble began. Daniel isn't on the premises most of the time, he's concentrating his attention on the IT project. He's oblivious to the corrosive drip-drip effect of Ashley's negativity towards me, and as a result he has withdrawn his support from me.'

'That's quite an allegation'.

'I'm telling the truth. I am kept busy processing large volumes of data which any junior out of school could do. It's a constant fight to maintain the status quo. My higher level job responsibilities are being stripped away and transferred to other people piece by piece, totally diminishing the complexity and variety of my role as a business analyst. I'm good at my job Robert, I don't deserve to be treated in this way.'

Robert leaned back in his chair and gave her a big smile.

'I agree with you Claire. I've always liked you and I've heard good things about the work you have done. I am going to ask for you to be transferred into my division. I have plenty of work to keep you going and I can certainly use you in ESI. We have a good bunch of people here and I think you will fit right in'.

Claire laughed with relief and delight, a huge smile on her face. She could have hugged him. She pumped his hand instead.

'Thank you so much. I won't let you down, I give you my word,' she vowed.

'I know that Claire. Between you and me, I can understand why you want to get away from Ashley. I don't exactly stop to chat with her on the stairway myself. Now don't say anything to anybody until the transfer is complete. I'll ring HR today to arrange it. Go and get yourself a coffee and relax, I'll let you know when the deal is done.'

Claire danced out of the room, feeling as light as a fairy. What a lovely, lovely man. She was going to love working for him. She could not believe it, her bad luck had turned to good at last. Robert had listened to her and believed her interpretation of events. More importantly, he believed in her as a person with ability and he was going to let her come to work for him in ESI. She would never give him cause to regret her decision, she would never let him down.

Her relief was immense. She did not want to look for another job outside Leictreach and, thanks to the divine Robert Blake, she did not have to. Leictreach had hundreds of thousands of employees throughout the world, surely she must be better than a lot of them. An organisation as big as Leictreach must have a place in it for an intelligent, well qualified, grafter like herself. Claire had invested so much of her energy and hopes for career progression in Leictreach during the last three years that she was loath to let go. She was proud to work for a company with such a strong brand name and, given the circumstances, she was strangely committed to it. She had worked hard to gain a measure of financial independence from her loving but aging parents and she did not want to let her job security go without a fight.

It must be true that people fight much harder to hold onto what they have, rather than fight to obtain something they did not have or may never hold. Claire was battling to hold onto the niche she had carved out for herself during the last three years. She had been happy in her job before Ashley had arrived to poison the atmosphere. She wanted to stay and develop her career in Leictreach, connecting with the many decent people who worked contentedly in the company.

The battle was over, Robert had given her a free get out of jail card. Her office was smaller than a prison cell but she would soon be waving goodbye to it. She ignored the 'have you got this, that and the other' emails sitting in her 'In Box' from Ashley and rang Andrew to tell him the good news.

'That is tremendous news Claire. I will come around with a bottle of wine tonight and we'll celebrate', he congratulated her.

'I am so happy, I can't describe it Andrew. I want to dance and spin around with my arms open wide. The relief is incredible,' confided Claire.

'It is no more than you deserve. Hold onto that feeling and I will see you later,' he replied.

It was truly wonderful news. It meant no more vomiting, no longer trying to hide her upset from Ben and her parents and no more of being busy but bored brainless at work. She would be able to laugh gaily again and find satisfaction in her job. She could reach out to grasp the next rung of the career ladder in Leictreach. She could leave her claustrophobic office behind and forget about the uneasy, guarded atmosphere which had taken hold of the finance department. A thought struck her like a thunderbolt and it left her breathless; with her problems in work resolved, she could make the phone call to Luke Elliott and invite him to hop on a plane and come on over to talk about their son. With her confidence in the future restored, it was time to face the main ghost of her past.

On her way home Claire impulsively popped into a shop and treated herself to a pink and blue patterned top and skinny jeans. Later that evening, when she was safely home, she left Ben watching a film on the television while she went upstairs to have a refreshing shower. Afterwards she looked her body over critically in the mirror, noticing how her waist and hips had shrunk. Those skinny jeans were going to look fabulous on her. What surprised her was the way in which her face had become smaller, with her eyes taking up half of it and her cheekbones being more defined than ever before.

'Funny', murmured Claire, cupping her face in her hands. 'I always figured I had a better balanced face. My skin has gone to hell, look at those spots. I had better put on make-up to cover them up.'

A transformed woman greeted Andrew Kennedy when he came knocking on her door. Claire's vibrant curls bounced around her head, her make-up successfully covered up any skin blemishes, the skinny jeans showed off her size ten figure to perfection and the patterned top complimented her blue eyes and golden red hair. Best of all, her glowing smile lit up her face, making her the happiest Andrew had seen her in years.

'Wow', Andrew whistled. 'You should get a new job every day'.

'Isn't it wonderful?,' Claire replied, taking the wine bottle from him. 'You have been an incredible support to me during the past months Andrew. I cannot thank you enough.'

'I only listened, it's what friends do. You're welcome Claire', smiled Andrew.

'Hi Andrew. Doesn't Mommy look pretty ?' asked Ben.

'She certainly does', agreed Andrew. 'As pretty as a Disney princess'.

'Mommy has been a bit sick but she says she is all better now. I'm glad, I didn't like her being sick', the child confided.

'I can see she has recovered, she has never looked better. We are men, we notice these things. Do you know what makes your Mom laugh? Pirates and tickling! Arragh!', said Andrew. Both Ben and Andrew launched themselves on Claire, until she was breathlessly begging them for mercy. The three of them enjoyed a very happy evening together, relaxed in each others company. At Ben's bedtime, Andrew gave Claire a quizzical look and asked her should he stay or go. She hesitated, giving him a shy smile, but suggested that it might be better for him to go as she had to read Ben a story and get him into bed. Andrew looked disappointed but shrugged his shoulders and gave her a light kiss on the lips when he was leaving.

'Maybe the next night I can stay longer, you gorgeous woman. I will go for now. Onwards and upwards Claire. You did great getting that new job. You are conquering mountains', he complimented her.

'I cannot do it by myself Andrew, I need the help of good people like you and Robert Blake.'

'Robert Blake, hmmm, smooth name. Is he married?' queried Andrew.

'Very much so, I guess he is in his mid-forties. He has three children I believe. I'd say he was quite a catch in his day.', said Claire, half laughing.

'You can never be sure but, it sounds like I can trust him with you. Goodnight Claire, sleep tight'.

'Will do. You too, ' said Claire, waving him out.

'Wait for me', she whispered to his retreating back, knowing he could no longer hear her, wondering why exactly she had suggested he leave her on this special evening.

Andrew was sweet and lovable and knew her well. He was usually clean shaven but tonight he sported stubble on his chin and it suited him, it made him look more mature. Andrew looked good in jeans too, not surprisingly given that he was able to run marathons. It was getting harder to close the door on him. All she had to do was step up close to him, put her arms around his neck, tilt her face invitingly up to him and let nature take over. She could feel him, taste him, delight in him, if only she took that one step forward to share his space. But she felt too cautious to commit, too timid to seize the man. She knew she was edging ever closer towards having a romantic liaison with Andrew but a part of her wanted to wait until she was absolutely certain it was the right thing for her to do. Before she could wholeheartedly commit to Andrew Kennedy she had to know for sure that the obsessive attraction she had once held for Luke Elliott was dead and buried. She sensed that Andrew was the man she was destined to be with, the one she could easily overlook in a crowd but who she was capable of loving very much.

Claire enjoyed her best night's sleep in months. She went into the office the next morning in fine spirits, eager to get an update from Robert Blake. She snatched up the phone when his call came though and listened in disbelief as he imparted the worst possible news. Robert had put in the transfer request to Human Resources but very unusually, the finance director had intervened and flatly turned the request down. This was very unusual as the finance director busied himself with meetings and took no part in the day to day running of the department or in the production of the reports. He gave no explanation but said the transfer request would not be revisited upon Daniel's return to the office and that it had no chance of happening.

It was crushing news. Claire understood that she had won a battle but lost the war. She had no future in Leictreach. With an internal transfer denied her, she had no option but to leave and find another job outside the organisation.   With genuine regret in his voice, Robert Blake confirmed this reality by ending the phone call with words which would haunt Claire for a long time:

'I am sorry Claire, but it is apparent that your face does not fit in here anymore'.

CHAPTER TWENTY EIGHT

The realisation that her internal transfer had been blocked by the powers on high in Leictreach hit Claire hard. She realised that senior management in the company no longer considered her to be a valued employee. They did not want to train or invest in her and they were not interested in developing her business expertise. The decision makers in the company were unwilling even to have a dialogue with her, meaning there was no chance that they were going to suddenly turn around and start a conversation about the best ways to facilitate career progression options. Claire had to let go of her legitimate expectation that she had a long term future in the company. This was a hard thing for her to accept as she knew that Leictreach was a good place to work for many thousands of employees and she did not understand why it should be any different for her, given her strong work ethic, reliability and competency. Nonetheless, her option was to stay, stew and stagnate or leave and hopefully progress someplace else. Out of fundamental sense of self respect, there was only one real option for her to take.

She set about the task of securing herself an alternative place of employment in a determined fashion. She booked herself a couple of days off work to set aside for interviews. One valuable thing Leictreach had given Claire was the all-important two to three years work experience, which was a requisite to apply for any of the advertised jobs which interested her. It was certainly an added bonus that her experience had been gained in a well known, highly regarded company. Claire took great pains in composing her two page Curriculum Vitae and she sent it off to the main recruitment agencies. She used every spare minute on her home computer in the morning and evenings for searching the job sites on the internet for suitable employment. She did not want to take any dead end job for the sake of leaving her current post quickly. She still aspired to obtain a financial analyst post in a reputable company with decent promotion opportunities. She had the advantage of not having an expensive mortgage wrapped around her neck and she took heart from the belief that she offered a prospective employer great value for the salary she was willing to work for. If anything, in her eagerness not to price herself out of the market, she was probably pitching her salary expectations too low. It was difficult to gauge the salary level she should accept because she kept receiving conflicting information about the going rate. One agency told her that many companies had gotten used to paying interns in their twenties peanuts during the recession and were reluctant to significantly increase the salary level of young business professionals given the plentiful supply of labour while another enthused that the fast recovering economy was providing wonderful opportunities in financial services for the well qualified. The most promising salaries and bonuses appeared to be in the banking sector.

Claire quickly recognised that permanent jobs with a pension for people at her level were extremely thin on the ground and that most positions were for specific purpose contracts such as maternity leave cover or for fixed term contracts of up to one or two years duration. She was reluctant to leave her job (bad as it was) for a maternity leave contract and was not keen on the one year contracts either. However, the two year fixed term contract was of real interest to her. A person could focus on gaining valuable job experience in a two year time frame and who knew what type of job such new knowledge could lead to? There was no point in giving her loyalty to a company if she could be displaced easily by the arrival of one unpleasant manager. The decision to concentrate her job search on ones which offered the opportunity for new learning on a fixed term contract defined the parameters of her job search and threw up a surprising number of interview options for her. When Claire received an interview offer she tried to arrange for it to be held during her booked holiday time off. It was difficult to factor in interviews during the working week as an inordinate number of them were scheduled to be held during normal working hours and there were only so many dental appointments a person could claim to be having on teeth which looked the norm. The doctor kindly facilitated her by writing her a sick certificate for nausea and general aches and pains and sent her off for blood tests for good measure. She was genuinely concerned about Claire's constant vomiting and weight loss and believed a change in job could only be good for the betterment of her health.

Claire did not give a toss for Ashley's tantrums. If Ashley was that worried about Claire's work falling behind, she could arrange for agency relief to pick up the slack or, (here is a novel idea) she could do a bit of the hard compilation graft herself instead of merely reviewing final figures. Any doubts that Claire was doing the right thing in concentrating on her job search were put to rest on Daniel's return from holiday. Claire was on tender-hooks for days, expecting the Big Boss to call her into his office, demanding to know why she had initiated a job transfer request in his absence. She relaxed when she realised that Daniel did not intend saying a word to her about it, even though she was certain he had been informed. No good comes from pouring oil on a flickering flame so Claire held her tongue and was as quiet as a Church mouse as she concentrated on her tasks in Leictreach during the day and conducted a thorough job search on her computer at night. She practiced answering interview questions at home in the mirror and accessed advice on positive interview techniques. Top tips were to be confident and never to admit to any weakness.

Q. We've talked about your strengths but what do you think is your greatest weakness?

Danger, red alert, be super confident, admit no weakness……..

A. I set such high performance standards for myself that I have to force myself to be more understanding of the fact that not all members of my team have the ability or the motivation to achieve the same level of productivity.

Q. What do you do when management have a different expectation of your job performance compared to your own?

A. I lower my expectations.

Having a positive interview technique did not include hinting that there existed a mutual dislike bordering on hatred between you and your immediate line manager and as a result you found yourself unsupported, isolated and with nowhere to go in your current job. Claire noted that nowhere in any of the books or manuals did it say that honesty was the best policy for getting her hands on an elusive prized post. The challenge for her was to sound effortlessly confident about her ability to take on a new job successfully, after being denigrated and downgraded in her existing position for the past year.

As Claire lined herself up for interview for perspective new jobs, she was given final proof that she was being forced out of her current job. Authorisations were being given out for the new IT system, which was on the cusp of going live. After a long and expensive development period, people in the company were buzzing at the prospect of operating the new IT system. A practice sandpit icon for the new system was put on every computer and staff were encouraged to make time to access the sandpit to familiarise themselves with how it worked. Claire was as eager as the next person to delve into the mysteries of the prized IT system which had cost millions to design and implement and she wasted no time in logging onto the sandpit. She did not want to be accused of being disinterested in utilising a key work tool. She liked to learn about new IT systems, discovering their logic, usefulness and reliability. It was going to be a pleasure to engage with something different to the norm after months of fielding repetitive work.

Despite recent events, Claire logged onto the sandpit with a sense of tingling anticipation to explore the areas of the management reporting section of the system she had been granted access to. She found herself in a situation where, once again, she had to do a double take and experience a sense of gasping disbelief. She had not been given access to the reporting module. She had no authority to go in and review the data on any of the cost or profit centres, nor could she access the profit and loss accounts or balance sheet of the company. She could not go in and export a single file into an excel format from the system. She used to maintain all the accounts on the general ledger in the old IT system and here she was not able to even create or edit an account on the new one. In short, the only thing Claire could do in the new IT system was data entry. The tools she required to carry out the type of work she had been engaged in on a daily basis up to a year ago had been taken away from her. Unless a big oversight had been made, it was nothing short of constructive dismissal. Her job had been wiped out and she was redundant in all but name. Together, Ashley and Daniel had caught her like a fish on a hook and were gutting her entrails.

Claire was no fool and she did not believe for a minute that a hideous mistake had been made. The fact that she still had a job and was on the monthly payroll was nearly a miracle if this deliberate oversight was anything to go by. She took a moment to let the stark truth of her rapid descent through the ranks of the finance department sink in. Was she feeling her stomach heave and a burning sensation in her throat? No. Claire realised she was not about to vomit; instead she was rapidly getting over her initial shock and becoming cool, calm and collected. She was nowhere near as upset as she had been mere weeks ago when she had been denied her transfer to the ESI division, reporting to the shrewd Robert Blake.

Shutting her out from the reporting functions confirmed what she had already painfully learnt from the transfer debacle, which was that senior management did not want her to continue working in the company. They were too mean spirited to make her properly redundant with a fair settlement. They did not expect a person of her age and qualifications to remain on working within Leictreach as a mere data processor. Initially, it had only been Ashley who had wanted her out the door but, over time Daniel and his allies had rowed in behind her. Ashley had been remarkably adept in winning Daniel over to her side of the argument. People in the wider organisation usually referred to Daniel as being a gentleman but he had proved himself to be ruthless in the dirty business of dispatching an unwanted employee. Ashley had reduced a clever man like Daniel, who had worked hard for years to be held in high esteem by his colleagues, to the status of a duped fool. Claire had always generously shared her knowledge with others in the department and been pleasant and courteous to those around her. On every level, it was shameful that Ashley's bullying tactics had resulted in Claire's isolation and ultimate banishment. Ashley had succeeded in diminishing people's perception of Claire but Claire believed that she had also reduced Daniel's stature as well, albeit in a different way. Daniel may not be able to see Ashley as the bully she was but other fair minded people in the organisation were becoming aware of her grave limitations as a manager. Ultimately his support for Ashley's actions would lessen the regard in which he was held by others in the company. Robert Blake already thought less of Daniel because of his dealings with Ashley and others would follow, as surely as night followed day.

The latest revelation did not kill off Claire's fighting spirit. She was not going to accept the extreme limitations of her access to the new IT system without comment. She opened her office door and kept a close eye out for Daniel, determined to catch him when he walked by. Daniel always moved as swiftly as a panther, never mincing his steps. When she spotted him striding along the narrow corridor she had to leap out of her chair and go after him, calling out his name loudly to attract his attention. Reluctantly he turned around and came into her office. His head kept turning towards the door, making it evident that he did not want to be there. Whenever Daniel and Claire conversed, they were usually facing each other on opposite sides of a big desk but this time she stood directly in front of him, blocking off his pathway. Daniel was a tall thin man and Claire was noticeably inches shorter in stature but she was well able to hold his eyes with her own.

'I have tried out my access to the new system, Daniel. I find I can only process data, not review or report on it'.

Daniel looked down at her unblinkingly, saying nothing.

'It means I cannot do my job as a business analyst'.

'What can't you do?' asked Daniel. Claire deduced that he was stalling for time.

'Just about everything. I don't recognise my job anymore. I can't see a complete income and expenditure account or balance sheet. Since I cannot access any cost centres it means I am unable to do the facilities budgeting or analyse and distribute the central departmental costs. I can't access or download the information I need for basic reconciliation work or for reviewing the fixed asset register or for filling in the CSO forms. My access is so severely limited it is difficult to know what I can do in the system.'

Claire could hardly believe that she was complaining about her lack of access to the fixed asset register or her inability to update CSO forms but in truth these were desperate times. She knew that the mind bogglingly boring fixed asset register was on Daniel's radar because of the millions tired up in assets.

'You are paid to do the work we ask you to do. Joan is going to take over the facilities budgeting and the central cost allocations, she has been trained up to do this already on the new system. Liaise with Ashley about the information you need for the CSO returns. You will be forwarded any files you need for reconciliation work. I agree that you need more access to the fixed assets register and will arrange it', directed Daniel.

Joan had never once mentioned that Claire's core accounting work was being reallocated to her whenever the two happened to meet in the office areas or canteen. She had not even the grace to blush or look away in discomfort. What a weasel! Was there any ray of sunshine to this debacle, any hay to reap? Come to think of it, Ashley disliked filling in the forms for the Central Statistics Office nearly as much as being responsible for the fixed asset register, though she had never mentioned this fact to Daniel.

'Since I am currently locked out from the information on the system and Ashley has full access to all the data needed for the CSO forms, she may as well fill them out herself. She can certainly do it more accurately than I and, after all, she is responsible for the balance sheet accounting and has a more top down knowledge of the company than I have', suggested Claire brightly.

Companies had to routinely complete lengthy government statistical forms and many of them only did it under duress, considering them to be a waste of their time and resources. Daniel did not want his senior management team tied up in non-productive, time consuming activities.

'No, you can continue doing the CSO forms, ask Ashley for the information you need. I have to go now,' he said tersely, determined to leave her.

Claire gnawed her lip as she gazed into the empty space. She was no employment rights solicitor but she was sure she was experiencing a case of constructive dismissal. She could no longer call herself a business analyst. Management were hedging their bets that she did not have the support and resources needed to fight for her legal rights and they expected her to put up and shut up or to quietly leave. The system was hard to fight. Claire knew she had been given the minimum amount of training on the new system but even that warning had not prepared her for her total shut out from the reporting function. Piece by piece, the ability to do her job was being stripped away from her and given to other people. All her support structures and tools of the trade had been ruthlessly pulled away. Joan had been trained up to take over Claire's reporting responsibilities in the new system. There was a good chance that Joan was delighted with herself, perceiving it as a type of promotion. The fact that it stabbed Claire in the back was merely an unfortunate side effect. Claire acknowledged to herself how much she had depended on Daniel's goodwill and support for her standing within the company and how bitterly disappointed she was in him for the manner in which he had let her down. He was an active participant in her public humiliation.

It was not Daniel's fault that somewhere in her head she had made him her father figure in Leictreach. Her own father had never let her down at home and by extension, she had thought she could depend on Daniel in the workplace. At a very basic level she had believed that if she was a good girl and worked hard for Daniel and did everything right, he would support and defend her as a valuable member of his team. She had imagined him to possess fine attributes and placed him on a pedestal to admire and emulate as a role model. She had been very wrong in her thinking and in her expectations.

One person she had been right about was the odious Ashley.

'I've just seen that you have written off a computer worth less than 500 euro over three years instead of one,' stormed Ashley, entering the room minutes after Daniel's departure.

'So? 'Claire looked up at her nonchalantly. The amount involved was immaterial given the scale of transactions and she could not give a fiddler's curse about it, considering her real job in Leictreach was well and truly finished. She was much more concerned with her urgent need to secure a new, decent position in record time.

'Honestly Claire, your attitude is appalling, you just don't seem to care at all. I'm not going to waste my time with you. Just fix it', barked Ashley, giving the door a good slam on her way out.

Claire shook her head in wonderment, it was beyond her how Ashley could get that worked up over a minor error. If something important ever did go awry, she was likely to blow a gasket and rocket off to the moon. Claire could not have cared less about Ashley's low opinion of her, the dislike was entirely mutual and she had known for ages that she did not want to work for her. No, today's big revelation had been that she no longer respected Daniel enough to want to continue reporting to him either. The big boss was a bust.

CHAPTER TWENTY NINE

Claire managed to line up five interviews, scheduled to take place during a two week period. She was nervously aware that it was often who you knew rather than what you knew which secured a decent job for a person in this country. Thankfully, the growing economy in Dublin was boosting job creation, although it seemed employers still did not want to pay accountants much money compared to solicitors. As wages increased so too did the cost of living in the capital city. Nevertheless, Claire got her hair and nails done and invested in a smart navy dress and matching tailored jacket which subtly showcased her newly acquired slim line frame. She had to be careful during the interviews to allow no trace of the difficulties she was experiencing in Leictreach to emerge. Depending on the organisation she was interviewing for, she gave her motivation for seeking a new job as being driven by either the desire to   broaden her work experience, preferably at a more senior level holding managerial responsibilities or to secure a role which allows her to gain a more top down insight into the financial workings of the company or alternatively to grow her role in a small but expanding organisation with a flatter organisational structure compared to Leictreach.

Claire could truthfully say at interview that it was difficult to rotate between jobs in Leictreach in order to get a more rounded experience of the business because people were protective of their clearly defined roles. Claire wanted to take the valuable work experience she had gained in Leictreach and apply it to another organisation, while she continued to up-skill and develop her career. Much as she loved Ben, she gave no indication that she was a single mother with one child during the interview. She was afraid her child care responsibilities would count against her if the decision to hire came down to a choice between her and a person with no dependents and she was thus relieved that employers were not allowed to ask personal questions.

Claire's first interview was for a job in an insurance company and it got off to a bad start when she entered the room to find herself looking at two women across the table.   The women presented themselves pleasantly during the interview but Claire realised she did not want to report directly to another women in her next job. She much preferred to take her chances with a male boss rather than a female one.   She believed that a male manager was more likely to look at the end result as all that mattered whilst a woman boss was more likely to micro manage the process of getting the job done. Claire knew rationally that there must be plenty of women in the workplace who were great to work for but she did not trust herself to identify such a paragon at interview stage. After her destructive relationship with Ashley, she wanted to give women managers a wide berth. She knew she was being paranoid as a male manager could be replaced at any time by a female but she could not ignore the sinking feeling in her stomach at the thought of reporting once again to a female boss.

The second interview was disheartening because it threatened to shoot to pieces her preference for choosing a male manager over a female one. The man who interviewed her was aggressive and unprofessional and suffered from an acute case of small man syndrome. One of the activities the company was engaged in was the distribution of mobile phones. She could hardly believe her ears when the weedy, pasty faced tosser guffawed:

'a mobile phone is the only gadget I've ever seen where a group of lads will slap theirs down in the middle of the table and boast about whose got the smallest one, haw, haw , haw'.

He must have been telling that 'joke' for years because mobile phones were bigger than they used to be. Claire would not have worked for him if the offer came served up to her on a silver platter. Surprise, surprise, no refusal was necessary because she 'was not successful at interview'.

The third interview was much more to her liking. She was interviewed by a man and a woman for a job in the finance department of a multinational company called Lemcein plc, which had an organisation structure very similar to Leictreach. It was coming up to their company's year end and they were rushed off their feet with the volume of work they had to get through. If offered the job Claire would be put in charge of the Accounts Payable section, monitoring it for the year end accounts. They were not promising permanency but if all went well it was intended to move the new recruit into a project management change role. Claire chuckled to herself when both the man and woman interviewing her went to pains explaining that there was one particular woman who worked in the Accounts Payable section who had been there from the year dot and who did things her way or not at all. Claire translated this to mean that Ms. Immovable must be as awkward as hell and she would have to dance around her to keep things running smoothing. Still, Claire could see the attractiveness of working for a multinational company with deep pockets in an environment which she was used to and, if offered the job, she would probably accept it. It was located in Sandyford Industrial Estate on the south side of the city and the increase in travel time getting to and from work was a cause of concern but it could be done. The company was well established and Claire could see the potential for her career to develop in the place. Ironically enough, what was giving her pause for thought was its similarities to Leictreach, given that part of her craved a completely different set up from the company which had driven her out.

The fourth interview Claire had was with a man called Mark Enright and the job he had to offer did give Claire an alternative career route from the one she had been following in Leictreach. From the offset of the conversation Mark Enright struck her as being a total gentleman, pleasant and professional. He and his wife owned a small Irish indigenous firm called CogitCuras which was supported by Enterprise Ireland and was in the business of researching and developing, manufacturing and selling specialist medical equipment worldwide. The accounts department was tiny, consisting of himself and one other person who did everything from payroll to debtors to creditors to cash control. The Girl Friday was leaving to travel the world and he urgently needed a replacement to help him keep his thumb on the pulse of the day to day business operations of the company. It was a busy but varied role, offering the opportunity to learn about the total financing activities of an expanding, export orientated, organisation.

Claire's natural enthusiasm bubbled up in her as they talked about the role and she sensed that she had a realistic chance of securing the job. Working in a small growing company would be very different from her current role as a cog in a wheel of a department comprised of over thirty people. She would be in constant contact with Mark Enright but she instinctively liked the man. He had been reserved but agreeably professional and had a warm smile and firm handshake. She was struck by his height as he unfolded himself from behind the desk; she gauged him to be over six foot tall but built like a bean pole, with a full head of brown hair, a wedding ring on his finger and thin rimmed spectacles which framed his face. Mark Enright had the aura of a fit college professor about him. The company did not have deep pockets but Claire could learn a lot about what factors went into building up a successful business and her role could expand with the company. The job involved a learning curve but the plus was that if she made a success of it nobody else was there to steal the credit away from her. She had not met Mark Enright's wife but surely a nice man like that would be married to a real lady? From what she understood from the interview, his wife and business partner was more involved in the scientific research part of the business whilst he took charge of the money, manufacturing and marketing activities.

The fifth and final interview was to provide cover for an accountant taking a two year career break in the finance section of a university. Claire was interviewed by a panel of three people, encompassing a human resource executive, the finance officer and a representative from its School of Business. An interview with three people at the same time was a novel experience. She got chatting to a person beforehand who was going for a lecturing position who told her he had to do a presentation before a panel of six people. He was disheartened because he had spotted an ex GAA county player going for interview ahead of him for the same job. A person must either be highly experienced or have held a temporary post in the college for years and consequently been promised the job or have a serious amount of pull and a word in the right ear to secure one of those coveted, permanent, lecturing positions.

The experience of having gone through four interviews already in a ten day time span stood to Claire during the tough interview for the two year contract. She was asked to explain a difficulty she had encountered in her job and how she had overcome it, she was questioned about her IT proficiency, her strengths and weaknesses, her five year career plan (sneaky as the position was only for two years), her flexibility, her experiences working as part of a team, her intentions for future study, the wisdom and rationale of her moving away from a multinational environment into the state sector for a couple of years. Claire got the impression that it was to her advantage that she had experience of working for a big multinational. Claire likened the interview to a hotly contested tennis match, with them lobbing probing questions at her over the net and her tossing back the answers right back at them. There was no room for fear or hesitancy, confidence and calm equilibrium was the only way in which she was going to win match point and claim the prize. At the end of the hour long interview the HR manager impressed on her that it would be a couple of weeks before they could advise her if she had been successful or not in securing the position. She was also at pains to ensure Claire understood that the position was for two years only and that there was no possibility of it being made permanent after the expiration of the period.

Claire knew straightaway that her first two interviews had not been successful. She was reasonably optimistic that she had a chance of securing one of the other three jobs. She only needed one offer to be able to move from Leictreach. Searching for a new job was a dispiriting quest and she would be upset beyond words if all five interviews ended in failure. The best that could be said about working in Leictreach these days was that they were still paying her salary.

Back in the office, the phone rang and Claire picked it up without enthusiasm.

'Hello Claire, can you talk?'

To Claire's surprise, it was Anna on the other end of the line. She had gone to ground and had been refusing to answer calls from any of her colleagues at Leictreach for weeks.

'Anna I'm so glad you called. Have you been sick? Where have you been? You've been out of work for ages!' exclaimed Claire.

'I know. I'm sorry, I know I should have called you before now. It's stress Claire, I just couldn't go on. I know I can talk tough but I'm not. I was having panic attacks. I couldn't go back to work', said Anna emphatically.

'But what are you going to do?' Claire asked in worried tones. Anna was a mother of four and teenagers burned up money like there was no tomorrow. Her husband was in his fifties and finding it difficult to re-enter the job market after his redundancy. Her family could not live on fresh air alone.

'I have just been talking to Daniel and I told him that I can't go back and work one more day for Ashley. I'll put my whole family on welfare before I'll do it', vowed Anna.

'I understand how it is Anna and I am sorry. It should not be this way. The way in which Ashley schedules work and the amount she expects to be done in a day is impossible. She wants it all to be perfect every time, even when it's unnecessary. She's incredibly rude and disrespectful. But Daniel does not see it. What did he say to you?' asked Claire anxiously.

'He went quiet, then he said we'd work something out, for me to come in and have a chat with him, just him and me on our own. I said there was no point if he was still going to put me working with Ashley. I won't see her, I won't talk with her. I can't stand even saying her name, I'm finished with her. I let him know in no uncertain terms that I wasn't going next nor near the place if I had to have any dealings with her, that we'd all go on the welfare first.' Anna's trembling voice was laced with anger but then it lightened up remarkably as she continued her story.

'He said that I didn't have to do any such thing, that I had been a great worker all these years and he was going to put me working in Debtors, reporting to Peter. He said I was the best he had ever seen at reconciliation work. I was to come in when I was feeling better and we'd talk about it and arrange it and because my work was going to be different, I'd be due a pay rise', said Anna, her voice lifting with incredulous delight.

Wow, the world was surely changing! Daniel was not in the habit of offering pay raises outside the formal performance management protocols.

'That's great Anna, it is wonderful news,' replied Claire, pleased and surprised that Daniel appeared to have turned up trumps for Anna.

'I can't believe it, I'm shaking here, I feel like crying. Two months out of work with stress, trying to make my mind up on what was best to do. The kids were great, right behind me, unbelievable they were. Said they'd live on half nothing if they had to. They're only kids, they shouldn't be seeing their mother in bits. I was all ready to turn my cards in. I can't believe that Daniel says no, that he'll fix it. I thought he'd be waving me out the door. You know what she's like around him, butter wouldn't melt. He has no idea what an evil bitch she is, with no proper feeling in her.'

'I feel the same way about her Anna, I hear her voice drilling away inside my head in bed at night and I can't switch it off or get away from it. You are not to worry about her anymore, she will leave you alone if Daniel is supporting you and you are working for Peter. His people like working for him. You will hardly see her as Debtors are located on a different floor and there is a totally different atmosphere down there.'

'I know, I can't believe it. The relief is something else, I'm near dizzy with it. I'm going to sit down and pour myself a whiskey.'

'Good idea and be sure to take it neat. Remember what the funny little man in 'The Quiet Man' said 'When I drink water, I drink water and when I drink whiskey, I drink whiskey' teased Claire.

Her attempt to lighten the mood was rewarded by Anna emitting a snort of laughter.

'The whole bottle will be gone. It's a wonder I didn't drink it all before speaking with Daniel, and not afterwards.'

'Relax and take care of yourself Anna. It is all good news, very good news. Thanks a million for ringing me. We will meet up for a chat before you come back to work. It's great that Daniel listened to you and moved you out of Ashley's reach.'

'You should get out of there Claire, you are young and want a career and she's ruined it for you in Leictreach. I'm different, I'm middle aged with no qualifications, I just want a job to keep things ticking over for me and the kids. A job is a job, money is money. I don't care what I do as long as they keep paying me. I just want to be treated normal, not like a dog. You are very bright and could go far somewhere else. Get out of there now before any more harm is done to you,' urged Anna.

'I hear you Anna and you are very good to be concerned about my welfare. This place has become toxic for me. I think about Ashley and the bad management and people jockeying for position when I'm walking to the shops or driving the car. I feel angry enough to explode. But I also feel helpless because, however much I try, I can't change my situation here. Please do not say anything to anybody but I am actively looking for another job. I'll fill you in when we meet up for coffee and have a chat. Take care of yourself until then. Well done with Daniel, he obviously thinks a lot of you when he has pulled out all the stops to keep you here,' replied Claire.

Claire put down the phone and looked out the window. As always, the sparsely covered tree branches standing firm against the wintry blue sky, dotted with fluffy white clouds calmed her thoughts. She was deep in thought, truly glad that Daniel had acted to rescue Anna from Ashley but puzzled as to why he had thrown her to the dogs. A steely determination entered Claire's soul. Ashley was not going to get away unscathed from messing about with Claire's life. Managers in Leictreach were not like Mark Enright and his wife, creating a company and building it up with their own money and sweat. Ashley and Daniel had created nothing, they were merely paid employees on the payroll, just like herself.

Ashley was so destructive, she had to be stopped and she, Claire, was going to play a part in it, however small. How dare she wreak havoc and upset in good people's lives? Ashley may be competent with figures but that should not be sufficient for her to be put in a position of authority over other people in the workplace. Ashley did possess cognitive intelligence but she had zero emotional intelligence. What could Claire do to stop Ashley in her tracks in the present circumstances? Although Daniel had listened sympathetically to Anna, Claire doubted that he would give her the same audience, it was evident that he did not want to listen to a word she said anymore.

'There must be a way, there has to be a way' mused Claire. A plan of action flew into her mind, like an eagle bearing down on his nest. Claire evaluated the plan as having a chance of working and that was good enough for her to give it a go. It was better to do something than nothing. The famous motto of the four musketeers 'All for one and one for all' jumped into her head. The workers needed to group together for social solidarity. It was time to call up the back up soldier reserves to fight the good fight. To hell with all those people who were only out for themselves!

Claire was reaching out for the phone when it rang out loud, as if on cue.

'Is that Claire? Hello Claire, this is Mark Enright. I am pleased to say that you were successful at interview and I am offering you the position at CogitCuras. Would you like to accept the position?'

Would she like to accept it! The job offer was causing her to float on air. It was going to be a complete change from Leictreach and that could only be a good thing for her at the present time.

'Yes, absolutely, I am delighted to accept the position. Thank you so much. I won't let you down', Claire said emphatically.

'The job offer is on the provision that your references are good but I don't foresee that as a problem. You should receive your contract of employment in the post by the end of the week. How soon will you be able to finish up at Leictreach and start work for us?'

'I do have to work out my notice but I will be ready to commence my new employment in a month's time. Thank you again for the job offer Mr. Enright, I look forward more than I can say to joining your team'.

'Likewise. You will hit the ground running, it is getting busier by the day. By the way, the name's Mark. I'll see you in a month's time Claire', her future boss rang off.

'Yes, I'm free,' whooped Claire gleefully, jumping up out of her chair, pumping the air left to right with both fists, giddy with happiness.

Freedom! There was nothing like it.

'I'm free of Ashley! I'm free of Daniel! I'm free of the whole miserable place', crowed Claire. 'They have no power over me. I never have to see or talk to any of them again. I did it. I got myself a new job, a good job.'

The Gods were smiling down on her, she must have done something good to somebody, somewhere. Claire's joy and relief at the impending liberation from her spirit sapping workplace was similar to the feelings which Anna had experienced when Daniel had promised her, she no longer had to report to Ashley and that she still had a job to return to.

She let herself savour her proud moment, head held high, her bow shaped lips curving upwards in a huge smile. The majority of jobs on offer in the current labour market were for short term contracts and this reality made her doubly delighted to receive an offer of a permanent job.

The phone rang again and once more Claire reached out for it. For an awful moment she wondered if it was Mark Enright ringing back to say he was terribly sorry but he had changed his mind and was rescinding his job offer. But it turned out to be the exact opposite for the HR executive of Lemcein was on the phone, pleased to inform her she had been successful at interview and the job was hers if she wanted it. Claire asked for one day to consider it and they agreed to her request after she admitted she had the offer of a permanent contract with another company to deliberate on as well. Was she right to accept the position with CogitCuras instead of the multinational Lemcein? Opting to work in a relatively new start up Irish company instead of a big multinational corporation was in biblical terms similar to backing David over Goliath. True the CogitCuras post was for a permanent job and the Lemcein post was for a fixed term contract but was there really such a thing as a permanent job anymore or was that an illusion? Most people her age were switching jobs every two to three years to gain experience but then the majority of them had not the responsibility of being a single parent. If she worked for Lemcein she would be directly building on the type of work experience she had garnered in Leictreach and she would be remaining within the multinational sector. CogitCuras offered a different type of experience and she was taking a gamble that it would work out better for her in the long run. But she was very tired of the politics she had seen in Leictreach and, politics being politics, there was a good chance that they would be replicated in Lemcein. She could have a far bigger impact working in a small company compared to a huge one. Her instincts were to follow up on her acceptance of the CogitCuras job offer from Mark Enright and go forward in a different direction.

Claire had been offered two jobs in quick succession because she was well qualified and had been involved in responsible account reporting in Leictreach until recent weeks. Ashley and Daniel had tried to infer that her years of study and business analysis counted for nothing. Her sense of outraged justice reasserted itself, clouding the sparkle in her blue flecked eyes.

'I would not have needed a new job except for Ashley making my life hell here for no good reason. I am going to reclaim back some of the self respect she has taken away from me. I will try to even up the score with Ashley before I leave and do her whatever damage I can', Claire vowed.

The pledge was not in accordance with the loving Christian sentiment of 'forgive those who trespass against us' mantra which Claire had grown up listening to but it did fit in rather nicely with the 'eye for an eye' reference in the old testament part of the Bible, which after all had been written first. It gave Claire some comfort that she was not a horrible person for wanting vengeance and it proved she was a mere human and not a saint.

Before Claire could do anything, she had to wait until her references came through and she had signed and posted off her new contract of employment with CogitCuras. She felt a momentary panic at the thought that Daniel might scupper her precious job offer by giving her a bad reference. Hopefully he would remember all the good hard work she had quietly done in Finance over the last three years ago and recommend her warmly to Mark Enright. On a practical level, Daniel wanted to shut of Claire and he needed to give her a good reference for her to secure another job, enabling her to leave Leictreach.

Claire typed out a three line resignation letter and put it into her bag, ready to submit it to Daniel when both Mark Enright and she had signed the contract of employment with CogitCuras. The relief was tremendous when a signed copy dropped through the door. She added her own signature to the contact with a flourish and posted it off immediately. The feeling of lightness was incredible. She could not believe it, she wanted to shout her good news from the roof tops. Freedom! There was no other feeling like it in the world.

There was also one more thing she had promised to do once her work situation had improved and that was to make the big decision about whether or not to actively introduce Luke Elliott into Ben's life. In truth, she had already made the decision but had been waiting for the right time to act. Claire and Luke had to come face to face with each other and square up to the challenge of forging a new type of relationship for the sake of their son.

Claire texted a message to the phone number she had memorised months ago but had not used until now.

Luke, I am ready to meet with you to talk about our son Ben. Claire.

She blinked as a message came winging its way back to her from across the Atlantic Ocean.

Brilliant news and timing. I am free to fly over for a week. Due to start a new job. Can I see you next Sunday 14th? Luke

Claire was shell shocked for after all her procrastination and agonising about whether or not it was a wise move to meet up with Luke, she had unwittingly picked a time to make contact when he was free between jobs, like herself. His new job was most likely more lucrative and high flying than her own but, still, it was a weird coincidence. Typical of Luke was his suggestion that they meet up together in a mere week and a half; he had always been action orientated when it suited him. Cometh the hour, cometh the man. Claire had a wry sense that the Heavens were pushing Luke and herself together.

Claire hesitated as she pondered over where was the best place for them to meet. It had to be an established public meeting place, one which she could get quickly in and out of. She wanted it to be comfortable surroundings, not too crowded. It was best for their encounter to take place in the morning rather than the evening time as she needed the cold light of day to keep her mind clear. She keyed in the fateful message and hit the send button.

Breakfast 10am, confirm Sunday 14th, Bewley's restaurant, Grafton Street. I will be alone. Claire.

There was an instant acceptance of her proposal.

Agreed, see U then. Thank U. Luke

It was incredible to think there had not been one word of direct communication between Luke and Claire since Ben was born, and suddenly, they had arranged a meeting in a matter of minutes. It had turned out to be a truly momentous day.

CHAPTER THIRTY

Sunday sunrise signalled the colourful dawn of a new day. Claire downed one cup of coffee after another, feeling intensely nervous about the upcoming meeting with Luke. Her mother had agreed to look after Ben while Claire met up with a friend, whom she had not seen for ages, for breakfast that morning. Claire was careful not to mention any names when she put forth her babysitting request but, nonetheless, Eileen threw her a startled stare before mutely nodding her acquiescence. Claire normally tried to keep Sunday free for spending quality time with Ben, in an attempt to make up for all the hours she worked away from him during the week. Tom leapt at the opportunity to bring the child along to Croke Park to support his precious Dublin GAA football team against arch county rivals Meath. Ben was wild with excitement at the prospect of this special treat and her old man was looking forward to the outing almost as much as the child.

The night before, Claire had agonised over what to wear. At one stage, in her desire to project a business like impression, she had even considered wearing her interview outfit. She wanted him to immediately recognise that the soft, pliable girl in the hippy skirt, with the big adoring eyes who had sought favour with him at every turn, was well and truly gone. She eventually opted for loafers, skinny blue jeans, white top and brown leather jacket, hoping the outfit conveyed a casual but smart look.

Claire tried to look calm, cool and collected when she stepped into the restaurant on the stroke of ten o'clock, her eyes scanning its busy interior for the face etched indelibly into her long term memory. She spotted him sitting at a table by the window, tucking into a substantial breakfast but keeping a close watch on the doorway. An instant fusion of recognition flowed between them, causing Claire to feel her stomach lurch and forcing her to tighten her muscles to control it. She tilted her head slightly to the left, like a bird poised before flight, her senses fully alert as she drank in the sight of him.

Luke appeared familiar to her but there were distinct differences from before. He used to have long, wavy hair which he wore tied back in a pony tail, which many girls coveted and admired. It was much shorter now but still longer than the norm, tousled and thick. His face was clean shaven and well defined, the lips were full, the jaw line strong. He was undoubtedly handsome, with regular bone symmetry, full lips and a nose which was exactly the right size, noticeable but not dominant. His teeth were whiter than white, structurally perfect, signalling cosmetic dental work performed by a top orthodontist, covered by expensive health insurance. Were great teeth part of the American dream or an offshoot of it, a stamp that the person had become financially successful? Luke's previously slightly crooked teeth may have been transformed but his eyes had not, for their slanted shape and cobalt blue colouring were replicated in her darling Ben's eyes, a mark of genetic inheritance from biological father to son.

Ben bore the stamp of the Howard heritage line except for the sapphire colour of his eyes. Like any mother, Claire had witnessed her child's eyes dance with merriment as well as swim with tears on different occasions. Some people believed that the eyes were the entry point into a person's soul and, if this was true, then perhaps her little boy was more like his biological father than she had ever acknowledged. It was not the most comforting thought in the world. She tried to ignore the knots of trepidation knitted together in her stomach and to concentrate instead on moving her legs in small steps towards Luke, without suffering the embarrassment of falling over or turning tail to run out the door.

Luke stood up politely to greet Claire and she was struck by the height of the man, his leanness and broad shoulders. Even in the confined space of a restaurant, it was apparent that he could move with the grace and fluidity of an athlete. Claire felt unfit and inadequate standing opposite him but, had Luke ever truly made her feel good about herself? His clothing was stylishly causal, every item showing off an admirable USA brand, adding to the perception that he had become more American than Irish. Luke reached out to take her hand but Claire evaded it by sliding down rapidly into a chair, not wanting them to shake hands, kiss cheeks or embrace.

'Hi Claire, it is great to see you again,' said Luke, giving her a gleaming smile.

'Hello Luke, it has been a long time', replied Claire politely. She had no wish to be bitter or accusatory.

Up close, his skin was clear and lightly tanned and the jet black hair was a striking contrast to the indigo hue of his eyes. A part of Claire was gratified that he was gorgeous looking, he was the father of her son after all.

'Coffee?' asked Luke.

'Please', said Claire, thankful that she did not have to pour out a cup of the piping hot beverage from the pot with her nervous hands.

'They give a fine breakfast here', said Luke, nodding towards the menu. He was munching through a full Irish breakfast, savouring eggs, bacon, sausages, hash browns, tomatoes and beans. There was obviously nothing wrong with his appetite.

'I had something to eat before I left the house. Coffee is fine for me', replied Claire.

She was not going to risk having anything to eat during their tête-à-tête or she might throw up. How could he be so relaxed in the circumstances?

'Please tell me about you and Ben. Forgive my curiosity but I have so many questions. Is Ben healthy and well? And where are you both living?' Luke questioned eagerly.

Claire realised that Luke knew as little about her as she knew about him. Andrew had told him nothing.

'Ben and I live together in a small house in Donnycarney, the same house my Dad was brought up in. My parents wanted us to have somewhere stable and secure to live and it is located close to their house. My parents look after Ben when I'm at work, the three of them adore each other. After you left, I could not have coped on my own with Ben, without the help of my parents', emphasised Claire, wanting to impress upon him how much his abandonment of her had forced her to rely on her parents for assistance in rearing their baby son.

'I am sorry I was not around to help you with Ben, Claire, truly I am', replied Luke, looking uncomfortable. 'You mention that your parents look after Ben when you are working. How are they keeping? They must be getting on in years.'

'They are fine, not a bother on them. They maintain that Ben keeps them young and fit. I'd be lost without Mam and Dad. It is thanks to them that I was able to study for my accountancy qualification and hold down a job as financial analyst in a multinational called Leictreach for the last three years. I'm finishing up there in the next couple of weeks to start work in an indigenous Irish company, which exports medical instruments abroad', explained Claire.

'I've heard of Leictreach, they are a massive company and reputed to be a good company to work for. Are you sure about leaving it to work for a much smaller Irish based operation?'

'Absolutely. I will get a much better all round experience of how a business operates and grows organically. It is easy to get pigeon holed in big companies. I can always move back into the multinational sector in a couple of years', said Claire smoothly. She was only going to admit to him over her dead body that the departure had been forced on her.

'It's impressive that you have managed to have a successful career whilst being a single parent Claire. It cannot have been easy for you. Can you show me a picture of Ben please? I really want to see what he looks like,' commented Luke eagerly.

Claire had deliberately printed out a photograph of Ben and tucked it away in her bag, ready to present it to Luke upon request. A real photograph was more tangible than an image on a phone. The picture depicted six year old Ben wearing his sports gear, a huge grin on his face because he had scored the winning goal of the match. He looked confidant and fit, happy and healthy.

"You can keep it. I have got plenty more', she proffered.

Luke studied it closely, an indefinable expression flickering on his face.

'Thanks Claire. He looks a fine boy. Tell me about him please', said Luke, placing it carefully into the fold of his leather wallet.

'Ben is amazing and we are all very proud of him. He is well behaved and has an inquisitive mind. Test results classify him as being academically gifted and he is advanced in all activities for his age. He loves school and football and he has lots of little friends. He is funny and kind and smart. He is competitive and brave when it comes to sports. He is only young but he is a real thinker, he observes a lot.' enthused Claire, smiling for the first time. Ben was her pride and joy and it showed.

'He sounds great, everything a parent could wish for in a boy. I'd love to meet him Claire. Will you allow me to say hello to the little guy?' entreated Luke.

'You are not a parent to him Luke, at most you are a small figment of his imagination. You disappeared into the horizon for seven years. Seven years is a long time Luke, a life time for Ben. All you wanted to do was go to

America. We did not matter to you. You did not even reach out to us through social media. We might as well have been living in the dark ages, as far as communication went,' said Claire, refusing to excuse his misdemeanours.

Awareness of their past history and mistakes hung in the air between them. They were not kids anymore making big choices about their lives, they were two fully grown adults living with the consequences of their behaviour.

'I made mistakes. I know it. I always wanted to live in the States. I grew up captivated by images of America. Ireland is too small a country for me to live in and be happy. I was afraid if I delayed and stayed until the baby was born, I might never get away. I did not have enough money to financially support you and a baby and pay medical insurance and high rents. I was just starting out and I did not know how things would pan out for me over in America. You were better off here. I took the easiest option and bolted. It was easier to stay away and say nothing while I was making my way. But America has been good to me, I am earning real money. I do not regret going but I do regret the manner of my departure. I am here to apologise to you and to try to make amends', said Luke sincerely.

'You are here to see Ben and not me. Did you ever love me Luke?', asked Claire bravely, steeling herself not to wince if she got an unpleasant reply. There was a long pause as their eyes locked across the table.

'Probably not,' admitted Luke. 'It is not my intention to say anything hurtful to you Claire but I think it is important that we be honest with each other. I may not have loved you but you did matter to me. When you became pregnant with Ben, I was finishing college. I was mixed up and restless. I certainly was not ready to handle the responsibility of being a father. I had never held down a real job, hell, I was more like a kid than a fully grown man. But you want to know if you and Ben mean anything to me? Of course you do. I want nothing more than for Ben and me to get to know each other and for the two of us to be friends. You are the mother of my son'.

'I am not sure if we can be friends', breathed Claire softly.

'We can at least try, can't we? Plenty of relationships break down and the parents get along together for the sake of the kids', cajoled Luke.

'One parent normally does not disappear into the sunset for seven years', pointed out Claire sardonically.

'Life moves on Claire, people can change with time. I promise you I will not disappear again. Once I am back in your lives, I am back for good', promised Luke.

'But you are not back, you have just told me that Ireland is too small a country for you to live in. You have no intention of settling down here again. What are your plans Luke?' queried Claire.

'We have something in common, we are both moving from major corporations to smaller companies. I was working on product innovation for multinationals based in Seattle and Chicago but I have signed up with a rapidly growing company based in New York which specialises in developing innovative products for the banking sector across multiple IT platforms. Naturally, share options are part of the deal. If the company designs, develops and launches products successfully on the world market, there is potentially a huge payout to be made. It will be all the greater if I become a key player in developing a successful prototype.'

'Congratulations, it sounds exciting', said Claire, impressed. She had always believed that Luke had the capability and personality to succeed on a grand scale in the business world. He had the ability to swim with sharks if it was required of him.

'It is, I have ideas buzzing around my head day and night. I can't wait to get started'.

'Do you see yourself staying with the company long-term?' asked Claire. New York had the advantage of being easily accessible to Dublin by aeroplane.

'It will depend on how well the trails for the new products go and if there is real money in it. I will give it two years and then review the situation.' Luke had never been the type to let the grass grow under his feet.

'I'm sure you would not give up a good job without the firm prospect of something better Luke. I wish you every success with your new adventure'.

'That's big of you, especially in the circumstances.' Luke drew a breath, steadying himself. He momentarily appeared to be stressed out by this encounter too.

'I know I have not helped you out financially with Ben in the past but I am in a position to contribute to his upbringing. I want to transfer money on a monthly basis into an account set up especially for him', said Luke.

Claire was genuinely surprised by Luke's offer to make a financial contribution to Ben's upbringing, given that he had never met the child and she had never asked him for money. The offer made her more willing to accept the possibility that finally Luke wanted to commit to their son and bear a real responsibility for his well being.

'Why now Luke?' she asked the simple question which had been tormenting her since he had reached out to her from the shadows. 'Why now and not before?'

'Claire, the last couple of years it has been eating away at me, knowing that I have a son over here who is growing up without me, who does not know me at all. I am truly ashamed of myself and my actions. I cannot be the man I want to be, unless I put things right with you and Ben,' said Luke, achingly honest.

'There is a lot about you and not much about Ben in that statement', Claire observed.

'I will spell it out so there can be no further misunderstandings. I am sorry I treated you badly Claire and gave you no help in bringing up Ben. Please let me make amends as best I can. I want to get to know Ben and for him to know me. I admit it, for the first years of his life I blocked him and you out of my mind. I put everything into developing my career in America. You either make it or you don't over there. But I could not maintain it Claire. The more time went by, the more I thought about my son. I dreamt of him, getting older and knowing nothing about me, about his own father.'

'The truth wins out in the end', thought Claire.

'I know I can be a selfish bastard but I am not being selfish this time. I am convinced it will be a good thing for Ben to get to know me. I am his father. I will not hurt him Claire, I want to take care of him', entreated Luke passionately.

But instead of appeasing Claire, his use of the phrase 'take care' infuriated her.

'I take care of Ben, not you. My parents and I love Ben and watch out for him and see that he comes to no harm. That will not change if I introduce him to you. You cannot take care of a child if you live in a different country, on a different continent, it does not work like that. A child needs to be fed and clothed and held on a daily basis. What gives you the right to come here now and demand access to Ben, upsetting the life we have together?'

'I know I have no legal rights but I am the boy's natural father. He is his own person but I am still a part of him. There is a higher natural order Claire and that is why I am here today. I made a big mistake in walking away from you but, what is done is done, I can't undo the past. I am asking you to be the bigger person Claire and do the right thing. There is nothing to be gained from being bloody minded. We don't have to perpetuate the mistakes of the past, we can do better as we go forward', urged Luke earnestly.

'How righteous you sound Luke. For the record, I have done mighty well bringing up Ben for the past six years and you have been the miserable failure of a father. Have you discovered religion? You will be telling me next 'let he who is without sin cast the first stone'. Any boulders lying around, to atone for your seven year itch?' said Claire caustically, using sarcasm to procrastinate, as her mind struggled to come to terms with this mature stranger who presented himself as Luke.

Luke laughed, easing the tension.

'Religion is big in America Claire and, as I have been there for seven years, anything is possible. But please, can we switch the boulder throwing for pebbles?' parried Luke. It galled Claire to see him speedily regain control of his composure. He reached into his coat pocket and pulled out a thick envelope marked with Ben's name and placed it on the table.

'Please open it Claire', he entreated. Slowly she opened the envelope and took out its contents. Her eyes widened as she grasped a cheque for a large five figure sum made out in Claire's name, together with a bank statement showing a regular amount of money going into the account every month for the last sixteen months. No money had been withdrawn from the account in that period of time and the amount of the cheque equated to the balance of the bank account.

'I am not acting on the spur of the moment, I have thought long and hard about making a commitment to Ben. I remember what it is like to be a child and to have your feelings hurt by adults. I will be careful of his feelings in my dealings with him. Ben growing up without me featuring in his life bothers me more than I can say. Let us get to know each other Claire'.

'What if I say no?' questioned Claire.

'Then there is nothing I can do about it, I owe it to you to accept your decision. But I would like him to know I exist and think about him. You might allow me to send him cards on his birthday and at Christmas time. Either way, I will continue to put money aside for Ben. One day he will know that at least I cared enough about him to contribute to his financial well being. Education can be horrendously expensive, especially in America. I do not intend my son to start out on his career with a huge college debt around his neck if I can help it', replied Luke, sounding much older and more responsible than Claire had expected.

Claire wondered what on earth had happened to him in the intervening years to turn him from an irresponsible, callow youth to a considerate, mature man. Something was going on here that she did not understand. She remained silent as Luke continued to speak.

'Will you set up a bank account for Ben, enabling me to transfer money into it on a regular basis? The account should give only you the authority to withdraw funds from it. I want you to have peace of mind that nobody but you can ever come along and empty it out', said Luke reassuringly.

Luke had considered all the options and understood that money liked to change hands and seldom stayed still in the one place. He needed Claire to begin to trust him if he was to get close to Ben. Claire had to be able to depend on the money being there for Ben to part fund his life choices as he grew older.

'I will set up the account and forward the details onto you, thank you' agreed Claire.

'I appreciate you doing that for me Claire, thank you.'

It would be good for Ben to have a nest egg to draw on when he was older. Any judge in the country would agree with her that Luke, as the biological father of the boy, owed a financial contribution to his upbringing. The cost of college education was increasing year on year. Claire knew she could look after Ben's day to day needs but she was by no means certain that she would be able to support him financially through university when the time came. What happened if she became sick or she lost her job when she grew older? She already knew to her cost that a person could be deliberately managed out of her job and it could be disastrous for Ben if that happened to her again when he was on the cusp of going to college. She did not want Ben to refuse to further his education because he believed it to be too big a financial drain on her. Medical insurance was expensive as well. She could use Luke's money to pay for the big ticket items of health and education for Ben and it was a lie to say that was not a source of relief.

Claire eyed Luke keenly across the table.

'I am trying to figure out what makes you tick Luke, I need to have some understanding of you and what happened in the past in order to know if I can trust you enough to come near Ben. Your actions are going from one extreme to the other in relation to him, from actual physical abandonment to promises of future emotional commitment. I can't help feeling that I am missing a piece of the puzzle. And don't think that I have not noticed that you have never talked to me about your own family. We haven't heard a dickie bird out of them, a big fat zilch, which makes it very suspicious. If Ben gets to know you then he will also come into contact with your parents. Tell me something about them please,' directed Claire, wanting to find the key which unlocked the door to Luke's past. Even in their carefree college days, Luke had always refused to discuss his parents with her, consistently turning the conversation onto a different topic.

Luke sighed deeply and stretched out his shoulders, as if weary of carrying a heavy burden.

'Okay Claire, here it goes. I had not intended mentioning it to you because it is not important anymore. I don't see it as a big deal but it may be what you want to know'.

Finally, she was going to be wised up, Luke might actually be ready to open up and give her an insight into his guarded private life. Claire suddenly felt ravenously hungry, as if she could eat twelve sausages and rashers all at once. She leaned forward, chin resting on her hands, elbows on the table, giving him her full attention. She had waited a long time to hear his story and she did not expect it to be boring.

CHAPTER THIRTY ONE

The waitress approached with a fresh pot of coffee for their table. Claire could not remember ever having such attention from a waitress at breakfast time and she wished the girl would buzz off and leave them alone. Luke thanked the blushing girl for the beverage, saying it was exactly what they needed to start the day off well and he slipped her a generous tip. Once she was gone, he turned his keen eyes back to Claire.

'Do you recall that I am an only child?' prompted Luke. Claire nodded, eyes wide. It had been one of the few personal details about himself that he had divulged to her. She had not reckoned on him going back as far as his childhood. Please God he would not tell her he was abused as a child or anything else horrible.

'I never told you I was adopted, not many people know about it. I was adopted in England by Florence and Henry Elliott when I was a few months old. They are good people, you are going to like them. I clearly remember the day my mother told me about my adoption. I was seven years old and the two of us were in the garden on one of those sunny days which you think will go on forever. My mother and I were wet from spraying the lawn and she chased me around the garden. We flopped down laughing on the rug and she reached out and gave me a smothering hug.' Luke paused before continuing, a faraway look in his eyes, not finding it easy to speak about.

'My mother told me that she loved me very much and that she had waited a long time for me. She assured me that of all the babies in the world they had chosen me to be their little boy because I was incredibly special. She knew from the moment she learned of my existence that I was meant to be her baby. No other child was more loved or wanted by their parents than I.'

'She broke the news to you in a loving way', commented Claire.

'She did,' agreed Luke, 'except that I was seven years old and I felt the ground quake under my feet. I did not really understand what it meant, I only knew that my mother was the most important person in my world.
I remember I did not like to be away from her, I wanted her to keep close to me. After the initial revelation, my mother found it difficult to refer to the adoption again and it was rarely mentioned. In her mind I could not have been more her son if she had given birth to me herself and she

preferred to blank out the other woman's existence. It took me a few years to fully grasp the fact that I had another mother and father out there somewhere in the world'.

'How did that make you feel?' asked Claire.

'Angry and confused. I knew my mother loved me completely but I also realised that another woman had chosen to give me up at birth. I could not reconcile being loved totally by one mother with being rejected by an unknown one. My sense of self importance was outraged. It did not help that Henry was kind but distant from me. He seemed only interested in my mother, his work, his boat and not in me. I barely impinged on his life. My mother and I went to places all the time without him. I grew to believe that he had only agreed to the adoption because he adored my mother and she badly wanted a child. He regarded me primarily as another man's son, not his own.'

'That must have hurt', acknowledged Claire.

'When you are a teenage boy you often feel the anger instead of the hurt. I resolved that once I was an adult I would go and find my real father. I already had a perfectly good mother and did not need another one. I was intent on finding myself a new and improved model of a father, in place of boring, staid Henry. To this day, we have nothing in common with each other and we continue to disappoint.'

'Did you find what you were looking for?' breathed Claire, intrigued despite her intention to remain cool and detached.

'I realised that to find my real father, I had to trace my biological mother first. I was not a hundred percent keen on that course of action since I knew it would upset my mother if she got wind of it. It was Henry's refusal to buy me a car for college which spurred me on. We had a huge row about it because he had promised me a car on the conditions I got through my exams and kept away from drugs. Henry insisted that he meant to give me a car after I finished my college exams, not my school ones. He was lying through his teeth, the dickhead, he knew I understood him to be referring to the leaving certificate examinations. He pontificated that I was too young to be driving and he was not going to be responsible for breaking my mother's heart by having me speed around the country lanes in the car and end up dead in a ditch. I was as mad as hell with him for breaking his word and got my revenge by restoring a junk motorbike for next to nothing. Eventually, I set out on it to find my real Dad.'

'I loved being on your motorbike, it made me feel reckless and free,' said Claire, wistfully remembering all the journeys they had taken on it together. She had burned with zeal and passion for Luke and delighted in clinging on tight to his back as they explored the by-roads of Ireland, every sense alive and tingling. It had been the most fun filled time of her life and the memory of it had featured in her ethereal dreams for years.

'I was a ghost rider on it, I made it my business to give Henry the finger by speeding on every road, whatever the condition. Somehow, I survived the experience and went on to track down my biological mother. I set off to meet her but I really should not have bothered.'

'Was that because she could not measure up to your adopted mother?' Claire felt sympathy for any woman who had to outshine Luke's sainted mother.

'I don't think that was it at all, it was more like she was nothing like me. The meeting was as awkward as hell. She had me when she was only sixteen and did not want to know. When I found her, she was living in an end of terrace house in Manchester with her husband and two kids.'

'Had she told her husband about you?' queried Claire.

'I dunno for sure. The dude certainly got a shock when he opened the door to find a six-footer towering over him, looking for his Mum. He seemed to be a decent enough bloke, worked as a mechanic in a local garage. Not entirely useless.'

'How did your mother react?'

'Her name is Carla. She asked me in for a cup of tea. She was slight and fair skinned, looked as if she ate half nothing. She could have been pretty if she took an interest in her appearance. I think it freaked her out to have me staring at her so intently but I could not see a resemblance between us and I felt gutted. She worked part time in a shop. She doted on her two kids. The girl was cute enough but I could have strung the boy up; he was a cheeky, spoiled brat. Probably robbing cars as we speak, as fast as his old man fixes them.'

Claire glared at him, not at all impressed by his description of his much younger half brother.

'I am sure Ben is nothing like that nightmare kid', said Luke hastily, aware that a comment about stringing boys up did his case no good with Claire. It was apparent to her that there had been no bonding with his blood family in Manchester. For Luke, his real mother was Florence, the woman who had lovingly adopted him and brought him up.

'What did Carla tell you about your father?'

'That is the rub of it, she could tell me very little and nothing that could help me locate him. What a loser she turned out to be', said Luke scornfully. 'Her story was short and not very sweet. She met an Australian dude at a house party who was travelling around Europe for a year. They talked, downed bottles of alcohol, as you do at a party, and had sex together. She let him walk her home and then waved him goodbye without knowing his surname. She did not consider it important to know his full name, she never expected to see him again. They knew nobody in common. He might be from Brisbane but she was not sure. She thought his name was Jared. Jared and Jarred, my father and mother.' The words were bitter, not joking.

'She was very young at the time, no more than a child herself really' said Claire gently.

'I know. She actually told me that I should thank her for keeping me alive, that all the girls she knew who got pregnant around the same age had abortions. She hid her pregnancy from her mother until it was too late for her to get an abortion easily. She was glad that I had been adopted by good people. She had to get on with her own life and I should get on with mine,' said Luke, looking vulnerable.

'I know it is hard to deal with but it sounds like Carla did the best she could in the circumstances she found herself in. She obviously did not have the incredible support from her parents that I had from mine. It would have been very difficult for Carla to bring up a baby on her own at sixteen. Was part of you not a smidgeon grateful that she carried you to full term and allowed you to live this amazing life? You have no right to be indignant about her reference to abortion, bearing in mind your suggestion to me about getting rid of Ben when I told you I was pregnant. How dare you do that, knowing me and my religious beliefs?' queried an impassioned Claire.

'It was an option', shrugged Luke. 'You never struck me as being overtly religious. I believe at looking at all the available options, whatever the scenario. It is irrelevant in terms of my own birth, I have been alive a long time. If I am being honest, I pushed aside thoughts of your pregnancy and refused to have deep feelings about it, preferring to focus my attention on other concerns.'

'You were so selfish you did not even have a flicker of feelings for Ben after he was born. You think you are clever but you get basic things wrong. Your poor mother probably did not know what to make of you, talking with an upper cut glass accent, dwarfing and judging her as you sat in her small kitchen. Don't blame her for the choices she made Luke', said Claire compassionately.

'I don't blame her but I don't have to like her', retorted Luke.

'You don't know her Luke, she could be a lovely person. She might be a kind, gentle person who would not hurt anybody. You feel superior to her and it is on shaky grounds. You hide this story from me all through college. Why are you telling me all this now? Your adoptive father is distant from you and you think he has never loved you. Your biological father unknowingly leaves you behind as a baby so you in turn knowingly abandon Ben?' asked Claire ruthlessly.

'I don't know Claire, I'd get therapy to understand it but most of the therapists are fucked up themselves. When I heard I was going to be a father, I ran scared. I am nothing like Carla, which means I must resemble my biological father. I will never have the means to meet him or discover what kind of man he is. At the most basic level I do not know if he is a good man or a bad man. I am trying to become a good man myself and part of that involves me having a meaningful relationship with my son. I know we will be living in different countries most of the time but we can use technology to stay in touch. I will try my best to be a good father to Ben and I cannot do more than my best. I know I need you on board for Ben and me to have any kind of a meaningful relationship.' Luke sat back in his chair, looking more strained than before, raking his fingers through his thick hair.

'Technology will only assist contact with Ben, not cement it. How often do you intend coming back to Ireland for a visit?'

'I promise you that I will come over to Ireland to see him a minimum of once a year but I want to visit much more than that amount of time. We don't get as many holidays in America as are commonplace in Ireland but I will work it out. I will have seniority and money in five years time and that brings with it more flexibility. I'm kind of hoping that when Ben grows older and you trust me more, you and he might visit us in America during the holidays'.

Everything pointed to Luke forging a successful career in America. He was a handsome man with intelligence, persuasiveness and charisma. He had been awarded a first class degree in physics and not many people with his level of mathematical ability were good at social interaction. His failure to be a proper father to Ben was the big blight on his behavioural record to date and he wanted to rectify that before it was too late. Claire hoped that one day Luke would make peace with his long suffering adoptive father since he sounded like a nice man. That thought gave rise to another question which had tormented her.

'Do your adoptive parents know about Ben?' she asked.

Luke squirmed uncomfortably in his seat.

'No, but I swear I will tell them. They will be pissed off with me for not telling them of his existence before now. They are getting older and I do not want to upset them more than I have to. Henry is recovering from prostate cancer, which has put my mother in a flap, and she is on at me to come home more often'.

'I knew it!' The words burst out of Claire's mouth, regardless of how infantile they sounded. 'I always knew deep down you had not told your parents about Ben, otherwise they would have wanted to see him'.

'My mother probably would have wanted to adopt him as well', commented Luke wryly. 'No, I have never them about Ben. I knew they would disapprove strongly about me going off to America in those circumstances so I kept my mouth shut. They were happy for me to go off on my adventure, they certainly did not try to stop me. I did not want them to be disappointed in me. Like I said, I'm not proud of my behaviour.'

'Holding your hands up and admitting you behaved badly does not make everything alright', shot back Claire.

'I admitted I did not love you Claire but, believe it or not, I did care about you. It was not easy for me to go', he asserted.

'It was easier for you to go than to stay', snorted Claire. 'Do you have a serious girl friend in America, Luke? I have to ask because, if things work out as you hope, Ben will have contact with her.'

'I do have a girlfriend and her name is Ally, short for Alison. She is a consultant who goes into companies and advises on changes in work practices and efficiencies to cut costs. She can work anywhere. She knows I am over here talking to you and she is super excited about Ben. Ally is great with kids, she loves them. What is it to be, Claire? Can I see Ben?' Luke's voice was full of eager anticipation.

It was not in Claire's nature to play power games. She had wanted this meeting with Luke to reassure herself that he was a good person who, at the very least, would do no harm to Ben and might possibly turn out to be very good for him. His openness and honesty during their conversation had surpassed her expectations. He had convinced her that he wanted to make amends and build up a meaningful relationship with his son over time. Claire believed that a child has a fundamental right to know the identity of his birth parents and this was the reason she had named Luke Elliott as Ben's father on his legal birth certificate. Luke's search for his birth parents had illustrated to her that he too considered it important for a person to know his origins. Her instinct was to trust her intuition and give her consent to Luke and Ben meeting up and getting to know each other, keeping a watchful eye on their interactions.

'I appreciate how honest and open you have been with me today Luke. I know that cannot have been easy for you to do. It does not make me excuse your past behaviour but at least it enables me to understand it a tad more. I am inclined to allow you to meet Ben but, before we make any arrangements, I want to speak with Ben and see how he feels about meeting you', said Claire magnanimously.

'Forgive me Claire but isn't Ben too young to be making those kinds of decisions for himself? It is your call, not Bens', replied Luke.

Luke was right on the button, of course, but that did not stop Claire's heckles from rising.

'He may be little but he is still a person with his own thoughts and feelings. I don't own him. Ben feels things deeply. I can guide him but, I am not going to force him to meet you if he does not want to,' said Claire firmly.

There is a sage maxim that if an individual cannot say the right thing it is best to say nothing at all. Luke clamped his mouth shut; he was not the first man to benefit from staying silent in a dispute with a woman.

'Look, I know you have to go back to America and your time here is limited. I promise to ring you tomorrow and let you know what is happening one way or the other. I expect Ben will want to see you,' said Claire, extending an olive branch.

Luke's expression lightened and he nodded his acquiescence, knowing full well that the balance of power lay with Claire.

'It is not good for Ben to grow up in ignorance of who I am. He will come looking for me one day but by then it could be too late. I know this from bitter experience. Whatever your decision is, Claire, I will abide by it. I respect you and trust you to make the right decision.'

Claire wondered if Luke's wholesome praise of her was true or fake. His glib words were practiced in achieving his goals.

'I have never given you any reason not to respect or trust me. I have always acted in Ben's best interests,' replied Claire pointedly, gathering up her belongings to leave the restaurant. 'Once upon a long time ago, you were my boyfriend for a short period of time. Big, bloody deal. The only reason I agreed to see you again is because I love Ben and you are his biological father. I never loved you, not in the true meaning of the word. Whatever it was that I once felt for you has wasted away with the passage of time.'

It felt good to publicly declare she had never truly loved him, as if she was reclaiming a piece of herself which she had given away too naively a long time ago.

'I hear you', said Luke, totally unperturbed. He deliberately turned the conversation onto a lighter note.

'I meant to ask you, what made you decide on the name Ben? I was surprised it was not William or Harry. You were always fascinated by the royal family.'

It was true, she had always avidly read magazine articles about the Royal family in Britain. Despite herself, Claire was gratified that Luke remembered some of the quirky details about her interests.

'True, I am a big fan of the princes, they have big hearts and do a lot of good. Mam always admired Prince Philip and suggested it as a name. I decided to name him Benjamin Philip, Benjamin being my grandfather's name on my father's side. The name pleased Dad and Mam no end and they have adored Ben, our little prince, since they set eyes on him. Look, I have to go now but I will contact you either tomorrow or the next day with my decision. I need time to reflect on what you have told me today.'

Claire marched away from the man who was the lost love of her life. She might be satisfied with her declaration about never having truly loved Luke but it was a false statement. Claire had not given a thought to the need for respect while they conducted their passionate affair at college. She had found it easy to love Luke but she had discovered that love needed respect and trust to sustain it. A leaf needed to be attached to a rooted tree to grow and flourish. The leaf of love needed respect and trust to root it, otherwise it withered away and died. For a relationship to work for Claire, she needed the three branches of love, respect and trust to be all present and interwoven tightly together.

'Love, trust, respect, how they all entwine; and the greatest of these is love', she mused.

Was love truly the greatest quality? Luke had broken her heart and the love was gone, but she wanted him to prove to her that she could respect him. She wanted him to prove to her that she could trust him with Ben.

A more immediate, flashing thought caused her to stop in her tracks and groan out loud.

'Damnit! How on earth am I going to tell Dad that Luke is back!'

CHAPTER THIRTY TWO

Claire was dreading telling her parents that Luke was back in Ireland and wanted to see Ben. She played out different scenarios in her head of how best to go about breaking the news to them but, curiously enough they all ended up the same way, which was with her father blowing his top. Her mother's reaction was harder to gauge and, in Claire's imagination, Eileen was as likely to adopt an outraged 'get him away from my boy' attitude to expressing an 'it will work out for the best if Ben gets to know his father' sentiment. Eileen preferred not to go against her adored husband and they usually shared the same values and acted as one unit but, very occasionally, she could break ranks with him and stand her ground alone, the epitome of a woman not for turning. If Eileen supported her daughter's decision to allow Luke and Ben to meet, then discord and disagreement with Tom was inevitable in the household, which was a state of affaires she normally worked assiduously to avoid. Eileen was worried about Tom's heart acting up and, at this stage of their lives, even if she was sympathetic to Claire's position, she might choose to say nothing and go for the peaceful option of agreeing with her obdurate husband.

Claire knew her father well and she had realised from the beginning that Tom would not be in favour of introducing Ben to Luke. Her father had earned the right to voice his opinion, given the love and attention he had lavished on Ben since the day the child was born. It was going to be difficult for Claire to stand by her decision in the face of Tom's staunch opposition but she had to be her mother's daughter and have faith in her own reasoning and instincts. The best Claire could hope for was for Tom to respectfully acknowledge that she had the right of final say as Ben's mother and primary carer. Whereas once she had feared her father would ostracise her if she broke his moral rules, she had grown wise enough to realise he would never cast her adrift because she did something he disapproved of. Claire hated to cause her aging parents' anxiety and upset but she judged it to be unavoidable in the circumstances. She brought Andrew up to speed on recent events and he offered to babysit Ben while she had the tough discussion with her parents. He arrived at the door, brandishing two toy guns which shot out pellets at high speed but which were too soft to do any harm. Andrew pretended to dodge the bullets before shouting out that he had been hit and tumbled onto the floor, a handy target to be jumped upon by a gleeful barrel of six year old boy.

'You're dead Andrew, I shot you, you're dead'. Ben could not have sounded more gleeful if by some miracle he had managed to do ten lengths of the swimming pool, filled with sharks.

'Thanks Andrew, you are a great friend', called out Claire as she headed out the door, barely noticing him.

'That's me alright, a great friend', said Andrew deadpan.

Claire's thoughts were racing forward to the contentious discussion she was about to have with her parents. She opened the door to her parents' house with the key she had never relinquished. Her parents looked up at her with surprise and pleasure when she walked into the sitting room.

Claire took in the familiar scene of her father sitting in the fabric armchair reading the newspaper and her mother reclining on the matching couch, diligently knitting a gorgeous red sweater. The fire was burning low in the grate and the pendulum of the hand crafted wooden clock caught her eye as it swung rhythmically on the wall over the mantelpiece. The crumbling statue of the Virgin Mary had been in her mother's family for generations and it stood atop the mantelpiece, draped in blue and white rosary beads. The television was on but her parents were not paying it much attention. A Waterford crystal vase, filled with a bunch of sweet smelling lilies, rested on top of an embroidered cloth which covered the coffee table. The big red plastic container holding Ben's toys was neatly tucked away in the corner of the room. There were no mirrors or bookcases in the room because neither Tom nor Eileen spent their time reading books and they considered mirrors to be functional items, best saved for the bathroom and the bedroom. If the room needed brightness then turn on the light switch. Eileen was slow to change the fixtures and fittings of her home. The floral wallpaper and the thick thread of the coffee coloured carpet contributed to the warmth and cosiness of the room. Claire felt a heel, knowing she was going to launch a rocket into their comfortable domain.

She took a big breath and ploughed on with her story in double quick time. She told her stunned parents that Luke was in Ireland for a holiday and wanted to meet Ben. It was his intention to have regular conversations with Ben over the phone and internet. He had pledged to financially contribute to his son's upbringing. He had never known his real father because he was adopted. He believed that it was in the best interests for both Ben and himself to develop a meaningful father/son relationship with each other. She then sat back and waited ten seconds for her father to explode.

'What do you mean you intend to let that no good wastrel back into your life! Have you no sense at all? Has he not done enough damage to this family? And now you're letting him weasel his way back in for a second go! It's worse than before, because now he's after Ben as well,' Tom roared, fit to be tied.

'He is not after Ben, Dad. He just wants to see him, to make amends for the past and to let Ben get to know him'.

'Ben is better off having no father than a bad one. What kind of man is this Luke fellow? You say he was adopted and that was the source of his trouble? Stuff and nonsense. Half the lads in school with me were adopted and there was nothing wrong with them. They were fine lads, in most cases you could not ask for better lads. Your runaway could not have cared less if you had put Ben up for adoption. If you had done that, Jack the lad would not have any claim or contact with the boy until he turned eighteen. Let him wait until Ben is grown and big enough to take care of himself and see if the boy goes looking for the likes of him. I would not be holding my breath, if I was him'.

'It isn't as simple as that Dad', said Claire, cursing the weakness of her tone against the full-bodied strength and conviction in her father's ringing voice.

'It is as simple as that! There is nothing plainer than the nose on your face. Didn't he want you to do away with the child altogether, may God rot his soul? Didn't he walk away from you and your boy? What kind of man does that? Let him go to hell and not come back.'

'Dad, there is a whole body of research out there which indicates that a child is better off growing up knowing who both his parents are rather than not knowing about them,' said Claire desperately. This was going worse than she feared.

'Research be damned. A lot of people writing for the sake of writing, one will spout off twaddle today and another will find against it tomorrow. Money for nothing. It is basic nature we are talking about here. In the wild, do you think an animal leaves their young and expects them to survive? Expects them to be there, waiting for them if they happen to come back after abandoning them? No, not even the stupidest animal on the planet expects to do that and here you are telling me how clever this fellow is? He is not clever, he is stupid and weak and you are stupid to be listening to him and his mealy mouthed excuses. Ben and you could have died in a ditch for all he knew or cared.'

'It is not like that Dad, we live in a civilised world and Luke knew that the baby would be well taken care of.' Claire tried to mount a credible defence in the face of her father's burning anger because she was certain that she was going to introduce Luke to Ben, despite the validity of her father's concerns.

'Have you gone mad altogether? Are you telling me now that all babies in our so-called civilised world are well taken care of? You must never listen to the news. It is a jungle out there. Terrible things are happening to children every day, in every country in the world, including Ireland. A father's job is to be around to protect his child and to make good provision, not to be indulging himself as if he was the only person that matters.'

'Luke wants to provide for Ben.' Claire had been impressed by the financial arrangements Luke had made for his son during the last year, it had meant a lot to her.

'He could not show his face if he didn't promise money. He has nothing else to offer, sitting pretty in his pad over in America. He thinks he is the big man coming over here, promising us money we do not need. He is a little man, not capable of cherishing a child, the easiest thing in the world to do. He is not offering you his time and time is worth more to a child than money. Don't be making any promises to Ben or mentioning money to him neither, because you wouldn't want him to be growing up depending on it. The first time creditors or a bitter wife claws boyo for money, any promise of money to Ben will disappear. I'll believe nothing that comes out of that lad's mouth'.

'Luke is Ben's father Dad'. Claire pointed out the obvious in an imploring tone.

Tom looked as if he wanted to jump up and pound the sky with his bunched fist.

'He planted the seed alright but he is no father. Loser Luke the lad cried on your shoulder that he had no father growing up but that was one more lie he told you. There was a good man there who adopted him and worked hard to put food on the table and grow flesh and bone on his body. He had a father all right and no appreciation of him. He did damage to that good man and to the peace in his house, as surely as he caused trouble and worry in this home too. Let him stay far away in America, we want none of him here. Ben is fine with things the way they are and you are better off without a selfish hound pulling at your coat tails.'

'Luke won't hurt Ben, he wants to make amends for the past and build up a good relationship with him. I will monitor it closely. I am only allowing it because I fully believe that it is in the long-term best interests of Ben,' said Claire, trying to stave off a feeling of helplessness.

'You and your poor judgment have given our poor boy the handicap of a weakling for a father. Listen to me now, the boy does not need that type of father. There is a lot of Howard in Ben and he will see the rotten core of the man quicker than you will. Leave it well alone and don't meddle with things you don't understand and can't know.'

This was turning out to be harder than even Claire imagined it would be. Tom's words and criticism were punching into her head, making her wince with each forceful allegation. Her throat constricted and her words wobbled in the air as she sought to bring the discussion to an end.

'I think you are wrong about this Daddy. I have to do what I think is right for Ben and that means him meeting Luke. I know you love Ben and don't want to see him hurt but this is my life and he is my son. I admit I have made mistakes, but I must follow my instinct and conscience or I will not be able to move forward at all. I will promise you though that I will not let Luke hurt Ben in any way'.

'You can't make that promise child', said Tom in a suddenly softer voice, with a note of pity threaded through it. 'You are taking everything he has told you at face value and you are not able to separate out the truth from the lies. A man is judged by his actions not words. All you know for sure is that he treated you badly once. Don't give him the opportunity to make a fool of you again. And you need not bring that boyo through our door because I will put him through the wall if I ever see him. You tell him from me that if he hurts Ben, he will have me to reckon with, and I will hurt him. I will go after him and hurt him.'

Luke was toned and muscular from his workouts in the gym and if it came to a boxing fight with her father any sane person would bet on the younger man to win. It was as if her father read her mind because he came back at her with narrowed eyes and withering voice.

'I've retired, I'm old now and they can do little with me. Laddo ran away and abandoned you the one time in his life he was required to show some mettle. Armies the world over shoot soldiers for desertion. My father saw it with his own eyes travelling along the Fermanagh border during the second world war; a soldier was running away and another British soldier put a bullet in his back. He told me that the blood splattered on the ground and the man did not get up again. The onlookers shed no tears; people said he was deserting his post at a time of war and that is what the army do to deserters.'

'What are you talking about Dad?' said Claire perplexed but relieved that Tom had stopped shouting and they could at least have a rationale discussion about their differences. 'You don't own a gun. You can't seriously be telling me that if Luke hurt us again you would chase after him with a rifle in your hand?'

'Maybe, maybe not, nobody knows for sure what they are capable of when it comes to protecting their own. I will not stand idly by and allow that fellow get away without a mark on him if he hurts my family again. I made a mistake by letting him get away with it the last time. But you are missing the point Claire, don't you forgive and forget what that Luke fella did to you and Ben too easily. Desertion is seen as the ultimate cowardice and treated with contempt. Men, governments and armies the world over, for good reasons, don't treat men who desert with leniency and women, for their own protection, should take the same attitude.'

Although men certainly had a different perspective on relationships to women, it was unlikely that Claire would find her father's theory on the treatment of desertion within relationships in any academic texts. People ended up in jail for following through on such theories. Maybe her mother could row in behind her with a gentler standpoint.

'What do you think Mam? You have been very quiet,' she asked Eileen, who had been sitting still, silent as a stone.

'I think that you are following your heart Claire and I pray that it works out well. You are big enough and old enough to make your own decisions and bear the consequences. You are giving Luke a chance to redeem himself, which is the Christian way. Your father will see the inherent goodness of your intentions when he calms down. But I warn you, if Luke disappoints and hurts a hair on Ben's head, I am with your father all the way.'

Eileen's answer was worthy of a master diplomat or the Pope himself. Tom had always striven to live his life according to the teachings of his Christian faith and his wife was gently reminding him of the noble aspirations proclaimed in the Bible. In lighter circumstances Claire might have laughed aloud, for here was her remarkable mother supporting both Tom and herself with their diametrically opposing views to each other. The feminist movement had lost a powerful ally when they failed to recruit Eileen Howard to the official cause of the sisterhood. Claire never loved her mother more than in that moment when she lent her support to Claire in the face of Tom's strident disapproval.

Tom was having none of it.

'The old testament came before the new one, woman', exclaimed Tom forcefully. 'Plenty of Christians believe in taking an eye for an eye and I'll be following that advice before I see my daughter turn the other cheek to be slapped down twice by that useless punk. Claire is not doing the right thing, she is doing the wrong thing. She is going to let that no good fellow back into her life after being well rid of him for years and she is even foolhardy enough to fall for him all over again. No decent man will get a look in while she ties herself up in knots and wastes time with that runaway degenerate. She will be left alone when Ben is fully grown and flown the nest and we are dead and buried, with no one to look after her and keep her company.'

Tom swung from glaring at Eileen to face down his daughter.

'Let go of the past and organise your life without that spineless, selfish snake of a man pulling you down Claire, making you doubt yourself. He had his chance and he blew it. Don't be giving him another opportunity to ruin your young life. You don't need Luke Elliott in your life and Ben doesn't either. The boy has enough people around him who care for him and treat him well to be happy and content. You are gambling on the boy's father coming good and it is a bad bet.'

Claire's eyes were swimming with tears as she listened to her father's words hammering home all her worst, hidden fears. It was time she fled home to lick her wounds in peace. Her father had one last throw of the dice.

'In the unlikely event the boyo makes his millions and keeps up contact with Ben he might come after you for more access to the boy than you are willing to make and you won't have the money to fight him. I'd keep the boy's passport under lock and key somewhere safe just in case, if I was you.'

'That is enough Tom, you've had your say and you are upsetting Claire. The poor girl looks traumatised,' interjected Eileen sharply. 'Leave it alone now, it is her decision and she must do what she thinks is best. It is her life. It is wrong for us to pass judgment. The world and its values are changing fast. I don't pretend to like Luke Elliott but I do believe that there must be good in him because every cell in Ben's body is good and believe it or not, half of it comes from his biological father. Genetics and DNA are more powerful than we know. Besides, we reared Claire and I refuse to believe she has such low self esteem that she could fall in love with a complete low life. Give her some credit.'

'She is stupid when it comes to him', snapped Tom.

'I won't have it Tom. You owe Claire an apology. Not another word out of you or you will be making your own dinner for a month', threatened Eileen, furious with her husband.

'Thanks for the vote of confidence Mam', said Claire tearfully, while Tom stood there dumb founded by his wife's unaccustomed sternness.

'Your father is right in one thing Claire, it would be a mistake for you to fall for Luke again. Once the trust is broken, it is very difficult to repair. You are young enough to start afresh with somebody else, a kind honourable man who will never betray your trust. If you keep your head on and remember that two people together have to take care of each other, through thick and thin, then your instincts will guide you right', cautioned Eileen.

'Thanks Mam, your support means a lot to me. Dad, I am really sorry you feel the way you do but I will do everything I can to ensure Ben's happiness. I will let you both know what happens'.

'You need not bother, we will know by the boy. It is Ben you should be thinking of, not being ridiculous and using the word trust in the same sentence as a man who left you and your babe out in the bitter cold. If there is any doubt about whether an action will bring harm to a child you just say no, you do not take chances. There is truth in the old saying, 'Fool me once, shame on you, fool me twice, shame on me'. Let him bugger off and find himself a new family and leave this one alone.......and I don't care if I am eating boiled eggs for a week,' bellowed Tom.

There was no point in staying any longer and Claire fled the room before the tears started to stream down her face. Telling her parents about Luke Elliot had been hard going but it seemed nothing in her life, either at home or at work, was destined to be easy for the foreseeable future. Perhaps her memory was playing tricks on her but she did not recall crying much as a teenager. She had gone years without shedding a tear and yet here she was weeping enough teardrops to end a drought in Africa. She reached inside the glove compartment of the car to find a handkerchief and an emergency make-up kit to repair the ravages on her puffy eyed face. She had to make herself presentable before she arrived home, enough people had been upset tonight without adding Andrew to the list.

Andrew was such a good friend and she was relying on him for emotional as well as practical assistance. The boyish, unassuming Andrew was turning out to be a tower of strength in her time of need, a solid mass in a sea of uncertainty. Unlike Luke, Andrew had never let her down. She had entered into this game plan with Luke on the understanding that Ben's welfare and happiness came first and everything that happened between them must be within those guiding principles. Her father had made it clear that he did not believe she could control the situation and had labelled her a fool and Luke a weakling. If that harsh judgment was true, then Ben was deeply unfortunate to have such unworthy parents. She would be a fool to fall for Luke Elliott again, as both her parents had been quick to point out. But maybe the real question centred on whether she was a fool not to fall in love with Andrew? He was wonderful to Ben and herself and he had admitted his loving feelings for her. The sparks could burst into a roaring fire if the right fuel was used, thought Claire, grimacing at the less than romantic metaphor. She revved up the car and resolved that she must never again be fool enough to allow Andrew Kennedy to play second fiddle to Luke Elliott in her life; otherwise her father might threaten to kill her with the rifle he was brandishing about in his imagination.

CHAPTER THIRTY THREE

Claire took a deep breath as she knocked on Daniel's half-open door, holding tightly onto her letter of resignation. She was not looking forward to having an intense conversation with Daniel but it could not be worse than the one she had endured with her father. She was nervous but determined to re-capture some of the self esteem which had been bullied out of her. She realised that confronting the big boss in his den was not without its risks since there was a possibility that he could rear up and maul her if he felt under attack. Claire did not want to antagonise Daniel; rather she would much prefer to leave the organisation on better terms with him given that she used to hold him in such high regard. Overriding this consideration was her determination to cause Ashley some damage before she left. Ashley had used the power bestowed on her through her managerial role to halt Claire's career development in the prestigious company and to box her into a lower level position than she had been recruited for. She was blocked from appointment to higher salaried posts within the organisation. The damage to her professional life had not been confined to the workplace as the worry, hurt and anxiety it had caused had inevitably spilled over into her private life, impinging negatively on her relationships with family and friends. All the time the good ship Ashley sailed on, convinced of her own worth and invincibility. Claire did not have the power to sink her but she was going to attempt to put a hole in her starboard as a small pay back for the havoc Ashley had wrought in her life.

Daniel looked up uninvitingly from his computer, clearly not pleased to see her.

'Can I come in Daniel? I have something to give you,' said Claire, relieved to hear that her voice was steady.

He hesitated before nodding his head in affirmation. Claire told herself not to take his reluctance to talk to her personally, he could easily be preparing for a meeting or be pushed for time working to a deadline. Claire crossed the width of the room and handed him over her brief letter of resignation, which he took in with a glance.

'I wish you all the best Claire. Thank you for all the work you have done here during the last three years'.

Typical Daniel, polite and gracious but cold and remote. There was no mention of how sorry people in the department would be to see her go and there was certainly no suggestion that perhaps she could reconsider her decision and continue to work within the company because she had a promising career there if she choose to stay. Not a bit of it, Claire had the impression that if Daniel were the porter, he would be packing up her bags for her even as they spoke.

'Given that I'll be leaving here soon, I'd like to speak with you about the reasons behind my departure,' Claire stated.

Daniel walked out from behind his big rectangular desk and beckoned her towards the circular desk with chairs at the other side of the room, closing the door on the way. The older man and the younger woman sat down and eyeballed each other.

'I want you to know that I've had a very tough time working for Ashley. I have tried talking to her about prioritising work loads and changing unrealistic deadlines but to no avail. She hindered rather than helped me during the budgeting process. She has been rude, unpleasant and unprofessional to talk to on a daily basis. In regards to the fixed asset register, she has demanded that I input unnecessary data into the system which consumes processing time but has no useful output. The make-up of my work load has deteriorated under her management, with the financial analysis side losing out to an ever increasing number of administrative tasks. My role has changed beyond recognition, to my professional detriment. I have to say to you that Ashley has made it very difficult for me here and she is the main reason I am leaving. I believe she has been motivated by an unprofessional, personal dislike of me,' said Claire, not holding back.

Daniel's face remained inscrutable while Claire laid down her case; she was saying nothing new to him and he had already made up his mind to disregard her on these issues and support Ashley instead. Ashley had always been careful to be extremely pleasant to Daniel, he had never witnessed her obnoxious behaviour. Claire guessed that as far as he was concerned, Ashley was good at her job and it was easier for him to replace her rather than Ashley. Life was tough and everyone could not be a winner.

'But Daniel, I am not the only person who has left the department because of Ashley. Three more have gone because of her,' asserted Claire.

This statement got his attention, making Claire pleased to see that she had managed to rattle his cage.

'What do you mean? Who else has left because of Ashley?' Daniel demanded to know.

Claire went in for maximum effect, using her big guns first.

'Amy left because of Ashley', she stated.

'Amy left because she wanted to travel to Australia Claire, not because of her relationship with Ashley,' asserted Daniel.

'Amy did leave to go to Australia but it was only for a holiday. She told me that the timing of her decision to leave came down to the fact that she could not tolerate remaining here to work with Ashley. She had intended staying on for at least another year, probably more, because she really liked it here and was getting great work experience and she wanted to ask for a leave of absence, as oppose to resign, so she could return here after her travels.' Claire drew breath but, as Daniel appeared to be listening to her, she ploughed right on.

'It all changed when Ashley started to work here and Amy had to report to her. She quickly decided that as she could not work for Ashley and it was better for her to go sooner rather than later. She did not find Ashley honest or upfront in her dealings with her. Amy had no interest in sticking around to report to such an unworthy manager. She took a holiday in Australia while she applied for jobs and she discovered that her accountancy qualification brought her more opportunities if she lived outside Ireland. She succeeded in landing a job with an oil company based in Scotland, starting on nearly three times the money she was on here. Amy is doing marvellously well in her new job and has already been given a big promotion. But Leictreach lost her to another company primarily because she refused to stay here reporting to Ashley,' divulged Claire.

'Amy did not say any of this to me when she was leaving,' said Daniel.

'She will certainly say it to you now, if you talk to her. Amy instructed me to give you her phone number and here it is,' said Claire, pushing a slip of paper towards him. 'You can discuss her dealings with Ashley any time you want. Amy considers Ashley to be a liar and holds her in contempt and she also believes that Ashley spread a false rumour about her. Ring her and you will find out. Amy told me that you did not ask her the reasons behind her departure, you erroneously made the assumption that it was purely related to her desire to visit Australia. But one thing is certain, Amy left primarily because she refused to stay here reporting to Ashley, as surely as I am leaving,' stressed Claire, pushing her argument home.

Claire was heartened when Daniel pocketed the piece of paper which actually had the names and phone numbers of three people typed on it. She knew Daniel had been very impressed with Amy. Amy had been striking, possessing the height and figure of a model along with a good humoured, cheerful disposition and a practical, calm head on her shoulders. Claire knew that Daniel, more than most people, believed that every person could be replaced in a job but even he had regretted Amy's departure and had wanted her to stay. Amy had huge potential and her loss to the company was an ace in the hole in dealing this round of cards with Daniel.

'You mentioned that three people left because of Ashley. Who are the other two?' questioned Daniel, giving Claire his full attention.

'Aaron left because Ashley made him feel so tense, he could not switch off from work when he got home and it was interfering with the way he interacted with his girlfriend and the enjoyment of his hobbies', imparted Claire.

Aaron and Claire had started their employment in Leictreach within a couple of months of each other and, while they were never close friends, they had always got on well together. Aaron had confided in Claire that he knew he had to leave when he found himself sketching hideous caricatures of Ashley instead of nude drawings of his gorgeous girlfriend Bethany. Claire could never understand what a born artist like Aaron was doing working in the Accounts Payable section of a finance department but she guessed he needed the security of a nine to five job to put bread on the table and oil paint on his canvasses. He was a gentle soul who would not hurt a fly, although he could definitely sketch it.

'He is working in the finance office of Fruor, a five star hotel located no more than ten minutes' walk away from Leictreach. He is paid less money than he earned here but feeling much happier. There was no other reason for him to leave other than his dislike for Ashley and the oppressive atmosphere which gripped the general office in the aftermath of her arrival. Have you not noticed how the atmosphere has changed Daniel? It is quiet all the time and you hardly ever hear anybody laughing or joking anymore', commented Claire.

'It could be argued that a quiet room is a sign that people are taking their work seriously and concentrating on getting through it as best they can,' retorted Daniel.

'People in Finance worked hard for you out of respect and admiration, not fear and unhappiness. They always took their job seriously but they still managed to have an occasional chat and laugh together throughout the day. Nowadays the silence is deadly. Most people want to do their job well if they can Daniel and they will put in extra effort for a word of praise. There was never a question of people not pulling their weight in your department prior to Ashley's arrival and you know it,' said Claire bravely.

'I did notice that the joking had stopped and thought it a pity', admitted Daniel. 'I put it down to people like Emmet leaving and quieter people coming in to fill their positions. Who is the third person I should know about who had a problem with Ashley?'

'Paula Dobson', said Claire, playing her final card.

Paula had been the first to leave when Ashley started working in Finance. She had worked in the Payroll office efficiently for years and had been sorely missed when she left. When Paula qualified as an accountant, somewhat unusually she had opted to stay on working as payroll manager, because she enjoyed the role. She knew all about the allowances and bonuses, the individual contractual arrangements and perks, all about the pension administration, payroll processing and the accounting aspects of the job. Her mind was full of payroll information, built up over many years and it included her advising senior executives on how to minimise their personal tax liabilities. Daniel had totally taken her skillset for granted because payroll was an area which nobody mentioned if everything ran like clockwork but all hell broke loose if it was not administered correctly. Since Paula's departure, Daniel had found to his cost that there were many payroll clerks who could run a payroll but who were incapable of doing a reconciliation or understanding the accounting implications of the payroll function. The efficiency of the payroll office nose dived as soon as Paula was out the door and this had necessitated Daniel sending in a team to clean up the resultant mess.

'Paula Dobson left because she was spending too much time travelling to and from the office and it became too much for her. She needed more time to concentrate on her daughter. She wanted to only work part time and be closer to home, which would free up time for her to build up a private client portfolio,' said Daniel.

'Paula got her driving licence before she left, which meant she could make the journey to and from work in forty minutes by car. No Daniel, the deciding factor in Paula's decision to resign when she did was because she found Ashley too interfering and offensive. Ashley was incredibly rude to Paula when there was a delay in putting Alex Brennan on payroll after he took up the post as HR Director and she never apologised to Paula for her outburst. After that incident Ashley would not leave Paula alone to get on with her job and she bombarded her with emails. She did not know Paula's background and assumed she was a run of the mill payroll clerk. Paula was wonderful at her job and did not appreciate being micro managed. She had been toying with the idea of leaving and, after two weeks dealing with Ashley, Paula decided she could do better for herself and be happier outside the company and she left'.

Daniel looked stunned by what he was hearing. It was a real achievement because he had the ability to make his face as inscrutable as a secret agent.

'You can telephone Amy, Aaron and Paula anytime to verify what I have told you. I have spoken to them all during the last week and they have all confirmed that they welcome the opportunity to talk to you about their bad experiences with Ashley.'

Daniel looked across the desk at Claire.

'I'm glad you have told me all this Claire. You share an office with Anna. Are you aware of her situation?'

Claire nodded affirmatively.

'The information you have given me has helped me to understand her position much better. Anna has worked here a long time and has a sterling record. I am hoping that she will return to work soon. She has four children and is the main breadwinner for her family. She needs her job here. I had not realised the extent of the problem but I am glad to say that I have already told her that she will not have to work for Ashley anymore. I am moving her to Debtors where she will be reporting to Peter and, if she encounters any problems, she is to come directly to me,' said Daniel.

'You have been away so much Daniel, you have not been able to see what has been going on here in your absence. You let Ashley take over the interview process, which means she is choosing the staff who come to work here. They have immediate allegiance to her because she gave them a job. What you do not realise is that Ashley's behaviour and actions are dictating who gets to stay on working here. It is all very personal and work should not be organised through personalities, we are meant to be bigger and better than that.'

Daniel's face turned to stone but he said nothing.

Claire hesitated momentarily, wondering if she should shut her mouth and withdraw gracefully while the going was good for her or should she go even further and express other thoughts which had been troubling her but which placed her on shakier grounds. Eileen had a favourite saying of 'In for a penny, in for a pound' and on the wisdom of that old adage, Claire decided to go for broke.

'Daniel, you are losing control of your department to Ashley. She is ambitious and will want your job next. She has no respect for people and, at some level, that includes you. She can pretend empathy but she does not feel it. The company is also vulnerable to a bullying case in an employee rights tribunal. If Anna decides to press forward with her complaints she will not be alone. I will be standing with her, shoulder to shoulder, and other people will line up in support of her,' said an impassioned Claire.

'I think you have said enough Claire. I get the picture. I will say that it is clear to me that I have to change my working arrangements to allow me to spend more time here in the finance department', said Daniel, reasserting his authority.

'People will be delighted to hear it Daniel, your presence has been sorely missed within the department', said Claire, drawing in her horns.

There can only be one acting boss in the department. Given that he was only in the office one day a week, Daniel had become the nominal boss while Ashley was flexing her muscle to exert the real power and control. Daniel intended to sweep back and take full control of his department again. Claire did not know the manner in which he was going to do it but she was ready to bet a month's salary that it would involve a level of discomfort for Ashley.

'There is one more thing I think you should know Daniel. You remember Tracey Barnes? She was working for an agency but she was physically here on the premises for nearly a year. The day Ashley instructed the agency to never send Tracey to work here again was the same day Tracey miscarried her baby,' confided Claire.

'There was never a word about Tracey being pregnant', said Daniel, his face grave.

'She did not want to say anything. She was hoping to be made permanent and she was afraid that she would lose her job if you knew she was pregnant or she missed out time due to her pregnancy,' said Claire.

'Not only would that be against the law, it would be morally reprehensible. As far as I am aware, a young woman losing her job because of pregnancy has never happened in Leictreach. There are stringent safeguards in place to protect pregnant women and we have arrangements to support expectant mothers. It would never happen on my watch', said Daniel.

'But Daniel, you were not watching and it did happen', said Claire softly, the words lingering in the air. 'Tracey is only in her early twenties. She made me promise not to say anything about her pregnancy. She did not want anybody to know, including you and Ashley. She was already feeling scared and insecure before she got pregnant. She was on the agency payroll, making her rights here during her pregnancy much more tenuous than if she was on the company payroll. Tracey believed she had no rights. Ashley fired her for being unreliable, when she was actually fighting severe morning sickness and meeting doctor's appointments'.

'I had no knowledge of Tracey's pregnancy. If I had known she was pregnant, an entirely different course of action would have been taken. If what you tell me is true Claire, I am sorrier than I can say. I will make contact with the agency and enquire about Tracey's whereabouts. Leave it with me. I will take up the matter from here', stated Daniel.

'Her medical records will confirm the timing of her miscarriage. She had to go into hospital for treatment. If you had called her in and had a chat with her about her sudden disappearances, she might have told you she was pregnant. She could have been helped out, not fired, if only you or another manager had asked', said Claire sadly. 'I was not going to say anything due to the promise I once gave her, but it has been on my conscience. She was heartbroken when she lost her baby.'

'I can imagine, I have children myself Claire and know something about these things. I am not completely heartless. It is also apparent to me that we should be carrying out exit interviews as a matter of routine, to uncover the real reasons behind a person's resignation.

Daniel paused, raking his hand through his thick mane of grey hair.

'Before you go Claire, I do owe you an apology. I have been away too much, tied up with developing the new IT operating system and handling my other responsibilities in the wider company. I placed too much trust in my managers, without it being earned first. I put the increase of the staff turnover rate in the finance department down to opportunities opening up in a growing economy. I admit I have not noticed what has been happening here in my own department', said Daniel.

Although Claire was painfully aware of Daniel's limitations as a people manager, hearing the longed for apology still brought a lump to Claire's throat. She was surprised to find that Daniel's apology meant a lot to her.

She got up from her chair to shake Daniel's hand.

'People often leave a job because of a manager, not the company Daniel. I appreciate you taking the time to listen to me. I'd like you to know that when I reported directly into you, I enjoyed the work and held you in the highest esteem and respect', she said.

'I wish you the very best of luck and good fortune in the coming years Claire', said Daniel graciously. He clasped her hand warmly and gave her a big, sincere smile. 'You have put me back on the right track. It will be no trouble to you to sort out your new company. I have no doubt that you will be successful in your future career.'

'Goodbye Daniel. All the very best to you too', replied Claire sincerely.

Claire left the room with her dignity intact and a deep sense of satisfaction that the bullet she had aimed at Ashley, activated through Daniel, had struck home. She had reclaimed her own sense of self respect and was able to revel in the lovely, bubbly feeling swelling up inside her. It was a long time since she had felt free and happy. Amy, Aaron and Paula were all likeable, high calibre people who had worked harmoniously in the finance department for a minimum of three years each prior to Ashley's commencement with the company. Poor Tracey had been treated appallingly by Ashley, there were dogs in Ireland who were treated with infinite more kindness and understanding. Claire had succeeded in making Daniel realise that valued members of his department were opting to leave the company rather than stay and report to Ashley. Why stay and report to a bad manager with an appalling attitude, one who treated staff members very differently depending on whether she liked you or not? If conditions were better in the wider economy, then even more people might be legging it out the door.

Ashley had believed herself to be impervious to harm, because most of the subordinates who disliked her, for good reasons, had obligingly and quietly resigned their posts and gone. Out of sight meant out of mind; they were ex colleagues as opposed to present colleagues and so appeared to have no voice. There had been no nasty disputes and settlements. The ones who remained were mostly falling over themselves to please and appease her. Deirdre was the sole person in the department who stood her ground with Ashley and, by some miracle, was still treated with civility. Ashley had thought herself to be safe, with the resources of the company behind her, but it was an illusion which could be shattered by a disparate group of people coming together to challenge her or alternatively, a more senior company executive publicly withdrawing his support.

Nobody likes or easily forgives being walked upon or disrespected. There were people out there lying in the grass, ready and willing to pounce on Ashley if the opportunity presented itself. Claire thought of people who had suffered harassment by Ashley as being like beads on a necklace, which needed somebody to bind them all together in a chain to tighten and pull around her neck. Although it was possible for a bully to pick on a solitary person and to be perfectly pleasant to everybody else, Ashley had not been content to confine her bullying behaviour to just one person. The fact that more than one person had been affected by her bullying behaviour gave her victims leverage in seeking redress. It had taken time but people were ready to spring into action against Ashley and the company which employed her, if they were asked to unite together to tell their stories at an employment tribunal hearing. Claire reflected that it was a great pity that it was much easier for a person to speak out about their experiences of bullying once they have left the employ of the company, rather than when they were actually experiencing it from within the organisation.

A key question which teased her for an answer was why had Daniel listened to her today, when he had not heard a word she had tried to tell him for months? Even as Claire felt light headed with jubilation because Daniel had finally listened to her and apologised, she noticed that he had not asked her to withdraw her letter of resignation and stay working on with Leictreach. The answer suddenly dawned on her; Daniel had listened to her only after she had presented him with her letter of resignation. He had decided to grant her one last audience, after which he would never again have to listen to a word which came out of her mouth. Yes, he seemed to accept the truth of what she had told him but he did not like it. Daniel was not comfortable with the message or the messenger and hence, he preferred her to be out of the way.

Claire had once had blind faith and trust in Daniel but he had let her down badly. She knew from bitter experience that it was difficult to mend a relationship once the trust had broken down. Daniel was an excellent accountant who balanced the books brilliantly but, he did not know his people. If he did not know his people and recognise what motivated them, how could he be a good people manager? He was so busy with the technical demands of his job and putting financial information together to meet relentless, repeating deadlines that Claire doubted if he could ever learn to understand and manage his staff well. Daniel may be glad to see the back of her but Claire was more than ready and willing to take her chances with a new senior manager and face fresh challenges somewhere else. She squared back her shoulders in a super woman pose, before relaxing them to half skip light heartedly along the empty corridor.

CHAPTER THIRTY FOUR

Claire put a lot of thought into choosing the venue where Ben and Luke were going to be introduced to each other. She had decided against inviting Luke into their own home at such a delicate point of proceedings, on the grounds that it would have revealed a huge amount of information about their private lives to him. The pictures on the mantelpiece and the possessions which filled the house told many stories to curious eyes and there was no need to allow Luke Elliot read the book of their lives. She wanted to keep the first meeting between father and son as low key as possible and prevent it from becoming emotionally charged or dramatic in any way. Luke's true identity was not to be made known to Ben. Claire was going to introduce him as a friend from college whom she had not seen in ages because he lived abroad. She reserved the right to tell Ben that Luke was his real Daddy if everything went well but she had to pick her moment carefully. It felt bizarre that at the end of this potentially life changing week Luke was going to return to America; he was literally flying into their lives and straight out again.

Claire decided it was best to meet Luke in a non-threatening, accessible, public place. She considered suggesting the local play ground as their meeting place but ruled it out on the basis that action packed Ben would be dashing from the swing to the slide to the climbing frame and Luke could consider himself lucky if he got more than a hello or goodbye out of the child. It was far better to choose a setting which could facilitate conversation rather than detract from it. She needed an indoor venue, if only to guard against the unpredictability of the Irish weather. After much deliberation Claire finally settled on "Books Doorway & Restaurant", a bookstore cum eatery tucked away on a side street in the city centre. It sold a sample of every genre of book in the store downstairs and had a winding staircase leading up to a bright, spacious restaurant on the second floor. Claire particularly liked the layout of the eating area, which was divided between a section containing standard tables and chairs and another area which held comfortable sofas and armchairs. The interior furnishings were warm and inviting, partly because the building had been handed down from one generation to the next, each adapting to their customers' needs and expectations as time passed by. The proprietors re-invested the profits into the business, providing their customers with a wide range of books to choose from and high quality fresh food sold at competitive prices. The customers felt relaxed and welcome and showed their appreciation by rarely leaving the store empty handed. The building was off the beaten track, hence a person had to either seek it out or have the good fortune to stumble on it by chance.

Claire mulled it over in her mind and came to the conclusion that 'Books Doorway' ticked all the boxes and was the perfect venue for the upcoming encounter with Luke. A plan of action formed in her mind and she briefed Luke on its key elements in a short telephone conversation. She would take Ben along to the bookstore at eleven o' clock on the Monday morning. Luke was to arrive on the premises at an earlier time because it was his job to lay claim to a sofa and a coffee table in the restaurant upstairs. Claire and Ben would select a handful of books in the children's section and enter the restaurant, where they would meet and greet Luke. Ben was to review the batch of books with Luke, then pick out his favourite one and the conversation would end with Luke buying the book for Ben and giving it to him. This sequence of events was to be followed faithfully by them every morning, Monday to Friday, exactly at the same time of day and in the same place.

Luke was not gripped with enthusiasm for the plan.

'Won't it be boring for the kid to come to the same place every day? Kids don't like to sit still, even I can remember that. I used to hate sitting in restaurants, it was as bad as shopping. Surely we can spice it up a bit and bring him to different places, like bowling or a circus or other places that kids like to go? A bookstore in the morning is going to be filled with boring old farts hiding from the cold,' he demurred fiercely, sure that if left to his own devices he could come up with a much better arrangement for them to enjoy.

Claire brushed aside his arguments.

'Books are wonderful for revealing both the real world and the world of imagination to children. You and Ben can get to know each other talking over the books, they will give you a focal point. There is no point dragging Ben around from pillar to post for a whole week in search of entertainment and, at the end of it all, he is exhausted and you both have hardly spoken a word to each other. Or do you not want to get to know your child?' she challenged.

Luke had no option but to reluctantly agree to her plan. Claire reflected wryly that if she had been as adamant in her dealings with her work colleagues as she had just been with Luke, then Ashley might have given a second thought to the wisdom of steam rolling over her. Then again, Claire had to go against her non-confrontational nature and manage Luke Elliott forcefully for one week only, not month upon worrisome month.

On Monday morning Ben could not believe his luck when his mother allowed him to gather up as many books as he could carry in the bookstore. His Mom and Granny usually made him put the books back in place on the book shelves after taking out two, saying he must be careful to treat the books with respect because they belonged to the shopkeeper and not to him.

'Now Ben, you can bring a handful of books upstairs to the restaurant but we are only going to buy one of them; you will have to choose only one' cautioned Claire.

'But Mommy, these are all really good, it's very hard to pick just one", he protested.

Claire seized the opening gratefully.

'Listen love, I'm meeting a friend here called Luke. You have never met him but he is very nice. If you show him the books, I am sure he will help you to decide on the best one,' she suggested.

'Alright Mom. But does Luke know anything about books?' asked Ben suspiciously. 'Like, what makes a good book an' not a bad one. Some grown ups like rubbish books. I want a good book, the best book.'

It was typical of her son to want the best quality product, observed Claire with amusement. It was a pity she could not afford to buy him more of everything. Her mother told her not to be ridiculous, the child could get more fun out of a cardboard box and using his imagination rather than playing with most of the bright, shiny plastic toys scattered throughout the house, which he hardly looked at most of the time.

'Luke is clever and he knows lots about books as well as plenty of other things. He is musical and is able to sing and play the guitar. You can start a party anywhere singing along with a guitar', Claire said brightly.

'Perhaps I can be friends with Luke too an' he can teach me how to play the guitar. I like parties an' I can sing really good. Is he a teacher?' asked Ben hopefully, for he had a huge respect for teachers.
'No sweetheart, Luke is not a teacher, I think he helps develop new products for computers. I'm sure he'd like to be your friend. I have talked about you to him and he is looking forward to seeing you.'

'Some grown ups like me to be quiet. Remember that ol' meanny in the cinema?'

'You can talk to Luke, no worries darling', reassured Claire. 'Look, he is over there.'

Claire smiled encouragingly at Luke as he unwound his long body up off the sofa, but her heart was racing and her mouth was dry. It was impossible to decipher the multitude of emotions pulling at her heartstrings, although concern and anxiety were certainly present. The stakes were high; what if Ben took against Luke? 'Please God, let it all work out well,' she beseeched. 'Steady on, be cool'. Cool? Where had that word come from? She had never played it cool in her life.

'Hello Luke, how nice to see you again. This is my son Ben. Ben, say hello to Luke, he is an old friend of mine from college.' Claire's voice was more high pitched than normal but her son did not seem to notice.

'Hello Luke, I don't know you but my Mom says you are good at picking out books.' Ben said politely, gesturing to the books in his arms. It could not be denied that Ben was a task orientated child.

Luke scrunched down to the child's level, smiling in gentle delight. As he scrutinised the boy's face, an incredulous flame of recognition and pride leapt into life, illuminating his own visage. For an adopted person, seeing a flesh and blood offspring for the first time packed an emotional punch. It was a definite photo frame moment but Claire did not want to intrude on its delicate intimacy by whipping out her mobile phone to capture it.

'Hello Ben, you have no idea how pleased I am to meet you. I see you have a fine collection of books there. I'd be delighted to go through them with you.' said Luke, speaking with great charm and warmth.

'Mommy says I can only have one but it's hard,' Ben responded seriously. 'They're all good. There's one about fighting dragons an' a dog who's lost and has to find its way back home. And Fireman Sam saving Norman Price, I mightn't get that one 'cos he's always saving somebody. This one's about dinosaurs but I dunno, Granny got me one of those already. This one's good about the trucks and cars, its' got mazes 'an stickers. What do you think? Mommy is carrying even more books to choose from, look!' he pointed to his mother.

'I can see the problem, it certainly is a tough job to narrow the choice down to one', agreed Luke. 'Here, let me help you with those', Luke reached out to take the books easily from Ben and Claire. She was totally startled when he bent down to lightly plant a kiss on her cheek. 'Thank you,' her murmured softly close to her ear, his skin clean shaven and his breath fresh. Claire detected a subtle smell of cologne and breathed it in, not recognising the brand but knowing that she liked it. She smiled uncertainly up into his gleaming azure eyes. Maybe it was going to work out well after all, despite her father's obdurate misgivings. There had never been any love lost between Luke and her father. She remembered Luke describing Tom Howard as an awkward old bugger who must be close to croaking it and that was well before she got pregnant with Ben.

'Ben sweetie, sit down and relax. I'm going to the counter to buy us drinks and cake but I will be back in a minute.'

Two pairs of eyes swung in her direction, identical in shape and colour. The shape of the eyes were unusual in that they were big and round in the centre but then also had an unexpected slant at the edges. What surprised her was how glad she felt that Luke and Ben shared that one strong physical feature. Ben's soft unblemished boyish face was stamped with the features which had characterised the Howard men for generations. He was going to be a handsome man when fully grown, with a square forehead, strong jaw, broad cheekbones, straight nose and full lips, capped with wavy chestnut hair. He could have been a replica of his Grandfather Tom or Uncle Martin except for the distinctive cerulean eyes he had inherited from Luke, blue as the deepest ocean sparkling under a hot Caribbean sun.

'Let me get the refreshments for you. What would you like?', Luke offered politely.

'Thank you but no', Claire refused pleasantly. 'I'd prefer it if you and Ben settled down and got started. Choosing books is a serious business and we don't have a lot of time', said Claire lightly. Luke understood that the real task she was referring to was of father and son getting to know each other in a restricted time frame.

When Claire returned to them bearing a tray loaded with food and beverage she sat down quietly, trying to be as still as possible. She did not want to intrude on the natural rhythm of their easy conversation with each other. She watched as Luke turned a page of the book and rested his hand lightly on Ben's shoulder and was surprised when the boy did not immediately shrug it away.

'It was a good idea to come here Claire', acknowledged Luke, gesturing at the books. 'These books are giving us plenty to talk about. I thought kids were born with a screen in their hands these days, not books.'

'It is inevitable that screen time will become the next battle with Ben but I am trying to delay it for as long as possible. Parents of older children tell me that controlling screen time is a real nightmare for them, as the kids switch between console, iPad and mobile phone. Boys get hooked on gaming and girls are more likely to become addicted to their iPad and phones. I love books myself and I read to Ben at bed time as often as I can. It is an activity we can share together', said Claire. She paused, realising she was opening up glimpses of their private lives to Luke but, she decided to plough on.

'Ben, why don't you show Luke the book about the Zoo and you can tell him about the last time we went there with Granddad', Claire suggested. 'The Zoo is one of Ben's favourite places.'

'I like the tigers an' the elephants an' the monkeys an' the giraffes. The giraffe are very tall, even the baby one is tall. Paul, he's my friend, went on an elephant's back at the end of a circus but we can't do that in our Zoo. Granddad says he went on the elephant's back when he was a boy, he even fed it once. He knows all about the animals,' commented Ben.

'The Zoo is a great place. Perhaps the three of us can visit it together this week?" suggested Luke, steering the conversation away from the tricky subject of Claire's father and onto the topic of going out and about with Ben. Claire felt a flash of annoyance at Luke's brazen attempt to change their rendezvous point. Before she could say anything, Ben surprised her by politely declining the offer.

'No thank you', said Ben, 'I go there with my Granddad and my Mom. It's our special place together. We'll have to find a different place.'

'What is wrong with meeting right here?' chimed in Claire. "It has begun to rain outside and we are nice and warm inside.'

It was true, the rain was pelting down against the window panes, drumming out a protest at being locked out of their cosy world.

'The incessant rain in Ireland, it never changes,' muttered Luke as he glanced out of the window at the sodden clouds dominating the skyline.

Claire got the distinct feeling that he was never nostalgic about the changeable nature of the weather in Ireland; it was one of the many things he was glad to have left behind him.

'The rain keeps the countryside spectacularly green and beautiful and gives us amazing lakes and rivers to enjoy. People are embracing outdoor activities and dressing appropriately for the weather. The kids are playing sports all year round', said Claire, defending the country Ben and herself lived in and from which he had chosen to flee.

Ben reached for a big slice of chocolate cake, oblivious to the subtle undertones in the adult conversation.

'Mmmmm, this cake is yummy. Good choice Mom.' Ben beamed his approbation at Claire before continuing his chat with Luke. 'I play GAA football and hurling. Once, Paul and me were in defence an' we saw a worm and we watched it for a long time and then the ball came our end and they scored a point. So now I'm in forward. Didn't want to be a back anyways.'

'Much more fun to watch a worm than play in defence, isn't it?', laughed Luke.

'Yeah, I like to score goals. An' I like splashing in puddles and putting my tongue out to catch the rain. Like this', said Ben, sticking his tongue out and making a funny face. 'But Mommy doesn't like me getting wet.'

'What else do you like?' said Luke.

'Lots of things, I like swimming but not getting' dressed after, that's bad. I like snow and playin' with my friends and making things with my Granddad. An' I like ice cream, I always like ice cream', he smiled mischievously.

'We had better get you some ice cream then. Three ice creams coming up', said Luke amused, levering himself easily out of the chair.

"I like your friend Luke, Mommy", nodded Ben in approval, licking his fingers.

'I'm glad you do darling. I think he likes you too', Claire's heart melted at the innocence of her son.

Luke came back with three bowls of ice cream, all a mixture of chocolate, strawberry and vanilla flavour.

'When I was your age, the kids in a nearby estate made the most enormous snowman. It had a carrot nose, a hat and a long scarf, everything a snowman could wish for. I climbed a tree, intending to throw snowballs down at the other kids, but instead I fell out of the tree, landing right on top of the magnificent snowman. I crushed it to the ground. I had to run for my life, being chased by very cross children, pelting me with as many snow balls as they could lay their hands on,', recalled Luke.

'Did they get you?' giggled Ben.

'They did, they pinned me down to the ground and made me eat the carrot nose of the snowman. Yuck, it nearly broke my teeth, it was so hard. I felt very sorry for myself when I got home. It was a long time before I went into that estate again', confided Luke with an exaggerated shudder.

Ben chuckled at the cartoon absurdity of the story. Pow, pow! It was obvious Luke had no trouble bringing his conversation down to the level of a six year old. The ability to communicate and gather people around him was one of his many talents. He was fully engaged with Ben, his eyes taking in every detail, wanting his son to like him. Claire was content to sit back in her chair, saying very little but pleased to observe the man and boy swap stories and share a laugh, facilitated by the books acting as a trigger to the conversation. Two hours sped by and suddenly it was time to go.

Ben was torn between a beautifully illustrated book concerning the adventures of a boxing kangaroo and one about boys befriending dragons. Usually, if it was not the end of the month and she was not flat broke, Claire would have caved in to Ben's pleading and bought the two story books for him, justifying it on how beneficial it was for a young child to learn how to read. Luke was itching to step in and buy Ben the whole bunch of books on the table but she stood firm and resolute in her resolve to stick with the plan. Ben could leave with only one book today but all three of them would come back tomorrow and choose another book for him. Ben settled on the desperate dragon tale and they all stood up to leave. Luke put his arm around her shoulders, his height and the width of his muscular shoulders making her feel like a dainty doll beside him. She stepped out of the half embrace, feeling that he was getting too chummy for comfort.

'You are different to how I remember you Claire', murmured Luke.

If she could only say the same! Luke Elliott, with his muscular six foot two frame, jet black hair and searing sapphire eyes, could still cause her knees to buckle when he came into close physical proximity to her. She had to steel herself to talk naturally and breathe normally when he came near her in a room but she could not afford to let him know that she still responded to the rays of animal magnetism which emanated from him. Luke must believe that she was immune to his sexuality, in a pure 'I'm the mother of your child manner', not a 'riding shotgun, let me shake your bones way'. Claire wished fervently that she could just relax and feel comfortable in his presence and not have to weigh up carefully her every word and look.

'I am different Luke, I am first and foremost a mother now,' she retorted primly.

'And I'm a father', he replied, looking down at Ben.

'Have you a little boy like me?' asked Ben.

'I have a little boy, exactly like you', said Luke, dropping down on his hunkers to the child's level.
.

'What's his name?', asked Ben.

'My little boy's name is Philip', replied Luke steadily, aware that Claire was looking daggers at him.

'Can we play together? Has he a Mom? I have a Mommy but I haven't got a Daddy. I have a Granddad and Mommy always says lots of boys have a Daddy but not many are lucky enough to have a Granddad as good as mine', said Ben.

Claire caught her breath sharply, recognising that her son had unwittingly presented them with the perfect opening to reveal Luke's parental identity. Luke sprang up and his eyes bore into hers, pleading with her to seize the moment and tell Ben of his true relationship to him. After a split second's hesitation, Claire's eyes hardened and she shook her head. She was not ready yet to break the news to her son that he was looking straight at his real Daddy; Luke's identity must remain in the shadows. Luke read the decision implacably pasted on her face and acknowledged it with a disappointed nod of his head and twist of his lips.

'You do have the best Granddad and we have to go home to him because he is waiting for you to help him build a model garage. The best boy in the world has the best Granddad. Say goodbye to Luke and we will see him again tomorrow. He is on holiday and is glad of the company,' directed Claire.

'Bye for now Ben, I can't wait to see you again. You are a great kid, a real character,' said Luke, bending down to give the child a hug.

'I like you too Luke, you're funny. Most big people aren't funny, even Mommy isn't, but that's alright 'cos she's my Mom.'

The compliments were flying between man and boy. The first meeting had gone as well as Claire had hoped for, despite the conversation treading on dangerous ground near the end. Now there was only the small matter of the rest of the week to get through. Claire spun around for one last glimpse of Luke before they turned the corner and the look of determination she spied on his face caused a shiver to run through her. Luke had changed too in the intervening years and had matured into a successful, accomplished man of the world. He was not a man prepared to be dismissed or ignored easily, nor was he one who she could influence or lead for long. Luke intended Ben to know his real biological identity sooner rather than later. He had been bitterly disappointed when he failed to identify his key character traits in the persona of his biological mother but his experience with Ben had been completely different. For the first time in his life Luke had seen himself reflected in the face and spirit of another person and the effect it had on him was as powerful as water being released from a dam. Claire realised that Luke Elliott was not the type of man who was going to permit even the best of mothers to play God with his child and his destiny.

CHAPTER THIRTY FIVE

Surprisingly, Claire managed to fall into a deep sleep during that Monday night, the one following on from her fateful encounter with Luke. She awoke feeling revitalised, pleased that she could not have had a better nights' sleep, even if she had swallowed a fistful of sleeping pills. She immediately became aware from the sounds in the house that Ben was already up, watching television in the sitting room. She was soon up and about herself, having a refreshing, spray splattered shower to kick start her day. They were due to meet up with Luke again and Claire intended to always look her best around him. Her curly red hair spun burnished gold, mascara applied to the thick lashes highlighted her big, blue eyes and rose blush lip gloss accentuated her bow shaped mouth. Mercifully, her skin had returned to its white porcelain smoothness once she received her new job offer and she had stopped throwing up. Now was not the time to look poor or bedraggled or beaten down by the grind of daily routine. Claire diligently ironed her jeans and she bought herself pretty new tops to wear, determined to put her best foot forward, with a perky smile on her face. Her efforts paid off and she looked as pretty as a picture as she stepped over the threshold of 'Books Doorway' with Ben, bristling with anticipation for their second meeting in the week with Luke Elliott.

Ben rapidly swept a handful of books into his arms and headed upstairs to the restaurant. 'I'm sure I'll like some of them books. Look Mom, there he is, over there', said Ben, pointing to the best corner table and sofa in the restaurant. Luke had thoughtfully already purchased a selection of drinks and tasty treats for them to savour.

'Damnit, why does he have to be so gorgeous!' groaned Claire for the umpteenth time, taking in the handsome chiselled features, softened by the warmth glowing in his cobalt eyes as he reached out to welcome Ben. She tried to project a pleasant, reserved demeanour, making up her mind that there was going to be no more kissing or touchy feel malarkey today.

The encounter progressed, following the same sequence of events which had occurred the day before. Claire sat back in her chair and withdrew as much as possible from the conversation, wanting to give Ben and Luke time and space to engage with one another. As she leafed through a stack of magazines, she tried not to show much interest in the animated conversation coming from Luke and Ben, touching on topics as diverse as friends and You-Tubers, toys and computer games, animals and sport. It was all entertaining stuff and Claire had to bite her lip to stop herself breaking out in a laugh more than once.

'When we go to the park Mom tells me that I can only look at a dog an' not touch him unless the owner says it's okay to pet him', explained Ben.

'Your mother is right. Only last week, when I was out walking my friend's Labrador and we were minding our own business, all of a sudden a tiny terrier comes up and starts to snap and jump all over me. Larry the Lab is a gentle mutt, excellent with babies I hear, but he grasped that bad tempered fur ball by the neck and threw him off me. It went up in the air and bounced back down hard on the ground. The stupid dog did not have the sense to stay away, it actually came back for more. You would nearly think the dogs were playing together until the terrier's owner started shouting and jumping up and down about the Labrador hurting his 'defenceless little dog'.

'Did you tell him you were sorry his little dog got thrown up in the air?' asked Ben with interest.

'I certainly did not' said Luke indignantly. 'I informed him coldly that Larry the Lab was a
superior sort of dog, who would not have so much as *sniffed* at his runt of a dog, if he had not first attacked me.'

It was all ridiculous stuff of course but Claire and Ben could not help but be entertained by the mental images the stream of stories conjured up.

Once again the two hour meeting flew by and it was time for Ben to choose his book and go home with his mother. He picked a book about a magician defending his King's castle against a rival clan and was happy to leave with it tucked under his arm.

'I will see you again tomorrow?' asked Luke, scrutinising Claire keenly, at odds with his relaxed poise moments before.

'Same time, same place', confirmed Claire.

'Thank you Claire, you are the best', said Luke, his white dentures flashing her a megawatt grin, happier than she had ever seen him.

Claire did not read much into the compliment. If he believed she was the best, he would never have left her. She had spent the last two hours reminding herself that she did not mean anything to Luke and that he would never have looked her up again but for his desire to get to know Ben. She hid the bitter memory of how her Herculean efforts to please and satisfy him during their sexual relationship had come to nought with a vivacious smile.

'I do try on occasion. When it is worth the effort'.

This time she left him without a backward glance, not wanting to feel unsettled. When Ben and herself were about to descend the stairway, two girls entered the restaurant together and one of them nudged the other in the ribs.

"Hell's bells but he's a ride. He's on his own. Come on, let's go over and one of us might get lucky.'

They headed straight over in Luke's direction and Claire had to fight an impulse to trip them up. She cast a pitying thought towards Luke's girlfriend Ally, who should have to keep a broomstick by her side to sweep away all the competition. Ladies were drawn to Luke as inevitably as bees were associated with honeycomb. They were attracted to his rugged physique, handsome face, fashionable clothes and quick intellect. Claire's mind boggled at the thought of the fanfare which would engulf Luke if he succeeded in amassing serious wealth on top of his personal charisma.

The next day was Wednesday, halfway through the make or break week for Luke and Ben.

For the third day in a row, Claire and Ben met up with Luke in the restaurant of 'Books Doorway' at exactly eleven o'clock. Claire was surprised and pleased to find a real fire burning in the grate of the old fireplace. A waitress informed her that it was a family tradition to light the fire in the grate on the anniversary of the date the store first opened for business in 1928. If anything, the warmth generated by the crackling coals made it even easier for Ben and Luke to be comfortable in each other's company. They reviewed the books together, bound by their mutual determination to find the best one to buy. The twosome talked and laughed, ate and drank, explained and entertained. Towards the end of the two hours, Luke pulled out his mobile phone and showed some pictures on it to Ben. The child was not very interested in them and he passed the phone over his mother, who quickly became engrossed in them -but that was grown ups for you.

The pictures were mainly of Luke and a tall, blonde woman striking a variety of poses in different places; there they were by the sea, at a glamorous ball, dressed smart casual inside an immaculate apartment and another one of them hugging each other in winter coats on top of the Empire State building. Claire found herself staring hard at the pictures of the statuesque, strawberry blonde woman with the easy, confidant smile. Together, Luke and his lady formed an athletic, high achieving, attractive partnership. They had most likely met at the gym.

'I take it that the woman in the photographs with you is Ally?'

'Yes, she is beautiful, isn't she?' commented Luke complacently.

Somehow, Claire refrained from giving the insensitive clod an utterly filthy glare. It was evident that Luke had no intention of dumping the absolutely fabulous Ally of New York in the same manner that he had ditched her, along with the rain water of Ireland. What was she, the dog's dinner? True, she looked nothing like Ally but Claire knew she was pretty. Acid thoughts crossed Claire's mind as she scrutinised the photograph: hair dyed blonde and groomed to the last centimetre of its life. Bleached teeth cemented in by the best orthodontist on the market, plucked eyebrows, skilled use of cosmetics and (the supreme fix) the same long, narrow nose as seen on the faces of US actresses on prime time television screens, undoubtedly produced by one of the best plastic surgeons in the business. How wealthy was Daddy to pay for all this enhancement?

Claire considered that she was naturally better looking than Alison but acknowledged that when it came to beauty, men were more interested in the end result; they did not want to know the details behind a woman's quest for polished good looks. Fear not, robots would never take over the world while there were glamour models around. The more the world changed, the more the basics remained the same. Attractiveness contributed to the theory of the survival of the fittest.

Claire pondered if any point could be proven with targeted research methodology. Apparently there were studies which indicated that good looking, clever women in organisations outperformed their equally intelligent but less pretty counterparts. Claire tended to mentally separate out her intelligence from her appearance and she was reluctant to accept the notion that good clothes, a good figure and the use of a stick of lipstick and mascara at work could be the deciding factors on whether or not a person got a promotion. In fairness, the maintenance of a polished appearance took effort and discipline, it did not happen on its own accord. It might help certain people to emit a confident aura and this aura got them noticed, both at work and at social gatherings. She was coming around to the realisation that countless women strove to enhance their looks for more reasons than a sense of personal well being.

'I can see she is tall and fit', commented Claire politely; but it was impossible for her to resist the impulse to taunt him lightly.

'Her eyes appear to be small but they could be screwed up because of the light. Her face is narrow but, then again, that may be caused by the angle of the camera or perhaps some shadow. She has a very different face to me; my eyes are big and my face is heart shaped in photographs.'

Luke was shocked and snatched back the phone, intently checking out the photographs, all of which were crystal clear and in high definition, taken with the highest specification mobile phone on the market.

'Your big eyes must need glasses. Take it from me, there is a real 'wow' factor when you see Ally in the flesh. It is actually hard to get a photograph which does her justice,' he declared with indignation.

Claire bit back a laugh; beauty was definitely in the eye of the beholder. To be fair, Claire had to admit that Ally was striking, however she managed to pull off the overall image. She turned her attention back to flicking through the magazines, gauging it was safer for her to criticise celebrities than the majestic Ally.

That night Ben smiled up at her after she had read him a good night story and tucked him up in bed.

'Today was a good day Mommy. I like Luke and I want to see him tomorrow and get another book.'

'We can do that, angel. Luke is here for a couple more days and I don't have to go to work this week', informed Claire, kissing him gently. 'Sweet dreams, my best boy. I love you'.

'An' I love you too Mommy. Lucky you don't have to go to work. I don't like your work', said Ben drowsily. 'I don't like it either', thought Claire. If only life was magical and she had a money tree growing in the garden, signed Claire. She turned out the light switch in the bedroom, making sure to leave the door ajar, allowing the light from the nearby open door in the bathroom to beam through. It scared Ben to be in complete darkness and Claire firmly believed that it was wrong to frighten the small child unnecessarily, especially in his own home. It was one of the reasons why she had hated vomiting in the bathroom while Ben was in close proximity and within hearing distance, fearing it threatened his emotional security. When he sensed her pain, it caused him anxiety. Let the innocent child's sweet slumber be undisturbed.

As she descended the stairs Claire's mobile phone notified her that a message had arrived from Andrew. He was on the way over, agog to know how the grand reunion with Luke was progressing. Sure enough, she spotted his silhouette on the door step five minutes later and ushered him inside with a smile.

'And they say women are curious! You couldn't stay away, could you?" Claire teased Andrew good naturedly as she led him into the sitting room, glad to see her friend.

'Not a chance', he replied. 'I had to check up on you to see if you were still standing or if you wanted me to beat up Luke for you'.

'Thanks for the kind offer, gallant sir, but he as he is bigger than you and built like an Olympic boxer, I will relieve you of that duty. However, you can pour me out a glass of wine from that bottle you are holding in your hand, I surely deserve one.'

'An Olympic boxer, you say? Impressive, he must have been working out. He may be bigger but is he better looking? Before you give me the answer, remember, I have the wine', parried Andrew.

'He is good looking Andrew, there is no denying it, but to me, you will always be the better looking one', replied Claire light heartedly if not altogether truthfully. Luke could still make her breath quicken with a knee touch but Andrew did not have to know it.

'Good to know', said Andrew, throwing her a quizzical glance as he made his way into the kitchen to search for the corkscrew and wine glasses. Claire choose to switch the focus of the conversation onto the interaction between Luke and Ben.

'The two of them are getting on very well, better than I dared to hope. I thought they might run out of things to say to each other but the opposite is happening, they are bouncing off each other and could talk for Ireland. They are playing board games and cards as well as reading books. Today they played Cluedo and Ben loved it, although it must have nearly choked Luke to let him win, he was always unbelievably competitive.'

'Is there going to be another week of meetings?' Andrew appeared in the doorway with the wine glasses in hand.

'No. Luke flies back early Sunday morning, which means that Saturday is the last day'.

'Then will Saturday be the day when you tell Ben that Luke is his father?' asked Andrew directly.

'You don't beat around the bush, Andrew. The answer to that question is ...... I don't know the answer. I watch from the side and see them interact together and it seems absolutely right to tell Ben about Luke. I can feel certain that I will break the news to him. Then Luke will say something to annoy me and the old resentments resurface to tug at me. I come home and put Ben to bed and I am torn to pieces again. I am so grateful I can talk this over with you. The only thing I am sure of is that Luke will be mad as Hell if I do not tell Ben that he is his real father.'

'Why are you tearing yourself apart if they are getting on well together? Is that not the most important thing? Or is that the problem, are you feeling jealous about the possibility of Ben and Luke growing attached to each other? It would be understandable if that was the case; Ben has been the most important person in your life since the day he was born.'

'No, I am not insecure in my relationship with Ben, a child realises who takes care of him. If Luke and Ben are to know one another, then I want them to get on well and enjoy being in each other's company.'

'Then what are you afraid of?' probed Andrew. Claire looked downwards as she pulled at her fingers.

'What if I tell Ben that Luke is his father and then his new found Daddy goes back to his life in America and in the next few years he gets busy with his job and maybe has a new wife and more kids and the bunch of them are happy to forget all about Ben? And my child will be sitting here, talking and crying about his missing Daddy, his Daddy who does not give a shit!' Claire looked as if she was going to cry.

'I can't tell you that won't happen Claire but, for what it is worth, I am going to go out on a limb and say I don't think it will play out that way'.

'But why not Andrew?' said Claire, needing to hear solid reassurances from her friend.

'He was my friend too Claire. I knew him for four years in college. I always liked the bloke, thought there was good stuff in him. I know he tended to suit himself but he did his best to make sure the whole group had a good time. He organised and brought the group together. He made things happen. We all looked up to him, we admired him. There was always a laugh to be had around him but I don't recall him ever hurting or humiliating anybody. All through his time in America he has kept contact with a few of the college crowd and he has even maintained contact with friends he had in school. I think Luke will make a real effort to maintain contact with Ben in the years ahead.'

'He kept contact with all those people but he cut me off', whispered Claire.

'We know he did and it was wrong of him, very wrong', said Andrew gently. 'He behaved as selfishly and recklessly as a misguided Norse god but he is only human and he makes mistakes. He wants a second chance to do better; he knows he can do better, that is why he is here. It is hard Claire, but relationships break down every day of the week. Shit happens. Maybe the time was not right, or your personalities were not compatible for the long term. That does not make him a bad person, it makes him a bad partner for you.'

'Your view of Luke is too altruistic. I will never fully forgive him for abandoning us. By past form, he is not likely to ever win a father of the year competition', said Claire steely eyed.

'Whatever you decide, it won't change the fact that he is Ben's father. Don't sell Ben short, he is a terrific boy and it is easy to get attached to him, to be proud of him. Luke will enjoy keeping contact with him. If the worst happens and Luke disappears off to America and is never heard of again, Ben will know he has met his father. He is young enough to adapt to circumstances and forget the details of the encounter.'

'You have got it all figured out?' probed Claire caustically.

'No, I wouldn't say that but I do know what it is like to lose a father at an early age. I remember my father's death vividly whereas all my other memories under the age of eight are faded.' Andrew was normally a laid back, even keeled guy but he looked pained as he racked his fingers through his hair, allowing Claire a glimpse of the bewildered child who nestled in the soul of the grown man.

'Believe me, it is easier to tell a child he has gained a father rather than break the news to him that he has lost one,' he said.

'You are a very nice person Andrew. Luke does not deserve a friend like you,' said Claire, impulsively putting her hand on his arm.

'Luke is not my friend these days Claire, you are', replied Andrew. 'I'm not telling you what to do, I'm just trying to make you see that your fears are zoning in on the worst case scenarios. Legislation based on worst case scenarios makes for bad law.'

'You mean bad decisions.'

'Some people argue that there can be no bad decision when it is made out of love Claire', Andrew parried.

'Love itself can be a bad decision', Claire's reply was tart.

'Not everybody agrees that love is based on a decision', said Andrew. He considered her for a moment.

'Luke sent me a text message.'

"Let me see it", demanded Claire at once. Andrew passed his phone over to her.

Thanks mate. Can't tell you what it means to see Ben. Blows my mind. Owe you big time. Luke

'He has no idea how much he owes you. If it was not for your good influence on me, he could go swim with sharks, coated in blood, before I'd let him near Ben. But the meetings this week are revealing things about Luke which he never told me before. For instance, did you know he was adopted?'

Andrew whistled, shaking his head.

'He went looking for his real parents but was not impressed by what he found out. He is bitterly disappointed with his biological mother but, from the sound of it, there is nothing wrong with her. She gave birth to Luke when she was a teenager and had to give him up. Later on, she got married and had two other children and is doing her best to live a perfectly normal life with her family in Manchester. Luke saw her and dropped her like a hot potato. Now he has come looking for his son. I'm afraid that it is in his nature to be restless and to move on when he is bored or disappointed. Human nature is a funny thing,' said Claire.

'You are not responsible for Luke's behaviour, you did not cause it and you certainly can't control it. All you can do is stay true to yourself and Ben and see how it all plays out', advised Andrew.

'You'd make a great counsellor Andrew. And you definitely still think that I should tell Ben about Luke being his Dad?'

'On balance I do. He is going to find out sometime and you will probably never have as much control or say about how it is handled than you do now. The older Ben gets, the harder it might become to explain it to him', said Andrew.

'Goodnight Andrew, and thanks. I'll take on board what you've said and mull it over', Claire reached out to hug her friend.

'You're welcome, just don't think about it too hard. And remember, no matter what you decide, whether for or against, it will be the right decision for you and Ben.'

'I can't be wrong huh? Can I have it in writing? You should be in one of the caring professions Andrew. I can't think why you work in banking, you're definitely in the wrong job'.

'Aren't we all, sweetie? The best of luck with Luke for the rest of the week. Get some sleep, you look awful.' He bunched his hand up to touch Claire's chin gently.

'You say the nicest things. Did I mention that Luke was showing me pictures of his drop dead glamorous girlfriend today?'

'I'll try again. Goodnight beautiful.'

'Goodnight Andrew.'

'Did I mention that Susie wants to get back with me? Apparently the longer she is separated from me, the more she misses me', said Andrew.

Claire's heart throbbed.

'And will you get back with her?' she asked stepping closer to him, staring into his eyes.

'No. There were reasons why it did not work out for us the first time', said Andrew. 'They all involve a certain person with the most vibrant, curly, golden red curls; hair I have never seen on any other woman.' He wound his hand through her hair, twisting a tendril over his finger, memorised as he gazed at it. He bent down and pressed his lips softly onto hers, holding the promise of much more. His tongue darted out, delicately tracing the contours of her mouth, until she imperceptibly opened it to allow her tongue to entwine with his. Claire wrapped her arms around his neck and pressed closer to his body, responding to the hard bulge she felt through the fabric of his jeans. The fact that she had the ability to arouse him so quickly excited her. She felt her own pelvis tighten and quicken, the nipples of her pert breasts tingle and her body elongate and surge against Andrew's body, until they were pressed tightly together.

'To me, you are the most beautiful one of all, nobody else comes close', murmured Andrew in her ear, his hazel eyes darkened with passion to near black. They half fell on top of the sofa, with Andrew below and her on top, and she slipped her hands under his shirt, running her fingers through the hair on his chest, pressing the flesh on his ribs, teasing his nipples. His hands dived under her top and he loosened her bra, going on to cup her generous, unblemished white breasts in his hands, flicking his tongue out to kiss the engorged nipples. He was gorgeously hard. His kisses became deep and urgent and Claire reciprocated by opening her mouth wide and drawing his lips fully into the cavern of her moist mouth. Andrews hands massaged their way down her back and one unzipped her jeans, spanning out to knead one soft buttock. It was Claire's turn to groan with delight and longing. Andrew moved both his hands to gently push her jeans down her legs and in turn her hand trembled when it went to the belt buckle on his jeans, ready to free him from all clothing confines, wanting him to plunge into her, to feel every inch of him inside her. Nothing was going to stop them now, they were past the point of return. Once Claire had unbuckled his belt, Andrew took over, throwing his jeans off but also managing to produce a condom and roll it on. They both stripped off until they were gloriously naked, running their fingers and hands hungrily over every inch of their bodies, familiarising themselves with skin and bone, scent and contour. Andrew was in the missionary position, about to take the greatest care in entering her, when Claire suddenly decided she wanted to be on top, bucking and squeezing and riding him energetically, exhilarated that he felt so satisfyingly big inside her. She felt him come and was joyful when his semen flooded into her and his fit, lean frame shuddered into her softer, voluptuous one. Andrew hugged Claire tightly as the waves of the after climax ricocheted through him, cupping her buttocks in his hands. He was not finished yet. He turned sideways until she was lying flat down on the sofa and he brought his hand down to the wet triangle of hair which curled in the mound above her legs, his fingers skilfully probing her pulsating core, stroking delicately until she fully opened up to him, physically and mentally. Her back, buttocks and legs lifted in a semi arc, while her heels and toes dug into the fabric of the sofa to help balance her slightly swaying body. She clutched him tightly to her as intense sexual sensations vibrated and ricocheted exquisitely throughout her entire body. She desperately wanted him to continue his magic finger movements, feeling that she could implode if he stopped before she reached climax. She suddenly experienced a delicious sense of release and she relaxed limply against him, laughing with pleasure. He ended as he had begun, gently stroking her head and dropping little kisses on her mouth, waiting patiently for the quivers emitting from her responsive body to subside. Minutes passed as they lay happily and contentedly together, allowing their fingers to trail lazily over the contours of their naked flesh, enchanted with each other.

'I guess this changes everything', she smiled up at him from the crock of his arm.

'Not everything, but a lot', said a satiated Andrew, nestling her closely to him. 'I wouldn't have it any other way, my beautiful Claire.'

CHAPTER THIRTY SIX

The next day was Thursday. Claire and Ben hurried up to Luke in Books Doorway.

'Sorry we are late. The bus broke down and we had to wait until another one came along.'

The tension lines on Luke's handsome face relaxed.

'That is one of the reasons why I refuse to do public transport in Ireland. I was beginning to think you had changed your mind about coming to meet me.'

'We are only ten minutes late Luke. If it was going to be any later, I would have sent you a message about the delay.'

'It is easy to over react in the circumstances', said Luke.

'Hi Luke. I liked changing buses, it was something different,' Ben piped up.

'Hiya buddy. Did the tires blow? The horn honk?' asked Luke playfully.

'No', replied Ben. 'But an old man blew his nose very loudly into his handkerchief, louder than a horn and a lady got very cross with the bus driver and said it was a disgrace an' she was late for an appointment.'

'What did the driver say to that?' Luke was amused.

'He said it wasn't his fault, he only drove the bus and she was cuttin' it a bit fine and maybe she should have left earlier. The lady said it was atrocious service an' she was going to report him. Another bus came and we all got off our bus and went on the new one. Mommy had to keep our tickets. There was lots of people on the new bus,' said Ben continuing his tale.

'Did you get a seat?'

'Yep but I had to sit beside an old lady. All the people on the bus were old, it was full of granddads and grannies an' no children. She patted my head and said I was a good boy.'

'So you are.'

'I try to be good but not always. I told her to stop petting me, I can talk and I can walk an' I wasn't a dog an' she was to stop petting me.'

Luke put his head back and roared with laughter.

'You have a good point there, little man.'

'Mommy didn't think so, she wanted me to say sorry to the lady but I wouldn't 'cos I don't go around petting people I don't know an' they shouldn't do it to me. An they do!' explained an indignant Ben.

'The lady was being nice to you Ben and you were rude to her.' Claire tried again to explain her point of view to the child.

'I wasn't rude, I just told her to leave my head alone!'

'I'm with Ben on this one Claire. You don't really want strangers to feel free to touch your child?' said Luke.

Claire was furious with him.

'Shut up Luke, she was a woman in her seventies who loved children and you are making it sound something completely different and unacceptable.'

Luke gave her an ironic bow.

'Like Ben, I stand corrected'.

Perhaps Claire had reacted too forcefully to Luke's throw away comment but he had a knack of putting her on edge. She drew in a breath and forced herself to speak calmly to defuse the tension in the air.

'Why don't you and Ben go and take another look at the books in the shop below? I can sit here and enjoy my cup of coffee. Being a man, something is sure to catch your eye which would escape me.'

'C'mon Luke, let's go,' said Ben, needing no second bidding.

'We had better steer clear of old ladies, geriatric gents and broken down buses Ben. Let's go and search for cars, tanks and super heroes', suggested Luke.

Man and boy went off sanguinely together, leaving Claire with time to sort out her feelings. She was mortified that she had told Luke to shut up, she had not uttered those words since she was a kid playing on the street with the other neighbourhood children. She did not want any tension to ignite between Luke and herself while they were spending time together with Ben, hence she resolved to smile sweetly and say little. Her ploy worked well and the reminder of the time in Book's Doorway passed by speedily. Ben shared his new joke with Luke, which was the start of plenty of laughs shared between them.

'Hey Luke, what's over there? A finger.'

One of the books Luke had picked out is was a music book for children, showing them how to read and write the different notes. Claire ruefully observed that father and son were bonding more with every meeting, something which could not be said of Luke and herself but, hey, two out of three was not bad.

Claire kept very much to herself but did agree to play a game of cards called pick up two near the end of the session and was pleased when they all won a game each.

The next day was Friday and Claire resolved to make an effort to get on better with Luke, since they were coming close to the end of their social experiment. Ben and herself entered Book's Doorway close to 11am and proceeded as normal to choose the books for browsing through with Luke. They always came across new titles in the well stocked shelves and Ben's enthusiasm for the search to find the best book did not dim. They joined up with Luke in the restaurant to find that he had bought all the food and drink they could possibly consume. Claire sipped her coffee and could not resist nibbling an almond slice as Luke and Ben settled into an easy conversation, holding a secret manoeuvre up her sleeve. When she judged the time to be right she stood up to excuse herself.

'If it is alright with you Luke, I will leave Ben here with you for an hour. I am back in work next Monday and there are a couple of things I need to buy. You can ring me if there is a problem and I will come straight back, I won't be far away. Please don't take Ben away from this restaurant while I am gone. I think Ben is happy to stay with you on his own for a while.'

'It's fine with me, we'll make out well together, won't we buddy?' smiled Luke.

'Yep, you go Mom, me an' Luke are going to play cards as soon as we pick out my book an' I'm gonna beat him. Better watch out Luke, Granddad says I'm born lucky.'

'It makes you a winner. But as Lady Luck is an acquaintance of mine, it will be quite the challenge to beat me.'

'Granddad says that the more a person practices something, the luckier he gets at it', said Ben.

'That is true, but sometimes it all comes down to the roll of the dice, my man.'

'I'll leave you two to get on with it, if you promise to keep him away from gambling. I'll be back in an hour. Have fun', Claire threw over her shoulder as she walked away from the pair of them, who hardly noticing her leaving.

Tomorrow was Saturday which was the day of the last scheduled meeting between Luke and Ben and this fact had influenced Claire's decision to allow Luke time alone with Ben. The pub next door had set out chairs and tables on the pavement outside its premises to facilitate the smokers amongst its clientele and it was here that Claire headed to sit and sip hot chocolate in freezing discomfort. Luke would have no chance of leaving Books Doorway with Ben without being accosted by her. The hour dragged by, although she broke the monotony by making a flirtatious phone call to Andrew, which cheered her up. They were going to hold off meeting up again until after she waved goodbye to Luke.

When Claire rejoined Ben and Luke, her son rushed to give her a hug. She was used to him lavishing her with a warm reception; he usually greeted her as if she had returned from a five day holiday when she arrived at her parents' house to pick him up after a day at work. Older colleagues bemoaned the day their sons discovered screens and henceforth hardly turned their heads to acknowledge their arrival.

'Mommy, we didn't play cards, Luke taught me a song when you were gone but it's a surprise until he sees us tomorrow.'

Claire threw Luke a quizzical glance.

'I know you have a large repertoire of songs at your disposal but I didn't think it included   children's tunes.' she commented, throwing Luke a quizzical glance.

'I was tempted to teach him 'We are the Champions' by Queen but then I remembered that kids' songs are the best', said Luke deadpan. 'We will perform it for you tomorrow as a special treat.'

'I look forward to it', said Claire sincerely. She realised that music was an integral part of Luke's life and he wanted to connect with his son in the medium he loved before he flew away. He was most likely curious to find out if his son shared more than the colour and shape of his eyes with him. If Ben had musical ability then it must come from Luke because the Howard family had singing voices which were capable of stripping paint off walls.

On Saturday, right on cue at five to eleven o' clock, with trepidation in her heart and butterflies in her stomach, Claire walked Ben purposely into Books Doorway, facing into their last encounter with Luke before he flew back to America. It was D-day, the make up her mind day, the day she had long been dreading. She had layered on foundation to conceal the sleep deprivation damage. The shop and restaurant were noticeably busier than during the weekday mornings. Ben was aware that they were going to say their goodbyes to Luke today as his holiday was over and he had to return to his life in America, a country far away.

'You get the books Mom, I'm going for Luke', exclaimed Ben, racing up the winding staircase.

Luke had arrived early and secured a sofa and coffee table, which were being eyed enviously by all the passing shoppers, who resembled circulating vultures ready to pounce on the furniture and claim it as a prize. Ben ran over to Luke and was welcomed by being swept up high in a huge bear hug. Claire's strategy had worked to perfection and this comfortable café, in the middle of a busy city centre, had become their special safe place; a peaceful oasis where routine, familiarity and open communication lines helped turn strangers into friends.

'Mommy says that this is the last time we will see you for ages, that you're going home to America on an aeroplane. I don't want you to go. Stay here longer, it's nice with you here', entreated Ben.

'I like it here too buddy, but my holidays are over. I have to go back to the States for work', replied Luke.

'Mommy has to go back to work too. I like it better when Mommy's with me. An' work's boring, she doesn't even like it. Why do grown ups have to go to work all the time?' said Ben, frustrated that he could not change such an unsatisfactory state of affairs.

'I have told you before Ben, big people have to go to work to earn money so we can buy food and clothes and toys. Adults go to work to earn money and children go to school to learn,' said Claire, hoping the child would understand her meaning one day.

'But you go to work even when I don't go to school', said Ben. 'An for some people, their job is stealing. I heard Granddad say it when John from next door had his car broken into an' his laptop taken. Stealin' is a job an' it's easier than your job an' its quicker 'an you can get the things you want. Why don't you switch to a job like that?'

Luke gave a snort of amusement at the boy's logic. Claire, well used to Ben's argumentative prowess and his determination to win an argument, decided to employ the tried and tested tactic of diversion, which had always proved useful to her.

'We don't ever steal Ben, it is a wrong thing to do. When people steal, they hurt other people who work very hard to earn the money to buy nice things. We don't hurt other people, we treat people well and with respect. Talking about nice things, do you see that Luke has a present for you?' she asked, pointing to a small guitar with a big red bow tied around its wooden frame which was standing upright at the far end of the sofa.

'Is it for me?' asked Ben with eyes the size of saucers.

'It sure is', affirmed Luke. 'Care to try it out?'

'Yes please'. Ben took the guitar eagerly into his hands but then looked uncertainly at the tall man settling himself back down on the sofa. 'But I don't know how to play it.'

'Well, it just so happens I have my own guitar here and I can show you how to strum a few strings', said Luke easily, clearly itching to teach him.

Man and boy were not interested in reading any books today. They had served their purpose of helping Luke and Ben to converse and relax together. Music and song were taking over, a natural progression where Luke was concerned. Wherever he was living, Luke reached for the guitar in the evening time, to unwind from the stresses of the day. He rarely went a day without playing the instrument and it was debatable if he was more attached to it than to any person. Music was as much a part of Luke's daily life as conversation and he wanted to share the love of it with his son. It was not lost on Claire that he had never tried to teach her to play a musical instrument, back in the day when she had considered them to be a couple. Now she eased herself into the tub chair and watched as Luke showed Ben how to hold the guitar and strum its strings, their heads angled close together.

The fun continued as Luke started to play and sing a medley of classic songs on his guitar. This was unheard of behaviour in Books Doorway but it quickly began apparent that people were listening with pleasure to Luke's beautiful, rich baritone voice pay homage to classic songs in a range of musical genres. He did not seek to command the room but every phrase was clear as a bell and every note was pitch perfect, causing her senses to heighten and the hairs on her arms to tingle. She had always considered Luke to be remarkably talented and sexy when he sang and played the guitar; they were abilities which held magnetic appeal and which had singled him out from the other guys in the crowd at college. Would she have craved him so desperately if he had not possessed this glorious musical talent? It was a moot point because it was impossible to separate out Luke from his music. Music stirred emotions and much had been forgiven Luke for his gift of song and chiselled good looks. Perhaps it was his melodious voice and skilful hands which she had fallen in love with and not his personality at all. It was clear to her now that she had never really known the essence of the man, never understood the impulses which triggered his decisions and actions. He had kept too many of this private thoughts hidden away from her.

Claire refocused her attention on Ben and Luke, still unsure as to whether to not she should reveal the truth to the little boy. This Saturday was the last time man and boy would see each other for God only knew how long. No matter what decision she reached it was only fair to give Ben and Luke time alone together and it would also allow her to calm herself and control her growing agitation. The stakes were high and she had to trust Luke not to tell Ben the real nature of their relationship while she was away.

'I'm going for a walk around the shops, you guys. Luke, you will keep an eye on Ben and say nothing to upset him?' she asked, eyeballing him.

'Of course,' Luke acquiesced, nodding his head. Ben's azure eyes sparkled up at her.

'Don't forget to come back Mommy, we have a surprise for you', said a glowing Ben.

'I'd never forget to come back for you, sweetheart. I might have a big surprise for you too', she said, immediately regretting her wry words when she saw hope spring into Luke's expression.

Claire went back to the pub next door and on this occasion she treated herself to a hot whiskey. She felt guilty to be drinking early in the day but this was no ordinary day; she was stressed and she was not driving so where was the harm in it? Her father always maintained whiskey was good for warding off colds and as it was still freezing, it was practically medicinal. To tell or not to tell, that was the question, she mused. She dragged her feet back to the restaurant in Books Doorway when an hour had passed, cursing her dilemma. 'Help me God, please help me,' she prayed fervently. 'I'll start going to mass again on Sundays, if only you will please help me now.' Unlike her mother, Claire was not fully committed to her religion but often desperation and prayer went hand in glove together. Miraculously, her prayers were answered by the scene which awaited her in the restaurant.

'Are you ready Mommy?' Ben struck a pose, guitar in hand, not noticing that his mother's answering smile was weak and watery.

Ben belted out the song 'Bear Necessities' from the Jungle Book, strumming his new guitar and tapping on the wood to accentuate the beat of the chorus with panache.

'Wonderful, darling', Claire clapped wildly, totally impressed by his stunning, upbeat rendition of the Disney favourite. The other luncheon customers joined in the applause with enthusiasm, enchanted with the cute, talented young boy's performance.

'Wait, Mommy, there's more', said Ben.

This time Luke took charge of playing harmony on the guitar while Ben stood beside him and sang out 'Under the Sea' from 'The Little Mermaid', his feet tapping and his arms and hands moving to the beat. Ben often listened to a collection of classic children's songs at bedtime and this had made him familiar with both songs but, in the short time spent practicing with Luke, the boy had made them his own. His voice soared out pure and joyously and the radiance of it spread like a sunbeam throughout the whole room. Claire felt the hairs on the back of her neck stand to attention as the revelation of Ben's musical ability unfolded before her eyes. Claire had known her child could sing and carry a tune but, not being musical herself, she had thought it the sweet voice of a young child. Luke, his biological father, had quickly identified Ben's talent and effortlessly show cased it for all to see. The crowd clapped loudly and Ben bowed low to them with the confidence and exuberance of a child star of the stage. She felt incredibly proud of her child. She appreciated that Luke had deliberately chosen to teach Ben carefree, uplifting songs specifically written for children, songs he had taken the trouble to learn himself first. Claire knew then without a shadow of a doubt that she was going to tell Ben that Luke was his real father. Quite simply, magic had been created, senses had come alive and, for the three of them, it was the right thing to do.

'Do you like it Mommy? '

'I love it darling, you have the voice of an angel', replied Claire.

What other traits had father and son in common? she wondered. Life with Ben was not going to be boring.

After all her doubts and agonising, the simple truth revealed itself in the glowing face of the man whom she had once loved and lost and the delighted face of her young son, who held her heart in the palm of his hand. 'Please God, you have sent me your message, stay with me for the next five minutes' she continued to pray on her hot line to the Almighty. The truth always wins out in the end. Her father normally spoke words of wisdom and he had advised her to say nothing about Luke to Ben but once again, in the case of Luke Elliott, she was going to allow her heart to rule her head. It was a risky business because life was never going to be quite the same for Ben and herself again.

CHAPTER THIRTY SEVEN

Claire did not know if Ben was going to remember the day he learned that Luke Elliott was his biological father but she approached the conversation in the belief that the revelation might become the six year old boy's first long term memory. She sat Ben down on the sofa between Luke and herself and gently took his hands in her own.

'You are already an amazing singer and you have the talent to become a world class musician if you practice hard. Well done sweetheart. Now I need you to listen carefully because I have something very important to tell you. It is about you and me and Luke', she said, feeling her way carefully. She had not rehearsed a speech for explaining the situation to Ben since her imagination had been blocked by the brick wall of indecision she had erected around her thought processes. She drew in a deep breath.

'I love you very much,' she said urgently.

'I know that Mommy, you tell me all the time', said Ben impatiently. 'But what about Luke? Are you getting married to him?'

Luke was extremely interested in the way the conversation was going but wisely kept his mouth shut, his muscle's bunching tensely.

'Why are you asking me that question Ben?' probed Claire.

'Cos the lady and the man get married in films an' if you and Luke marry he wouldn't have to go back to America. He could stay here with us. An' with Granny and Granddad and Andrew'. Ben beamed at his mother and new friend happily, problem solved.

'They are make believe stories Ben, not real life. No darling, Luke and myself are not getting married and Luke does have to go back to his home in America; he lives there, not here. Do you remember me telling you that your Daddy lives in America?'

'I think so', said Ben uncertainly.

'The big, important news we have to tell you is that Luke is much more than our friend, he is your Daddy,' said Claire, attempting valiantly to keep her intonation and facial expression serene.

'My real Daddy?' Ben was incredulous.

'Yes Ben, your real Daddy. He wants to get to know you really well because you are very important to him', Claire elaborated.

'But how can he get to know me really well when he lives in America? He won't see me', pointed out Ben. The child must be in the top one percentile of his age group for logical and abstract reasoning.

Luke reached into a case by his side and took out a slim laptop, which he flicked open and connected to the internet.

'This is a computer Ben and it is linked into the internet. It is fitted with devices and software which enable us to see and talk to each other over screens, no matter where we live.'

'But I don't have a computer an' Mommy doesn't let me on hers much', replied Ben.

'If your mother allows it, I'd like to give you this laptop as a present, to help us talk to each other and keep in touch', said Luke, looking enquiringly at Claire, who gave her permission with a nod of her head. Luke handed it over to Ben, who was thrilled at receiving a brand new computer. The electronic device was a more concrete reality to him than the notion that Luke was his father.

'Thank you soooo much Luke, thank you. I'll look after it real well. I'll talk to you on the computer every day. Can we play computer games on it?'

'Definitely. We will play lots of computer games together as you grow older', said Luke.

Ben hugged the laptop to himself but then looked longingly at the guitar.

'But what about the guitar? The computer an' the guitar are big presents 'and it's not my birthday or Christmas. I want to keep both of them. I like the guitar a lot. Please, can I keep it? I want to learn to play it like you, an' the next time you come, we can sing an' play together, just like today', said Ben.

'Sounds like a good plan to me. I will pay for you to have guitar lessons to get you going. And I can give you tips on playing it when we talk together.'

'Mom, do you hear that?' Ben could not believe his luck. It seemed irrelevant to him that Luke had not been in his life for the past six years, he was living in the moment.

'I certainly do', replied his mother dryly. 'Careful Luke or you will be outdoing Santa Claus and that is not allowed with children.'

'I have a lot to make up for', said Luke regretfully.

'When will you be coming back here to see us Luke?' enquired Ben.

'I promise you I will be back to visit you in three months buddy. I know that sounds a long time away but it is a short time for grown ups. We will plan fun things to do. When you are older you can come out to visit me in America'.

'But I'm big now, I'm not a baby. I can go on an aeroplane with you', suggested Ben.

'You have to be a very big boy to go in an aeroplane to America, big like Robbie', Claire said firmly, naming a fifteen year old neighbour to help Ben understand that he had to wait a long time before he could visit Luke in the United States.

'Oh', said Ben, instantly crestfallen. 'But how will I meet my brother?'

Luke stooped down to the child's level to look him directly in the face.

'I said you were just like my little boy Philip because you are my little boy. Your name is Ben Philip and you are my only son. You don't have a brother yet but one day in the future it is possible you may have one. You are very special to me Ben. Will you let me be your Daddy, please?'

Ben's face looked solemn and intent as he gazed intently at the face of his new found father.

'I've had to wait a long time for my Daddy. I wanted a Daddy. I waited and waited but you never came 'an then I didn't want to think about a Daddy anymore,' the child said simply.

There was the truth as the child perceived it; an adult never knew what was going on in a child's head.

'I know it and I'm sorry Ben. I'm going to be honest with you. I can't be your typical Dad, living close by and seeing you every day. I live in America. But I can promise you that we will talk often together and see each other at least once a year. So what do you say buddy? Will you let me be your Dad, who loves you but happens to live far away? Or if it is easier for you, you can think of me as a great friend and call me Luke.'

Luke and Claire both held their breath as the question hung in the air for an eternity. Then Ben nodded, a wide smile splitting his face in two, his distinctive sapphire eyes dancing.

'I guess we could give it a try', he pronounced. 'You can be Dad Luke'.

Luke let out a deep, relieved laugh and lifted Ben up into a bear hug.

'That's my boy', said Luke, proud and happy.

Claire bit down on her lip as she watched Ben and Luke laughing and holding onto each other. She should be feeling glad they had reached an understanding but hearing Luke spell out the limitations of his future parental involvement with Ben had upset her.

'He thinks he is the lucky man but what a loser he really is', she reflected bitterly.

The type of father and son relationship he was offering Ben was paltry and much less than the big hearted child deserved. She would follow her son to the ends of the earth and back again but Luke was making a big deal of just talking to Ben via the internet. He promised to see his son at least once a year.....bloody marvellous. Luke was doomed by his own personal decisions, ambitions and choices to be an inadequate father to little Ben. Luke did not have to live in America, he was bright and well qualified in science and technology and he was sure to secure an excellent job in Ireland if he went looking for one. But living and working in Ireland was too ordinary and too mundane a life for Luke, he wanted something bigger and more exciting, even if it meant cutting himself off from his child. He was chasing the American dream, big bucks in the land of opportunity. She breathed in deeply to calm herself and to count to three, before exhaling. Despite her anger and recognition of Luke's selfish nature, she still believed she had done the right thing by her son on this momentous day. She could only hope that while Luke and Ben would never have a traditional familial father/son relationship they could still develop a close bond in the years ahead, one based on liking, love, respect and common interests.

Her eyes were drawn to a little old lady of about eighty who was approaching Luke with a glint in her eye and a ramrod back, holding a neat, black handbag over her arm. She tapped his arm imperiously, impossible to ignore.

'Excuse me', she said, the steely voice belying her advanced age and tiny frame. 'I was sitting down over there in the table behind you last Monday, when you met this child. I've been here most mornings this week and I've overheard a few things. There is nothing wrong with my hearing, thank God, and my eyes can see that you are a fine looking man, I'd have my eye on you myself if I were fifty years younger. We all have to look out for the little children, it takes a village to rear a child. Because I wish you and the lady and the little one all the best in the future, I want you to be in no doubt that there is a limit to the number of fresh starts a person can have in life. Treat people in your life well. Bear it in mind and you will be all the better for it.'

With an emphatic nod of her head the old lady took herself off, leaving Luke to shake his head in disbelief and mutter the words 'only in Ireland' under his breath. For her part, Claire's mood lightened considerably and she allowed her laughter to ring out, but only when she judged the old dear to be safely out of hearing range. She would not have offended her for the world. Such women were the last of a generation of strong characters who had grown up in hard times and asked little for themselves but whose generosity of spirit was such that they would give the clothes off their back to help a neighbour in need.

Claire's attention turned back to her little man.

'I'll miss you Luke, please don't go,' sniffed Ben, his cobalt eyes swelling with tears.

'I'll miss you too buddy', said Luke. 'I'll think of you every day. You are very important to me. Hey, we'll be hanging out together again before you know it, shooting the breeze. Next time, you will have to teach me a song.'

'I will, a real good one', vowed Ben. 'Bye Luke. It was good seeing you.'

It was time for them to go. Luke swept Ben up in his arms to give him a giant bear hug. Claire felt close to tears herself. Luke reached out to pull her into the embrace. He smelt divine, this gorgeous hunk of a man who was not her destiny. He retained an ability to churn up emotions in her because, in spite of everything, she was still intensely aware of the potency of his manly sex appeal. His smile was as dazzling as the sun breaking through the dawn skyline, causing the bleak blackness of a harsh winter's night to fade into memory.

Ben was upset as the two of them walked away from Luke but he found real consolation in the marvellous presents Luke had given him. His world was still intact, because his stalwart mother walked by his side, holding his small hand tightly in hers. On impulse, Claire decided to hail a taxi to bring them to her parents' house. It was better to immediately tell Eileen and Tom about what had transpired with Luke and to get all the drama over with on the same day. Tom was busy hosing down the front driveway when they got out of the taxi and Ben rushed over to him, stealing Claire's thunder.

'Granddad, Granddad, guess what? I have a Daddy and his name is Luke and he lives in America an' I'm going to talk to him on the computer every day an' he's nice an' he's very tall.'

Not a bad summation of events, reflected Claire, wryly amused despite the real trepidation she felt facing into her father's disapproval. Tom straightened his back and spoke gently to the child.

'Well, that surely is a big story to tell your Granny. You had better go in and find her in the kitchen, she is baking scones for our tea. Go on in now, I'll follow you in when I put the hose away.'

Tom looked on as Ben galloped obediently inside the house to find his grandmother and the cakes. He turned to his daughter with a taut face and tightly controlled voice.

'So you told the lad. The deed is done and can't be undone. What made you do such a foolish thing?' asked Tom.

'It is the truth Dad, you always said it was best in the long run to tell the truth,' Claire lifted her chin up proudly but her grimace was apologetic.

Their eyes locked until a heavy sigh shuddered through Tom.

'Aye child, it normally is the best policy but sometimes it is best to shield a young 'un from the truth. We will have to go on from here as best we can.

You say you trusted in the truth, eh?'

'I did Dad, there seemed to be no other right way round it.'

Tom put his arm protectively around Claire's shoulders.

'God bless your innocence child, there are always different ways of dealing with the truth. I hope for all our sakes that your way is proved right. Only time will tell. Your mother had a strong feeling you were going to go that way. Come on in and we'll have some of her cake; she was expecting you and baked it special.'

'I love you Daddy', Claire sniffed.

'I love you too my dear, and the youngster as well. Stop your worrying now, for no good will come of it. It will be far better for the boy if you are at peace with your decision. Ben will do fine as long as we Howards stick together', said Tom gruffly but with true heart. He steered his daughter inside the warm haven of their family home. With or without Luke Elliott, Tom fully believed his daughter and grandson would indeed fare well while he and his beloved wife Eileen had breath left in their bodies. The Howards looked out for their own and family always came first.

CHAPTER THIRTY EIGHT

By the time Claire returned to the office after her week off work, news of her resignation had taken wings and everybody she knew there seemed to have heard that she was leaving the organisation. She was surprised and touched by the number of exceptionally nice emails sent to her by staff members based in other departments of the company, saying how much they had enjoyed working with her and wishing her all the best in her future career. She was thinking about the many good people working in Leictreach when the bold Ashley barged unceremoniously into her office, as unwelcome as a stinking skunk. Claire tightened her lips and straightened her spine because she did not intend to allow Ashley to verbally attack her again without retaliation.

'You went away for a week without completing the stock report Claire, that was shoddy of you and proved how undependable you are', she charged.

'I could not get around to doing everything before I went on holiday Ashley, I had to prioritise. You don't get the concept of holidays. We use them to carry out our family responsibilities, not to deliberately inconvenience your work schedules. It is your job as manager to arrange cover for absences from work, whether planned or unforeseen. I emailed you that I would update the stock listing upon my return to work. The report is not due till tomorrow and nobody looks at it anyway', Claire defended herself wearily.

'We do not run a last minute dot.com outfit in *my* department Claire', sniped Ashley.

'Given that I am practically out the door of *Daniel's* department, I suggest this is an opportune time for the job to be delegated to somebody else ', suggested Claire, thoroughly fed up with her.

'The disregard you have for your work responsibilities is atrocious Claire. Normally a manager is in a position to say that they are sorry to see a valued employee leave the organisation. It pains me to admit that I do not regret your imminent departure; in fact, I feel sympathy for your next manager as he has no idea of how difficult you can be. I don't know what addition you are going to be in your new company. If you had twice the brain, you would merely be twice as thick,' said Ashley bitingly.

'Your brain has its wires crossed Ashley, it is a wonder you don't electrocute yourself. I have a very responsible attitude towards my work, often putting in unpaid overtime hours to cope with multiple tasks and deadlines which are set needlessly early by you. I am meticulous in producing reliable reports but you take an inordinate amount of time to review them. You cannot distinguish between work that has to be prioritised and the less important tasks. You have no feel for the numbers and need them proved to the nth degree before you accept them because you are insecure about your own abilities, You are constantly afraid you have overlooked something important in the material and will be caught out by the senior management team. I've news for you, senior management don't want perfect reports, they want reliable data contained in short reports which they can read quickly and make informed decisions on.'

Ashley's pale face flinched with rage.

'What you produce is barely worth my attention. You think you're so clever, don't you? You do not do what you are told, when you are told to do it. You have too many opinions. You don't grasp the simple fact that what you think is not important. Nobody cares. It's a pity that Leictreach has not got a policy for ordering you to clear your desk and escorting you off the premises immediately after you handed in your resignation. It is not as if you intend to do any more work here, is it?'

'On the contrary Ashley, I have been very conscientious about my job here. A good manager might have arranged a suitable replacement for me to train up before I leave, therefore facilitating the smooth operation of the department going forward. But you are not a good manager, are you Ashley? You have no appreciation of what I do or how long it takes to do it. Let us agree that you don't think much of me and I certainly do not think much of you. It is best that we stay away from each other until I go. You have got what you want, there is nothing more in it for you. Don't worry about my farewell speech, you are definitely not the right person to deliver it. Don't forget to close the door behind you', challenged Claire.

'The company and I are both glad to see the back of you Claire,' retorted Ashley.

'You are not the company Ashley, you are a paid employee here. You may be a manager but your services can be made redundant at any time. You did not create this company and you do not own it. It is highly debatable if you add real value. You are not as important here as you think you are', thrust Claire.

'You are the one going and I am staying right here. The others will take note of that fact and fall into line,' said Ashley scanning the office, which had always been too small a work space to be suitable accommodation for two professionals.

'You and Anna were never important here. This place needs de-cluttering. I think I will move Karen into this office next week and recommend her for a pay rise. She should be quite comfortable here on her own. You will never have your own office in this company, you are finished here. I heard you were downsizing, going to a small company which does not have the financial resources or career opportunities Leictreach offers to its valued staff members. Goodbye Claire. Best of luck.'

Ashley smiled maliciously as she exited the office with style, relishing having the last word.

Claire sagged against the desk, her energy depleted. The woman was truly horrible and Claire must not allow any of her spiteful darts to find their target. Claire had done her best to fight back but her comments had bounced off Ashley's thick hide. For Ashley, it was always the other person who was at fault, she never saw the problem as originating from within herself. It was shocking how much Claire and Ashley's perceptions of the same events differed. Their view of themselves compared to their perceptions of each other were diametrically opposed. For Claire, it was sickening to think that Ashley was charm personified to the generals holding influential positions in the organisation while she treated the foot soldiers in the trenches like muck.

Susan, who worked downstairs in Accounts Receivables, popped her head around the door when the coast was clear.

'I was passing by and I heard how Ashley spoke to you Claire. I knew she did not like you but what I heard her say was something else. She should not be allowed to talk to you like that, it's terrible. I'm glad for your sake you are going, you can't stay here and work for her. I'll miss you though.'

'Thanks for your words of support Susan. You're right, I can't remain in an atmosphere like this, it is too toxic for me. I'm glad I'm leaving. Are you coming to my going away do?'

'Wouldn't miss it Claire, most of us will be there. We'll have a blast, give you a really good send off.'

Her demeanour turned solemn as the warm smile left her face.

'None of us have liked what has been going on Claire but people are afraid of speaking out. They are comfortable in their jobs and with their terms and conditions of employment and they want to remain working here. Leictreach is a well-regarded employer and the pay is as good, if not better, than anywhere else for most of us. Unless you work in an area of skills shortage such as information technology, companies are keeping wages as low as they can get away with for new recruits. The economy is performing well but people are paying high rents and mortgages and wondering when the next recession will hit. They don't want to take a chance of leaving secure employment, unless it is to go travelling.'

'I know Susan, when I had a decent job here I did not think about moving. Leictreach employs thousands of people and it should have career opportunities for me, given my qualifications. It is not your fault that Ashley has ruined my chances for advancement in the company. I am better off out of here. On a positive note, I have a good feeling about my new job. I realise people have to look after themselves and their own interests. I don't blame anybody here in Finance for what has happened to me'.

Claire paused briefly before continuing to express her thoughts.

'Not quite true, I do blame Ashley for what has happened and, to a much lesser extent, Daniel. But honestly, nobody in the general office has anything to feel bad about, except perhaps Joan. I know people are here because they have to earn a living and everybody is doing the best they can.'

'It is generous of you to see things in that light Claire. People have noticed how Ashley treats you but they pretend that they see and hear nothing. There is an element of people believing it is better to deal with the devil you know than the one you don't, when it comes to Ashley. Thankfully, she ignores a lot of people. We hope she will get bored here or be offered a better deal somewhere else and move away herself, sooner rather than later. I'd better go, Peter is waiting for these invoices.' She shook the bunch of paper she was holding in her hands. 'See you later on.'

Susan was one of the many decent people who worked in Leictreach. Daniel, for all his faults, had always been courteous to Claire and he would have been appalled to pass by her door and overhear Ashley's rant, as Susan had just done. He had been much warmer to her since their private conversation about Ashley and he was more visible in the department. Daniel would soon be prowling up and down these corridors with the stealth and speed of a panther, gathering information and making ready to pounce on those who threatened his territory. He was sure to catch Ashley unawares spitting venom at her next victim and he was ready to intervene to stop the abuse of power. There were finance managers who acted all the time purely out of self interest and who were more than willing to stand idly by as their subordinates were downtrodden but Claire did not count Daniel amongst the 'Grab, Gobble and Go' category of manager; he was too much the quintessential company man for that type of crassness. It was unfortunate that Claire was not going to be around to see it, but she was sure that Daniel was going to clip Ashley's wings, curtailing her reign as the Queen Bee of Finance. She chose to put her trust in Daniel one last time, hoping that he would ruthlessly box Ashley into an uncomfortable corner. The unscrupulous, manipulative hag did not deserve to get away scotch free for bullying Claire and ousting her from a job she valued, in a company where she had expected to build up a long and respected career. It comforted Claire to believe that Ashley's words of bile were going to come back to bite her in her skinny ass.

The one thing that could prevent Daniel from taking immediate action against Ashley was if he needed her to get the departmental reports out on time or otherwise his own neck was on the chopping block. He had to lessen the dependency which had built up around Ashley whilst he was away from the finance office developing the IT project before he could deal decisively with her bullying. There might have to be a transitional period whereby Daniel reorganised the operations of the department and gradually shifted responsibilities away from Ashley. Claire wondered how long it would take Daniel to make Ashley redundant sliver by sliver; from her own experience it should take no more than a year at most. Hopefully Ashley would not get a big, fat, payoff as she was propelled inexorably out the door, for she did not deserve to be rewarded for her bad behaviour and certainly nobody had offered Claire a wad of cash to cushion her own departure from Leictreach.

Claire's mother Eileen was glad to see her leave the company.

'I didn't want to say anything Claire, but your whole personality changed during the last year. You went quiet and tense and your smile was gone. It was not good for you or Ben. I'd see the child looking up anxiously at you with his big blue eyes and then he'd try to say or do something to make you smile. I'd say to myself, "give it up girl, it's not worth it". There are other jobs for those willing to work. We only have one life and we don't get back wasted time.'

'I don't know where it all went wrong Mam. I worked really hard and delivered all my reports on time but it was not enough, it was never enough. It did not matter what I did or produced. They didn't want to keep me in the end. It could happen again because I don't know what I did wrong. I might make the same mistake again', confided Claire.

'You did nothing wrong darling, don't you be worrying your head about it anymore. You were far too good for them and you are better off without them. Why should you waste your precious time and energy on the likes of them, petty low life who want to keep you down? Work for a man in future, stay away from bitchy women. You don't need to be micro managed by a mean minded woman, one who is jealous of your personality and ability.'

'There are all types of women managers in organisations, some of them must be good. I've heard other women giving out about male assholes in their offices. I think I was just very unlucky having Ashley as my manager,' responded Claire.

'There are good and bad managers everywhere but I believe you are better off working for a man. A man is more likely to give you space and room to flourish,' said Eileen, unmoved from her position.

'Daniel was alright, until those bad young 'uns got to him. It was too many hens around the one cock', said Tom sagely, joining in the conversation.

'What do you mean Dad?' asked Claire, startled.

'There were too many women around one man in that office, like hens picking each other to death. Nature is nature, they can make as many policies and regulations as they want but nature will win out. They need more men in offices to help sort out that kind of behaviour. Real men, not men who are more cissies than the girls themselves'.

'Like Emmet?' said Claire.

'Yes, like Emmet, although I don't know how all those women together didn't drive him mad. Now there is a man who will be enjoying his retirement. But there are some men who are so long working with women, they turn into women themselves'.

'I don't want to turn into a woman, Granddad', Ben piped up, having slipped unnoticed into the room.

'There will be no fear of that happening to you, my little man. Stick with me and I'll have you taking charge of building sites. Or a doctor in a hospital, you have the brains for it. You aren't going into an office to be pecked to death by a gaggle of women,' asserted Tom, lifting up the child in a protective bear hug. 'The Jesuits have a saying 'give me child until the age of seven and I'll give you the man'. Ben is six now, going on seven. I already know what type of fine man he is going to be.'

'Dad, you are not with it at all. We won't be able to let you out of the house with those views, you will be asked to leave places for fear of offending people. The talk nowadays is about transgender and binary and gender fluidity; that is the world Ben is growing up in. You will get Ben into all kinds of trouble with your old fashioned theories', said Claire, half teasing her conservative father, half serious.

'The Howard men are not complicated. Give us food, work, rest, sport and a beautiful woman and we are as happy as any man can be. Ben will not have to take much notice of all that other kind of thing,' said Tom dismissively.

The grandfather gently traced his finger down the side of his only grandson's unblemished cheek, the elasticity of the skin proof of the purity and perfection bequeathed to extreme youth.

'We're nearly there now, aren't we little 'un? The way you can build with blocks, kick a ball, climb a tree, ride a bike, do your maths, you are a great little man altogether. Fearless you are, but clever with it. Brains to burn, you love your sports but we have to make you put aside the gadgets and screens when you get your hands on them. You're gentle with animals too, always a good sign.' His other arm reached out to also enclose Claire in the warmth of his embrace.

'Don't you be afraid anymore, sweetheart. Your mother and I are proud of you, always have been, always will be. Same goes for Ben. We love you and are proud of you. Maybe I should have said it to you more often when you were growing up and then you'd know the truth of it', confided Tom.

'I love you too Dad', affirmed Claire.

She turned her face into her father's shoulder, close to tears but not wanting him to see them. She knew Tom Howard had a horror of female tears and would think he had said the wrong thing if he saw her crying. His words of love and respect were more precious to her than nuggets of gold. She knew her parents had been proud of her through her childhood and adolescent years, but she had secretly feared she had lost their respect when she had become pregnant with Ben and they had reason to form such a low opinion of Luke. One of the reasons she was driven to succeed in her job was to make her parents proud of her again. After her son, her parents were the most important people in the world to her, although Andrew was rapidly becoming close to her innermost heart as well. Claire wanted to make her parents proud, because one thing was for sure, she had always been proud of them.

CHAPTER THIRTY NINE

It turned out that the remaining two weeks spent working in Leictreach was all about salvaging Claire's pride and self-respect with her colleagues until her final day there announced itself with the date ticked in her calendar. She had smiled as she diligently went through her files, being gracious and positive to everybody who passed her way, excepting Ashley, who she ignored. As she made her way into Leictreach for the last time, Claire opted to take the longer route through the park, where she admired the bright blue sky interspersed with wispy cloud and noticed how the golden rays from the sun brightened the browns, reds, orange and yellow coloured leaves heaped beneath the trees and along the hedges. She was in a good mood when she entered the building. Her work was being split up between four different people and they were welcome to it. Claire was doing a comprehensive clean up of her office when Deirdre arrived to escort her to the general office, where a presentation in her honour was to be made. Claire was touched to see that every person in the busy finance department, excepting Ashley, had gathered together to bid her farewell; even Karen Woods was there, smiling at her from amongst the crowd. She was surprised to see that Daniel himself had taken on the role as Master of Ceremonies and was going to do her the honour of making the goodbye speech. It was unusual for the financial controller to be the main speaker when a person left the department, unless it was for a manager or to mark the retirement of a long serving member of staff.

Daniel gave a warm and gracious speech which Claire found gratifying to listen to, especially the part where he said that he had only realised the sheer volume of work she had done whilst tucked away in corners of the finance department over the last three years when he had sat down and made a list of it all. He went through the different projects she had been involved in since the start of her employment in Leictreach and thanked her for all her hard work, which had made every project she was involved in such a success.

Claire was touched by the praise Daniel publicly heaped on her and held her head high, knowing she had regained his respect. This realisation was more valuable than money to her. She had accomplished it by securing a new job for herself and by making him realise that it was not just her who had experienced major work difficulties with Ashley. Claire did feel a tinge of annoyance when she noticed that her work on the de-merger of TvQuinno was not given a mention, which confirmed that Daniel had wrongly accredited the project to Karen Woods instead of herself. Besides that slight, which was only going to be noticed by herself, it was all very pleasant and she followed on from Daniel with an impromptu speech, thanking everyone for their help and support at Leictreach and wishing them all well. There was not a trace of begrudging hurt or criticism or ill will to be found in Claire's speech to her colleagues. She remembered all the reasons why she had once loved her job in Leictreach and concentrated on them, (almost as if the last year had not happened) before finishing up by thanking Daniel for the valuable work experience she had gained working there under his guidance.

'Thank you Daniel for giving me a job in Leictreach three years ago, when I had the accounting qualification but not the experience. It has given me the confidence to take up new opportunities when they present themselves', said Claire. 'Onwards and upwards, for one and all.'

 The warmth and applause in the room was palpable after Claire closed off her perfectly pitched speech, making her the undisputed star trouper of the show. It also marked the end of her relationship with Daniel; it was unlikely that they would ever encounter each other again.   How often Claire had thought of Daniel and Ashley when she was at home with her family and friends and let vivid images and imagined conversations with them adversely affect her well being, health and sleep. Now she was leaving the organisation and it was as if 'puff' they were disappearing into a cloud of smoke. She resolved that from this day forth she would cast out their tiny phantom forms chattering inside her head, never again allowing them to exert power over her mind, mood, appetite and decision making.

In the meantime Claire had a party held in her honour to go to. The girls pulled her away from the filing and boxing of folders in her office, telling her it was not her problem any longer. Everybody went to the hotel bar straight from work, picked because of its close proximity to Leictreach and because it had a club for them to dance the night away. Looking around at the friendly faces thronging the hotel bar and pushing drinks into her hands, she realised that she was better known and liked in Leictreach than she had known. Daniel only ever turned up to retirement parties so it was no surprise when he did not appear in the hotel but there were people from a significant number of the other divisions in the company. Most of them could be classified as being fair weather friends but their faces definitely went beyond the people who worked in Finance and it was good of them to take the trouble to turn up and wish her well on the night. She knew better than most that it was not easy for people to juggle jobs, children and relationships and more than one person here tonight had put themselves out and deprived themselves of precious family time to say a final goodbye to her. Claire was bemused by how much her place in the popularity stakes had soared once the news of her resignation and new job had broken; she might not understand it but for one night only she could certainly enjoy it.

Ashley did not put in an appearance but that was no surprise as it was common knowledge that there was no love lost between the two women and people were mightily relieved to discover their manager was not there to spoil their fun. When she noticed Karen Woods blending into the crowd, it struck Claire that today was the first time she had seen Karen make moves independent of Ashley, first by attending the farewell presentation and secondly by joining the drinks party. Claire had a hunch that Karen was a wily customer who had sensed that change was in the air in Finance and that maybe it was better for her to hitch her horse to a wagon of a different hue. Claire had judged from the beginning that Karen was a tough nut under her polite reserve and she chuckled to herself at the prospect of Ashley's golden protégé morphing into her nemesis and likely successor. As far as Daniel was concerned, everybody could be replaced in their jobs and he could well ask Karen to step up to the plate if he chose to get rid of Ashley, given that the girl had finally managed to pass her accountancy exams. It was all fun and games and jockeying for position in Leictreach's never ending merry- go- round.

Claire was particularly pleased to see that Declan Carroll from Telecommunications and Robert Blake from ESI had both turned up for her going away party; she was surprised the date of her departure had even registered with such busy divisional heads. Declan made a point of coming over to say that he had always thought highly of her and that although he was sorry he could not offer her a job on this occasion, Dublin was a small place to do business and they could well end up working together in the future. Claire thanked him sincerely, saying that it would be a real pleasure to work for a gentleman like himself and she appreciated him coming tonight. She did not explain to him that as the powers on high had blocked her from availing of an internal transfer elsewhere in the company, it was highly unlikely they would have authorised her taking up a post in Telecommunications and so there was no need for him to regret not offering her a job. She kept it sweetness and light and Declan's opinion of her went even higher.

'You are exactly the sort of girl Leictreach should be hanging on to Claire. It's unfortunate that I needed somebody with more experience in the telecommunications market but we're operating in a cut throat environment and there is no room for learning on the job. I wish I could have done more for you, you have bags of potential. You only have to look around and see the amount of people here to know you are well liked', he squeezed her hand lightly.

Declan Carroll was a portly man, with thinning hair and a moon shaped face but his eyes were kind behind his heavy rimmed glasses. He looked around, mopping his sweaty forehead with a cloth handkerchief; it was too hot and loud in here for him and Claire sensed that he wanted to go home once he had said his piece.

'I don't like making mistakes and I don't like to see the company making them either. Poor judgement brings a company to its knees. Get the wrong people at the top of a company making mistakes and the inevitable result is a loss of competitive advantage. There has been talk about Ashley Scanlan being promoted but that type ends up giving a chap a heart attack. It does not bring out the best in people and it is no way to do business', said Declan.

Robert Blake approached and slapped Declan on the shoulder with one hand, holding a glass of wine for Claire with the other.

'We can still teach the Young Turks a thing or two Declan', said Robert.

'We can. I'll leave this lovely young lady for you to look after and go home to my long suffering wife. Before I go, I want to say that I think Ashley Scanlan had something to do with you leaving Claire and I don't like it. Robert and I will take Daniel out to lunch and have a word in his ear. I wish you all the best in the future Claire.'

Claire shook hands with Declan but could have hugged him for his kind words.

'Thank you for taking the time to come tonight Declan', she said. 'It was always a pleasure dealing with you. Best wishes to you and your family.'

Once Declan took his leave Robert arched his eyebrow from his considerable height.

'What about me? I actually did offer you a job,' he teased.

'You are the best Robert. Knowing that you had confidence in me and were willing to let me join your team meant more to me than you will ever know. It is not your fault that the transfer was blocked at the highest level of the company, by people who normally would not be familiar with my name. It made it crystal clear to me that I had no other option but to leave the company and get on with my career somewhere else', said Claire.

'I'm surprised and disappointed by what has happened to you in the company Claire. I've seen people shafted before, but never at your level. There was no way back for you once your internal transfer was blocked. I've given it some thought and come to the conclusion that a lot of people in Finance were jealous of you and their jealousy caused them to work against you', said Robert

'But why should anybody be jealous of me? I gave them no cause. I was just quietly working away in a corner on whatever work Daniel gave me to do. If anybody asked me for help I tried to give it to them. I was not in charge of people and, because I was inexperienced when I started working in Leictreach, I was not paid very much. Why on earth should any of them be jealous of me?' asked Claire in total confusion.

She desperately wanted to understand what had happened so she could learn from it and do everything possible to integrate well into her next place of employment; she could not afford to be frozen out from another job. She needed to be able to hold onto what she had, to not let another person come along and take her precious job away from her. Ireland was a small open economy which could speedily lurch from cycles of boom to bust. Whenever the employment market tightened in Ireland, who you knew appeared to count for more than what you knew when it came to securing a decent job. Her wonderful parents were aging fast in front of her eyes. She needed to be able to stand on her two feet like a grown-up and protect her job, otherwise she would not be able to take proper financial care of herself and Ben in the future.

'You've hit the nail on the head without realising it Claire. The close relationship you had established with Daniel is the key to understanding it all. The others were envious of your relationship with him and set out to break it. And they succeeded in achieving their objective.'

Claire still looked up at him, not fully comprehending the truth of what he was trying to tell her. She considered her relationship with Daniel to be professional and polite, she had never perceived it to be a close one.

'It is very unusual for somebody at your junior level to have a close working relationship with the financial controller of a large multinational company', explained Robert. 'How many people are employed in Finance? Thirty two? Thirty three? Most of them report to a manager and the manager in turn reports into Daniel. The majority of people working in the department have minimum contact with him. But because of your involvement with the merger and de-merger accounting and your project and budgeting work, you reported directly into Daniel. You could walk in and see him anytime and he would listen to what you had to say. Other people who were there longer than you and considered themselves more senior noticed your access to Daniel and resented you for it. You were oblivious to their ill will as you worked quietly at your desk, concentrating on meeting the next pressing deadline, not realising you were in a privileged position. So they grouped together to break your relationship with Daniel. Certain people knew exactly what they were doing. They executed the hatchet job nicely, hence we are here tonight.'

He tilted his head and pint glass at an angle, as if taking a bow to his audience. Claire weighed up his words carefully, finally acknowledging the truth of the situation. Claire had focused all her enmity on Ashley but it had taken more than one person to bring her down.

'My Dad told me there were too many hens around one cock', said Claire shyly.

Robert Blake's deep throated laugh rang out, making people nearby wonder at the joke.

'Your old man had it exactly right, he has not put it in the most politically correct way and I would not be allowed to phrase it that way myself, but yes, far too many hens around one cockerel. And what a cock-up we have!'

His tone sobered. 'You're a good kid Claire. I know Daniel a long time and think highly of him but you have been treated shabbily and I'm disappointed in him for allowing it.'

Claire found herself defending Daniel, still loyal to him.

'Ashley is very clever Robert and she makes sure to be always charming to Daniel. She is technically proficient at her job and he relied on her expertise to get the reports out. He did not realise what she was really like or how badly she treated people'.

Robert responded rationally,

'Ashley could only treat the people under her badly if Daniel allowed it to happen Claire. As a manager myself, I contend that the blame lies primarily with Daniel and not Ashley. When complaints against Ashley started to come his way he chose to ignore them, instead of carrying out a full investigation and putting a stop to the inappropriate behaviour.'

'But what happens to the victim of bullying whilst the investigation is being carried out? I'll tell you, when they lodge a complaint they still have to remain there day after day, reporting to the very person they have publicly accused of making their life hell. There is often nowhere else in the organisation where they can move, which is what happened to me. The only good thing to come out of this is that I think Daniel eyes have been opened and he might take action against Ashley the next time there is a complaint ', confided Claire.

'Unfortunately it is too late for you Claire. But take heart, I have managed a lot of people down through the years and I don't doubt that you will do very well in your next job. Now enough gloom and doom talk. How is that little guy of yours keeping these days? Broken any limbs climbing tables and trees recently?'

Robert's change of subject was rewarded by a wide smile from Claire and the bright light came back into her blue eyes. She had no idea how pretty she looked in her crushed velvet green dress, with her distinctive cork screw copper curls framing her heart shaped face.

'He is growing big and strong, running and jumping everywhere. I don't know who I should be worrying about, my son who thinks everything his feet touches is a trampoline or my father, who is busy trying to keep up with him.'

'I wouldn't worry about either of them, boys that age are made of elastic and he is keeping your father active and alive. Relax and enjoy them,' said Robert.

'How many children do you have?' asked Claire.

'Three boys, all rascals but life would be much duller without them. You are being called away', he nodded towards a group of girls rapidly approaching them.

'Thank you very much for everything Robert, particularly the job offer. I won't forget you', said Claire squeezing his arm in farewell.

'You are welcome, Claire, it was the least I could try to do for you and I am

351

sorry it did not work out. It was a safe bet for me, I knew you would be great at the job, just as you will be in your new one. Enjoy your night', said Robert as the girls from the office grabbed hold of Claire's shoulders excitedly and instructed her to come with them. The night was going splendidly well and fingers crossed, it appeared it was going to get even better.

Claire followed the girls into the reception area and was stunned to see Amy standing there, looking like a supermodel in killer high heals and a skin tight shimmering purple dress, laced with crystals to the throat but cut low at the back, her black hair swept away from her face and straightened to fall sleekly to her shoulders. A guy walking past nearly tripped over his feet when he beheld Amy's long legged sophistication. Amy laughed at Claire's surprise, reaching out to give her a warm hug.

'Surprise! I didn't trust them to give you a good send off. My own was rubbish so I knew I had to come along and take charge of your party. I flew in today from Scotland. You had better ring your mother and let her know you are not going home till we've had breakfast in city centre.'

Claire pinched herself to make sure she was not dreaming. All these people were here for her tonight, to show that they had liked and appreciated her in Leictreach and that many of them were aware of and disagreed with her constructive dismissal. The last time so many people turned out to see her was at her twenty first birthday celebration. The night was getting better and better and taking on a surreal quality.

Amy dragged her away into the ladies' restroom and worked wonders on her make up, using a deep rose coloured lipstick to draw attention to her bow-shaped lips and lashing on the mascara and smoky eye shadow to compliment the intensity of her dark blue eyes. Her eyes were sending out a sparkling come hither invitation to the world. Nobody suspected from looking at Claire's vivacious face that her heart was tinged with sadness and regret over the manner of her departure from Leictreach.

Claire looked at herself in the mirror standing beside Amy and admired her slim but curvaceous figure silhouetted in her belted crushed velvet dress. Her new improved figure had been sculpted out of vomit but nobody present was privy to that nugget of information and all they could see was how fabulous she looked tonight. It was as if Amy read her thoughts because she reached out and gave Claire's hand a squeeze.

'You own this night Claire. Look at you, you're gorgeous You've had a rotten time of it but what does not kill you makes you stronger. I am having a blast with my new job and you will too,' affirmed Amy kindly

'I can't believe you came all the way from Scotland to be here tonight Amy, I have to pinch myself to know you are really here. You have changed too, you were always stunning but you've gotten so confident in the last year. Ashley wouldn't stand a chance if she went up against you,' said Claire.

'Not a chance', agreed Amy cheerfully. 'The world is a big place and if you move around you can grab opportunities that never come your way if you stay too long in the same place. I'm on loads more money than I was on in Leictreach and you can be too Claire, you are every bit as good as me at figures. Of course it helps if you are working for a giant oil company making obscene profits. Now let's get out there and make some guys happy.'

Claire laughed and followed her back out to the disco bar.

'Look over there at ninety degrees Claire because that guy is very interested in you', instructed Amy, nudging her.

It was Stephen Murray, the financial director of the newly de-merged company TvQuinno, standing alone with a glass in his hand and smiling straight over at her. It had not entered Claire's head that Stephen would be at her party but she was glad to see him. Claire was nothing if not single minded and there was one final thing she wanted to settle in her head before she laid the ghosts to rest.

'He is cute, go for it', said Amy approvingly, as Claire excused herself for a few minutes to go to talk with Stephen. Amy did not realise that Claire was in a relationship with Andrew and she wanted her to enjoy the music and muscle on show.
Stephen was about thirty; he had grown a neat beard since Claire had last seen him and it suited him, making him appear older and more distinguished, somebody to be taken seriously around the business table. Claire thanked him for coming, she had not expected it.

'I wanted to come Claire. I enjoyed working with you and I really appreciated the work you did on the de-merger. We were able to rely on the figures you produced and that made life a whole lot easier for me.' he replied.

'Stephen could you tell me something please? Who did the main work on the de-merger project, was it me or Karen Woods?,' asked Claire, who had suffered a burning sense of injustice since Daniel had attributed the project to Karen and stopped her involvement in high profile analytical work.

'It was you of course, Claire.   What Karen did is not worth mentioning. Why are you even asking the question?' replied Stephen.

'I needed to hear you say it Stephen, call it a reality check.   Daniel accredited Karen with the project, not me. I wanted to make sure my perception of events was not lopsided. It is in the past now. How are you finding your new job as head of a subsidiary company?' asked Claire. Stephen had given her the final reassurances she craved to put balm on her wounds and she was prepared to focus on the positives.

'I like it, it is incredibly busy but there is a buzz to it. We have put a good team together. I'm over and back to London every week since our data feeds into their system and most of the business meetings take place over there.'

'Will you have to relocate?' probed Claire

'Not yet, but it may be a possibility for the future', said Stephen.

'Will your girlfriend mind?'

'I don't have a girlfriend. She got fed up with all the long hours I work. That is what I tell myself anyway. It is either that or she just got fed up with me', retorted Stephen good humouredly.
The fact that Stephen was not going out with anybody surprised Claire, he was a good guy, had an impressive job and was the perfect age for marriage. He was also giving her a sexy grin, which he never displayed in the office. Caught off guard, Claire flushed and swept her hand through her hair, feeling an unexpected flirtatious charge sizzle between them. What had happened to her hormones in the last month?

'Would you like a drink Claire? I certainly owe you one', offered Stephen.

'Yes please, it is hot in here and a glass of lager will cool me down', acquiesced Claire nervously. She was relieved when Stephen refrained from making the obvious pun about preferring his women hot rather than cold and went off courteously to buy her a drink. She had never viewed Stephen with amorous eyes when they had worked directly together and it stunned her to realise that he was an attractive man who might possibly fancy her big time.

'Here you go Claire, enjoy', said Stephen, handing her over a drink. 'How about you, are you looking forward to starting your new job?'

'Definitely. It will be very different from my work in Leictreach, it is a girl Friday role in the finance section of a small but growing organisation. I'm hoping this role will broaden my experience and I can make a difference to the bottom line,' replied Claire with regained composure.

'Never say never Claire, get your broad experience in the next two years and then consider moving back to the multinationals', smiled Stephen. 'Don't leave it too long, the multinationals operate in a certain way and it will be more difficult for you to get back into them after a certain time elapses. Anyway, enough about work, would you like to dance?'

Claire agreed, it would have been rude to refuse. The music was slow and she felt Stephen stiffen and his arms around her waist tighten as they moved rhythmically together on the dance floor. Claire felt a pang, recognising that Stephen was attracted to her. Where had all these gorgeous men been in the last lonely five years? She had been blind to their presence, she had been stupid. She had refused to let go of her obsession with Luke Elliott. She could have been out having fun but instead she had chosen to embrace misery and rejection. Stephen was the finance director of TvQuinno and she certainly did not want to smooch the face off him on the dance floor, surrounded by everyone she knew in the office and allow that to be the talk of the place come Monday morning. A vision of Andrew leapt into her mind and Claire kept her head down, feeling horribly disloyal to him. She was dancing with an admirable man but....... he was the wrong man for her. The tempo of the music changed to a rock beat and only then did she break away and look up, noticing that Stephen looked disappointed. He slipped his business card into Claire's hand.

'If you ever want to go out for another drink Claire, without the presence of this mob, give me a call', he said, backing away. Claire fingered the card, he was a nice guy and it was reassuring to know that there were attractive men out there who were willing to ask her out. Her mother Eileen would be delighted to know that Claire had options. She could have grabbed hold of Stephen's hand and arranged a time and a place for them to meet together, just the two of them but, instead she stood back and watched him leave the room on his own. The reason why she had let Stephen go without even the lightest of kisses was because of her thoughts for Andrew, her constant friend and newest love.

Suddenly Claire spotted Andrew shouldering his way steadily through the crowd, making a bee line for her, his dear familiar face alight with anticipation. He had not told her he intended to come tonight. She was immediately glad he had not seen her dancing with Stephen, even though nothing untoward had happened. What caught her completely unawares was the way her heart leaped upwards, sending an imperative message to the circuit lines of her brain. It was Tarzan and Jane like in its simplicity: Andrew loves Claire and Claire loves Andrew. Andrew was destined to be her lover, her true friend, her companion and her rock in the months and years to come.

'Don't let this one get away Claire, your expression is completely different compared to when you were talking with the other guy', said Amy, giving her the thumbs up.

'Hello beautiful. I thought I'd call in and see how you are enjoying yourself with the gang', smiled Andrew, folding her into his arms.

'Hi you. I'm glad you came. Don't wait any longer Andrew, kiss me', she breathed softly into his ear.

Andrew did not need a second invitation, dipping his head to lightly kiss her mouth, coming back a second time to go deeper with his mouth and tongue but keeping it light, coming back a third time to thoroughly kiss Claire, the love of his life. Claire let her weight be supported by him as she threw back her head in delight to drink in the kiss.

'You're the one that I want Andrew, only you', pledged Claire.

'What about Luke?' probed Andrew warily.

'I never really knew Luke. I obsessed about him but he was more a fantasy figure I created in my imagination than the real man. He is Ben's father but he can't compare with you. I need you, not him, in my life,' said Claire sincerely.

'You are the one who I have always wanted Claire. You're gorgeous, I can't look at you without thinking how beautiful you are', said Andrew, sliding his fingers through her curls and bringing them down to caress the side of her face. He swooped down to capture her lips again, sure of what he was doing. Claire was the only woman in the world for him.

'I feel incredibly lucky tonight Andrew. I have you and Ben, my parents and some friends.' Claire scanned the crammed, throbbing dance floor. 'It is time for me to leave this place and these people and start afresh.'

'You have fought the good fight Claire. It has been hard on you because you dislike confrontation and avoid it when you can. Your gentleness is one of the things I love best about you. You deserve to work in a place where they will appreciate your talents and warm personality. But you can't leave yet, this is your big night and lots of people from Leictreach have turned out to wish you well,' commented Andrew, observing the crowd around them.

'I want to dance the night away with you. I feel happy, as light as air. For one night only, I am the belle of the ball, the winged angel on top of the Christmas tree', laughed Claire.

Andrew rocked her close, responding instinctively to the uplift in the rhythm of the beat.

'Bully for you, Claire'.

ACKNOWLEDGEMENTS

I want to thank my fabulous friends Geraldine and Bernadette for editing the "Bully For You" manuscript for me and for their wise advice. I would also like to give particular thanks to my dear friends Marie and Stephanie for their staunch encouragement and belief in my ability to bring this story over the line. The topic of workplace bullying is not an easy one to describe realistically and my friends always encouraged me on in my mission, believing in its worth.

I want to acknowledge the general support I have received for most of my life, throughout all my endeavours, from my oldest friends, namely my 'Orange and Biscuit' group, consisting of Geraldine, Paula, Fiona, Aine, Catriona, Fionnuala and Ann Marie.

Thank you to every friend who has encouraged and supported me while I wrote this story, you know who you are. I also want to acknowledge the Parnassus drama group, who have brightened up my life with the glow of their creativity over the years.

I have to thank my parents, brothers and sisters for their constant love and support. I particularly wanted to complete this book for my father, who has infinite faith in my ability. Most importantly, I owe huge thanks and gratitude to my incredible husband and best friend, as well as to my darling children, who generously and good humouredly gave me the time and space to write this story.

I have witnessed bullying in my years of work experience, firstly as a teacher and secondly, in my career as an accountant. I have reached the conclusion that bullying is dealt with badly in society. This book aims to bring comfort to those people who have experienced bullying in the workplace by knowing they are not alone, that it is not a figment of their imagination and that it has happened to others. For those lucky enough not to have direct experience of workplace bullying, the story strives to broaden their understanding of the actions which can underpin bullying behaviour and to explain why it can be difficult to stop it from happening, perhaps to somebody they hold dear.

For make no mistake about it, the person being bullied faces challenging odds and needs all the help he or she can get. Be kind, be patient, be supportive; bully for you for reading and for at least trying to understand.

Bully For You,

Kind Regards,

Jeanette Clyne

Printed in Poland
by Amazon Fulfillment
Poland Sp. z o.o., Wrocław